THE LAST
DANCE

THE LAST DANCE

Paul Charles

NEW ISLAND

Previous Titles

Detective Inspector Christy Kennedy Mysteries

I Love The Sound of Breaking Glass
Last Boat To Camden Town
Fountain of Sorrow
The Ballad of Sean & Wilko
I've Heard The Banshee Sing
The Hissing of the Silent Lonely Room
The Justice Factory
Sweetwater
The Beautiful Sound of Silence

Inspector Starrett Mysteries

The Dust of Death
Family Life

Other Fiction

First of The True Believers

Factual

Playing Live

www.paulcharlesbook.com

THE LAST DANCE
First published 2012 by
New Island
2 Brookside
Dundrum Road
Dublin 14

www.newisland.ie

P/B   ISBN 978-1- 84840-142-6
ePub   ISBN 978-1- 84840-154-9
mobi   ISBN 978-1- 84840-155-6

Cover design by Nina Lyons
Typeset by JM Infotech INDIA
Printed by Bell & Bain Ltd., Glasgow

New Island received financial assistance from
The Arts Council (An Comhairle Ealaíon), Dublin, Ireland

10 9 8 7 6 5 4 3 2 1

To the memory of Gerry McGinley,

a true gentleman who was never ever too busy to stop and help his neighbours.

PROLOGUE

Towards the end of the dreary 1950s, the number one recreational occupation in Ireland was dancing in ballrooms. We're not talking about ballroom dancing here; we're talking about dancing in ballrooms. On St Stephen's day – aka Boxing Day – it was reckoned that one in every four people living in Ireland went out to a ballroom to dance to the sounds of the new fad: the Irish showband.

The showbands were so named when the Clipper Carlton became the first group of musicians to dump their seats and their music stands and start to move around the stage, thereby putting on a *show*. At one point in the late 1950s, there were as many as 760 such bands criss-crossing the length and breadth of the land, putting on shows for the new generation.

This phenomenally successful trend came into being after the Second World War, when a whole swathe of young people simply wanted to get out of their houses, let their hair down and dance. Or maybe they sensed that 'the troubles' were just around the corner. But it didn't really matter what the reason was… they worked hard but were paid little, and so they needed to enjoy themselves. And enjoy themselves they did.

At the top of the showband pile was The Royal Showband, who were so successful that The Beatles actually supported *them* in Liverpool. Then you had The Freshmen – with their perfect, soulful harmonies they were Ireland's answer to The Beach Boys, and they certainly gave the American band a run for their money on the night they shared a stage in Belfast. Next in the pecking order were the aforementioned Clipper Carlton; followed by The Dixies, with their crazy but talented drummer, Joe McCarthy; then The Miami; The Drifters; The Capitol; The Cadets; The Mighty Avons; The Plattermen and, down in eleventh position, The Playboys. They were followed by The Melody Aces and the remaining 748 bands.

There's a good chance that you or your parents – or some of your Irish relations (absolutely everyone has Irish relations) – will have heard of one or more of the showbands, but there is an equal chance that they will have forgotten about The Playboys, or never even known about them in the first place.

The Playboys from Castlemartin, to give them their full name, were a good showband – a great showband by all accounts – and that coveted number eleven spot out of 760 is certainly not to be sneered at. At one point they were closing the doors with 2,500 people inside the ballroom and sometimes just as many outside! They were doing this in every corner of Ireland, six nights a week, all year long – excluding Lent of course, when dancing was strictly forbidden by the church. During that time of year, Castlemartin's finest would try to replicate their Irish success outside of their homeland, in Scotland, Canada and even as far away as Australia.

The band released several single records, which, we are assured in various press cuttings, outsold their competitors by three to one. They had their own weekly 15-minute programme on Radio Luxembourg, and their lead singer, Martin Dean, was on three consecutive occasions voted the most eligible Irish male in the *New Spotlight* poll. At one point, there were even mutterings of The Playboys competing in the Eurovision Song Contest.

If we were to put the band into some kind of modern perspective, I'd say The Royal Showband (safely nestled in the top spot) was the equivalent of the great rock behemoth that is U2, while The Playboys would be on a par with Westlife or similar. Whenever U2 tour, they arrive at the venue in their private jet with an army of personnel, trucks and buses to perform sell-out shows. At the other extreme, The Playboys would have showed up with their entire entourage *and* equipment in one small van. However, unlike their modern counterparts, the *entire* village would have turned out to greet them.

The Playboys' entourage consisted of Martin Dean, the lead vocalist who also doubled on guitar and keyboards. He was young, handsome, single, talented and clean-living. Martin Dean was his stage name, chosen in homage to one of the all-time great chanters and founder member of the Rat Pack. Dixie Blair was the bandleader and saxophonist with ambitions so huge he rarely admitted them, though at one point it looked like The Playboys were going to fulfil these for him. Gentleman Jim Mitchell, the band's smooth, mysterious manager, was also a bit of a gambler. The rest of the band was completed by Brendan, lead guitarist; Davy, bass guitarist; Maurice (Mo), drummer; Robin, trombonist; Barry, organist and alto saxophonist; and Andrew (Smiley), trumpeter. This was 'the band', and as band members they seemed to enjoy a single personality – a united voice.

The Playboys' harmonies – their united voice – came second only to The Freshmen and, like their contemporaries, they were a musician's showband, constantly drawing praise from their peers.

So why is it that the band has been all but forgotten, even written out of the history books? Why was the Irish showband circuit so keen to forget The Playboys' obvious talent? And not just their talent, but also their story?

To find out, we should get back to their story. Let's see now… it all began with a single mother, a gambler, two choirboys and one girl. We are talking about the mid-fifties in rural Ireland here…

THE LAST DANCE
BOOK ONE

CHAPTER ONE

I wasn't a showman;
I was just a musician

Dixie Blair

When trying to define the beginning of a story, it is vital that you pick its real genesis. In all human dramas there are many players. Some have bit parts, while at the same time they can be the stars in some other drama of their own. Some, on the other hand, are the main players, the *stars* in a way I suppose, but at the same time this seems to imply that their involvement is an enjoyable experience and, to a certain degree, that they've agreed to being involved. The surprising thing you find is that the main players at the start of a story will not always remain in such a position throughout, which is probably why it's difficult to identify that pivotal character at the outset.

I suppose in this instance it is relatively easy to pick out our pivotal character, for without Dixie Blair there would be no Playboys, and without The Playboys we would certainly have no story. It could be argued that the principals in this story could have met under other circumstances, which might have produced a similar outcome. I'm not so sure I subscribe to that particular theory. I think we all make our own choices, each and every day of our lives, which bring us into contact with a unique set of characters who, in turn, will affect our individual life choices. So, by process of elimination, Dixie Blair is our man and our starting-point.

Dixie Blair was born on the day the *Irish Press* was published for the first time: September 5, 1933. He was christened Desmond Peter Blair after his father and his uncle respectively, both of whom played saxophone in the Castlemartin town band. Desmond, the father, called his son 'Dixie' from his first birthday onwards. By the time wee Desmond was five, Dixie was his accepted and acknowledged name. By the time he was nine, he was average at schoolwork but was successfully drawing scales out of his father's tenor saxophone. He received his own instrument, albeit second hand, for his twelfth birthday. In 1948, when Dixie was 15, he started his own band, Desmond and Uncle Peter completing the brass section. Desmond christened the band 'Dixie's Teatime Orchestra' in reference to all the tea dances they played.

'I think my dad and Uncle Peter went out of their way to keep me tuned into the music, primarily to keep me out of trouble, you know, with all the Northern Irish/Irish politics,' Dixie recalls. 'The only arguments we ever had in our house were never over religion or politics, no, but our heated discussions were always over the virtues of the great players. The only time I can remember my dad being genuinely upset over politicians was through that incident in 1945 when Éamon de Valera, head of government of the Irish Free State, offered his condolences to the Nazi German Minister on the occasion of Hitler's death. My father felt he was being disrespectful to the 50,000 southern Irish soldiers who'd served in the British Army during the war and that all was lost. He didn't want me involved in any of that auld stuff. So he and his brother, Peter, would round up their mates, some of them well past their sell-by date to be honest, just to make sure I had a full complement to make the concert dates.

'Looking back on it now, I can't believe I was leading the Teatime Orchestra when I was 15 years old, but I don't believe I thought like a 15-year-old would think now. As far as I was concerned I wasn't too young, and my father, God bless him, supported me to the hilt. He wanted to make sure I'd stay interested in and committed to the music. He needn't have worried; but I loved him for it anyway. I'd never any interest in settling down with a real job.'

Even when Dixie's contemporaries were starting their budding careers, in *real jobs*, Dixie was working the petrol pumps in his older brother's garage to help finance his musical endeavours.

'It was never that I'd a grand plan or anything,' Dixie admits. 'I was young and I loved to have a blow. I'd even bring the saxophone into the garage and practise scales while waiting for customers. I got a lot of practice, I can tell you – there weren't many customers in those days. The first post-war motorcar to be seen in Ireland was the Austin A40; I think that was in 1948. The Austin wasn't really a popular car with the Irish drivers. They were more into the Morris Minor, and my brother, who owned the garage, sold the first Morris Minor in Castlemartin – maybe even in County Derry – but I'm not 100 per cent sure about that. I do know it was in April 1949 and it cost £397.'

Dixie certainly had the look of a bandleader, even at that age. He had a light frame, but his enormous hands were out of proportion with the rest of his body. He was constantly trying (unsuccessfully) to straighten his thick, black, wavy hair with water or large dollops of Brylcreem. He was known around town as a 'Derry American' because, like his hero, Glenn Miller, he wore rimless glasses. Some say the lenses were non-prescription, plain glass, and that Dixie wore them only to cultivate the look of the great American bandleader who had disappeared on a wartime plane flight, or at least Jimmy Stewart's interpretation of him in the 1954 film *The Glenn Miller Story*.

'People say I was ambitious; yes and I agree I was most certainly driven but, to be quite honest, I have to tell you I never saw it that way. I'd never a grand plan and, if anything, in 1956, when the Clippers threw their music stands away, I thought my days were numbered. I never figured I would ever have the confidence to do anything like them. I wasn't a showman; I was just a musician.'

After the First World War, the only way to socialise outside of the family unit was to attend barn dances, which became the main arena for the mating game. These gatherings played a crucial role in the social structure of rural Ireland. The only other way in which boys could meet girls was on more formal and rather contrived 'dates' organised by local matchmakers. For the price of a small registration fee you could go on the matchmaker's books. Here you would list all your worldly goods, your qualities and faults (not surprisingly, this particular section was usually left blank) and dictate the qualities you were seeking in a partner. The matchmaker would then do his research and endeavour to put you together with your perfect mate. Sometimes this system was successful, but those wanting a more natural courting process preferred the barn dances.

Barn dances almost always followed the same pattern. The early sessions were led by an accordion player or a couple of fiddlers, or maybe even both, who would get the audience dancing. Then the local singer would get up to do a song or two. A céilidh band would follow, playing traditional tunes, jigs and reels as the caller shouted dancing instructions. It was a wonderful sight, not to mention sound, and was hugely popular with the Irish dancing crowds. At the end of the proceedings a collection plate would go round, with the majority of the take generally going to the farmer (who owned the barn in which the proceedings were taking place). The musicians would receive a bit of drinking money if they were lucky.

Eventually, these dances moved into the slightly more salubrious surroundings of the parish hall, where the village priest acted as promoter. There was a strict admission charge, part of which went to parish funds with the remainder going towards the musicians' expenses. Soon, céilidh bands such as The Malachy Doris Band were joined, and eventually replaced, by travelling orchestras, including the Johnny Quickly Allstars and Hugh Tourish & The Clipper Carlton Orchestra.

Once the wireless became a popular form of entertainment, the dancers began demanding to hear the English and American pop songs that were being piped directly into their homes. Inspired by the new beat of this more expressive up-tempo music, and feeling restricted by their chairs and music stands, the legendary Clipper Carlton Orchestra decided to commit their sheet music to memory, thereby giving themselves the freedom to move around the stage and put on a real show, acting almost as a human jukebox. Their performances became known as 'the band show', which in 1956 morphed into 'showband'.

It was a smart, not to mention revolutionary, move. Suddenly the Clipper Carlton were demanding more attention and getting it from their ever-growing audience.

Around this time, they introduced their famous Jukebox Saturday Night routine, during which the audience would stop dancing for around 20 to 30 minutes and crowd around the stage to be entertained. The Clippers were certainly versatile: their routine incorporated Laurel and Hardy impressions, comedy sketches and musical items with a couple of skiffle tunes.

When The Royal Showband came along in 1957, they were, in a certain inhibited kind of way, considered sexy, setting them apart immediately from the likes of the Clipper Carlton, who at that point ranged in age from 25 to 55, which seemed positively ancient to the younger audience.

While the showbands grew in popularity, so too did the motor-car. This was a newly mobile generation, whose youth didn't mind driving to a nearby village, or even down into Belfast, to hear the new music. In fact, some preferred to endure the extra two-hour drive each way so they could do their dancing and (hopefully) courting away from the local busybodies. In turn, this new mobility meant the bands could ply their trade across the circuit of 2,000 plus capacity ballrooms springing up at every crossroads in the country. The most popular bands were able to play to something like 10,000 people a week, nearly half a million people a year. As a result, their fame spread like wildfire. Most of the old-school musicians, such as Dixie's father, would have seen but a tiny fraction of this audience share in their entire career.

Dixie Blair expected the Clipper Carlton's ballroom revolution to signal curtains for his band and their like. In actual fact, The Clipper Carlton proved to be a one-band boost for the entire Irish ballroom circuit. When a ballroom couldn't book the Clippers, they went searching for the next big draw, and when the ballrooms in the Castlemartin area couldn't book any of the top-ten draws, they started knocking on Dixie's door.

Following suit, The Teatime Orchestra were forced to dump their chairs and music stands and, sadly for Dixie, his father and uncle, who were already running on empty in the stamina stakes, had to give up their places to younger members. The Teatime Orchestra became The Teatime Band, and if you had £5 to spare you could book them to play for four hours at a location of your choosing. Initially, the ever-changing line-up settled on the name 'The Teatime Showband', and Dixie upped the fee to £10.

'Around about 1957, we started to enjoy a regular line-up for the first time', says Dixie. 'Let's see… we had Maurice on drums and Davy on bass. Now they were a really tight little rhythm section. They knew the biggest secret in the showband world: you don't need to be loud to be tight. Barry played organ and alto sax and sang a bit; I played tenor and sang a bit; Brendan played lead guitar and was lead singer. He was great at the country songs, but not so hot on the pop material. We'd always had trouble with trumpet and trombone. The players would either be cronies of my dad and my uncle, which meant they were too old for the one-nighters, or the younger chaps who would prove to be either unreliable or Bengal Lancers, you know, chancers – chancing their arm by saying that they could actually play their instruments when they most definitely couldn't. Eventually we filled the spots with two mates who grew up and played in the local brass band together, that would be Robin on trombone and Andrew – known by everyone as Smiley – on trumpet. They were great chanters as well, perfect for the harmony vocals.

'Me dad and Uncle Peter would still come down to the rehearsals to make sure everyone was shaping up. The boys in the band all liked the two old boys – I mean, they'd a reputation around town as being the greatest players of their day, and give them the slightest encouragement and they'd be off on one of their Dixieland tunes. We actually did a tune of my dad's in the early days: 'Dixieland Brothers Swing'. Eventually we had to drop that, along with a lot of the old-time songs – not much demand for it really, but at the same time I think me dad and Uncle Peter gave the band its initial musical base. It was solid, you know, musically speaking.

'To be perfectly honest with you, I was completely happy with that line-up – it might even have been the best band I've ever been in. The Teatime Showband became Dixie & The Teatime Showband and then Dixie & The Prayboys in 1958. I can't remember the exact reason for the change. Someone thought the 'Teatime' bit of the band name sounded a bit old fashioned, and several of the band had come from various choirs around Castletown, and that's where the Prayboys idea came from.

'The name thing was always a bit of a problem for us in the early days. On the other hand, the Royal, who had started up in 1957, took their name from the Theatre Royal in Waterford – easy. You see how easy it can be? Then there was The Dixies, shortened from The Dixielanders – I'd been considering that one as well at one time – maybe a wee bit too much of an ego trip, but it turned out to be a good name for the Cork boys. And The Clippers; they got their name by running a competition which was won by a barman, who pocketed a ten-bob note by nicking the name from the Pan Am planes. Then there's The Freshmen and The Plattermen and The Cadets and what have you, but The Prayboys didn't really have that kind of a professional ring to it.'

They may not have had a professional-sounding name, but the band formerly known as The Teatime Orchestra did have a full diary. Inspired by his father and his uncle, Dixie had no time for women, liquor or ciggies, instead spending all his waking moments planning for and practising with his band. Dixie was paying each of his men a tenner a week at this stage, cash in hand as it were. Most of the lads would only have been receiving about £2 a week from their regular day jobs.

As a band they were good, but not great; they were working the third level of the circuit, picking up £60 on the weekend and £50 mid-week. They were putting in the hours – as many hours as the big bands – but they weren't getting anywhere, and were fast discovering that it could be extremely exhausting being average.

Although inwardly Dixie Blair was concerned about his band's lack of progress, outwardly he was beginning to show all the signs of a prosperous young 1950s Ulsterman, and he wanted an image to match. Dixie was continuously lecturing his boys that they had to look as good off stage and around town as they did while performing on the bandstand, like their heroes The Royal Showband.

'[They] had this fabulous image,' Dixie says. 'I remember the time – they were starting to get big at this point, mind you, and were packing out ballrooms absolutely everywhere – they drove into Magherafelt, that's the next village to us, in their fabulous kitted-out Commer van, you know, with the name "The Royal Showband, Waterford" in a neon light up on the roof in front of the roof rack, which carried their equipment. They parked up outside Agnew's Café and went in for a coffee. They were all dressed in these amazing sheepskin jackets with silver-blue drainpipe trousers and winkle-picker shoes with white socks. They were like a gang of laughing and joking gunslingers hitting town. I swear to you, mothers would take hold of their children's hands and pull them closer, crossing to the other side of the street. Schoolgirls would pull their white socks up over their knees and hoist their skirts up a bit further into the belts and accidentally happen by Agnew's window once every two minutes or so. The shopkeepers would be walking out onto the pavement, still attired in their aprons, and scratching their heads in bewilderment trying to figure out what all the fuss was about, and the corner boys would be examining the van in great detail to see if they could see Jim Conlon's guitar, Eddie Sullivan's trumpet or Brendan Bowyer's trombone. But they just looked so… "cool" is the best word to describe it. They looked like they belonged. Do you know what I mean? I think that's exactly it. They were leading a romantic life. Yes, because we were also in a band, we knew the reality of hours cramped up in the back of the van together, four hours on stage, no dressing rooms, cold drives home, grabbing a bite whenever you could, but mostly only managing to get potato crisps, Jacob's biscuits and chocolate, so we knew all of that. But that wasn't the public image. They looked class – and that's class with a capital "C" – and although they were outsiders, in that they didn't hold down a regular job, they looked like they belonged. You know, in this life it's important to belong, and then when you do feel that you do belong, it's equally important to be *seen* to belong.'

Image was, therefore, all important to Dixie. To prove his point, he began giving each band member a clothing allowance of £1 a week for shoes, socks, shirts and off-stage clothes. They always wore suits, which were apparently secured for free from Willie Bradley, the Magherafelt-based tailor who also supplied the band's uniforms.

However, belonging and looking good wasn't everything: you also had to feel that you were going somewhere, getting somewhere. There were a hell of a lot of bands out there, and when Dixie stopped to consider the professional and musical progress of The Freshmen, for instance, it could get pretty depressing.

But just as Dixie & The Prayboys were on the brink of losing their momentum and enthusiasm, they played their first date for local ballroom owner 'Gentleman Jim Mitchell'.

CHAPTER TWO

Every crowd has a silver lining

Gentleman Jim Mitchell

Gentleman Jim Mitchell looked like he'd never been a young man, like he'd been born in his mid-thirties so comfortable was he in his classic horse-racing fraternity garb. Fashions came and fashions went with consistent regularity during the fifties and sixties, but not for Jim Mitchell: he was always dressed in brown brogues, dark brown corduroy trousers, country check shirts with gold armbands (to keep his cuffs secured at the perfect length), a green mohair waistcoat and a dark brown – so dark brown it looked black – weather-beaten and well-worn felt hat. He always carried a fawn camel-hair coat with a black velvet collar, which some say had secret pockets sewn deep within the timeless garment which concealed his racetrack earnings and his ballroom takings. The only variable was his choice of tie – red, blue or green – but, winter or summer, spring or autumn he always wore one with a Windsor knot tight up to his top button.

No one knew or could even remember when he had arrived in Castlemartin or where he had come from. There were no known family members to ask, and such personal questions were never welcomed or entertained by the great man himself. His exact date of birth was a mystery, for he never knowingly celebrated his birthday, but an educated guess would have put it somewhere around 1924.

Jim lived in a very grand house he had built for himself halfway between Castlemartin and the Lough Shore. He owned all the land from his house down to the Lough, and the only other building in his immediate vicinity was his beloved Dreamland Ballroom, the jewel in his ever-expanding ballroom crown. 'To me,' Jim would say in his accentless baritone voice – more Henry Fonda than County Derry – 'it's not like it's brain surgery. You have a ballroom, and if it's successful you either pocket the money, and through time it will disappear, or you use the money to build another ballroom, which will continue to stand, thereby protecting your investment, and if the ballroom itself is a successful enterprise it will also earn you money, and so on and so forth.'

By the time Dixie Blair and The Prayboys played their first engagement in the Dreamland Ballroom (this would have been during July 1959, when Derry City's teenage football sensation John Crossan discovered that the only way to beat being banned for life by the English Football League was to pursue his football career in Rotterdam), Jim Mitchell had seven ballrooms around Northern Ireland, and he was also quite a player in the showband circles. It was rumoured that he might have as many ballrooms again in the south of Ireland, but no one really knew for sure. Like all great gamblers, Mitchell had a habit, not to mention a great desire, to play his cards very close to his chest. Even if the rumours that he had ballroom partners running his operation for him in the Free State were untrue, he seemed happy to neither confirm nor deny the stories, thereby conjuring the myth of his substantial extra clout on the circuit, perhaps without owning the hardware to warrant it. If Dixie Blair's philosophy was that he had to be seen to belong, Jim Mitchell's was the exact opposite.

In a rare interview with Russell McLernon, local boy making good as a journalist with Belfast's *City Week* magazine, Mitchell said,

'I'm from the racing world. I love to gamble, but like the majority of gamblers I know I don't see what I do as gambling. You study the form of the horse, the jockey, the trainer, the owner, the track and the going, and you bring to bear all your experience and your expertise and you make a decision and you invest your money in your decision. But I always treated the horses as a business. I'd never get emotional about it. I'd go to the racetrack, and I'd have a certain amount of money in my pocket that I'd already decided to invest that day. And I would work with only that amount of money. If, say, I won money on the first race, then I'd immediately replace my initial investment money in my pocket. I'd actually have different pockets. I'd use one for my pocket money, out of which I'd took my original investment, my float as it were, and one for my winnings and, as I say, out of that one – if there was anything there – I'd immediately replace my invest-ment money. If and when my original investment money ran out, I'd stop then and there. No matter how sure I was, no matter how great a filly looked down in the show ring, I'd walk away. It's a golden rule I've never broken, and a rule I believe to have served me well.

'How'd I get into showbands? Probably due to a racing friend of mine who owned a couple of ballrooms down in Wexford and ran a couple of his own bands. Sorry, I won't tell you who he is if you don't mind. Anyway, he told me he found that working with a show-band was just like gambling on the horses. You did your research on the band. How good were they? How well did they look? Were they punctual? Did they play well? Did they have an image? Did the girls like the singer? Did they have reliable equipment? Did they have photographs and posters? Did they have a good reputation? Could you get the right function room to hire on the right night? Would there be any other bands playing on that night? Would you have enough time to promote the dance? And so forth. You do your research, and you'd invest your money, and if you got it right you'd get a hall full of people turning up, paying their five bob each, and you'd make a tidy profit.

'Initially, I'd let my mate book the bands, and I'd book the halls for him. And then he said, "Right, I've got you started. I'm not holding your hand any longer. Go and do it by yourself now." And I did. And pretty soon I was running shows every Friday and Sunday. I spent the other five nights of the week checking out all the big showbands. Then I discovered things that I hadn't even considered: things like the local priests or other long-serving showband promoters would be able to block you from getting bands in your area. So then I decided that what I had to do was to spot my own bands before they had a loyalty to these other people, these other promoters, and I also had to build my own ballroom rather than being at the mercy of the letting committee or whoever was responsible for booking out the various halls I was using. On top of which, I figured out that if I had my own ballroom I wouldn't be losing out on all the money coming in on the bits we sold to the kids, you know, the tea, coffee, milk, minerals, potato crisps and chocolate.

'Now, the majority of the bands I used would rave about how great the Flamingo in Ballymena was, so I went over there and met the owner, Sammy Barr – a great fellow altogether – and I was far enough away from him that he didn't see me as a competitor so he was supportive, and let me hang out with him every Thursday night at his dances. He was great fun. A great man, very funny. The bands would rib him unmercifully. Like he'd say, "Sure I've got the biggest ballroom in Ireland." And they'd say, "With trousers that size we're not surprised." And so on and so forth. Sorry. But they loved him. They loved him because he had a nice, clean ballroom and he had nice, clean dressing rooms, and he gave them tea and coffee and minerals and the best hotdogs in Ireland. Pretty basic stuff, but you'd be surprised how some of these bands were treated backstage – very primitive, I can tell you.

'Eventually, I got my ideas and my plans together and we built the Dreamland Ballroom. We built it knowing that we wanted to look after our bands and our patrons. We built it to accommodate, we thought, 2,500 dancers, but we've had 3,000 in on a good few nights. We could probably have squeezed another couple of hundred in, but then it would have been chock-a-block, which is no fun for anyone.'

Mitchell ran his empire from the Dreamland Ballroom, and took great delight in telling people to 'call him up in Dreamland'. Like the majority of the ballroom fraternity, though, he conducted his business in person and concluded all his great deals with a handshake and a spit (for the sake of pretence to hygiene we might not have mentioned that sequence in the exact chronological order).

He started his day at 6.30 a.m., when he'd cook himself a breakfast, a traditional Ulster fry, the substance of which was so filling that it would last him through the day with only a sandwich and a cup of tea at lunchtime. He would arrive at the Dreamland at 9 a.m. sharp, by which time his current ballroom manager would have been expected to have opened up shop and have a fresh copy of *The Irish Times* and the *Racing News* laid out for him. If the manager, or anyone else, committed the mortal sin of glancing through his papers first, Mitchell would immediately throw the soiled rumpled copy into the dustbin and send them out for another mint copy. He had to carry out his threat only once with each manager, whereupon he'd find the papers miraculously folded neatly and unread for the remainder of that particular manager's tenure. Most days, irrespective of the time, he'd retire to a contented, deep, trouble-free sleep at the end of the day.

Mitchell had many more foibles. He detested making a request of a staff member – no matter where they stood in the employee hierarchy – and discovering that they had delegated the task to someone else. Again, Mitchell would deliver a stern, one-time-only lecture: 'I employ you. When you prove to me that you are capable of employing someone else at your own expense, then and only then can you delegate. Until then, sir, *you* will do as I request when I request it.'

He disliked cliques and inner circles, and moved his staff around continuously to ensure no such relationships formed under the roof of any of his establishments. To keep a constant check on this he had his office built over the entrance to the Dreamland with four 1-foot-diameter portholes installed, so that from one side he could see out front, while from the other he could observe the comings and goings in the ballroom. He expected his employees to be diligent and go out of their way to find things to do, which was why, thanks mainly to the Dreamland Ballroom odd-job man Scotty Connolly, he had the best-shined car in Northern Ireland: an overtly American-influenced Vauxhall VX490 – green with a distinctive white flash. He demanded loyalty from each and every one of his staff and he paid well, very well in fact, which was why he never had a problem finding replacements.

If there was one member of his staff who was indispensable, it was his long-serving, tight-lipped and fiercely loyal bookkeeper Kathleen McClelland, but more about her later.

Mitchell: 'So, as I was saying, we got the Dreamland up and running, made a few mistakes along the way in the building process and had to backtrack to get it right. I mean, I knew all the time we were doing it that we could have gotten away with less, but I'll let you into a little secret here: I figured we were still going to have trouble getting the big bands, so I thought if I could make the Dreamland a patron-friendly venue, then they'd still like to come here even when I didn't have the biggest of bands playing… We would also serve as a kind of social venue, a community gathering point.

'You have to realise that ballrooms were springing up at every crossroads in those days. I mean, I'm not exaggerating one iota when I tell you that the showband explosion was a phenomenon. So I felt it was important that the people around here felt as if the Dreamland was *their* ballroom, not just *another* ballroom. We take care of the details, which sets us apart. For instance, I always try to use local relief groups, you know, the smaller local bands that would get the crowd warmed up for the main event. And I definitely wanted girls to know they could come here and that they wouldn't be hassled. There's no messing in my ballrooms. I look at it as though I'm inviting someone into my own home; while they're under my roof I'm not going to allow anyone to mess with them or be rude or ignorant to them, now, am I? So while you're in the Dreamland, you're in my house and I'm going to take care of you.

'Look, here's the thing: to me every crowd has a silver lining. Yes, the big boys, The Royal Showband, The Dixies, The Freshmen, The Capital and The Miami are all going to fill your ballroom for you. But we have to accept the fact that there are, say… what… 20 of that calibre of band at the most, you know, a band you can close the doors with at 10 p.m. Now if you're very lucky, their managers are going to let them play for you twice a year. Okay? Well that's 40 nights of the years taken care of if, as I say, you're lucky enough to get them. But I run dances here about 160 nights a year. That's after taking into consideration that you have no shows during Lent and extra shows around Easter, Christmas and carnival time. So you see what I'm saying? You can't afford to be depending on the big bands. Heavens, if I did, sure I'd be out of business with the percentages the big boys are getting these days. The audience, though, they are the important part of all of this. Coax *them* into your ballroom and they'll pay all our wages. We, the showbands *and* the ballroom own-ers must never ever forget that simple fact.

'How much do the big boys get? Away with ye, that's not for me to tell, but I will tell you this: the majority of the boys and the girls who come to my dance halls don't come to see the bands. They come primarily to see each other – to most of them the bands are just the backdrop to the main event, which is getting to meet and talk with new boys and girls. Future husbands and wives are meet-ing every night in the Dreamland Ballroom, and the same applies around the rest of the establishments. So, you see, the more com-fortable you make them feel with your facilities and reasonable ticket prices, the more regularly they are going to come back to your ballroom for dances.'

Mitchell had been spot on in his assessment. There was fierce competition between the ballrooms. In the early days, the priests who promoted the dances were working under 'a higher authority', their priority being the parish coffers, usually at the expense of the patrons or the showbands. More than one ballroom owner – usu-ally a direct competitor – had suffered at the hands of a local priest declaring from the pulpit that the 'cloven hoof' had been seen in their venue. There was no statement more effective in permanently closing down a ballroom.

There was no fear that Gentleman Jim Mitchell would fall foul of local witch-hunts. He made sure he stayed on the parish priests' good side by giving them free use of his venues on Mondays, Tuesdays and Wednesdays for their various functions and clubs.

It was ideas like that that kept Jim one step ahead, and once he'd figured it out in one ballroom, he'd repeat it across his other venues. For example, when he introduced a new band to the area he would encourage a big crowd by giving free admission to the girls. He found, to the band's benefit and his own, that nothing brought the boys in quicker than a venue packed to the rafters with girls.

Furthermore, he discovered quickly that it was much more cost-effective to buy for seven ballrooms than it was to buy for one, and that applied to both general supplies *and* showbands.

Jim Mitchell's only known weakness was his love of the cinema. In fact, he was a movie buff. The nearest screen was in Magherafelt, but it sometimes took as long as a year for a film to open there, so he would drive the three hours to Belfast to see each new release. While he was in the city, he'd do a spot of shopping, have a bite of supper, see his movie and then head to the Floral Hall, where local promoter Jim Aiken would be presenting the biggest and best of the Irish showbands, or sometimes even visiting attractions from the UK. If he was *very* lucky there'd be one of Jim's personal favourites: Roy Orbison. It was the perfect way to mix business with pleasure. (Some said Mitchell was doing a line with a married woman down in the city, but the truth was that no one had ever witnessed him stepping out with a woman. He seemed comfortable enough in female company, mind you – he just didn't actively seek out their attention.)

It was during one of his visits to the cinema that Jim came up with a great idea for decking out his staff in his ever-growing chain of ballrooms. Even when pushed, he couldn't remember exactly which movie had inspired him – maybe one of Cary Grant's early films? It didn't matter; the important thing was that he wanted to replicate the look of American bellhops: the smart uniform, blue, waist-length jacket with silver buttons, grey trousers with a black stripe down the side of the leg and a pillbox hat. Within a month, all of his ballroom staff were dressed in the new garb for dance nights. The patrons loved it – staff were now immediately notice-able and accountable – but some of the staff themselves grumbled at the change. Mitchell absolutely detested negativity, and anyone heard moaning about the uniforms was given the option of leaving either instantly or immediately. He figured that when you could see a potential problem, the best thing to do – always – was to nip it in the bud. You might be right, you might be wrong, but either way at least you'd get a good night's sleep.

Bryson's pub in Magherafelt was 3 miles away from Castlemartin, which had four pubs of its own, but it was a firm favourite with musicians and the like who'd had enough of public houses where the patrons treated drinking as an Olympic sport in which they were representing Ireland. It was here that Dixie's father Desmond Blair crossed paths with Gentleman Jim Mitchell. Desmond, the old sil-ver fox, was subtle enough not to ask outright for a booking for his son's band, but he manoeuvred the conversation around to how well The Prayboys were doing.

Mitchell, having learned several tricks of his own, discreetly went to check out the band in Cookstown so that when Dixie came calling at the Dreamland a few days later he would be ready. Mitchell didn't have a problem with The Prayboys. He didn't particularly like their name, and he thought they were a good, if somewhat average, band, who would probably never be anything other than average, but there wasn't really anything wrong with that – every single band on the circuit couldn't be a good as The Freshmen, The Dixies or The Royal Showband – three of Mitchell's personal favourites – could they?

In fact, Mitchell actually made more money out of the 'average' bands. Thanks to the pioneering efforts of T.J. Byrne – the Royal's entrepreneurial manager – Mitchell and his contemporaries were forced to pay the big boys up to 55 per cent of the gross box-office takings. On a good night, that could be as high as £600, which was at that time, to put it into perspective, roughly equivalent to a teacher's annual salary. The average bands didn't draw as many people to the venue, but they were happy to take an upfront fee of between £50 and £150, meaning Jim actually retained a larger slice of the profit.

It might have been because Mitchell had just returned from the Cheltenham Races where he'd made a few bob on Fare Time, ridden by Fred Winter, trained by Ryan Price and coming in at 13-2. Or maybe he was well aware that Dixie would spend as much time as him promoting the show – the Blairs were a proud and ambitious family, and it meant more to Dixie to have a full house than it did to Mitchell. Whatever the reason, he agreed to give The Prayboys a try at the Dreamland Ballroom.

The Prayboys' first show was a Thursday night in June – the same day that Radio Éireann announced they were banning several songs from the musical comedy *Gigi* because they felt them to be unsuitable for Irish ears. They drew a very respectable crowd of 684, peopled mostly with their friends and families. At 6s. a head, minus the band's fee of £75, Mitchell had made a tidy profit for a Thursday night.

By the time The Prayboys had played their third Thursday, Dixie Blair's confidence had grown to the point that he was pushing Mitchell not only for a better night in the Dreamland but also for a run in his other ballrooms. Mitchell still wasn't convinced enough to give the band a shot at his other venues, but he had taken to both Dixie and his father, who was always somewhere close by in the background. This was reflected in the fact that, by the time they played their fourth date in early December 1959, The Prayboys' fee had risen to £125.

Around the same time, there had been a passing out parade for the first 12 Ban Garda (female Civic Guards) in Dublin's Phoenix Park. Dixie celebrated this very fact by announcing two 'ladies-choice' sets that evening, which was quite unheard of. Usually bandleaders would call the dances in three-song sets – three songs for a dance set of a similar pace or mood. For example, they'd say, 'This next dance will be a slow foxtrot' (or a waltz, or a ladies' choice, where the lady could actually choose with which male she was going to dance). The couples would take to the floor for the duration of the set, meaning they would have approximately ten minutes to make an impression on their dance partner. If they got on well, the boy would ask the girl to save the last dance for him – literally. If she agreed, there was a good chance she was going to let him walk her home. If she turned down his request for a last dance, he still (potentially) had enough time to make the same request with the next girl down on his list.

Some bandleaders viewed the dance-calling sessions as a small window of opportunity to sell their personality, maybe even throwing in a few jokes or wisecracks to make a connection with the audience. Dixie Blair was particularly good at calling the sets. He had an instantly warm, affable personality and the musician's unique sense of humour, which usually had the band members laughing louder than the patrons. He was in fine form on that December night, and for the first time in living memory he was seen to be chatting up a girl – a beautiful, leggy, local blonde – during his single-set break from the bandstand.

At the end of the night, he requested a further chat with Jim Mitchell and his father. They set a time of 1.30 p.m. the following day, and a place – the extremely comfortable Bryson's in Magherafelt for the meet.

'Okay Mr Mitchell,' the ever polite Dixie began, after his father had bought the first round of three pints of Guinness, 'I won't beat about the bush: we'd like you to be our manager.'

Mitchell was somewhat taken aback by this request – he had been expecting a concerted effort from both Blairs to get The Prayboys onto his seven-ballroom circuit. He was flattered by this unexpected turn of events, and stole some time to prepare his reply by taking a long, thirst-quenching drink. As he wiped the rich cream froth from his lips, he took a moment to study his two drinking companions. The youth had all but disappeared from Dixie's eyes, and his enthusiasm had been replaced by the look of someone who always has a long list of tasks to complete. His hair was longish on top and unruly, parted badly because of how thick and unmanageable it was, but it was clean. He always looked friendly, if a little guarded, maybe just slightly hesitant – in the same way a shopkeeper will always greet you with a smile, simply because he wants your business, but he'd never invite you into his house. Desmond was dressed for the weather and not to impress: he looked like a much older, more weather-beaten version of his son.

'Aye, you certainly don't beat about the bush do you?' Mitchell started, as he replaced his half-finished glass on the table. 'Well, in that case, I won't either. I will manage your band, but I have two conditions.'

'Go on?' Blair senior grunted as he fixed the ballroom owner in a sideways stare.

'I want you to change your name to "The Playboys". The Prayboys is neither one thing nor the other, The *Playboys*, on the other hand, sounds like there just might be a bit of glamour and intrigue about you.'

Dixie motioned to his dad, flashing him a 'That's okay isn't it?' look. Blair senior winked his right eye positively at his son.

'Okay,' Dixie replied, unable to keep the excitement out of his voice. 'What's your other condition?'

'This one might appear a bit more complicated, but it's equally important to me,' Mitchell started and paused.

'Go on?' gestured Desmond.

'I want you to add another member to your band.'

This drew a look of shock and surprise from Dixie, but not from his father, who repeated the only words he'd so far uttered. 'Go on?'

'I'd like you to add a singer, a lead singer.'

'But where are we ever going to find a singer around he…?'

'Go on,' said Desmond Blair, interrupting his son. 'Have you anyone in mind?'

'As a matter of fact, I have,' Mitchell said expansively. 'There's a wee band who rehearse in the Dreamland. They're okay, not great to be honest, but the lead singer is excellent. He's a good lad, he looks good, he's a first-class chanter and he writes his own songs. I don't know if the songs are any good or not. That doesn't matter at this stage – the fact that he's writing them is what's important. I have a hunch that, in the future, the really big bands will be the bands that do their own songs and not all these UK and American covers. Sure, when the record buyers can get the originals for the same price, why would they want to buy someone else's interpretation of the hits? But if you're putting out a record of your own songs – well now that would be a different matter altogether, wouldn't it?'

'What? You mean you want us to make a record?' Dixie blurted out, unable to contain his excitement.

'Oh, that would be a long way down the line... possibly even years.'

'And who is this wee boy we're talking about?' Desmond asked.

'Martin McClelland's your man, believe you me.'

'I think I know him,' Blair senior continued as he slowly trawled his memory. 'Yes I've got him now... he's Kathleen McClelland's son, isn't he?'

'Aye, that's right, my bookkeeper's boy.'

'Aye Dixie, he'll do well for you. He's a good chanter. I've heard him in the choir – he's got good range and a strong voice... you could do a lot worse,' Blair senior said as he finished his pint and wiped his lips. 'This is wild thirsty work, this talking.'

'Same again then, lads?' Mitchell offered, reading what Desmond was implying – not so much that he was after another drink, but that he wanted to have a quiet word with his son while Mitchell went to the bar.

Four minutes later, Mitchell returned with three brand new liquid minstrels.

'Okay, aye,' Dixie started, still less than a third of the way through his first pint. 'We're fine with that. I mean, I'm okay with all of that. So you'll be our manager then?'

'I will, aye,' Mitchell replied, shaking the hands of both men. 'It's a deal.'

'I'll tell you,' Blair senior said, 'if you'd said one of your conditions would be on the money side, we'd have walked. If youse all do your jobs properly there'll be money aplenty, but I wouldn't want Dixie working with anyone whose priority was how big a cut they would be getting.'

. Mitchell smiled and took a drink of his Guinness, graciously allowing the old man's compliment to waft around the table like a plume of smoke from Dixie's Senior Service cigarette. The Dreamland Ballroom owner wasn't a great one for accepting praise. He found it hard to accept compliments. He came across as the kind of man who liked people to think well of him, but who didn't particularly like them to say it. However, there at the table in Bryson's, he saw that old man Blair's remark was really his way of initiating the important part of proceedings.

'Are the boys on a split or a wage at the moment?' Mitchell asked, getting things going.

'They're currently all on a wage. A tenner a week... ' Dixie replied, 'cash in hand.'

'Okay. Here's what we should do. We don't want any of that back-of-the-van whispering nonsense about how much each of you is taking home, despite the fact that they're all on stage the same length of time and in the van the same number of hours and the rest of us are all on peanuts – all that nonsense can wreck a band.' Blair senior nodded in agreement and somewhat reluctantly Dixie followed suit. 'I suggest we have 11 shares..'

'But there's only seven in the band – eight if we get young McClelland?' Dixie protested, cutting off his new manager.

'Aye, but you'll take two shares as bandleader, and I'll take two shares as band manager, and if McClelland has any gumption he'll be after two shares as well.'

'But not from the start,' Blair senior interrupted.

'You're absolutely correct – he's got to earn it, but we need to make sure the other band members don't think McClelland's extra is coming out of their pocket down the line, so if we have 11 shares from the beginning...'

'So what happens to the eleventh share?' Dixie asked, obviously still confused.

'The eleventh share will initially go into the pot to pay for publicity photographs and posters and then, if you're going to play the big ballrooms, you'll be needing some new band gear and eventually you're going to need a van.'

'What, with a neon light on top with our name and all of that?' Dixie asked, clearly excited again.

'And all of that,' Mitchell smiled.

'The Prayboys from Castlemartin,' Dixie announced, lifting his pint to a toast.

'The *Playboys* from Castlemartin,' his father corrected him.

'Yes, of course – The *Playboys*,' Dixie replied, still obviously delighted and clearly caught up in the idea of all the new gear.

Mitchell assumed that every band member would fight tooth and nail for every penny they could get, and weep, moan and groan over every halfpenny they felt they'd been deprived of. But drop in a mention of publicity handouts bearing their likeness and posters with their names and faces splashed across them, not to mention new equipment and their own personalised van and, well… they're literally putty in your hands. He dwelled on this thought for only a moment that December morning.

Now that Mitchell had taken on this new role, he felt a certain amount of pride; not only was he the owner of a successful chain of ballrooms, but within 24 hours he had waltzed into the exclusive band manager's club. However, he warned himself that pride comes before a fall, and in so doing, he resolved there and then to make The Playboys not just one of the biggest bands on the Irish circuit, but he wanted them to compete with the best.

'Okay,' he said with a sigh, 'now the hard work starts. This thing with McClelland…'

'Yeah – you've got to try and persuade him to leave his band and join your crowd of comedians?' Blair senior asked, looking directly at Mitchell.

'No,' Mitchell said firmly, 'that *has* to appear to be a band decision. First, Dixie here has to persuade the rest of the boys that they need a lead singer in the first place, and then he's got to try and manoeuvre it so that it's one of the band who actually suggests McClelland.'

'That's fine, leave that to me – you book his wee group to play relief for us for a few dates and I'll handle the band,' Dixie said, as they all drained the remainder of their second pints and buttoned up their coats to leave, not before tidying up a few of the details. Mitchell would take over the band's diary immediately, and from January 1, 1960 they would officially be known as 'The Playboys from Castlemartin'. Mitchell advised Dixie that they should honour all existing dates at the already agreed fees. He would endeavour to raise these from Easter, on condition that they had their lead singer on board by then.

As they left the warmth of Bryson's, and stepped out into the cold, pre-Christmas winds, Mitchell was sure that Dixie could handle the rest of his band members, but handling Martin McClelland... now that would be a different matter altogether.

CHAPTER THREE

Take one fresh and tender kiss
Add one stolen night of bliss
One girl, one boy
Some grief, some joy
Memories are made of this

Terry Gilkyson, Richard Dehr and
Frank Miller (The Easy Riders)

On the day that the big meet between Gentleman Jim Mitchell, Desmond Blair Senior and young Dixie Blair had taken place, Martin McClelland was patiently waiting in his house for his former fellow choir member and current fellow group member, co-songwriter and best friend, Sean MacGee, to turn up to work on a couple of their songs. As he waited, his career was being discussed in hushed tones in Bryson's bar, barely 3 miles away.

Martin and Sean's group was called 'The Chance' – *group*, not *band,* because (a) with four musicians there weren't enough members to meet the early Musician's Union requirement for a band; (b) they didn't have any brass instruments; (c) they played (they hoped) more contemporary music than the showbands; and (d) they never played as the main act, but only as relief to the big bands in the ballrooms and on their own at local clubs and hops. The Chance had been together for about 18 months, playing a total of seven gigs during that period, three of which had been at the Trend Club in nearby Magherafelt.

Martin McClelland was a 17-year-old youth who was inclined to wander. He loved to walk, observing and noting everything that came into his view and into his mind. On the day in question, he was dressed in his usual James Dean uniform: dark, blue denim jeans, whiter than Daz-white T-shirt, white socks and slip-on black leather shoes. He had thick, black hair and, much to his mother's annoyance, avoided the barber like the plague. With the help of Brylcreem, the clever use of mirrors and not to mention *77 Sunset Strip* character Kookie's two-handed hair-combing technique, he kept his thatch in a Tony Curtis DA (short for duck's . . . well, 'posterior' would probably work better for the fainter hearted) by checking it at regular five-minute intervals. His trademark polished steel comb was ever present in, and visible from, the back pocket of his jeans.

At this point in his life, the puppy fat had all but disappeared from his face, and with his new sharply chiselled features and baby-blue eyes he started to draw admiring looks from the single girls and the younger married women alike. Not that he noticed such attention. No, Martin McClelland only had time for his songs and his mother.

Martin's father had deserted the family when Martin was just old enough to miss him, so he and his mother were tight, very tight – tight to the point that Sean MacGee often sneered at the loyalty Martin afforded his mother.

Martin sat on the edge of his bed, strumming his Hofner guitar, unfocused on the chords he was playing and staring absent-mindedly into the open guitar case on the floor of his congested bedroom. In it he noticed a photograph of his mother, which was turned away from him by about 120 degrees. The photograph had been taken before her accident, when she was a teenager, and at that obscure angle she looked unconnected – detached, as though she were floating through space. Martin tried to stare into her kind eyes, but because of the angle he found that he couldn't concentrate on her. He momentarily stopped strumming his guitar, and leaned over to straighten the sepia photograph. As he did so, he nearly fell off his unkempt bed, and he quickly steadied himself against his knee to avoid losing his balance and tumbling over on his precious guitar. Precious not because it was a particularly expensive instrument, as the receipt in the guitar case testified, but because he knew the sacrifices his mother had made to ensure that she was able to buy it outright for him and not on hire purchase. She was always lecturing him never to buy anything 'on the slate' or 'on tick', as the shopkeepers around town were fond of saying. 'Never buy anything unless you have the money in your pocket to pay for it,' had always been his mother's advice.

The young musician recalled the numerous times he'd walked the 3.5 miles into Magherafelt just to visit Tone Sounds at the foot of Broad Street and stare at the guitar in the shop window, the very same guitar that he now gently strummed. It was the first real guitar he'd seen in his life. Yes, he'd ogled a million photographs in the magazines, of stars caught mid-strum with their instrument. He had even sent away for Bell's catalogues so that the likes of Hofner, Gibson and Burns could flaunt their various wares at him. But he became obsessed by this one guitar in particular, which looked so cool with its variation in stains and varnishes, blending to create a warm, autumn-coloured soundbox. The colours contrasted pleasantly with the heavily polished tan neck, which stretched the six steel strings so tight you could hear the 'ping' just looking at them.

Martin became overwhelmed with love for this instrument, yet he wasn't sure where the obsession had come from. It wasn't that he had ever wanted to master the instrument or anything as honourable as that. On reflection, he thought it might have more to do with his inbuilt compulsion to write songs.

Ever since he could remember, he would occupy and amuse himself by walking around, singing little songs he'd made up on the spot. He'd tried to learn to play the piano, just so that he could find a way of grounding his songs in music to help him remember them. But he couldn't find anyone to teach him to play in the way he wanted: the three local piano teachers had each furnished him with boring scales and exercises while lecturing him with the line: 'You've got to creep before you can walk.' Every time he tried to improvise and work up the chords for one of the melodies in his head, they'd return him to the scales, with a hot ear for his troubles.

From the little he *had* learned, he soon realised the piano wasn't the instrument for him. Quite apart from the financial and physical considerations, he didn't think it would suit his songs. Learning the numerous finger positions to produce chords on a guitar, and then strumming them over and over in various sequences, was going to be a much better way for him to ensnare his melodies.

One particularly wet morning, as he stood outside Tone Sounds transfixed by his beloved guitar, the astute shop owner came out onto the pavement and invited Martin to have a closer look at the instrument. Martin was actually going to be allowed to hold the guitar and strum its strings. Despite his obvious excitement, he was yet to learn any of the wondrous chord combinations that would unlock the secrets of the pleasing harmonies he so desperately sought.

'Oh,' the shopkeeper offered on hearing Martin's first efforts, 'it must be out of tune. I wonder how that happened. I'm quite sure it was in tune when I bought it!' The shopkeeper and his assistant (supposedly his cousin, but apparently this was only a cover for them living together) – both fell about in stitches of laughter at his obviously oft-repeated joke.

However, Martin's mind was elsewhere: he had discovered a major problem in his plan. Should he ever be lucky enough to afford to buy this guitar – any guitar, in fact – how on earth would he ever be able to keep it in tune? The problem was quickly resolved by the shopkeeper who pulled out Bert Weedon's *Play In A Day* guitar book, pointing out the section on tuning the instrument. By now very aware of Martin's enthusiasm, the shopkeeper gifted him a copy of the book.

'Either this will make sense to you or, if you're like me, it will be like a foreign language. It might therefore be an idea that you give it a good read before you waste any money on the auld banjo there.'

Martin couldn't wait to get home to discover the secrets of the guitar. Before the day was through, he'd cut up a cardboard box, marking out a pretend fret-board by drawing lines for the strings. He immediately started to practise the finger positions of the various chords listed in Bert's handy wee book. By the time he put the cardboard fret-board down, the wrist of his left hand was aching so much he was convinced he'd never be able to learn to play the guitar, but by the third day he was feeling no discomfort whatsoever.

A week later, he returned to Tone Sounds.

'Well,' the shopkeeper began, 'was it friend or foe?'

'Oh, definitely friend,' Martin replied, his enthusiasm evident to the entire shop. 'Could I have another try on the guitar please?'

'Why certainly, Martin,' the manager replied, aping Stan Laurel by twiddling with his tie and scratching his crown from above.

This time, armed with his newly practised chords, Martin discovered that he was able to coax a bit of music out of the guitar, even if he had to press the strings down a lot harder than he'd expected to make the chord ring true. Using a set of tuning pipes, which he insisted on buying, and faithfully following Mr Weedon's instructions, he was even able to tune the guitar to some degree.

'Close enough for a céilidh band,' the shopkeeper gasped on hearing Martin's efforts.

Martin hadn't mentioned a word of any of this to his mother, but obviously other shoppers had. And so, on the occasion of his fifteenth birthday, his mother presented him with his first guitar. The sales receipt, revealing a cost price of £4/19s./6d., was now a permanent resident in his guitar case. Martin wasn't sure why he'd kept it; maybe he felt it was the only way to convince himself that his dream really had come true and the guitar was actually his.

Having long since resolved to keep the instrument for the rest of his life, Martin sat strumming the same guitar that morning in his bedroom. He didn't know enough about such things, but he was convinced that his instrument must have been some kind of fluke, so rich and warm was its natural tone.

He stared into the guitar case, and studied the rest of its contents. A photograph of himself and Sean MacGee with Norman, their drummer, and Eric, their bass player, was the first approved photo of the group, complete with the legend 'The Chance' in large letters at the bottom. Underneath that, in much smaller lettering, it said, 'For bookings ring Martin McClelland on Castlemartin 2450'. The contact telephone number was Martin's local telephone box. To date, no one had called to book the band as a result of the publicity handout.

At varying times, Martin viewed The Chance's efforts as either totally amateur or affording them a slight prospect of turning professional. From his point of view, it seemed it was he who was pushing them to get to a better station. Sean didn't seem to mind spending time writing songs – in fact he was great at polishing off some of Martin's more cumbersome lyrics and shoehorning them neatly into the melody line – but at the end of the day he was more interested in the comforts offered by the next bottle of scrumpy he always seemed to be magicking up.

Martin hadn't acquired a taste for alcohol, and was continuously annoyed by the amount of rehearsal time Sean wasted while incapacitated. As soon as Martin removed his comb from his back pocket, gliding it through his hair with one hand firming it into place followed by the other a split second later, you knew he was frustrated.

If Sean was the big disappointment in Martin's life, his mother was the complete opposite. Martin never ceased to be amazed by the many things his mother understood. They spoke as friends, as they had done since Martin was 9 years old when his dad left, and they were always talking – as quickly as Martin could find another question to ask, his mother would answer it. Her take on Martin's pal Sean was that he was going through a phase, rebelling as he thought he must. She could sense he was down, and if he could just meet someone who would make him happy again he'd surely give up his dependence on the drink.

Martin could discuss absolutely anything with his mother; anything bar his father that is. He'd asked about him on two separate occasions: on the first time, Kathleen had said his father had decided not to be with them any more; on the second time, she'd been much firmer, replying that it was better they didn't discuss the subject any further. That was fine with Martin – it was disrespectful to his mother to be preoccupied with someone who'd never been there for them when she had shown him nothing but unconditional love his entire life. On top of that, he didn't want to intentionally hurt her.

He was surprised at his own ability to block his father from his consciousness altogether. He'd even reached the point where he was no longer the slightest bit curious about the identity of his father. Despite this, as he grew older he could not help but be surprised that someone as ordinary and as good as his mother had a child out of wedlock at a time when it was considered to be the most taboo subject in Ireland. His mother was not an impulsive person, so she must have really loved his father to have borne his child.

As a younger boy, around 8 or 9, he'd set himself the task of finding out if his father had left his mother because of her accident. Kathleen McClelland had a 2-inch scar under her left eye, and the stretching of the skin around this area of her face had caused a certain amount of disfigurement. The bottom part of her eyelid was permanently pulled down to the scar. To Martin, it looked like she didn't have enough skin to close her left eye properly, but she always managed to do so. When Martin was young enough to still be sitting in her lap, his mother's scar intrigued him. He would amuse himself by getting her to open and close her eye, which would send them both into uncontrollable fits of laughter.

The accident had happened one summer. Kathleen had been trailing around the shops of Castlemartin, and had arrived back home exhausted and extremely thirsty. She decided to open one of the bottles of lemonade she had just purchased. During the walk home, the mineral had splashed around in the bottle and the gas had built up quite a head of steam. Kathleen couldn't remove the tight bottle top so, armed with the old fail-safe bottle opener, she placed the bottle in the gap between the kitchen door and the doorpost, which acted as a very effective vice. The secret was to ensure you didn't unscrew the top all the way, otherwise the lemonade exploded all over the place, so she carefully began to loosen it. However, the pressure of the gas build-up was enough to force the bottle top completely off, and it shot up, hitting Kathleen under the eye. The doctor in the hospital had said that if the ejected top had jumped half an inch higher, she would have lost her eye, maybe even her life. The resulting scar, Martin's mother claimed, served as a reminder to both herself and her son that you can never be too careful.

Martin concluded that, because the accident had happened two years before he was born, the scar couldn't have been the reason for his father leaving his mother.

Martin looked away from the publicity photo of The Chance, and focused instead on the well-worn edition of Bert Weedon's tutorial, also lying in the guitar case. To the left, and just visible underneath it, was a copy of Dean Martin's one and only UK number one hit single, 'Memories Are Made Of This' – a song written for the crooner by his backing band, The Long Riders. Apart from the song, Martin liked the sleeve and the way the name had been worked into the photograph and, though he would admit this to no one but himself, his dream was to have a record out some day and to use the same idea on his own sleeve. He'd tried to fashion The Chance's first publicity shot in this way, but whereas Dean Martin's single looked cool and sophisticated, his efforts were amateur, like the lettering had been cut from a newspaper headline and crudely pasted on.

Martin also kept a silver tuning fork, which had replaced his original tuning pipes, and several spare sets of Fender steel-wound strings, which were always carefully packed in a plastic envelope in a special compartment so as not to scratch the guitar. He liked it because it was hidden – just a raised-up section of the dark blue velvet housing that lined the inside of the case and a little piece of identical coloured ribbon, which, when pulled, revealed the secret compartment. Martin also used this compartment to store a few coins, a few plectrums and the first pound note he'd ever made playing his guitar.

That particular performance had been a bit of a disaster really. It was a friend's birthday party, and the partygoers were more into Elvis Presley and Cliff Richard than Dean Martin and Nat King Cole. Pretty soon, the novelty that one of their friends could play the guitar wore off, and they started to drift away. But Martin had kept his agreed fee, hoarding the pound note as a souvenir of his first professional engagement, and as a reminder always to be conscious of his audience.

Martin used his bare toe to flick the Dean Martin single in the figure-of-eight shaped guitar case, uncovering a light blue ribbon. It had dropped from the head of a girl he'd been infatuated with since he was 12 years old, and he'd hoarded it as a keepsake. In the early days, he'd even been guilty of occasionally sniffing it to enjoy the aroma of the girl who'd awoken this forbidden side of his life. All the ribbon smelled of now was the inside of the guitar case, the predominant trace being that of the varnished wooden instrument, which, for now, had taken her place in his affections.

Next to it lay a photograph of himself and the girl on the annual school excursion to the seaside town of Portrush. Martin clearly remembered the street photographer outside Barry's Amusement Arcade, where on impulse he'd caught the girl's hand and pulled her in front of the camera. The look in her remarkably beautiful eyes was in equal portions one of happiness and shock. Martin removed the photograph and smiled at it. There he was, barely in his teens and with a beautiful girl on the streets of Portrush. He smiled to himself, thinking back to the happiness of that summer morning.

He placed the photograph back down, and removed a couple of sets of lyrics lying in the body of the guitar case. He carefully balanced one of the sets on his knee, and removed the plectrum from between his teeth. He started to strum, very gently at first: C, A, F, G and then back to C. He played the sequence three times, and on the fourth he began to hum a very soulful melody with a Celtic influence. He continued to hum for another three passes of the sequence before adding the lyrics. Mostly he sang with his eyes closed, but occasionally he would open them when he needed prompting from the lyric sheet that was resting on his knee.

He called the song 'There's Always Another Song At The End Of A Teardrop', but the lyrics were still incomplete:

There's always another song
Waiting on the end of a teardrop
There's always another reason
Why I can forget you
Dada da da dadadada da da

I'm tired of trying to block out
All my sweet memories of you
I can never stop the pictures
From flooding back again
Last night I fell asleep hoping
You wouldn't come calling in my dreams
Like you did the night before
Like you always do

Yes there's always another song
Waiting at the end of a teardrop
There's always another vision
That won't let me forget you
Dada da da dadadada da da

And though you don't want me…

And here Martin broke off from the lyrics, and returned to humming, scatting, trying out words, repeating lines in a desperate effort to make them fit. Perhaps that was the problem; he was trying just a wee bit too hard to find a great lyric. He hadn't even sought any help from the now absent Sean MacGee, because it was a song about her, and it was too real, too personal, and he was very self-conscious about it.

Martin had a beautiful, rich, soulful voice influenced (unintentionally) by the aforementioned Nat King Cole and Dean Martin, the latter being McClelland's all-time favourite singer and his idol. Alone in his room, he struggled to find his voice, but on stage with a microphone he miraculously transformed into a magical singer.

He sang his lyrics again, still unable to find suitable words for the missing lines.

He stopped singing, and pulled another lyric sheet from his guitar case. This song had been a departure for him, another one written without MacGee's help, and the first he had ever written about a real-life, albeit tragic, incident.

On January 31, 1953, a large passenger ferry, the MV *Princess Victoria*, sank near the Copeland Islands at the entrance to Belfast Lough. A total of 128 people lost their lives on that tragic morning, and only 44 survived, making it Ireland's worst peacetime sea disaster. Martin was only 9 years old when it happened, but the image of all those people drowning gave him nightmares for months, and it had never been far from his mind whenever he took his favourite walk along the shores of the nearby Lough Neagh. He called the song simply 'No Time To Say Goodbye', because it was written from the perspective of the relatives of those who'd drowned, having been deprived of their final farewell.

He sang the song through once, which was enough to know that it was complete. If anything, he felt the song had written itself – it had taken as long to write as to sing the lyrics through. It was funny how some songs came like that, while others, like 'There's Always Another Song At The End Of A Teardrop', could take a month of Sundays of work and still wouldn't be there.

He tried another song, but he couldn't make any progress on that one either. Maybe it was due to his frustration with Sean not showing up, or perhaps it was down to the unresolved relationship with the blonde-haired girl of the 'Teardrop' lyrics, Miss Hanna Hutchinson.

Martin poked around in the bottom of the case until he found a large, brown envelope, which concealed a black-and-white photograph, no more than a year old, of the girl. She looked absolutely beautiful, but Martin thought it still didn't do justice to the real-life version.

Martin had known Hanna since the end of primary school. Hanna, being a bit of a tomboy, hung out with her brother, who was mates with Sean MacGee. Consequently, the circumstances brought Hanna and Martin together. She was the first girl Martin had ever been friends with, but this had never been an issue in the early days, and nothing would be neither made nor said of it. They were merely very close friends; she always made him laugh with her sharp dry humour and her anti-pigtails wit, and they would go to each other's houses for tea.

But one day – he'd have been 14, she 16 – Martin looked at Hanna and realised just how beautiful she was. He began to notice how her figure was filling out under her clothes. Her dark eyebrows – instead of being comical in contrast to her blonde hair like he'd once thought – were becoming a striking feature on an absolutely stunning looking face. For the first time in his life, he was *attracted* to a girl. He'd find himself stealing glances at her when he thought she wasn't looking, but she would sometimes notice and say 'What? What are you looking at?' thumping him in the arms or ribs as punishment.

Around the time of Martin's discovery, other boys were also starting to cotton on to Hanna's blossoming looks. At first, Martin was scared by this new attention, but later he was relieved to find that it actually drove them closer together. In lieu of having a better girlfriend, Hanna confided to Martin that she was concerned about the attention she was getting from boys. If anything, she was embarrassed by her good looks.

'What do you think I should do?' she asked in her husky voice.

'Do you like any of them?' he asked, crossing his fingers in his pocket and hoping that the nervousness in his voice wasn't evident.

'No, not really,' she replied, brutally honestly.

'Well then, why are you even considering it?'

'Don't be naïve, Martin. They're boys, I'm a girl, and that's the way it works. They ask me out. I go out with a few of them. Eventually, I meet one of them I don't actually find offensive, we get married and breed babies, and then in 18 years' time the babies end up doing the same thing all over again.'

The last statement stopped Martin in his tracks. 'You don't actually believe all that crap do you?'

'Oh, so now you're going to give me one of your lectures on true love and all that carry-on?' she replied, her frustration with Martin clearly growing.

'"And all of that carry-on?"' Martin said, unsure whether to be upset or amused.

'Martin, you don't mean to tell me that you still believe all that nonsense about true love and that "there's only one love for you and one for them" rubbish? Look, Martin, we're here on this planet, we don't know why we're here, or who put us here, but we're here, and it seems to me that while we're here we might just as well drop a few wains until such time as someone figures out exactly why we are here in the first place. At least this way this human zoo of ours can continue. You know, just in case we were meant to be doing something important in the first place, for instance like being the food for some creatures from another planet or something equally enticing.'

'But there's more to life than that!'

'Okay, pray tell.'

'Well, there's your mother and your brother and achievements and care…'

'No, no, Martin, don't be confused; that's all still part of the zoo – they die, you live on, you die and your offspring live on,' she said with an air of finality that scared Martin.

'Okay, if that's the case, why trouble yourself over whether it's Tom, Dick or Harold for you? It seems to me that, as far as you're concerned, it doesn't matter one little bit and it doesn't make any difference who you have kids with, so why bother yourself with all the problems of the selection process? Why not just take the first one who comes along?'

'And are ye volunteering?'

Martin didn't respond. He was trying to think of a clever answer because he didn't want to scare her with an honest reply. He was still searching when she cut back in.

'Oh I get it, you're saving yourself for Mrs Right, right?'

Martin was tempted to reply, 'Are ye volunteering?' but he couldn't quite find the confidence, so he said 'We're not talking about me here, we're talking about you. And I repeat my question… why don't you just take the first person who comes along?'

'Well, two reasons actually. The first is that, although I realise I'm only on this earth as part of the baby-producing machine, I want to be comfortable for my three score years and ten I'm on this planet.'

'And the second reason?' Martin prompted.

'Well, wee boy,' she started, coyly using her favourite nickname for Martin, 'if I were to step out with, say, Sixer Kelly or the like, wouldn't that mean we'd not be able to hang out together any more? You know, the old jealously factor would raise its ugly and essential – for the reproduction of mankind, that is – head.'

Martin took her point and decided not to push the issue any further, but he had been surprised and shocked by her reaction. He knew her well, at least well enough to know that she was a bit of a revolutionary and that she'd some pretty far-out ideas, but to appear to elect a life completely devoid of love? Well, that just seemed way out there, even for someone like her. Yes, he could in some ways understand it if she'd been a girl who looked like the back end of a bus, but she was blossoming into a goddess, giving the likes of Brigitte Bardot a run for her money. If it ever came down to it, there'd be no competition, no competition whatsoever. Hanna Hutchinson would win that particular beauty contest every single time – French accent or not. In Martin's eyes, Hanna looked even more like Barbara Parkins, the actress from *Peyton Place*. As far as Martin was concerned, that was probably an even bigger compliment.

Martin was bewildered by how little he really knew Hanna, and therein lay the problem.

When he was 16 and she 18, Martin McClelland and Hanna Hutchinson had enjoyed their first kiss. But it wasn't with each other. And since they hadn't shared their first kiss, they decided they'd better share their second.

How the whole thing happened was this.

Although Martin and Hanna had gone on to different high schools, they remained good mates and confided their deepest thoughts to one another, sometimes talking for hours.

Martin was forced into a double date as a favour to his best friend, Sean MacGee. Sean's current beau, Maggie Curtis, could and would only meet up with him if her sister, Colette, could come along 'because of Daddy's rule'. Colette turned out to be a fussy kind of creature, and she wouldn't be a gooseberry. She would, however, quite like to go on a date with Martin McClelland, whom she considered quite cute now that his voice had dropped and he sounded like Dean Martin.

Colette wasn't backward at coming forward, and within minutes she was tickling Martin's tonsils with her tongue. The kiss was pretty forgettable and very unsensual, particularly as her tongue tasted of cabbage (his least favourite vegetable). Not only that, she indicated that she was up for further examination and experimentation behind the bike shed at Magherafelt Tech. Martin wasn't having any of that – he left her standing there and, for all he knew, she might still have been there when he told Hanna all about it the next time they met.

Martin couldn't believe how unpleasant the experience, particularly the kiss, had been. He had genuinely thought his first kiss was going to be magic – the whole romantic blissful works.

Obviously Hanna didn't take much notice of Martin's misgivings, because the next time Sixer Kelly invited her out she accepted, and on the date she said that for her to go out with him again he'd need to be a great kisser. 'So… let's get it over with,' were her exact words.

So they did, with the result that she cut the date short and went to Martin's house to give him chapter and verse of her first romantic adventure.

'Well,' Martin said after hearing her tale, 'perhaps you were right. Perhaps it is all a functional experience and all the pretence of romance is only propaganda cultivated by society over the centuries to ensure that couples feel in the mood for mating.' She flashed him one of her 'I told you so' looks. 'What a let down,' Martin groaned.

'You're not kidding,' she replied. 'That's certainly been my belief, as you know, but even I was hoping for a little more from the procedure.'

'Tell me… ' Martin continued, 'what did your kiss taste like? Mine was like cabbage.'

'Coffee and KitKat.'

'Coffee and KitKat?'

'Yes, we'd just been to Agnew's,' Hanna answered absent-mindedly. 'Isn't it strange though, two people getting together?'

'What, meeting and dating?'

'No, I meant getting together for the reproduction process,' Hanna continued, maintaining eye contact with Martin. 'I mean it's just so…'

'Strange?'

'Yes, I suppose strange is a good word. Bizarre would work too. Probably even weird. Yes, maybe weird is the best word. If you just step back and look at it, it's too weird for words.' Hanna sounded like she didn't know whether or not to continue with her thoughts. Martin's silence and shrug was all the encouragement she needed. 'Right, we start by holding hands, skin on skin, right?'

'Right,' Martin agreed.

'Then we kiss,' Hanna smiled, 'again skin on skin. But can you imagine walking along the road and seeing two cows kissing?'

'Only if they were fruit merchants,' Martin replied. 'Well, I suppose they could be – they don't wear socks either.'

Hanna didn't understand Martin's joke but she continued, 'or dogs or horses. And then he puts his hand on her breast, again skin on skin. And then he puts his hand on her leg, more skin on skin. And then she puts her hand on his leg. *Skin on skin*. And then… and then he puts… ugh, I don't even want to think about it any more!' She rolled back into the sofa in fits of laughter. 'I get the shivers just thinking about how bad it felt to kiss Sixer Kelly.'

'I'm still trying to forget mine,' Martin replied. There was a certain amount of pride evident in his voice though. In a way, it was as if he too had been through the war of love and, although he was younger, it made him feel equal.

They were in his mother's room listening to *Frank Sinatra Sings For Only The Lonely*, already a classic Capitol Records album. His mother was out. The lights were low. Martin had not planned it that way – he just liked to listen to music with the lights down and no distractions, and that's the way it had been when Hanna came calling.

'Unless of course,' says he.

'We weren't trying it with the right person,' says she.

'Yes,' says he, 'I wonder should…'

'… should we try it with each other, you mean?' says she helpfully.

'Yes,' says he, 'perhaps we should?'

'Only as an experiment,' says she.

'Of course,' says he, hoping that the vibrato in his voice isn't noticeable, 'of course.'

It was a clumsy encounter at first, mainly because they were friends and were unsure of where to put their hands and arms and unclear of the angle, timing and even whether to approach each other's lips. But then, following a few seconds of awkward fumbling, their lips met and the shock of an electric charge blew away any unnaturalness of their contact.

The important thing was how gentle their first kiss was. Hanna would have described it as gentle. Martin, on the other hand, would have described it as loving. No matter how either of them tried, unsuccessfully, to capture the magic in words, the gentleness of their first contact was awesome and beautiful in equal amounts.

After a time, he found a parting in her lips and started to explore further with his tongue. He opened his eyes briefly to see if the new adventure was going down okay. Her eyes remained closed. He'd never seen her with her eyes closed before. Just as he was thinking how beautiful she was, her tongue made contact with his tongue and he wasn't prepared for how electrifying that was going to be. His eyes closed unconsciously and he lost himself in the kiss.

They kissed so much that their jaws hurt, and the more they kissed the more they hurt. It was a blissful kind of pain, though, which made the kissing even more enjoyable. Martin was experiencing pure joy in the fullness, softness and dampness of her lips. Although she felt that she had known Martin well, Hanna couldn't believe what a caring and considerate kissing partner he was.

Their future experiments never ventured beyond the kissing line. Martin wasn't sure he had the capabilities to withstand more pleasure than that he experienced when kissing Hanna. They never once discussed how they'd started kissing. They never once got soppy with each other. He knew that although she'd taken to tenderly holding his hand when they were alone, should the 'L' word ever be mentioned, she'd run a mile – at the very least – without looking back. Such was their joy that neither was concerned about what they should be doing to take their relationship to the next level. They were both equally and completely fulfilled. If they'd been able to capture that space, that time, forever, it would have been perfection.

But that's neither what society expects nor wants from its young mates. Under such conditions – lack of physical fulfilment – society would reach an end within four generations. So the primeval animal instincts are continuously at work whether or not we know about them, let alone accept them.

About three months into the kissing phase of their relationship, Martin realised that he hadn't seen Hanna for at least a week. The week became ten days, and the ten days became two weeks, and then, on June 14, 1959, he finally bumped into her on the steps of Agnew's Café. It hadn't been a planned meeting – made obvious by the fact that she was holding the hand of Sixer Kelly as their eyes met.

Martin always figured that if ever he tried to write a song about that encounter, it would need to be an instrumental. They said nothing to each other because there *were* no words to say.

To say that Martin's heart was broken was, in a way, similar to saying that Arkle was a great horse or that The Beatles were a brilliant group. While all three pieces of information are factually correct, none really conveys successfully or adequately the enormity of the situation.

CHAPTER FOUR

Life is sweet
Life is bitter
John loves Mary
Does anyone love John?

Martin McClelland

Hanna Hutchinson cannot remember any of the thoughts she had while she was growing up. All those of which she was conscious were from her late teens. She could never work out where her thoughts came from, or who was responsible for implanting the seeds of such thoughts in the part of her brain that was responsible for exposing them to her consciousness. They definitely didn't come from her parents. She had always felt strangely detached from them. Her parents were not of her, or perhaps more appropriately – but this wasn't the way that the thought first came – she was not of them.

She didn't really know why she felt this. She just knew that she felt it with such passion she convinced herself it was true. In the early days, she assumed her parents, particularly her mother, were amused by her ideas, but by the time she was allowed to go to the ballrooms – a week after her 19th birthday – she saw finally that her mother was scared and alienated by them.

Hanna examined the facts. She had blonde hair and dark eyebrows – she felt she looked kind of Spanish or Roman really. Neither of her parents nor any of her grandparents had blonde hair. Even her brother looked like he had come from yet another family altogether. Mind you, if push came to shove, he could probably have claimed to have inherited his father's nose and ears – not that anyone would have wished to have those features, excepting Dumbo that is, perhaps. Hanna spoke differently from her parents, and that was even before she went to primary school. She pronounced all her words properly, avoiding the laziness in speech the Ulster folk had made into an art form. She was taller than her mother and her older brother by the time she was 13. By the time she was 14, she'd even managed to outgrow her father.

The most important difference for Hanna, though, was the fact that she *thought* differently to any other member of her family. No, she didn't know where her thoughts came from, and she didn't particularly like them – sometimes they felt alien to her, or she to them. It felt like they were invading her body and fighting with her every logical thought for brain space.

Hanna in fact felt so different to her family in every way that her mother and father even went to the trouble of presenting her with her birth certificate, and yet she still wouldn't believe that she was their child. The only logical conclusion was that someone had made a mistake at the hospital when she was born and she'd been sent home with the wrong parents.

And then, all of a sudden, it didn't seem to matter.

Hanna was 19, and she wasn't anyone's daughter or sister any more. She felt like she was out of the chain. She had decided she was going to be the one to break the parent-to-child link.

At first, she celebrated her new-found independence by caring about no one. Then she found the one and only person she cared about as much as herself. But when she realised how *much* she cared for him, she cut him off immediately without even saying goodbye. She felt there would be no good in their byes, and so, in a split second, she erased him from her life and her mind, if not from her heart.

Why had she done that? The truth was that she really didn't know why. She wished with all her heart that she hadn't but, when it came down to it, she felt she had no say in the matter. She watched the damage she caused compulsively, in a manner similar to a spectator at a boxing match. You knew instinctively that you shouldn't watch and take pleasure from seeing someone pulverised to near death but, at the same time, you were always compelled to watch on.

And here's the strange thing: in a way she felt guilty for taking perverse pleasure in the way she'd dumped Martin; in the way she'd pulverised and humiliated him, using the art of ignoring him as lethally as any of Cassius Clay's right hooks. In fact, it looked like Martin would have preferred to have his head beaten in by Clay rather than see her walking hand in hand with Sixer Kelly.

In Hanna's time of self-doubt and justification, she'd consider the theory that it wasn't that she hadn't thought Martin was a nice guy, but that he was a committed musician: consequently, there was a good chance that he was going to be penniless. With this she puzzled even herself: normally she wouldn't have bothered to consider such a thing. It had never occurred to her that she wanted to be with someone who could guarantee her a comfortable lifestyle, although she accepted the fact that, given the choice, she would have liked exactly that. But if her decision had only been a financial one; then surely she should have been happier when she dumped Martin? At the very least, she should have been able to make sense of her actions.

Hanna didn't know that in this life you shouldn't try to change the course of what is mapped out for you. She did accept that there was a potential danger in trying to manufacture happiness; it was just that she didn't really care about such a danger. But she wasn't what you would call a bad person. No, far from it in fact; she was merely guilty of being the only person she knew how to be.

CHAPTER FIVE

Treat them mean and keep them clean

Smiley

The Chance had *their* first chance with The Playboys at the Dreamland Ballroom in Castlemartin on February 13, 1960, which was shortly after John F. Kennedy was inaugurated as President of the United States of America, the land of the free, and the home of the hearts of many of the Irish.

Although the opportunity had been orchestrated as a result of Mitchell, Blair and Blair's meeting in Bryson's pub, The Chance weren't aware of this. As far as they were concerned, they had been booked as a relief group for The Playboys, which meant they had a job to do, and an important job at that.

Relief groups began to play a vital role in the booming showband scene. Showbands were usually booked to play from 8 p.m. to 1 a.m., with late dances running on to 2 a.m. It was 5, maybe even 6 hours of dancing for about 6s. (30p), which was great value for money. The reality, however, was that after a maximum of 2 hours, boy, girl, man and woman had either (a) viewed the available talent, (b) danced and chatted up – or been chatted up by

– someone attractive, (c) paraded their new boyfriend/girlfriend in front of their mates, (d) met up with someone they'd become acquainted with at a previous dance, or (e) been downright rude/crude and (this applies only to the male side of the hall, mind you) gone up to a girl to ask them not if they fancied a dance, but if they fancied a ride. Nineteen times out of twenty, these efforts would be rewarded with nothing more than a set of ever-glowing red cheeks. But on the odd occasion, these males would luck out with a girl and would thereby avoid the long, drawn-out process of having to go through the whole courting palaver: asking the girl for a couple of dances, then chatting a bit at the lemonade stall, some more chatting and then dropping into the conversation nonchalantly the request that she might, 'save the last dance for me,' and then, only if she accepted, asking if a walk home was okay. After three successive nights of this you'd be semi-officially stepping out together. Then, and only then, you might be rewarded with a peck on the check, and 18 months later – when you became engaged – you just might cop a feel. Another 18 months after that, when you were married, if you were very lucky you might finally be permitted to do the wild thing. If that was all you were after in the first place, you'd have to admit that there was definitely a certain amount of charm to the 'Do ye fancy a ride?' approach, especially if you'd approached a merry widow or, even rarer, a frustrated divorcee.

Or, going back to our original thread, by the two-hour mark you'd also have had a chance to check out the qualities of the band, should that have been your want.

Consequently, as the boom continued unabated and the scene developed, the showbands discovered that their patrons were content to spend the first three hours of the dance topping up their evening's courage down at the local ale establishments. So, by and large, all but the major showbands found themselves playing to empty ballrooms until chucking out time at the pubs. When the magical 23rd hour arrived, the dancing and romancing establishments would miraculously spring to life. Some say the situation played out in reverse, and the crowds sat in the local ale houses *because* the showbands rarely took to the stage before 11 p.m.

Either way, the ballroom managers wanted music on their stage from the time the doors opened at 8.00 p.m., hence the necessary, and somewhat lazy, introduction of relief groups.

The showband leaders would book their relief group, paying for them out of their own salary. They'd usually pick a younger, often local group of up-and-coming musicians to play relief for them up to 11 p.m. It allowed the wee groups a chance to play through professional equipment and, at least for the final three songs of their set, they'd get to play in front of a full audience.

The showband leaders oversaw the relief group setting up on stage, leaving them with the vitally important instructions, 'Leave all of our settings on the equipment as they are and none of that exit music!'

'Exit music?' one of the relief group members would be compelled to enquire.

'You know, none of that auld "way out" stuff,' the bandleader would reply as he disappeared to a dressing room, card school or whatever his particular band did to occupy themselves during their time off stage.

The Playboys – no one seemed to notice that they'd subtly changed the spelling of their name, and even if anyone did it was never mentioned – had slipped back down to just over 700th position in the showband league table on their fifth night at the Dreamland. Mitchell assumed that it was more down to the traditional post-Christmas slump than having anything to do with the band.

This didn't worry Dixie Blair too much – he was flush with confidence from the Bryson's meeting. As they waited in the main dressing room just before The Chance took to the stage, he told the rest of the band that he was thinking of hiring Gentleman Jim Mitchell as manager. Taking the softly, softly approach recommended by both Mitchell and Blair senior, which 'included' the rest of the band in this monumental decision, each of the boys thought it an exceptional idea. 'First class man, he'd be a first class manager,' were the exact words of Brendan the guitarist.

Quite craftily, Dixie also advised the boys that he would change the payment system to the band's benefit. He was going to give them all a share of the band. As bandleader, he would take two shares and any manager worth his salt would want the same. He was also going to create a pot, equal to one share, to cover the additional expenses about which Mitchell had tipped him off. Advising the boys of this before officially appointing a manager meant that Dixie, and not Mitchell, would get credit for the windfall.

All the same, it took a while for Dixie and Brendan to convince Davy the bass player that the new payment system would be beneficial to each musician. Davy had valid concerns: his mother and father were also on a percentage or share-out of some kind or other with the local credit union, and when they received the money just before Christmas it had been a big disappointment. He didn't want any of that 'auld carry on'.

Dixie also used the opportunity of the band meet to lecture the boys on their futures. If they were to have a chance of 'going places' and 'competing with the big boys' – the likes of The Royal Showband from Waterford and The Freshmen from Ballymena – they were all going to have to be 'very professional' in the future. He hinted that all of them – and he went to great pains to include himself – should be prepared for big changes. He led by example: changing the band's name and dropping his from it altogether would be the first of many new ideas. He also wanted the boys to take a good look at The Chance. If they were any good, he wanted to hire them regularly as The Playboys' relief group.

The Chance gave a very good account of themselves that night. Under orders from Martin, Sean MacGee even agreed to keep off the cider, at least until after their performance. They played three of their own songs in the set. One was 'Did She Say Anything (To You)' from the pen of McClelland & MacGee, and the other two, '(Only) Your Way' and 'Broken For Good', were both McClelland songs. At the end of each song, Martin hid his nervousness by removing the comb from his back pocket and giving his hair a quick once over, à la Kookie. Whereas he looked totally comfortable in an amateur kind of way on the big stage, Sean MacGee was awkward, gangly and out of sorts. Norman and Eric were solid on bass and drums but a bit iffy on backing vocals.

Martin sang 'What Do You Want To Make Those Eyes At Me For', which had been released by Emile Ford & The Checkmates for Pye Records. The song, written by Joseph McCarthy, Howard Johnston and Jimmy Monaco, had the unique distinction of being the last ever to share the coveted top spot. During his 6-week reign over the charts during Christmas 1959, Emile Ford was joined at the peak of the pop tree by Adam Faith with 'What Do You Want' (Martin often wondered whether the joint number one status had anything to do with the fact that both titles opened with the same four words).

'What Do You Want To Make Those Eyes At Me For' was written in 1917, and had been revived by Betty Hutton in her 1945 *Invincible Blonde* movie. If Emile Ford had bettered her treatment of the song and managed to make it his own, then Martin McClelland had come close to trumping him. He sang it as though he'd written it for someone in his own life.

'McClelland's definitely got it,' Mitchell shouted to Dixie Blair above The Chance's racket. They were standing at the back of the hall on a partitioned-off raised platform, which Mitchell had built to afford his bouncers an overview of the dancers and, in turn, any potential problems that might be brewing in the middle of the dance floor. Mitchell had also taken to using this vantage point to watch the stage without having his toes trampled on by 75 quartets of feet.

'Aye, I'll give you that,' Dixie replied in open envy. There were about 150 people in the ballroom, and about 90 of those had formed an arc around the lip of the stage. 'That's a good sign as well,' Dixie added, nodding at the dancers. He knew to his own cost just how difficult it was to get people onto the floor at the beginning of the night.

Mitchell agreed. They had both noticed how some of the wee girls nudged their mates, never taking their eyes off the lead singer as he mouthed the words in their direction.

What do you want to make those eyes at me for
When they don't mean what they say
They make me glad
They make me sad
They make me want a lot of the things
That I've never had.

All harmless innuendo, but it made the girls weak at the knees.

'We're going to have to get him to change his name as well you know,' Dixie shouted in the general direction of Mitchell's ear. (In his relatively short time in the ballrooms, Dixie had learned that you never leaned in close to shout at the top of your voice.) 'Martin McClelland doesn't have the same ring as, say, Billy Brown, or Brendan Bowyer or Dickie Rock.'

'Aye, you're not wrong,' Mitchell agreed. 'But first you're going to have to get him to join up. I'm not sure that's going to be so easy.'

Martin announced The Chance's final song, one of his own called 'Broken For Good'. Bandleader and manager were impressed by the song, and particularly Martin's delivery of the lyrics. Although it was quite a sad number about someone's heart being broken forever, by placing the lyric in a joyous, upbeat musical setting and using 'Good' in the title, Martin had cleverly disguised the darkness of the tune.

'You're right you know,' Dixie began after a couple of verses and a chorus, 'he is a great songwriter too. My band, I mean The Playboys, could do a great version of that one.'

'Aye, as I said,' Mitchell cut in, 'never count your winnings until your horse crosses the finishing line. You've got to get the lad to join your band first.'

The Chance drifted off the stage at the end of their performance, Martin running the comb through his hair again as they left without a final goodnight to the audience. They twice returned awkwardly to the stage to break down and remove their gear.

Dixie excused himself. Making his way through the rapidly filling ballroom to the bandstand, he accidentally bumped into the blonde he'd met the last time they'd performed. Technically, that is not an accurate account of the encounter, for Dixie, his mind racing with thoughts of McClelland and his potential, wasn't aware of the girl until he'd started to excuse himself for the supposed blunder. The blonde, however, knew exactly what she was doing: she had spied Dixie on the platform with Mitchell, and upon seeing him dismount had made a beeline across the floor to intercept him. For the first time that month, Dixie was distracted from the world of The Playboys, dilly-dallying with the girl for several minutes longer than he really had the time for. The incident didn't go entirely unnoticed by one member of the relief group, quietly packing away equipment up on the stage.

It is impossible to say whether the new momentum of The Playboys, McClelland's impressive performance, or the blonde girl on the dance floor had raised the band's game that third night at the Dreamland. It was probably a combination of all of the above, but whatever the reason, The Playboys played an absolute blinder. Mitchell looked on contentedly: Dixie & The Prayboys had miraculously transformed... into The Playboys.

From the opening song, Dixie Blair was so *on* it, as in capital 'O' and 'N'. He egged on the band to keep up the pace like he'd never done before. 'Okay,' he began after the first three-song set, 'look, with all these beautiful girls here, surely we can get all of you lads up and dancing for the next set?'

'Sure, if we're that beautiful,' a nervous but familiar voice shouted out from deep within the crowd, 'why don't you come down here and dance with us?'

Uncharacteristically, Dixie rose to the occasion. He called the set to the drummer Mo who counted in the first song, 'At The Hop'. Dixie removed his tenor saxophone, placing it carefully on its stand before hopping down from the stage and confidently striding towards the blonde girl. 'Could I have the pleasure of this dance please?' Dixie asked, holding out his hand in her direction with a warm and genuine smile lighting up his face. The entire ballroom of dancers hushed to a silence as they waited nervously with Dixie for her decision.

'Sure, the pleasure would be all mine,' she replied, accepting his hand. Everyone broke into spontaneous applause. Encouraged by Dixie's success, a swarm of boys dived across the dance floor to invite their first choice to dance. Mega body-swerving ensued as some saw their intended taken to the floor by a competitor, whereby they'd subtly swing round 90 degrees to target a new lucky lady or victim, depending on the perspective and the size of the lad's feet. The manoeuvre was only considered successful if the second choice believed she'd been the first choice all along.

Some lads took a lot of encouraging before they would venture across the longest and loneliest 20 yards in the world towards the opposite sex. If you studied their thin shirts carefully, you could almost see their hearts trying to hammer out of their rib cages.

The old pros – those in their second season of dancing – would invite two or three girls to the floor before their top choice, their courage growing along the way. For this reason, it was not unusual to find some of the most gorgeous girls sitting out the first dance. It was a risky business: you couldn't afford to hang around too long in case another lad swept your girl off her feet for the last dance before you'd a chance to stub out your imaginary cigarette and make your way to her across the well-polished floorboards.

This tried and tested mating call wasn't the only one that lads had to interpret: they had also to deal with the girls' replies, of which there were many. If a girl looked over both your shoulders, she was either checking out your dandruff or holding out for someone better. A reply along the lines of 'I've got sore feet, but I'll dance the one song with you,' (as opposed to the standard three-song set) meant 'no', but she was too polite to say so. If she said 'I'm sorry, I've already promised this dance to someone else', it meant either (a) 'no', or (b) that she was a liar – the only promised dance was the last dance. A comeback of 'Ask my sister, I'm sweatin'' was an outright rejection whereas 'Clear off you wee skitter!' said it all. If she answered with 'I'd love to, what took you so long to ask?' she was far too desperate.

There was really only one answer you were waiting for: 'That would be nice' meant you had the perfect starting-point and her undivided attention for the 10-minute set. You were in with a chance to impress her, and you'd hope and pray that by the end of the three dances she wouldn't leave thinking you were a complete dork.

The only golden rule was that you *never* refused a girl who invited you up to dance during a ladies' choice. Do that, and you'd risk missing out on another partner all night, possibly even for the next few dances in that hall. Girls can have a very long memory…

This is most likely why people came to talk about that night for years to come. Gentleman Jim Mitchell marvelled at the spectacle: he knew that Dixie's uncharacteristic behaviour would probably add an extra 500 tickets at the box office to their next performance. It wasn't that Dixie was considered to be a particularly good catch, but were he to have walked on the water of the nearby Lough Neagh, it still wouldn't have impressed that audience nearly as much as his show that night at the Dreamland.

Mitchell needed to find a subtle way to ensure he made the most of the buzz. He was paying a lot of heed to T.J. Byrne, a clever manager down in the Free State, who was pioneering self-promotion by converting the buzz his band were creating into ticket sales. He was playing a blinder in press relations on behalf of his clients. As a result of his efforts, The Royal Showband were catching fire in a big way and filling out every ballroom they played. This is made all the more incredible when you consider they'd only been professional for less than a year at that point in early 1960.

The Playboys were off to a fair enough start of their own, but the next step – securing Martin McClelland – could prove a stumbling-block. Surprisingly enough, it was their then lead singer Brendan who first raised the subject.

It was March 1960. In the weeks following the historic Dreamland date, The Chance opened for The Playboys at a further three dances. By this point, Mitchell had agreed to the band playing his other ballrooms. On the way back from the third dance in a wee hall in Rasharkin, the conversation in the back of the wagon naturally worked its way around to McClelland. 'Look lads, there's no point in beating around the bush here,' Brendan said. 'If we're all gung-ho about the professional business, and we're trying to make a real go of it with this Dreamland man behind us…'

'I know what you're going to say, Brendan,' Robin interrupted. He usually opened in this way, but this time he shocked everyone by following up with: 'But no way!' Once he had everyone's attention, he delivered his point: 'We're not going to replace you with anyone.'

'Jeez, Robin, remind me never to introduce you to any of my girlfriends. That wasn't what I was going to say at all. What I was going to say was that maybe we should think of getting this lad from The Chance to be our chanter. I'm happy enough doing the country songs and playing guitar, but quite frankly I'm not comfortable with the pop songs, and they're beginning to get in the way of my guitar playing to be honest. That's what I was going to say, Robin, you begastard.' This last friendly insult was a product of an exclusive showband lingo called 'Ben Lang': people in the know would disguise words by adding 'eg' after the first letter, thus allowing them to 'secretly' communicate in the presence of outsiders. 'Doll' would become 'degoll', 'ride' would become 'regide'. 'Van' would become 'vegan', which was probably the least appropriate of all as there was hardly a vegetarian in Ireland, let alone in the back of the band van.

In this particular 'vegan', making its way back from Rasharkin, Dixie said nothing, in Ben Lang or otherwise. He couldn't believe his luck. He couldn't have orchestrated it better if he'd spent a month of Sundays planning it.

'Brendan megan, I wasn't suggesting…'

'I know, Robin, I know,' Brendan said, breaking into one of the big smiles he usually reserved for the girls who would stare up at him adoringly on his side of the stage. 'It's just that we've got a great chance here. We've got a great wee band. We've got the chance of a great manager – no disrespect, Dixie, you've done a brill job in getting us this far.'

'None taken, head.' Dixie had heard Billy Brown, The Freshmen's main man, address his bass player as 'head'. He wasn't sure what it meant, but he was prepared to run with it until corrected.

'And,' Brendan continued, 'we can either mess around like all the other Bengal Lancers or we can try for something special with the band, make sure it means something for us. You know, make us an important band. And I'll tell you something for nothing, there's no reason why we can't be up there with the big boys. I've seen The Drifters and they're a good enough band right enough, but apart from Joe, they haven't really got much that we haven't.'

'Aye, and all he does is sweat buckets on stage,' Smiley offered. 'I'll tell you what, I wouldn't join that band unless they were throwing in waterproof suits and an umbrella as part of the deal.'

They all enjoyed a wee laugh at The Drifters' misfortune before Brendan continued: 'So I'd say if we got young McClelland in now, well, there'd be no stopping us.'

'Aye, but then Dixie has always been saying it's important to keep it a small unit. What was it you used to say, Dixie?' Davy the bass player asked earnestly, '"The smaller the unit, the quicker you travel, the quicker you travel the farther you go."'

'Aye, that's right,' Dixie agreed from behind the steering wheel. He was happy to appear to have a distraction during this particular conversation. He changed down a gear as the old Commer, on its last legs at best, made very hard work of the small hill just outside Toome. He waited until he peaked the hill before changing the gear back up again so that he'd have a chance to be heard over the noisy engine. 'Aye, that's what I said, but no matter how small and fast you are,' Dixie continued, clearing his throat and choosing his words with the dexterity of a politician, 'it doesn't matter unless you've got a lough full of petrol in the tank. And, at the same time, Brendan does have a point. If he feels happier concentrating on singing the country songs and playing guitar, then I'd have to say we'd be fools to ignore him.'

'Now listen, don't get me wrong on this, lads,' Brendan cut in, 'I wouldn't be making this suggestion for any Tom, Dick or King Harry, but tonight when I heard McClelland, well… I mean, he's got a few rough edges we'd have to smooth over and he defo needs to be a lot more professional, but I def-in-ite-ly think he could be great for The Playboys.'

'You're not wrong, Brendan,' Barry, the usually sleepy organist and alto saxophone player, chimed in. 'And another thing I meant to say: the name, The Playboys – it works great for us, Dixie, that was a class idea as well.'

'Thanks, head,' Dixie replied as he negotiated Pear Tree round-about in the centre of Castlemartin. 'Right then. If we're all agreed, I'll go and see McClelland tomorrow morning then?'

'Aye, sound, head,' Brendan, the soon-to-be-ex lead singer of The Playboys chipped in, throwing Dixie's new sobriquet back at him. By the next band practice, they'd all be addressing each other in the same way, as though they'd been doing it for years.

***

So far, so good. Everything was going to plan, better even than Kennedy's design for his new America.

Martin McClelland, however, was about to put a great big spanner in the works. Dixie had presented his offer in such a way that he'd save face should the younger musician refuse the lead singer position. Still, the unthinkable happened: Martin wasn't up for joining The Playboys. Dixie immediately changed the subject to the upcoming engagement on the following Friday in Cookstown Town Hall.

Gentleman Jim Mitchell would have to have a word with McClelland before the weekend. He took the end of The Chance's rehearsal at the Dreamland a few days later as his opportunity.

'So, I hear the boys have invited you to join The Playboys.' The rest of the lads were packing their gear away, and Martin had taken a seat in a quiet part of the ballroom by the mineral counter to try and fit some of Sean MacGee's new lyrics into one of his tunes.

'Aye, sure they're a *showband*,' Martin replied. He said the word 'showband' with such complete and utter contempt that it was immediately obvious why he'd turned Dixie down: relief group snobbery.

'Now Martin,' Mitchell said, taking the seat next to the lad, 'is that a wee bit of self-righteousness I'm hearing there?'

'Agh, you know,' Martin smiled self-consciously, replacing his guitar in the case that was leaning against the wall behind them. The lid lay wide open, and looked from a distance like a double guitar-shaped hole in the wall.

'They're a good band, Martin, and if they get a good singer they're going to go places. I've just taken them on my books for management,' Mitchell said. He wasn't exactly sure what that meant, or indeed where those aforementioned 'books' were kept, but he'd heard this phrase before among managers and liked its ring – it sounded professional.

'Oh!' Martin replied, at least making a good show of being impressed. 'I'd always thought of them as a wee local band… but with yourself behind them, they'll get a good shot at it.'

Mitchell couldn't read Martin: was he backtracking because he was now interested, or was he just being polite because Mitchell had declared his managerial hand? He decided to try a different tack. 'Those songs of yours… I've been listening to them… I think they're good – what are you planning to do with them?'

'Oh, you know,' Martin replied, shifting about in a chair and looking like he was bored in a way only the young do when they're feeling inferior *and* resentful in the company of adults. 'The Chance… we do some of them with the group.'

'But hardly anyone's going to hear The Chance are they?' Jim suggested, signalling to the cleaner with a fist to the mouth and two raised fingers to order a couple of minerals. He could see Martin's discomfort, but it didn't put him off. He leaned back in his fragile-looking chair, appearing every inch the Don, and continued. 'Why not do them in a showband? If I'm to have any say in the matter, Martin, they're going to be a big band. I'm planning to book them out four nights a week from Easter and they'll be up to six nights a week by Christmas.'

'But sure, showbands only do covers. None of them have released a record yet, as far as I'm aware.'

'Exactly Martin, *exactly*,' Mitchell leaned in close over the table and dropped his voice a couple of decibels, 'so the first one who has a supply of good original songs will automatically move up a gear. There's no telling what you could do. England? America? Just listen to what's on the radio. There is no reason why that couldn't be The Playboys with you and *your* songs. I mean, they have to play some records, don't they? Well why not yours? They're as good as anything I'm hearing on the radio.'

Martin looked off into the distance and started to blush. Mitchell's statement had been made in a matter-of-fact manner, but it was the single biggest compliment Martin had ever been paid. Mitchell had been his mother's boss for as long as he could remember, and he'd just had his very first conversation with the man as an equal. He knew from his mother that Gentleman Jim never did anything for the money alone – if he was going to do it, he wanted to do it well. And if he did, he would probably make a lot of money in the long run.

'Sure, but what about the boys?' Martin said, nodding in the direction of the stage and his own group.

'Shall I tell you something, Martin?' Mitchell said, breaking into a warm smile. 'None of those lads are a quarter as serious about your group as you are. The drummer and bass player would take an engagement with the Cranny Pipe Band if they were paid ten bob a week for it.'

Martin sighed. He knew Mitchell was right, but regret washed over him.

'And then there's Sean,' Mitchell continued. 'Well, Sean likes the sauce a wee bit too much for his own good. I'd hoped he'd have grown out of it by now, you know.'

'It's not a problem; it's just a lark, something to do for fun.'

'Look, Martin, let's leave it there for now, but I would ask you to think some more about it before you say no – let's have another chat about it. But my view is that it would be a good move for you and a great move for the band.'

'Right, I'll think about it, I will,' Martin promised as he drained his mineral. 'I'll talk to my mother about it too.'

Only Dixie and his father knew what rested on McClelland's decision. After three very nervous days, Martin came calling at the Dreamland. It was a beautiful spring morning; the sun was sending golden beams of light through the regal, leafless oak tree, which sheltered the rear of the ballroom from the biting Lough Neagh winds.

Martin made the first move. 'And you say The Playboys will agree to doing my songs?'

'Martin – I know they will, but please don't make it a condition. There's nothing that would scunder the boys away more quickly than making it a prerequisite to perform your songs. You've got great songs, Martin – The Playboys will perform them because they're great, not because it's part of any side deal. Don't belittle your songs, Martin, let them stand for themselves. Hey, young man, apart from which if you were to join the band, I'd become your manager, and you'd hate to think that your manager would ever agree anything on your behalf behind your back. Now isn't that a fact?'

'Aye, I suppose so,' Martin said. He looked like he was about to say something else before pausing and appearing to change his mind. 'Okay. Go on then. I'll give it a go.'

Mitchell didn't know whether to be disappointed that Martin had been persuaded so easily to forsake the members of The Chance, or to feel proud because he was sussed enough to be ambitious for both himself and his songs.

'Don't you even want to know what you're on?'

'My mother said that you're a fair man. She also said that you'd never ever cheat me. That's good enough for me, Mr Mitchell.'

Mitchell smiled and shook Martin's hand. Privately, he was happy Martin hadn't haggled him over a deal; that would have been petty. Equally, Martin wasn't going into it blind. His mother had vouched for Mitchell, and that had been sufficient. Mitchell, for his part, took the opportunity to explain to Martin in great detail exactly the deal that he would be on, admitting that Dixie and the manager were both on a double share. Trust was a good thing as far as Mitchell was concerned, but never something to hide behind.

They agreed that Martin would go to Dixie to tell him he was in. As he left Mitchell's office, he turned to his newly appointed manager. 'Just one other thing…' Martin began and hesitated, '… and I've been thinking about this for quite some time.'

'Go on?' Mitchell prompted.

'I think I should change me name for the band. I mean, I'm quite happy with my name really and I'll keep McClelland for the songwriting.'

'Right,' Mitchell replied, in a matter-of-fact way, not wanting his young charge to be deterred in his line of thought. 'Did you have anything in mind for your stage name with the band?'

'I do as it happens,' Martin replied, raising his eyebrows in a 'gee shucks' gesture, 'I'm a big fan of Dean Martin.'

'So I've heard.'

'Well, I wonder what you'd feel about me changing my name to that?' Martin asked.

'Oh, I see,' Mitchell replied. Their relationship had quickly transformed, manager and client already practising trust, equality, openness and friendliness and, to a certain degree, dependency. The uneasiness that had initially clouded their first meeting had evaporated as completely as the morning mist rose from Lough Neagh. He smiled as much at this thought as he did at the suggestion, 'So, you wondered what *I* felt about the name Martin Martin? Novel, Martin, I'd have to say that. It's novel.'

'No, no… I meant *Martin Dean*. What do you think about the name Martin Dean?'

'I know, Martin, it sounds great to me,' Mitchell laughed, 'Martin Dean, yeah, it sounds very good to me. Now you should get off to tell your bandleader the name of his new lead vocalist.'

And that's how Martin Dean, lead singer of The Playboys, came to be. He had been in the right place at the right time, but he could just as easily not have joined the band if he'd said, or more importantly *heard*, the wrong things. Several years down the line, his monumental decision would come to have serious repercussions – even cause regret – but on that beautiful spring morning he had made a choice that would change the rest of his life.

The Playboys were complete. It had taken some time, and had happened more by accident than grand design, but they were now officially up and running; a professional band with professional management at the helm. Their adventures – in and out of Dreamland – were about to commence.

CHAPTER SIX

*Don't forget to be careful
out there, and buy as much
land as you can*

Gentleman Jim Mitchell

The Playboys from Castlemartin officially took to the road during Easter of 1960. They had spent the intervening month playing two gigs a week, and the rest of the time they rehearsed long and hard. Except on Mondays that is; in the showband world it was a more hallowed day than the Sabbath because no eejit in his right mind would want to go out dancing on a Monday night. On their day off they rested, washed their clothes, cut the grass, reacquainted themselves with their families and paid their taxes. Paid their taxes? Yes, paid their taxes! Although 100 per cent of their income was cash, Gentleman Jim didn't want the taxman sniffing around any door that might directly or indirectly lead to him, so they declared the 20 per cent portion to the taxman, which made them sleep easier at night. This had little to do with their clear conscience and everything to do with the softness of their mattresses, now that they were stuffed with tenners.

In the 1960s, buying your own house was a major status symbol. If you were also a young lad in a showband, even better. Once you owned a house, you could start to buy land, land and then some more land. This was the perfect place to invest your money; transactions were made in cash, meaning you protected your earnings against the taxman and inflation. If you were lucky, there'd be a considerable amount of interest thrown in to accommodate your initial investment.

Mitchell always tried to temper his long-term plans for the band against the limited shelf life the majority of people in the entertainment business had. He'd assure the band they had a future and some stability, but he'd conclude every chat with a warning: 'And don't forget to be careful out there, and buy as much land as you can.'

At the newly formed band's first rehearsal, Dixie made an announcement that delighted his lead singer. 'Right, Martin, we'll stick mostly to our set for the time being, just so we can keep some kind of handle on this, but I'd like us to do a couple of your tunes too and I think we should have a stab at your version of 'What Do You Want To Make Those Eyes At Me For'. I've got a great idea for a sweet brass fill during the verses and then I thought about a big riff under the chorus.'

'Excellent – I'd love to hear that!' Martin replied, and immediately tried to return the compliment: 'I love the harmonies youse guys do. Maybe we could work up some oohs and ahhs for the verses.'

'Bejesus, Martin,' Robin the trombonist exclaimed loudly for the benefit of all of the band, 'if you've got me oohing and ahhing out of one end and Dixie wants some brass fills, well... there's only one other place I can produce wind from and I'm not sure it's legal to do that on stage in this country yet.' Everyone, including Martin, fell about the stage in fits of laughter.

When the commotion had died down, Martin continued. 'I'd say with the size of that hooter of yours no obscenity will be necessary.

If you stick the end of your trombone up your nostril, you'll be able to sing and hoot simultaneously with the best of them.' This was followed by another round of raucous laughter.

Mitchell, who had been watching and listening to the proceedings from the vantage point of his office, found a smile move across his face as effortlessly as the shadows of the clouds passing over the fields on a windy day. He'd had no concerns about the band's ability to play well together, but now he could see how easily they were laughing and joking with each other and how Martin, by far the youngest at 16, was holding his own. Playing well together was one thing, but to be able to endure the endless hours cramped in the back of the van they also had to be able to laugh together.

Dixie and the rest of the lads were impressed that Martin already knew all the words to the pop songs he wanted to perform. And 'Eyes', as Emile Ford's song had been rechristened, came together remarkably quickly.

Even more impressive was how quickly the band managed to learn Martin's own compositions, 'Broken For Good' and 'Only Your Way'. 'Broken For Good' in particular was sounding absolutely amazing. The brass arrangement Dixie had come up with was so uplifting it brought a smile to everyone's face, even Robin the trombonist's. Martin sang lead on the verses, but insisted Brendan joined him on the chorus, and the blend of the two voices – one pop, one country – worked fantastically. In fact, by the end of the first week's rehearsal, they were confident enough to try all three songs at their next engagement.

The entire band seemed genuinely in awe of Martin's ability to write lyrics. You see, although all of them had been involved in and playing music most of their lives, they'd never met a real life songwriter before. Although it was left unsaid, they were all proud to be working with the composer – fulfilled, even, to be playing on his songs.

Martin, for his part, was delighted with what the band added to his compositions. He was pleased to admit, and admit it he did, that the arrangements they came up with were far superior to his original visions. He thought Dixie was brilliant at conjuring up catchy, sometimes cheeky lines, and he absolutely loved the sound of The Playboys. It was a joyous sound; there was something incredibly inspirational in hearing a four-piece brass section play such melodic lines, and he found it almost spiritual. He was flooded with musical ideas and potential arrangements for his other songs, and for the first time he realised exactly what Mitchell had meant when he said the first band to write original material would get a head start. Being as impartial as he could be, Martin thought that the Playboys' new sound had already set them miles apart from every other band he'd heard. All they had to do now was to ensure the rest of Ireland knew it too. They were in need of a diary full of engagements and a gimmick to draw the people into the ballrooms.

But most importantly, they desperately needed a better set of wheels to get them around the country.

The Playboys got their first wagon thanks to a horse.

Gentleman Jim Mitchell went to the races a lot. He applied the same logic to gambling on horses as he did to all other aspects of his business: 'Minimise your risk by doing your research properly.'

To build up a pot to buy their new wagon and the necessary equipment, The Playboys needed to be able to get to gigs. To get to gigs they needed a reliable wagon. It was a vicious circle. So, without telling the boys, Mitchell put an extra £160 on the nose of Merryman II at the Grand National. To the canny manager, it wasn't really a gamble. Merryman II had won the Liverpool Foxhunters Chase and the Scottish Grand National in 1959. The 8-year-old was trained by Captain Neville Crump, and was ridden by Gerry Scott, a former apprentice jockey of Crump's. To Mitchell, the combination on paper was unbeatable and, luckily for The Playboys, it proved to be unbeatable on the course as well, the horse winning by a triumphant 15 lengths at 13-2.

Five weeks later, The Playboys got their brand new Commer van, complete with customised seats in the back and a rooftop neon light proudly proclaiming 'The Playboys from Castlemartin'.

In 1960, the petroleum company Esso introduced a popular campaign to increase sales of fuel. Based on their tiger mascot, the logo 'Put a Tiger in your Tank' persuaded customers that if they filled their tank with Esso's fuel they'd get more for their money. They merchandised 'tiger tails' (furry tails about a foot long, which looked very sad in damp Irish weather), which you could tie to the vehicle's petrol cap. The boys staged a ceremonial tying of the tiger tail on their old wagon. With an even better tiger in the tank of their new wagon, The Playboys were finally able to get to their engagements and earn the wage that would build up their pot... it also made weekly payments to Mitchell to pay off the grand in cash he'd forked out for the Commer.

The Playboys' first big date outside of the Dreamland was at Sammy Barr's Flamingo Ballroom in Ballymena. Sammy was a larger than life character, and his hot dogs were famous the length and breadth of Ireland. Mitchell liked Sammy Barr a lot, and was indebted to him for sharing valuable information when Mitchell was starting up the Dreamland. Now that Mitchell had his own band, he was desperate to get them into the Flamingo, one of the best run ballrooms in the country. Sammy gave them a Friday in June, the same week, in fact, that the first scheduled jet airliner – a Pan Am DC8 – landed in Shannon having flown from Detroit, USA.

The word on The Playboys was that they were a good wee band, their leader started off the show by dancing with a member of the audience and they had a very young lead singer who wrote their songs. Due in part to the above, and in part to the fact that Sammy Barr had been giving The Playboys a big build-up in his on-stage announcements between the relief group and the main band on dance nights, they drew a very respectable 800 people on their first night at the Flamingo.

The band opened with a Martin Dean composition, 'Gone For Good'. With Martin's permission, Mitchell had told Dixie not to draw attention to Martin's compositions when announcing the song on stage. Although he wasn't religious, Mitchell quoted the Bible from St John to get his point over: "'A prophet is without honour in his own land in his own time.'"

'So you think because Martin is a local lad, the locals won't be impressed by his songs?' Dixie asked, somewhat bemused by Mitchell's approach.

'Exactly,' Mitchell agreed, hands deep in his famous overcoat. 'Let's not labour the point that they're Martin's songs. That's all I'm saying. They're great songs and the band do a fabulous version of them, so lets just leave it to the dancers to make up their own minds.'

There was no argument from either Dixie or Martin. If anything, Martin was quite happy to be out of that particular spotlight. On the night, it didn't even matter because an almighty cheer erupted as The Playboys strummed the final chords of 'Gone For Good'. Dixie, visibly impressed by the blend of Martin and Brendan's voices, called a change in the set five songs later. Instead of Brendan singing 'All I Have To Do Is Dream' as a solo, he had Martin do a shadow vocal à la The Everly Brothers, who had taken the song to the top of the UK pop charts in May 1958. It turned out to be a great call, because it sounded nearly as good as the original.

The final song of the evening was a Dixie standard, the song he'd ended all his sets with since the days of the Teatime Orchestra – a ripping version of Hank Williams' 1952 number one country hit 'Jambalaya'. At that time, Dixie had been known to have a stab at singing it himself, but that night in the Flamingo he was happy for his new lead vocalist to take on this duty. If Brendan was unhappy about Martin's swift ascent to the forefront on any song, it was this one. However, Martin, sympathetic to Brendan's feelings, took his Shure Skull microphone over to his bandmate's side of the stage and coaxed him to join in on the final verse. This magnanimous gesture was appreciated by the entire band, but by none more than Brendan.

That wasn't actually The Playboys' final song that night in Ballymena. No, they didn't return to the stage for an encore – they in fact signed off the way every band in the North signed off: by playing the National Anthem. Which National Anthem you played depended on which neck of the woods you were in, and the deeper into that particular neck of the woods you were, the more important your choice of Anthem…

The Playboys' debut at the Flamingo had gone fantastically well, and for that they received a fee of £100 and an unheard of additional bonus of £50, with Sammy sticking two more dates in the diary between then and Christmas. Although Mitchell was happy for them, he was worried they would be spoiled. In fact, it would be a long time before they were looked after so well by a ballroom manager.

But The Playboys, with their new wagon and new-found success, were on a high. If the band were a wee bit more excited than their manager, that was certainly forgivable – they were going to be doing this four nights a week for the rest of the year and beyond, so it helped that they had enjoyed themselves. They were bonding well, and were taking to life on the road.

The week after the Ballymena show, The Playboys commenced what was to become a monthly residency at the Dreamland Ballroom. Mitchell had moved a few dates around to be able to set aside the first Thursday in every month for the following 14 months for his band. He'd been accurate in his prediction of a good turnout: 1,200 had turned out to see The Playboys with their good-looking lead singer and the bandleader who danced with the audience. If Dixie was regretting his actions, he certainly wasn't complaining about having to repeat it at every dance as a matter of form. He even expanded on his 'trick', staying off the stage when he was called down and dancing each of the three songs of the set with a different girl. But every month at the Dreamland he danced the entire set with the same blonde girl who'd started the whole thing off. Dixie could always be found chatting to her at the mineral stall during the relief group's set.

When Martin had defected to The Playboys, his former band, The Chance, had split up. It was left to Dixie to book a replacement relief band for their gigs. Blues By Five, a wee group from Magherafelt, were heavily into R&B.

For Martin, it was sensational to have a group play relief for him when only a few months before it had been his job. However, what wasn't so sensational was witnessing Dixie with the beautiful blonde girl. For the girl was none other than the subject of his deepest lyrics and certainly all of his thoughts: Hanna Hutchinson.

CHAPTER SEVEN

Tell me, Dixie – does Hanna like The Playboys?

Smiley

For his part, Dixie Blair was getting into the relationship innocently enough. If in fact getting into a relationship was what he
was doing – he couldn't really tell because he'd never gone down
that road before. What made it all the more surprising for him was
that someone like Hanna Hutchinson would be interested in the
first place. At 19, she was 7 years younger than him. She was beautiful; he knew she was beautiful because everyone's tongue would be
tickling the floor when she walked across the ballroom. He rifled
through every magazine and could never find anyone who looked
as good as Hanna Hutchinson.

She was also smart, and never failed to answer any question he
asked her, no matter what it was. She wasn't loose, not that he'd any
real experience in that direction himself, but she had the reputation
of being a nice girl rather than a 'good' girl. She liked the buzz of
the dance hall, but she didn't seem to be a fan of the music, taking it
for granted the way you do a radio: if it's there, you listen to it when
you want to, and when you don't want to, you turn it off.

'What do you think of the band?' Dixie had asked her the second night they danced.

'Which band, the elastic band?' she ribbed him.

'The boys… us – The Playboys?' he pushed suspiciously.

'What do you mean, "what do I think of them?"'

'Well… ' Dixie stammered, his embarrassment shining through on his red cheeks, 'do you like them? Do you like us?'

'I mean, I think they're okay, I don't know a lot about music but I like it when you all do Martin's songs.'

'How do you know which are Martin's songs?'

'Agh,' Hanna started, appearing somewhat agitated, 'well, his wee band played them and I always recognise that song about "why are you looking at me?"'

'Ah yes, 'What Do You Want To Make Those Eyes At Me For'?' Dixie asked.

'It's nothing personal,' Hanna laughed.

'No,' Dixie stammered again. 'I mean, that's the title of the song.'

'I know, I know,' she said, sinking her head into her shoulders.

'Right,' Dixie replied, taking his rimless glasses off to clean them with his handkerchief. 'So you saw The Chance?'

'Aye, there's not many of them around are there?' Hanna started, and then appeared to think better of it. 'Yes, I mean, yes of course I did – they were on that night in here, the night you jumped down from the stage and danced with me.'

'Oh yes, of course,' Dixie said, putting his glasses back on.

The mineral area was filling up, so Hanna led Dixie over to the far back corner of the dance floor where they could enjoy more privacy.

'So… you like Martin's songs then?' Dixie asked as they reached the corner.

'Well, I think it's great that a wee lad from around here can write songs and then someone like your band can perform them on stage – I'm not sure I've thought any more about it than that.'

'Look,' Dixie said nervously. 'Would your mother be all right if I asked you out?'

"*'Would my mother be all right?'*" Hanna roared so loudly that some of the dancers looked back at them. 'What about me? If you want to ask *me* out, ask *me* out; if you want to talk to my mother, ask *her* out.'

'Yes, of course, I'm sorry,' Dixie said, seeing the funny side. 'I just meant because you're young and she knows my mother well.'

'Maybe you should come back and see me when I'm a big girl then,' Hanna replied dryly. She most certainly wasn't seeing the funny side, and didn't even attempt to hide her irritation. She stormed off, leaving Dixie to pick his jaw up from the floor.

Dixie sheepishly made his way back to the bandstand. A young, blonde-haired girl observed the final part of his journey, in fact the same young girl who'd been giving him such a hard time. 20 minutes later, when Dixie jumped down from the stage at the beginning of The Playboys' performance, she was back in her usual spot, perfectly positioned to forgive Dixie and join him on the three-song dance. The third song was changed from the usual 'Be My Guest' to 'Eyes'. Hand on heart, though, you'd have to say that Martin Dean didn't perform it with his usual passion…

Dixie was confused by the mixed signals he was receiving from Hanna. She seemed… well… 'keen' wasn't the right word. 'Receptive' was better, but only receptive in the way a flower is receptive to a bee, powerless against and accepting of the bee's advances. But Dixie was confused – which one of them was the flower and which the bee?

Dixie decided it was time to take action. He had woman troubles, and he needed help. He would have to consult 'the Oracle'.

The Oracle was Andrew, the trumpet player in the band, also known as 'Smiley'. It wasn't exactly that Smiley was a woman's man, more that he just loved women. All women. He adored them, worshipped them, he was amused and bewildered by them, enchanted by each and every one of them.

Equally, the girls, charmed by his permanent smile, flocked around Smiley. For his part, he never discussed his ever-growing fan-club behind their backs, so his success rate was unclear. But it *was* clear that he was the most unlikely of Romeos: he was gangly, so gangly in fact that Dixie had trouble finding him suits, made to measure or off the peg. He looked like he might have had the perfect build for a 4 foot boy but then he'd been stretched over-night on a rack to 6 foot 4 inches. His legs didn't seem strong enough to support him, and he looked like he would collapse at any moment when he performed his crazy dance moves on stage, which involved moving his knees violently in and out as his hands rode effortlessly from one knee to the other like a maniacal wind-screen wiper.

If was difficult to tell if the permanent smile on Andrew's face came from his love of music, or his love of women or his obvious contentment with his lot.

At 29, he was the oldest member of both The Playboys and his siblings. He still lived with his mother and father and his two broth-ers and three sisters down in the White City in Magherafelt.

Dixie picked his moment with The Oracle, choosing to drop him off last following that night's gig so he'd have the chance to speak with him alone.

'He's a great chanter that Martin, isn't he, head?' said Smiley.

'Aye, great all right,' Dixie replied, trying hard to find a thread to take him to his problem.

'He's young, but he seems to have his head screwed on his shoulders,' Smiley continued, oblivious to Dixie's agenda. 'I mean, sometimes he looks like he's so far away, you know, deep in thought. I suppose that's just the way of songwriters, isn't it?'

'I suppose,' Dixie replied, his frustration growing in direct pro-portion to the ever-decreasing distance they had left to Smiley's house.

'Maybe it could be down to him not having a father around. Have you any idea who his father was?'

'Nah. I wouldn't say that he was from around these parts or we'd know who he was from the gossips. I think his mum went away to the Free State – it was during the wartime, you know, so everything was a bit crazy, wasn't it?'

'What?' Smiley said as though hit by a sudden revelation. 'You don't suppose it was an American do you? You know one of those GIs?'

'Possibly…' Dixie smiled, 'that might account for his songwriting talent.'

'Oh, she's a fine woman, Martin's mother Kathleen,' Smiley said, 'a beautiful woman altogether.'

'You haven't, Smiley…' Dixie hissed, nearly driving off the side of Westland Road as they neared the end of their journey. They'd be in the White City in a matter of minutes and he still hadn't addressed the Hanna issue.

'Please, Dixie!' Smiley protested, 'Goodness, if you believed all that was said about me, you'd think I'd a hault with every single woman in County Derry!'

'Aye, and some of the married ones as well,' Dixie chuckled.

'Nah, not me, Dixie – never do to another man what you wouldn't want done to yourself.'

'You've never courted a married woman?'

'Never have, never will,' Smiley replied proudly. 'Besides which, there's no need to – there are too many beautiful single girls out there for there to be any need to bother.'

'First class, Smiley. First class, head.'

'Well it's simple for me. It's my only golden rule, and if I ever should be tempted there's my mother and the auld fella, and I look at them and think what it would do to everyone if she ever ran off with another man.'

'Sure, but what if it were only a one-night stand?'

'Even worse, man, even worse – at least if she ran off with someone you'd think that there was some kind of commitment shown on both sides.'

'Smiley, head, you've got this female thing well sussed,' Dixie began seeing a gift of an opening, even though they were pulling into the White City at that precise moment. 'I just can't get to grips with it at all.'

It was 3.20 a.m. and a full moon was lighting up, showcasing the breeze-block houses, built just after the war and painted with gallons of whitewash, earning the housing estate its famous nickname. Just before Dixie had a chance to pull into the White City, Smiley stopped him. 'Have you ever seen Slieve Gallion in the moonlight, Dixie?'

'Can't say that I have, head.'

'Drive straight on here then,' Smiley ordered, as they left the Rainey School behind on their right.

A few minutes later, they were parked at the peak of Mullaghboy Hill, and before them they could see the rich, mountainous countryside. Nature had provided its very own patchwork quilt using the 40 shades of green of the fields, trees and hedgerows very effectively.

'Just look at that, man,' Smiley said expansively. 'Can you believe how wonderful that looks even at this time of the morning?'

Dixie agreed with Smiley, although he wasn't really *seeing* what Smiley saw – he was looking past the view and trying to steer the conversation back around to girls in general, and Hanna Hutchinson in particular.

'Turn the engine off, man. Let's just sit here for a while and soak in all this spirituality, eh?'

'You're not going to try and convert me or anything?' Dixie said, genuinely alarmed.

'The only religion I'm into man is the religion of women.'

'Oh!' was Dixie's eager happy reply. Now that the door had been opened, he stepped straight in without cleaning his feet, let alone taking off his shoes, metaphorically speaking. He sighed, took a deep breath, and began. 'How'd you learn all this stuff about women, head?'

'Firstly, the one and only thing I've learned is that as far as women are concerned I know absolutely nothing.'

'But...' Dixie hesitated, his disappointment obvious, 'you always seem to get on so well with them.'

'Dixie, man, you're referring to them as though they are from a different planet,' Smiley replied, his amusement apparent. 'I tell you, man, it's like this. I get on well with you, don't I, Dixie?'

'Of course.'

'And I get on well with the boys in the band, don't I?'

'Of course.'

'Well that's it, Dixie, it's as simple as this: I like people, I get on well with people because I love them and I love finding out about them, men and women, boys and girls alike.'

'But how do you do that?' Dixie asked, turning to face Smiley, who was still enjoying the view.

Smiley wound down the window, the sharp morning air dispelling the smell of eight men who had sweated together on stage for two and a half hours earlier that night.

'Do what, man?'

'Just go up and speak to someone?'

'Well, you merely have to accept the fact that sometimes it's okay just to speak to someone – you know, they're happy to talk to you without wanting anything from you and vice versa, and then, before you know it you're involved in a conversation,' Smiley replied, putting his size tens up on the dashboard. A severely stern glance from Dixie had him sheepishly removing them again.

Due to his height, Smiley was the one band member who was always struggling to find a comfortable position in the van. His favourite position seemed to be with his feet up on the dashboard and knees tucked under his chin, and whereas Dixie hadn't seemed to mind in the old bus, an unwritten and unspoken set of rules – all of them enforced with the deft use of Dixie's arched eyebrows – seemed to be developing for the new van.

'Yeah, but you see, that's the bit I find hardest to do, you know, just speaking to someone – take Hanna for instance…' Dixie hesitated. Smiley waited contently for him to continue. 'I… I like her… I want to get to know her better, but she's very difficult to deal with. I mean, she's not your usual kind of girl, is she?'

'Aye, she's beautiful all right.'

'Goodness is she ever – she literally gives me the shivers when I see her,' Dixie gushed. 'I've never seen anyone who looks so stunning. I just want to… I just want to… I want to ride her every time

I see her,' Dixie admitted and blushed instantly. There it was. He'd said it. He'd finally admitted what had been preoccupying him for the last few months.

'Dixie, man, I have to tell you, once you lie with someone you'll still need to communicate with them, and to do that you need to find out all about them first. You need to understand their internal beauty as well.'

'I know, I know,' Dixie said impatiently.

'But do you, Dixie?' Smiley asked slowly and considerately. 'I mean, after you lie with her, what will you want to do? Will you still be fixated on her, or will you want to dump her and go off looking for someone else to "ride"?'

'No way, head,' Dixie blustered, 'I mean, I know I said every time I see her I want to ride her, that doesn't mean that I would – I'd love to court her a while and then get married…'

'But why would you decide you wanted to do that? You don't even know her!'

'But I know her a little and she's beautiful.'

'I know she's beautiful, Dixie, but what if that beauty is only skin deep: what then?'

'But we'd have kids by then!' Dixie protested.

'Tell me, Dixie; were you looking for a wife and kids before you met Hanna?'

'No, not really. I mean, I'd never really thought about it.'

'Okay, that's good,' Smiley replied, 'that's a good start. But why don't you just spend some time trying to get to know her, you know, let her get to know you as well? You're a good man, Dixie, aye, a sound man – there's a lot there for her to get to know and to like. And, yes, she's beautiful, there's no doubt about that, but equally when you get to know her, she might just turn out to be a right royal pain in the neck, she might be a moaner, she might be bossy, some- one who's always critical, someone who doesn't share your interests. Tell me, Dixie – does Hanna like The Playboys?'

'She says she likes Martin's songs, and she says she likes it when the band performs them,' Dixie offered.

'Does she like your records? Does she like Satchmo? Does she like Boots Randolph, does she like Tommy...?'

'She didn't know any of them. She likes Elvis because he's wild, she hates Cliff because she says he looks like one of the boys who goes to prayer meetings and does everything his mother tells him to.'

'And what else, what does she like other than Martin's songs and Elvis? What are her other interests?'

'She doesn't have any,' Dixie admitted somewhat sadly.

'She doesn't have any, or you haven't discovered what they are yet?'

'Nope, head. When I asked her, she said something like, "It's all boring, if you ask me."'

'You've got to be careful, Dixie. I mean, you've developed your personality, and you've got your interests. But Hanna has just recently started to blossom into a woman, and it could all be a bit too much for her at this point, what with all her hormones running wild. I tell you this because I've witnessed it in all of my sisters. You know, once they are aware that they have *a look* and that men and boys are *looking* at them, well... Sadly, Dixie, I have to advise you that there's an 18-month period when their brain just goes off on vacation, and the look and the new power that this look gives them takes over. I'd say you'd be best advised to take it very slowly with Hanna. That's what I'd do if I was you, Dixie, otherwise it could all end in tears.'

'But, Andrew, she seems interested in me – I mean *really* interested.'

'Yes, Dixie, and why wouldn't she be? Sure, you're a handsome young bandleader soon to have the world at your feet. From her point of view, less than a year ago she was running around with her school friends and now she's the belle of the ball because Dixie from The Playboys has come calling.'

'Animals, you know, they've got all this stuff more sussed than we have, head,' Dixie began, choosing to pick this moment to develop a thought of his own. 'They can't even talk, yet they always seem to know what to do.'

'Yeah, Dixie, but we're not animals, we're meant to be more civilised.'

'Not when it comes to riding we're not – that's so basic,' Dixie said with a slight hint of distaste creeping into his tone.

'Well, the animals only do it in a reproductive way, there's never any lust involved. Perhaps lust is the destructive element in all of this, eh, Dixie?'

'But what if I take your advice?' Dixie asked, ignoring Smiley's question and returning to his own agenda. 'You know, I back off and then she finds someone else… well, then it'll be too late won't it?'

'Not necessarily, Dixie. Not necessarily, man. There's a lot to be said for taking a step back and allowing her to make her mistakes with someone else, then you can be the knight in shining armour waiting in the wings to ride in and pick up the pieces.'

Dixie thought about this bit of advice for a few minutes as they both sat in silence and deep in thought.

'So, you think I should try and get to know her a bit better?' Dixie eventually said.

'Yeah, head. Take it slowly, just take it slowly,' Smiley replied with a frustrated sigh. 'Now, man, it's getting late, it's time I visited a more peaceful dreamland.'

CHAPTER EIGHT

I wandered lonely and not so loud

Smiley

There's this mate of mine, and he's interested in this girl and, well, I was wondering, you know, as you seem to, you know… get on well with girls, if you could tell me what I should tell him to do.'

The speaker was Martin Dean. The location was along a sandy beach just below the Arcadia Ballroom up in Portrush on the north coast. The time would have been late July 1960, a month marked by the fact that Charlie Chaplin, his wife Oonagh and family were enjoying a touring holiday in Ireland. The listener was none other than Smiley, trumpet player with The Playboys.

'This friend of yours, Martin – has he said anything yet to this girl, you know, *about* his interest?' he said, the smile still on his face but walking along the beach with the manner of it being a frown.

'Well, here's the thing – he used to kinda go out with her, but now she's kinda going out with someone else,' Martin replied, trying to speak loud to be heard above the buzz on the busy beach, but not so loud that any of the Ulster folk on their annual pilgrimage to the seaside would hear him.

The Playboys had driven the 30 miles from Castlemartin in two and a half hours. They'd unpacked their gear, set it up on stage and checked it over. Martin and Smiley had then left Dixie and the remaining members of The Playboys to oversee the setting up of the relief group, Blues By Five.

'So, do you know, Martin, if your friend dumped the girl or the girl dumped him?'

'Neither – you see it's like I explained – they weren't *really* going out, they hadn't *really* started, so there was not really anything to end.'

'Does your friend not like it, now that she's going out with someone else? Is that why he's interested again?'

'Do you mean do I think the girl is only going out with the other guy to make my mate jealous so he'll want her again?' Martin replied, showing that he had some kind of grasp of the situation.

'Yes,' Smiley replied, 'I suppose I did mean exactly that now you come to mention it.'

'No,' Martin smiled back, answering his own question. 'It's more than that – well I suppose this other fellow is kinda older than my mate and so my mate feels that she might feel my mate is too young for her now – which is why they weren't really going together properly in the first place. But my mate wants to know what he should do to prove to her that he's not too young to be going out with her properly.'

'Oh, is that all he wants to know? Well, that's easy, Martin.'

'Really?'

'Yes.'

'What should he do?'

'*You* should ignore her completely, Martin. If you're to stand any chance at all, that's the only thing you can do that will do any good.'

***

Martin tried ignoring Hanna. He ignored her in a way he hoped wouldn't look like he was ignoring her. His logic being that if he looked like he was ignoring her, in a way, she'd know that he was preoccupied with her. But if he treated her like she didn't exist, well then, that would be totally different and surely all the more effective.

It took him a while to perfect this ignoring lark. In the beginning, he'd always give himself away by stealing looks at her to see if she realised he was ignoring her. He reckoned it was a good 7 months before he'd perfect this art. 3 months later, when word was out that Hanna would be announcing her engagement to Dixie Blair, he figured perhaps it hadn't been the best bit of advice he'd ever taken.

CHAPTER NINE

Is that from an English or an American record? I'd like to buy that one

Gentleman Jim Mitchell

et's fast forward to June 1961. The Playboys were doing very well by then, in part because of their natural momentum, but tourism that year in Ireland was at its highest, generating £42 million, and ballrooms around the country were enjoying a piece of those record figures.

That summer, Gentleman Jim Mitchell, never a man to miss an opportunity, pitched a 5-pole marquee in a field he owned on the other side of town. He was going to run the first Annual Mid-Ulster Carnival. He asked all the local traders to get involved, taking money from some and goods from others in exchange for publicity, but no matter the small print of the various deals, all sides were extremely happy with the arrangements.

The Playboys did quite well out of it too. They played to one of the biggest crowds of the carnival, not to mention their career, when they sold 2,972 tickets. Dixie was extremely annoyed they didn't break the 3,000 barrier, feeling that it would have put them up there with The Freshmen and The Royal Showband.

He was, however, happy with the £557/5s. fee the band were paid that night. Dixie still worked under the counsel of his father. Blair senior was a proud man who never owed a penny to anyone in his life, and despised those who were slave to the tick. Jim Mitchell was not in the least bit surprised when the morning after their big payout at the carnival, Dixie, accompanied by his father, came to the Dreamland and handed over the £230 the band still owed him for the wagon. Mitchell couldn't help but note the look of pride on old man Blair's face as his son handed over the wad of warm, newly counted and recounted fivers.

Mitchell, for his part, gave to Dixie the traditional lucky penny, in the form of six blue notes, which seemed to please Desmond Blair just as much as his son being able to wipe the slate clean. It wasn't as if Mitchell was making anything on the van deal in the first place, and he'd already covered the original outlay thanks to the horse Merryman II, but since he was 'receiving' the payments for the van, it was still proper form. Besides, with his 15-night season at the first Annual Mid-Ulster Carnival he wasn't exactly short of cash that summer. In fact, he presumed that as Dixie and his father walked home that day, they'd probably be taking a guess at just how much he was making out of the 5-poler up on the Fair Hill. But even at their most exaggerated estimate, they'd only be crediting the canny Playboys manager with less than 50 per cent of his takings. Mitchell, discreet to a fault, never flaunted his wealth. He was well aware that folks never spent as much time trying to work out your losses as they did profits.

In addition to the success of his carnival, Mitchell was happy that all seemed well in The Playboys' camp. The band was making progress on the circuit – not as fast as some other bands, mind, such as The Freshmen, The Royal Showband, The Clippers and The Dixies, but he took comfort in the fact that each step forward was a solid step, and a step they wouldn't need to repeat. He believed the band would continue to raise their profile and their fee, slowly but surely. However, he could never have foreseen their next step: they were lurching towards one of the biggest arguments of their short career so far, an argument which would nearly take them off the road altogether.

It all started the week after Dixie paid off the outstanding balance on the van. It was a Tuesday in fact. The Playboys usually played dances on Thursdays, Fridays, Saturdays and Sundays, sometimes on the Wednesdays. Mondays was always a day off. Tuesdays, and sometimes Wednesdays, were rehearsal days.

As always, Dixie arrived with the wagon at noon – petrol tank so full the tiger's tail couldn't fit in. Mo arrived next: he had the most work to do in setting up his drum kit. The remainder of the band arrived in dribs and drabs, in ones and twos, but never threes. By 1.00 p.m. they were all set up and ready to go.

They opened the rehearsal with a new Martin Dean song, 'Still She Dances With You'. Martin was fast becoming a dab hand at using a bit of sugar to sweeten a bitter pill. Whereas the title, the melody and the arrangement were up-tempo, poppy and catchy, the lyrics' theme said it all: 'Why is she still dancing with you, when she should be dancing with me?' No prizes for guessing who this particular song was about.

Dixie, oblivious to the real focus of the song, came up with a beautiful horn part, which was as sweet as a strawberry milkshake. He, Robin and Smiley rehearsed the part to perfection in the dressing room while Martin and the rest of the band worked up the foundation of the song on stage. For this number, Martin wanted Barry with him on vocals, so he asked him to leave his alto sax in the wings and come up with something on the organ. Barry, inspired by what he could hear of Dixie's horn parts, muffled by two doors and the corridor that separated them, contributed an infectious Mexican-influenced piece.

When Dixie and the boys returned from the dressing room, they put everything together with the vocals and the harmonies. It was an exciting result. Even Gentleman Jim Mitchell made a rare daytime appearance in the ballroom to see what all the fuss was about. The band polished off the song over the next hour.

'Okay, heads, that's it,' Dixie said, content with their work. 'Let's call it a day.'

'Aye okay, how about calling it Tuesday?' Robin chipped in as he normally did. The band laughed, not at the content of Robin's quip, but at the fact that he should still be making the same joke two years on.

The lads began to pack the equipment up. Dixie packed the Shure microphones into their original cases. The brass lads removed mouthpieces and liquid, in the form of spit, from their instruments; Mo dismantled his drum kit and the two 6-inch nails he hammered into the stage to keep it from wobbling all over the place; Davy and Brendan returned their guitars and leads to their cases and Martin helped Barry break down the Vox Continental organ and Dixie dismantle the PA system. It was a well-rehearsed ritual, and one they routinely performed to perfection. They were so efficient because after each dance, the sooner they got the gear packed away and loaded into the wagon, the sooner they either (a) got on the long road home, (b) got to eat or (c) got to chat up the local talent. It had been a great day, and they were flush with the success of a fantastic new song.

The problem with euphoria is that a feeling of emptiness – not quite depression, but rather one of disappointment – can frequently follow. The boys had been on a creative high, and each of them had contributed in some way to the new tune. And if Dixie had thought the volunteering of his next bit of information was going to cause such distress and anxiety, he might, on reflection, have left it to another time, allowing the boys to bask in their collective glory. But Dixie didn't have the ability to compartmentalise issues. The song arrangement had been accomplished to everyone's satisfaction, and so it was on to the next point on his agenda: informing the boys that he'd finished off the payments on the van.

'So,' Dixie announced to no one in particular and everyone in general, 'for the first time we're going to be packing the equipment into our own wagon.'

'What happened to the old one, Dixie?' Brendan asked, rolling his guitar lead over his elbow and through the thumb and forefinger of his hand.

'Nothing, head, it's just that it's all ours now,' Dixie replied as he clicked shut the final microphone box.

'But it was all ours already – sure, we bought it,' Brendan replied, lifting his guitar and sitting on top of his Vox AC30. He then proceeded to polish his red Hofner Verithin guitar with the yellow duster he kept in his case.

'Yes, we bought it Brendan, but we were still paying it off,' Dixie explained painfully. This wasn't going to be as easy as he'd thought.

'I know what you're going to say,' Robin announced as he drained a few hours worth of spittle from the long U-bend of his trombone, 'you're going to tell us that you paid off the wagon with the extra dollars we made at the marquee.' Robin had never actually seen a dollar in his life, but his obsession with American movies inspired his new lingo.

'Oh Lordy, no,' Brendan said, stopping work on his guitar midshine. 'Ah, don't tell me Robin's correct, Dixie – I'm in need of a bit of cash and I was counting on that.'

'I bet you, head, that's exactly what he's going to tell us,' Robin said, packing the pieces of his Selmer trombone into his tattered hand-me-down velvet-lined case.

'So what does that mean Dixie?' Davy the bass player asked, the very mention of money, as always, capturing his undivided attention.

'Listen, lads…' Dixie sighed in frustration, 'we took a wild fee out of the 5-poler – just over 550 lids – and we'd 230 still left to pay on the wagon, so I paid it off.'

'What, without discussing it with us?' Barry said, making a rare contribution to a band conversation.

Mo continued packing away his drum kit. He hated any kind of unpleasantness, and whenever he spotted any on the horizon, he always stuck a Lucky Mine in his mouth. Lucky Mines were large sweets which cost a penny, but if you were very lucky you might find a threepenny bit in the centre. It took some effort to get through them, and Mo reckoned all that sucking strengthened his jaws, so when he'd be lucky enough to start kissing the girls, he'd be ready.

'Aye, he's right, head,' Davy chipped in again, 'there should have been a band meeting about this.'

Dixie, feeling as though he was about to take on seven men in a football match by himself, sighed. 'Ah, listen here a minute, lads. We owed the money, we'd a bit of a windfall, so we paid it off.'

'But Dixie…' Brendan began doing and undoing the top button of his white nylon shirt, 'the magic word you're using there is *"we"*. *"We* owed the money" and *"we* paid it off." I don't remember being consulted, and I'm a fecking equal part of this royal "we" of yours.'

'He's right, head,' Robin said confidently. By this point, the only people still working were Mo on his drum kit and Martin on the PA system.

'Jeez Dixie…' Brendan continued, 'you just don't know how much I was depending on that money. You're making me feel sick.'

'Now don't all be getting crabbit with me, don't be getting on my case. Isn't Jim always telling us to be careful with our money, never to spend it until it's in our hands? It's basic housekeeping, lads: you owe money, you pay it off. We owed money, we paid it off.'

'But *we* owed it to the guv,' Brendan protested. 'He wasn't exactly knocking on our doors demanding it back.'

'But that's not the issue, Brendan,' Robin started. Dixie's smile of relief soon disappeared as Robin continued. 'The issue here is that you spent our money without our permission.'

Smiley, Martin and Mo stared in silence, and Dixie looked to them for a glimmer of support. But Martin continued about his work, his body language giving absolutely nothing away. Smiley sat on a fold-up wooden chair beside Mo's drums, his long arms wrapped around his trumpet, the horn of which was resting on his thigh. His stern look suggested there was something more serious going on here, apart from the obvious facts that Brendan needed money and Dixie had taken an apparent liberty with paying off the van. Mo's mouth was still occupied by his Lucky Mine.

'Correct me if I'm wrong here, Dixie,' Brendan began expansively, 'but just before Gentleman Jim came in as manager, didn't you give us all a share of the band?'

'Not exactly,' Dixie replied, worry overtaking his face.

Robin and Brendan spoke at once. Brendan's statement contained mostly profanities, so it was easier to make out what Robin was saying. '"Not exactly?" How "not exactly?"'

'What *exactly* is going on here?' a very distressed Davy asked.

'Sure that's rubbish, Dixie, you've been giving us all an equal share,' Barry chipped in, ignoring Davy and appearing to suggest that Dixie didn't know what he was talking about and he was getting himself into trouble over nothing.

'Look, lads, I suggested paying you all a split because I wanted you all to feel part of it. But I'm still the bandleader, I still run the band, I still make the decisions about what we do. It's still *my* band.'

'Oh, so you're the boss?' Robin said.

'I don't give a feck who the boss is – no one's going to spend my money without my permission,' Brendan announced, the red in his checks now obvious. Brendan's statement was as confrontational as anyone's so far and no one dared speak as he continued. 'Okay, here's what I say we do. I say we take a vote.'

'Too late, it's already done, head – I've paid off the debt and I can't unpay it.'

'Dixie, you just shut the feck up. I'm calling a band meeting and I'm going to put this to a vote. If the band votes that the van shouldn't have been paid off without our permission, then you're going to owe me a split of that money and I just hope you're as keen to pay me off as you were to pay the boss off. Sure he's rolling in it; he's no need of our money.'

'That's still not the issue here, Brendan,' Smiley chipped in again, 'It doesn't matter how much money the Guv has – if we owe it to him, he deserves to be paid, no matter how much he may or may not need it. The issue here is whether or not Dixie can decide to pay off money without our permission.'

'Okay, fair play, fair play,' Brendan conceded. 'Let's take a vote. Robin, what do you say?'

'I say it should have been a band decision.'

'Davy?'

'Totally. I'm with you, Brendan. I don't want anyone spending my money without my permission.'

'Mo?'

'Band decision, I agree,' Mo replied awkwardly through his munching.

'Barry?'

'Sorry, Dixie, but I'm with Brendan. You should have asked us first.'

Dixie smiled in disbelief as Brendan gestured. 'Smiley?'

'Come back to me later… I'm still not sure on this.'

Brendan looked like he'd been kicked in the gut, but he continued. 'And Martin?'

Martin stopped his packing and looked up at the portholes on the front wall of the ballroom. He thought he could see Mitchell but he wasn't sure. Either way, he was finding neither support nor interruption there. 'You know it's easy for us to get carried away here,' he began, his voice a bit shaky. 'Ehm… did any of you guys sign for this loan?' He looked around at everyone but Dixie. Each of them shook their head. Martin sighed. He looked at Dixie, who was still wearing a smile, maybe a smile of shock but a smile nonetheless. 'Dixie, did you sign a bit of paper with Mr Mitchell for the loan on the van?'

'I did Martin, I did,' Dixie sighed.

'So, say for instance the band split up, would the band have been responsible for the debt or would you personally have had to pay it back?' Martin continued. Unlike a barrister, he asked the question as though he genuinely didn't know the answer.

'Me and me auld man would have been responsible, it was our name on the note,' Dixie replied, his lone voice echoing around the empty ballroom.

'That's not the fecking point,' Brendan cut in.

'Whisht, hold your horses a minute, Brendan!' Smiley hissed. 'Let's hear what Martin's got to say.'

'Well, that's it, really,' Martin sighed. 'Dixie took on the debt – he didn't ask any of us to sign and accept responsibility for it. He took responsibility, therefore it was his responsibility to pay it off. I tell you I wouldn't be happy to have debts like that hanging over *my* head.'

'But he still should have told us,' Robin cut in.

'Aye, well that's another matter,' Smiley said.

'So you're saying that you still run the band, just like you did before you gave us a cut?' Brendan asked Dixie in disbelief as he saw the tide ebb away from his stance.

'I'm the bandleader. As far as I'm aware, there's never been a dispute about that,' Dixie replied.

'But I thought we became a co-op outfit when you agreed to give us a split,' Brendan said, seething. 'Tell me… what would happen to the equipment if the band split up?'

'Well that's simple, all the equipment the band bought would be sold and the money would go back into the pot and then be divvied up under the normal share structure.'

'So what would happen if a band member left?' Robin spoke this time. 'Would he get a share?'

'No,' Dixie replied plainly.

'No?' Davy asked.

'No,' Dixie said, and then offered an explanation. 'If someone leaves the band, it would still continue, so paying out money or selling equipment would seriously jeopardise the future of the band.'

'I think you should have explained all this from the beginning,' Smiley said, echoing the thoughts of the others.

'So you run the band whatever way you want?' Brendan asked, the wind now extremely low in his sails.

'Well, obviously I have to take everyone's views into consideration and consult with Jim Mitchell, but yes, essentially I believe that to have a successful organisation, at the end of the day there has to be a lone voice calling the shots.'

'That's news to me, head,' Brendan said. 'I think we should take a vote on it.'

'But can't you see that would be a waste of time, Brendan? It's not a co-op band. The vote doesn't count,' Dixie said, sounding more like he was pleading than telling.

'Well. Maybe if the vote doesn't count, Dixie,' Brendan began, scanning the other members, 'we should form our own band where the vote does count, and replace you with another tenor player?'

Dixie clicked his tongue in a tutting sound.

Smiley looked at Martin, who was about to say something, but he spoke up before Martin had formed his words. 'Ah now, this is ridiculous, Brendan. Sure none of us want that. Starting all over again, after all the progress we've made?'

'We've done it once, we can do it again,' Brendan began. 'It'd be the same band... ' he stared at Dixie, 'well, very nearly.'

'Aye, but it would be with a different manager – Jim Mitchell's not going to want to work with us again. He'd run a mile from a bunch of messers,' Smiley said, shaking his head very slowly from side to side. 'Oh Lordy, no,' he continued in time with his head movement. 'I'm happy with things the way they are, and you know what? Now that the air has been cleared and we all know where we stand, I'm happy with that. Dixie and Jim Mitchell haven't exactly done badly by us with the way they are running the band. And you want to know what else? No disrespect, Dixie, but I couldn't be bothered with all this organisational crap – you're welcome to it, head.'

'Smiley's right, Brendan,' Robin continued seamlessly. 'The band is well run, we're doing well and we're making serious money. I'll let you into a wee secret: I earned more money last month than my dad does in an entire year!'

Dixie found a spot in the changing tide to jump in. 'And we're only just starting, lads! The Guv reckons that once the news gets out about the business we did in the big marquee, we'll get a lot of prime Christmas shows coming in!'

'I heard from someone in the *Mid-Ulster Mail* that we did more people in one night than Fossett's Circus does in a whole week!' Davy piped in, crossing back over the imaginary line to Dixie's side again.

Brendan finished polishing his guitar in silence. He packed it away in his case, and announced to no one in particular: 'Don't pack my amp in the wagon, I'll come by later and pick it up.'

'What do you mean?' Robin asked. This was from the man who always knew what people were going to say before they said it. He appeared to be offering Brendan a chance to clarify the situation for the rest of the band.

No one heard exactly what Brendan said in reply. It was mumbled, and he was grabbing his guitar case and leaving the stage as he spat the words out, words that sounded something very like 'That's me, I'm finished with ye. I'm off.'

***

Martin Dean's earlier suspicions had been spot on: Gentleman Jim Mitchell had not only been watching the encounter, but he'd also edged the porthole window open a little, just enough to hear what was going on. He was happy to let Brendan go off and cool down, choosing instead to avoid a direct confrontation with him – there was only one guaranteed outcome to such an attitude. He did, however, stroll down to the ballroom and lean across the front lip of the stage so that he looked like a dismembered head plonked down as an eerie footlight. 'Congratulations, lads! I suppose Dixie's told you the wagon's your own now?'

'Aye, we just heard,' Smiley said, electing himself as the first band member to put on a brave face. 'We knew something was up, even the old tiger's tail was wagging this morning.'

'Not only that, but he also blagged me into giving you a 30-quid discount because he claimed youse had paid it off so quickly,' Mitchell continued, bringing his hands up to support his chin. 'I'm going to need to keep my wits about me with that one I can tell you – there are certainly no flies on him!'

'A discount?' Davy piped in. 'First class, Dixie. Well done, head.'

'Aye,' Robin said with a tut, 'we know he's got our best interests at heart.'

'As long as youse appreciate what he's doing for you, that's all that's important,' Mitchell said. 'That new song you were working on sounded very strong to me. Is that from an English or an American record? I'd like to buy that one.'

'Aye, that's one of our...' Robin replied immediately and then corrected himself, 'I mean it's one of Martin's. It's first class isn't it?'

'Is that a new one, Martin?' Gentleman Jim asked. He was keen to ease the band back to basking in their recent glory.

'Just wrote it at the weekend, sir,' Martin replied, pride obvious in his voice. 'The boys did an amazing arrangement on it. I can't actually believe how good it sounds.'

A bit of general discussion about the song and the virtues of the arrangement, and all but Dixie and a faraway and fuming Brendan had forgotten about the fracas.

CHAPTER TEN

.... sticks and stones will break my bones, but the first cut is the deepest

Martin Dean

It's astonishing really how the politics of a band work. You have two musicians: one totally comfortable up on stage, dedicated to the guitar and country music and with a very pleasant voice; and the other not quite as comfortable up there, committed to the saxophone and jazz and, although an accomplished musician, unable to sing a note to save his life.

If you had to hazard a guess as to which one would do the bidding of the other, without knowing the personalities of the characters involved, you'd be forgiven for thinking that the singer-cum-guitarist would have the upper hand. But you'd be wrong. You'd be wrong, not because of anything to do with musicianship, no, but because of everything to do with ambition. Now, contrary to popular opinion, ambition has absolutely nothing to do with sitting around all day dreaming about wanting to be as big as Brendan Bowyer or as great a musician as Billy Brown. Ambition is all to do with setting your sights on, and working towards, your short-term and long-term goals. Dreaming doesn't come into it. People who are ambitious are not, as a rule, dreamers; however people who are ambitious – Dixie, for instance – sometimes have to use dreamers, such as Brendan, to help them achieve their ambitions.

In Brendan's mind, The Playboys' dilemma could have been solved by a unanimous vote to replace Dixie. Looking back, it's hard to think he really believed this was all it would take to live happily ever after. To reach his goal he'd have had to lose Smiley, who with his bubbly personality and feelgood smile, not to mention his A1 musicianship, was a valuable asset to any band. He would have sacrificed the unique talents of Martin Dean, and the powerful management of Gentleman Jim Mitchell.

Had it gone that way, it might have ended up like the very true story of another warring band, a famous showband leader who sacked all of his boys on the spot when they wouldn't agree to his unreasonable demands. Since he owned the band's name, and couldn't face the process of building up a new band from scratch, member by member, the bandleader nicked an entire set of musicians from under the nose of another local semi-professional leader.

A few months later, both leaders met by accident in a local pub. 'Look, I'm really sorry about all the problems I've caused you,' said the famous leader.

'Oh, no bother,' replied the genuinely elated semi-professional. When he spotted a look of confusion on the man's face, he continued: 'Really, now *you've* got all of my problems!'

Dixie, however, knew what he wanted – he knew his assets and he went out of his way to protect them. He wouldn't have been happy that Jim Mitchell overheard the band row. He wouldn't have been happy that Martin Dean might worry about the band's stability. He knew that some of the Dublin showband heads were already paying close attention to The Playboys' young singer-songwriter. But Martin had stood up against the band to side with his bandleader, a positive sign of loyalty. He also reasoned that, as long as a man as powerful as Mitchell was their manager, nobody would dare make a move to steal their singer.

They'd have to make real progress now, though; he knew the kiss of death for Martin would be for him to witness the passing of too many Christmases without seeing an advance in his career. People could be cruel, and if Dixie and Jim Mitchell didn't push the band upwards, once the novelty of a young singer-songwriter wore off, the whispers would begin: 'Oh, if he's been around this long and he hasn't made it, he can't be all that good.' Perhaps before that started, others would appear and start to bend Martin's ear with talk about English publishing and recording contracts and what have you, and no matter how strong Mitchell was in Ireland, the English connections might start to look more attractive.

But that was down the line. Dixie had time in hand to deal with everything. The important thing now was to carry on. Brendan had to be made to believe that the band was moving on without him, and that they were going to be equally successful without him. If he did, he'd start to feel isolated, self-conscious when he walked through town, having to answer all the questions about why he'd left the band. Surely people would start to whisper behind his back?

In a village, small talk was important. The majority of village-dwellers didn't have a clue what it was *really* like to be in a band. They only saw glamour. Musicians were lucky because they got to travel outside the village limits, something a lot of locals never got to do, and to them it seemed a romantic life. Musicians were also part of an exclusive club: they name-dropped members of The Royal Showband, The Freshmen and The Dixies. Sure, didn't The Playboys from Castlemartin drive down to Dublin and Galway at the drop of a hat? Didn't they get their names and photos in the local newspapers, their posters plastered all over the place – in shop windows, on telegraph poles, on derelict buildings around the countryside, on school and church noticeboards, on the Fair Hill walls? Hadn't Dixie Blair bought the several plots on the shores of Lough Neagh that Jim Mitchell didn't already own? Couldn't The Playboys, *particularly* Barry the organist, sleep in all day and, not only that, but didn't they get paid fabulous amounts of money to do so?

Jim Mitchell decided he would take care of Brendan, calling round to his house the next morning with the amplifier. He didn't feel it was safe lying around the stage of the Dreamland, he said. He was friendly but casual. He acted like he believed that Brendan had definitely left the band. He asked him if he intended to work out his notice or if he was going to leave immediately. If Brendan could give them a week, they'd all appreciate it – Smiley and Martin (he went out of his way to avoid mentioning Dixie) wanted to bring Sean MacGee in on guitar, and it would take a week for him to learn the parts.

Brendan listened to all of this in silence, and then said with a laugh, 'It's all a misunderstanding, I never said I was leaving The Playboys. I might have said something about being done for the day and needing my amp to work on it – one of the valves is loose or something… there's a terrible rattle through one of the speakers.'

Mitchell, for his part, was gracious, and said that the misunderstanding was surely all his.

Some damage had been done. Scars had appeared, mostly on Brendan, but they'd mend. The marks would always be there to see and feel – no matter how faint – as a reminder. From Dixie's point of view, he wasn't the type to dwell on whether he was at an advantage or a disadvantage through winning this battle. He wasn't going to be preoccupied about whether or not Brendan would hold a grudge, about whether or not he would want to get his own back, or even in redress the balance altogether. This time, Brendan's little uprising had been cut off at the pass, and the status quo had been maintained. The problem with keeping people down, though – holding them back as it were – is that eventually seeking justice in equality is never enough. No, the danger is actually that the oppressed eventually want to ensure their oppressors get a taste, at least in equal amounts, of their own medicine.

CHAPTER ELEVEN

Ah jeez, Martin, for heaven's sake kiss me

Hanna Hutchinson

Meanwhile, back in Castlemartin, Martin Dean was trying to make the whole sorry business rhyme. As he busied himself working on the lyrics, he realised that it was during moments like this when he missed Sean MacGee the most. He was someone to bounce ideas off, someone who was not scared of laughing at his lyrics if they were too coy or flowery, and equally someone who could pull an average set of lyrics into a tight song without offending the sentiment of what he was trying to say. To Martin, it seemed that coming up with lyrics was second nature to Sean. His former songwriting partner could do a set on demand, and the scary thing was that the majority were first class. Strange, being that they were both of a similar age – just turning 17 at this point in our story – and both had enjoyed a similar upbringing, excepting the fact of course that Sean had two parents. Both had been average at school and, if anything, Martin had always done a bit better at English, so he felt he should have the upper hand with lyrics.

There was perhaps one incident in Sean's life that might have given him the ability to look deep inside and set his thoughts on paper; the very same incident that was also most likely responsible for his need to consume vast quantities of alcohol.

When Sean was 11 years old, he'd been sitting by his front window taking his normal sinus treatment, his head over a bowl of steaming hot water, into which his doctor's weird and wonderful potion had been mixed. He had come up for a moment's air when he happened to see a local shop van pull up on the grass outside his house. Two men hurriedly jumped out of the van, one ran towards the door and banged on it, the other started to open the back door of the vehicle. His mother let out a scream. Immediately, he ran out to find that she'd fainted and was lying on the floor. The man ran back to help his cohort lift something from the back of the van. Sean thought it was a delivery of some sort. He continued to comfort his mother.

But then he caught sight of what the men were carrying – it was not a delivery, but the crumpled figure of his brother's bloody and bruised body. Sean stayed with his mother as the two men carried his brother into the living room. He'd been knocked down by a lorry, they said as they left, closing the door quietly behind them.

Sean's mother eventually came round. They both returned to the living room. He felt a bad tremor through his body when he saw his brother on the floor. Why would they not have put him on the sofa, which would have been more comfortable? Sean went to pull him up. There was a lot of dried blood around his head, but he was no longer bleeding, which Sean took as a good sign. And then he felt the coldness of his brother's skin.

That was when Sean realised that his 10-year-old brother Pat was dead.

Sean never really got over the death of his brother, and Martin couldn't help feeling guilty for thinking it was behind his ability to write great lyrics. It was not a price anyone would want to pay for such a gift. And even if it was, why was Sean being continually asked to keep paying with repeated run-ins with alcohol?

Sean had approved of and praised Martin's, 'No Time To Say Goodbye'. Martin himself was particularly proud of the lyrics because he'd been able to tap into the tradition of using songwriting as a means to record history, in this case a major shipping disaster. He wished that he could write more of the same; in other words, songs that weren't about Hanna Hutchinson. Nearly every single word he created with the blue ink of his cheap Biro had Hanna lurking in the background and mostly, he thought, sneering back at him from between the lines of his school exercise book.

So you can surely imagine how shocked he was when, exactly one week after the Brendan voting episode, his current prolific spate of songwriting was interrupted by a knock on the door and who should be standing there – larger than life and twice as pretty – but the very same Hanna Hutchinson.

The image of Hanna immediately sent a sensual shiver down his spine; if anything she was even more beautiful than he'd remembered. Except now it was clear that she was conscious of her looks and had subtly enhanced them with touches of make-up, particularly around the eyes, and had allowed her straight, blonde hair to fall unrestrained to her shoulders. Her cheeks were as naturally rosy as ever. She was wearing a light blue, loose-fitting, ankle-length summer dress that buttoned up the front.

'Are ye going to stand there all day gawking at me or are you going to invite me in?' Hanna asked, obviously pleased by the reaction.

'Ah goodness, Hanna, of course… come in.'

'I've missed our chats, Martin,' Hanna said a few minutes later in the kitchen as Martin attempted to make them a pot of tea.

'Aye. Me too.'

'I'd say from the look on your face that's not all you've been missing.'

Martin blushed. She was standing so close to him now he could smell all her scents. He recalled them, each and every one – all natural except for just the slightest hint of a heather perfume.

'Not been kissing the girls behind the ballrooms then, Martin?'

'No, of course not.'

'What do you mean *of course* not? I've seen all the wee girls gawking up at you on stage, Martin. They'd all give a month's pocket money for a quick kiss from Martin *Dean*.'

Martin smiled.

'Martin McClelland, you vain basket, you know it too, don't you?' Hanna tickled him in the ribs.

Her touch nearly took the knees out from under him. It was meant to be playful, and, yes, it sure was playful, but it was also sexually charged. Well, at least that was Martin's reading and reaction to it. 'I haven't, Hanna, honest, I never…'

'I know, Martin, I know,' she said, taking over the tea-making process from Martin, 'I have my spies in the camp.'

'Ah – Dixie?'

'Ah Dixie,' she agreed.

'What's this I hear about you and him?'

'Martin, please let's not talk about Dixie.' she swung around, taking Martin's hand. They stood staring at each other for a few moments. She looked like she was considering whether or not to tell him something.

'Dixie wants us to become engaged. I haven't said yes…' she began, contradicting her original request to not speak about Dixie. She paused, just enough to see him smile, and then continued '… and I haven't said no.'

The smile dropped from Martin's face as quickly as a child loses interest in last Christmas's toys.

'Martin, I miss talking to you about things, rubbish things – about how Sixer's breath smells, about Colette's cabbage kiss and important things like what's happening in our lives. I liked it when we were friends. I know it is my fault we fell out.'

'What happened?' Martin began, obviously still oblivious to the reasons behind Hanna's actions.

'Ah, Martin, we both know I'm weird sometimes, it's nothing personal, believe me. You should see how I behave with other people. Remember when I told you I'd told my parents I thought they weren't my *real* parents and sometimes I think to myself, "How could you be so insensitive as to say something like that?" Other times, I'm so preoccupied with the fact that I think they really aren't my parents that I don't care about their feelings. I scare myself sometimes, Martin, I really do, and then other times I'm so strong and single-minded I don't give a fig about anybody.'

Hanna looked directly into Martin's eyes as she spoke, as though she was challenging him to look away if he didn't have the bottle for her craziness. Martin held her stare. She rubbed her hands, not exactly in glee, but more in some sort of acknowledgment that he'd passed a test. She continued: 'I don't honestly have anyone I can talk to the way we used to talk, Martin. Even when we weren't talking we still had some kind of connection. I don't know what that means, I really don't, but I didn't want to let it go any longer without at least talking to you about it. Do you know what I mean?'

'I know exactly what you mean,' Martin replied, acknowledging his preoccupation of the previous 12 months. He knew because everything he did, he did for her. If it wasn't for Hanna and what she meant to him he would never have joined The Playboys, he just wouldn't have – there'd have been no need to, would there? She unwittingly gave him that extra bit of a spiritual push when he needed it. *She* was the difference between him being content to confine his songs to his bedroom and having the courage to get up on stages throughout the country to sing his heart out to her. It never mattered that she wasn't actually in the ballroom: it was her he was singing to.

In fact, Martin suspected that 95 per cent of the audience didn't really get what he was singing about. But that wasn't the point; the ballroom circuit was all about entertainment, and inside the structure of a 3-minute song you had to make your point, musically and lyrically, while at the same time being able to *entertain*. There was no use being intellectual and snobby with your audience. Martin and Sean MacGee had long since agreed that all the great artists, the truly great artists, were able to accomplish both seamlessly. Actually, the main difference between Dixie and Brendan came down to this very thing: Brendan would get annoyed when the audience didn't stop dancing to concentrate on the songs the way they did with the big boys, but Dixie was more than happy to have the crowds simply enjoy the music and dance along to it. He was happy just as long as there *were* crowds. His aim was to send them home with a collective smile on their faces and, thanks mostly to Dixie, The Playboys did send their ever-growing crowds home happy, not to mention with an extra coat of sweat on their backs.

When bidding their audience goodnight prior to performing the National Anthem, Dixie would announce: 'We're The Playboys from Castlemartin; if you enjoyed us please tell all your friends, if you didn't please keep your gobs shut!' But he knew and liked his audience. They came out to escape all of their own troubles and worries, and they were prepared to hand over their hard-earned cash, wanting nothing in return but to be entertained and to dance. Boys wanted to meet girls and, equally important to the success of the ballrooms, girls were just as keen to meet boys – they could be fussier, but they were certainly just as keen. Martin knew exactly how important he and his songs were in this equation; he was an acceptable backdrop to their budding romances.

The other thing about an audience is no matter how much some band members might berate them as culchies, no matter how rural the crowd or how gentrified they'd claim to be, an audience always knew when they were in the presence of true greatness. It had been an absolute joy for Martin to witness The Freshmen's Billy Brown singing 'When Smoke Gets In Your Eyes' at the Arcadia Ballroom in Portrush at the beginning of June that year. When he sang, something tribal travelled infectiously throughout the audience. They instinctively stopped and listened: all 1,799 of them. They were subconsciously moved by the power of this great man's ability to interpret a song, a good song made great by the spellbinding performance that night in Portrush.

For Martin, Billy Brown was the best there was in Ireland, possibly even England as well. No disrespect to the Brendans or the Dickies or the Joes or the whomevers, but Billy Brown was *the* man: he was a great musician, a good songwriter and he could freeze a ballroom crowd two or three times a night with his soulful singing. Billy Brown was one of the few who could distract them from their dancing. Hell, he could even distract them, albeit temporarily, from their romance.

And it was the potential of romance that was *the* thing in all of this. Martin supposedly went to ballrooms to entertain and play for these crowds, but in doing so he was searching for his own romance, the romance he felt he'd lost. Despite this, he still put himself out there every night, baring his soul and his heart only for her. He wasn't sure if it would help his chances, but he just had to do it, although he wasn't sure he could tell her any of this without scaring her off for good.

'What is it about you, Martin?' Hanna asked, breaking into his thoughts. 'I haven't spoken to you for a year and here we are as if just yesterday we were hanging out together.'

Martin blew air through his lips.

'Very articulate, Martin,' Hanna laughed, 'I see the old songwriting skills haven't deserted you.'

'I don't know, Hanna. I suppose, for me, it's like… because you've been in my thoughts each and every day, so you're no stranger to me.'

'Ah jeez, Martin, kiss me for heaven's sake.'

Now if Martin had dreamed up this little scenario, and he certainly wasn't beyond dreaming about it, 'Ah jeez, Martin, kiss me for heaven's sake' was possibly the line he'd have had Hanna say. On consideration, he would have preferred 'Ah jeez, Martin, for heaven's sake *kiss me*.' Either way, it didn't matter: for her to just come right out and say it, there in his kitchen in real life, his biggest wish in the world had been granted.

So they kissed.

It started in the kitchen and continued in the good room, the front room, the room you brought visitors to. Hanna was a visitor after all, not to mention the fact that there was a rather large, comfy sofa in there. It was possibly 5 minutes before they came up for air.

'I missed kissing as well, Martin.'

Martin grinned.

'I hope those wee girls never get to realise what they're missing behind the ballrooms.'

'I wouldn't…'

'I'm kidding, Martin. Was it as good as you remembered?'

'Better,' Martin immediately countered.

'Me too.'

Martin didn't feel it appropriate to mention that 'better' might have had something to do with the fact that the fuller contours of her body were evident against his, through the soft material of her dress.

They lay in each other's arms, side by side, eyes closed, in silence for a good time, and then he felt her move. His eyes remained closed as Hanna started to kiss him again. This time, the kiss wasn't a test; it was a kiss they both lingered on, the most intimate of kisses. She rolled over and lay on top of him. His stirring in the nether regions didn't seem to offend or scare her. He was convinced he could hear an 'mmmm' through the kisses. She didn't shy away from him.

'Well it's great to know that somebody's still attracted to me,' Hanna began, as the kiss came to an end.

'Sorry?'

'Well, sometimes I get the feeling that Dixie thinks I'm going to break in two if he holds me.'

Martin couldn't hide his discomfort at this sudden intrusion.

'Oh, don't be such a goof, Martin! Dixie and I don't do anything like *this*. He's never even kissed me properly. I was beginning to wonder if there was something wrong with me, but then I remembered our kisses.'

Martin remained stony-faced.

'I think he's more interested in intellectual stimulation,' Hanna said, pushing herself gently into Martin's nether regions, and when he involuntarily responded, she smiled: 'This is the stimulation I prefer though.'

This time Martin smiled.

'Well I'm young, Martin, me hormones are raging; I don't want to be sitting bored out of my brains on a pedestal. I want… ' Hanna paused and moved her mouth very close to his ear and whispered, '… I want to experiment.'

They both seemed to consider her last statement for a while. She was gently rocking backwards and forwards on him.

'Do you want to experiment, Martin?'

Martin nearly choked trying to get a word out, 'Erm, aye, I mean yes… yes, of course.' He didn't exactly know what she meant by experimenting. Part of him, a lot of him in fact, was scared what Hanna might mean by experimenting. It had now become clear why she'd come round to see him: she missed their chats. Dixie was probably proving to be a bit of a fuddy-duddy for her and, more importantly, he was probably as scared of her physically as Martin was.

Martin followed the flow of her rocking backwards and forwards for a short time before he started to counter her movement with an opposite one of his own. It just seemed to be a natural thing to do. She seemed to enjoy this. She closed her eyes, barely, and lay on him, appearing to enjoy the motion. Her legs had parted on either side of him and her dress, while still protecting her decency visually, was offering no resistance physically.

They started to kiss again. He was tempted to move his hands but he wasn't quite sure that she wanted him to experiment to that degree. He never did get to find out, because a few seconds later they heard Martin's mother fumble around with her key in the front door.

Martin and Hanna made themselves decent, as they say in Ulster, by quickly rearranging their clothes. Hanna immediately started talking in a loud voice: 'Go on, Martin, play me this new song of yours. What's it called?'

'Oh… 'Still She Dances With You',' Martin replied, falling in with her pantomime and adding a bit of his own. 'How did you know about that?'

'I have my spies. Oh. Hello, Mrs McClelland!'

'Hello, Hanna, we haven't seen you for a long time. What have you been up to?' Kathleen offered very warmly.

'Oh you know, Mrs McClelland, finishing off college, trying to work out what to do next.'

'What *are* you going to do next?'

'Oh, I was thinking about going to Queen's University.'

'Really?' Martin replied, unable, or unwilling, to hide his surprise from his mother. He withdrew his comb from his back pocket and gave his hair a couple of surplus strokes.

'Well, I'm thinking about it, Martin. I mean, I'd have to do another year at Magherafelt Tech and go to Belfast in September next year.'

'What are you going to study?' Kathleen asked as she took her shopping through to the kitchen, returning to the front room door before she'd finished her question.

'Well, I thought I'd do a degree in English Literature.'

'Maybe then you'll be able to help Martin with some of these lyrics he's always struggling over.'

'Oh, that's not what I'm hearing, Mrs McClelland. I'm hearing he's written another classic for The Playboys and they're going to perform it at the Flamingo Ballymena this Friday,' Hanna said proudly. 'I'm hoping he's going to play it for me today though.'

'Course he will,' Kathleen replied proudly as she returned to the kitchen. 'Martin, take Hanna up to your bedroom and play her your new song.'

'Maaaam,' Martin moaned.

'Go on, Martin,' his mum tutted, 'the wee girl wants to hear the song, so play it for her! Go on, and I'll make you a cup of tea, just like the old days. I'll give you a shout when it's ready.'

'Come on, Martin?' Hanna pleaded, taking his hand and dragging him out of the sofa. However, when she spied Martin's denim tent and his discomfort, she pushed him back down into the sofa, playfully. 'Sorry, Martin, first I have to use your toilet.'

A few minutes later, they were kissing in the safety of Martin's bedroom. Hanna was leaning against the door and Martin was leaning against her. She broke free to come up for breath and announced, 'You better play me this song, Martin, your mum will be listening out for some noise.'

Martin did as he was bid, and Hanna listened, transfixed.

Love was gentle,
Then love was gone
But the memory lingers on
You were once here
And now you're gone

Sure he holds you
Like I used to do
But she don't hold you
Like she used to hold me
But still she dances with you

Still love's unforgiving
It acts like we never met
If we never ever met
Then why all the regrets
Now that you're gone

Yes now he holds you
Like I used to do
But she don't love you
Like I used to love her
But still she dances with you

Let the sad clouds
Block the blue sky

Let the persistent waves
Stop kissing the beach
Now that you're gone

Now he holds you
Like I used to
But you'll never ever
Break each other's heart
But still she dances with you

'Is that about us?' she asked after he returned his guitar to its case.

Martin was intrigued that she'd said 'us' – he figured anyone else he knew would have said 'Is it about me?' He flustered to find a reply. Eventually he found one. 'Well, it's kinda about you and Dixie and your dance, you know?'

'Ah Martin, don't worry, please don't worry about all that stuff – that's just window dressing.' When Martin didn't appear to be taking much heart from her words she added, 'Martin, you and I will enjoy our own dance and no one else will ever share it.'

'Your tea's ready!' Kathleen shouted from below, shattering her son's daydream.

CHAPTER TWELVE

Martin McClelland, I do believe you got me

Hanna Hutchinson

The Playboys played on, and if Martin felt any awkwardness about the Dixie and Hanna situation, he certainly didn't show it. He and Hanna were discreet because she insisted on it. Martin was totally besotted with her and so he didn't object. She rewarded him by allowing him to be party to her experiments and then, as an additional reward, he even got involved in a bit of experimentation himself.

Their second encounter also took place in Martin's house. Again, out of the blue, Hanna knocked on Martin's door, only this time Kathleen was at the Dreamland Ballroom at work for the rest of that Monday afternoon.

Hanna asked to hear the song again. He obliged, taking her up to his bedroom and, when he stood up and put his guitar away, she started to kiss him. She was dressed in a cream, flowery dress, of the same flimsy material as last time. They were leaning against the door but then moved to the bed. 'It'll be more comfortable,' Hanna reasoned.

Once again, Martin's feelings were predominantly those of fear with just the slightest hint of excitement. He wasn't sure how far she would go, not to mention how far he would follow. This time, instead of rolling on top of him Hanna manoeuvred so that he rolled on top of her. All the while they kissed. He pushed against her. She responded. Although neither knew exactly what they were doing or what they *should* do, they both followed a predetermined animal instinct.

She took his hand and guided it down the top of her dress and onto her right breast. Instinctively, he made a grab at the mound of flesh. Her hand was still holding his and she broke from their kiss to whisper 'Gently.' He obeyed, and soon her hand guided his hand to her nipple, which he started to caress. This time she instructed him to be 'less gentle' and then, when her nipple started to respond, 'more gentle again please'. They repeated the process for the other breast, and this time he knew the pressure to apply and she merely whispered 'beautiful' between the kisses.

They had another similar session the following Monday. The Monday after that, they didn't manage to meet up because The Playboys were on their way back from a very successful jaunt at The Showboat in Youghal, County Cork. The following week, Martin's mother nearly surprised them again, so for their next meeting Hanna suggested they go for a walk across the fields.

They ended up in Old Man Hutchinson's (no relation) hay shed, far away from man and beast. This time, as Martin fondled Hanna's breasts, she actually touched him through his trousers. Martin felt a wee bit uncomfortable at that, but tried not to show his discomfort. They were lying side by side so he rolled over on her and pushed himself against her. She responded, and the next time he opened his eyes, as he sometimes did to steal a look at her as they kissed, he noticed just how flush her cheeks were. She was struggling to catch her breath now. He felt he should stop pushing against her to see if she was okay – she was acting like she might be in some kind of pain, but her pushing against him became more fanatical and eventually she bucked up against him and froze solid in that position as he continued to push down on her. Hanna cried aloud 'Agh, Martin!' and gave out a large sigh of air as she collapsed into the hay.

'Martin McClelland,' she whispered, 'I do believe you got me.'

They returned to the hay shed one afternoon a few days later. The Playboys were only playing over in Cookstown, and the pick-up wasn't until 6 p.m., so they had time to continue their experiments. Martin got Hanna to explain what she meant by the phrase 'I do believe you got me'. He still didn't know if he'd hurt her.

Hanna explained just how exquisite a feeling it had been. She asked him if he'd enjoyed any similar experience with her. Martin explained that although, as ever, he'd enjoyed their kissing, he'd been a bit sore when he'd tried to walk home. 'Oh, poor wee boy,' she teased, 'are you still sore?'

'No it's… sorry, I'm fine now, thanks.'

'Are you sure, wee boy?' Hanna continued unperturbed, touching him gently around his trousers.

Martin decided it just might be better to keep quiet. He lay his head back in the hay and closed his eyes. She kissed him gently on his eyelids and continued to comfort him through the material of his trousers. He felt her unzip them and he was nervous, very nervous and very scared, but he couldn't stop her. He felt her manoeuvre her hand through his flies and very tentatively touch him with one finger. Her touch betrayed the fact that she was also petrified. She touched him like she was scared – scared of what she would feel, in the way someone might touch something that might burn them. But she didn't get burned, and soon all her fingers surrounded him and he felt himself grow in her hand.

He reached up to touch her breasts as he surged himself in her hand. Her fingers were around him as she feathered him ever so gently. Pretty soon, both his hands had found her breasts and he was caressing her nipples to a peak. She seemed preoccupied with what she was doing to him and hadn't made any move to stop his hands. He too was getting adventurous and starting to undo the buttons at the front of her dress. Soon he had it down to her midriff, and then, very clumsily, he removed her bra, freeing her beautiful snow-white breasts and enjoying free access to her amazingly sensitive nipples.

'Oh please kiss me, Martin,' she whispered.

Martin couldn't really get up to her mouth to kiss her; apart from anything else he figured he'd lose the spectacular view of her breasts if he did.

'They're burning, my nipples are burning, please kiss them, Martin, oh please just kiss them,' she moaned.

All this time she continued to feather him so gently he barely even noticed, except, that is, apart from the feel of his own pulsing against her hand. He leaned up to her breast and kissed it. He supposed you just kissed a breast the way you kiss a mouth so he just pecked at it nervously.

'Put my nipple between your lips, Martin.'

He did, and found it to be as responsive as it had been to his fingers. When he started to play with it, using his tongue, it became so hard. He lost his grasp of it a few times and as his nose rummaged around her breast to recover it again, he could smell her sweet scent of heather and recently washed skin. Had she planned this, he wondered – was that why she smelled so good? He wondered how he smelled himself.

He moved to her other nipple and did the same. Hanna seemed to enjoy this even more. She was moaning. God, her breasts are so beautiful, Martin thought, so firm and so full. He worried that once he had a chance to see breasts in real life he'd think they were ugly. Maybe some people's were, but not Hanna's.

Martin's left hand lay alongside Hanna, who was on her side, her toes to her hips flat on the straw and the remainder of her torso held up, supported by one hand with her other occupied by her continued experimenting. She pushed her hips into the side of Martin's hips and, on sensing his hand come into contact between them, she pulled back again, appearing slightly nervous. A few seconds later, he felt her once again push against his hand, this time with a more assured movement. Martin didn't move his hand for fear that she would pull back from him. She continued gyrating against his hand

and now Martin flexed his fingers to avoid cramp. She seemed to enjoy that because she moaned some more and he pushed the palm of his hand into her dress, at the top of her legs. All this time he continued to kiss her breasts. Now and then, he would blow on them. He didn't know why he did this. Maybe it was because she said they were burning and he should be helping cool them down. It didn't matter what the reason was because it seemed to give her pleasure, so much pleasure in fact that she was allowing him to put his hand in a place where a girl was never supposed to allow a boy to put his hand, or indeed any part of his person. Admittedly, there were two layers of material between his hand and her skin, but he could feel the texture of her.

Hanna was sighing just like she had done last time. Her nostrils flared, and her cheeks grew deep red. For some reason, Martin found himself becoming extremely excited by the way she was looking and acting and he found himself sucking on her nipple, pushing his hand harder against her and grinding himself in bursts through her fingers, which held him and gently feathered him. She tightened her grip.

At this point, they were a mass of uncoordinated limbs and movements. On and on they pushed, until Martin was overcome by a strange sensation of wanting a release, a release of some kind, he knew not what – he just seemed to know that the more they pushed and sucked and kissed and clung to each other, the sooner it would happen. Hanna 'got' Martin first but Martin 'got' Hanna a few seconds later.

He sure felt the release mentally. Physically as well, it transpired, because he ejected just as Hanna managed to direct the warm, milky liquid away from both their persons and their clothes. The moment after could have been embarrassing, had it not been for the fact that Hanna started to kiss him gently and, as she did so, she started to do up his trousers and the top of her dress.

They discussed their adventure in great detail on the way back into Castlemartin.

'Jeez, Martin, it was such a beautiful feeling wasn't it?' Hanna said as she took his hand in hers. 'I never want to feel it with anyone else but you though, Martin.'

Martin wondered about Dixie, but didn't say a word. He felt they were as close now as they'd ever been, but he also felt it was a closeness brought on not by their sexual awakenings, but by the fact that they were truly soul mates. This recent need to pleasure and take pleasure from each other was just a manifestation of this.

They met the following Sunday at lunchtime. Again they went to Old Man Hutchinson's hay shed, and were kissing each other the minute they arrived. Martin was getting a little more adventurous, and immediately unbuttoned Hanna's dress to below her breasts, clumsily removing her bra. He knew it was an awkward moment, but he didn't feel the need to stop and say, 'Okay, Hanna, could we just stop here for a moment so that I can practise undoing your clasp a few times.' He was too keen to kiss her nipples the very second they were free to bother about any of that. Soon, Hanna was making the purring noises like before. Martin found her sounds to be as stimulating as their kisses.

He was aware that Hanna was leading him towards the far corner of the shed where they could in fact make themselves cosy and hide behind a few tall bales of hay. He didn't care where she was leading him; he was just enjoying her breasts so much. She pulled his head up so that she could kiss him on the lips. When they broke from the kiss, she pulled him down beside her in their special corner.

Hanna took his hand and pushed it down to where it had been last time, and he started to push against her softness through the double layer of light material. She tugged his elbow in the direction of her toes, all the time exploring his mouth with her tongue. He felt she was trying to get him to touch her knees for some reason. He couldn't quite reach her knees, but he grabbed a handful of her dress and pulled it up. She didn't resist. He pulled the dress up even further until he could feel the bare flesh of her thighs. This touch was electrifying! He felt the buzz of pure electricity as if he had just stuck his hand into a mains socket. He caressed her thigh for a few minutes, totally turned on by the cool touch of her skin. She tugged at his elbow again, this time in the opposite direction. Perhaps that was as far as she'd allow him to go today. He brought his hand back and placed it around her shoulder. But she immediately tugged on his elbow again. Okay, Martin thought, maybe not. He started to caress her thigh again. Once more she tugged gently on his arm, so this time, instead of removing his hand, he caught the hem of her skirt and started to raise it slowly, very slowly, all the time letting the back of his hand trail against the inside of her thigh. He fully expected her to stop him at any second, but on and on he was allowed to go, and then his hand came to a stop as he touched the material of her pants. Mind blowing! Fecking mind blowing, he thought. In a way, he hoped she would stop him. The honest truth was that he was petrified to go any further. But, if anything, Hanna seemed to be kissing him more passionately, with more abandon.

He left his hand still by the edge of her pants, as if it was a POW waiting for a sign or cover of darkness to make a run for it and escape. Martin was as scared as any of those POWs had ever been, but for totally different reasons. He didn't really know why he should be scared. He was with a girl, and she seemed happy to be there. Very happy, in fact – she was now wriggling her bottom against his hand, which was still motionless. Was this the sign he'd been waiting for? He moved his hands over her pants, which felt extremely soft, and he kept moving his hand over the top of them, happy to feel the material. She didn't seem to mind. He let his hand slide down and touch the top of her thigh. He could feel her strain against his hand. He didn't know what else to do so he let a single finger slip under the elastic of the bottom of her pants. She dropped her hand down onto his. Ah, great, Martin thought, relieved that it was time for the 'that's enough of that young boy, behave yourself' reprimand.

But no such reproach came. She gently caught his hand in hers and pulled the offending hand and finger away, bringing it back up over her pants to the top, on up towards her navel. Ah right, she wants me to touch her nipple again, Martin thought. That's okay, I do nipples. I just don't do the other things, no matter how sweet they may be. She stopped both their hands and then, using her own finger, lifted the elasticated waist of her pants and slipped both their hands down, deep down so that soon his fingers touched hair. He couldn't believe how soft and smooth her hair was down there. She moaned as they kissed. Through their kiss it was as if they'd become one: by joining their breath they joined their bodies, and their lives. At times it felt as though she was trying to climb into him through his mouth. Every now and again he would hear a rattle as their teeth crashed together.

She skilfully guided his fingers through her hair, and at the same time he could feel her parting her legs. Oh jeez, he thought, oh jeez I gotta stop this, how embarrassing – she's going to be so annoyed with me but I gotta stop. At the exact moment he was trying to work out the logistics of stopping and the repercussions, she stopped the kiss and whispered in his ear, 'Please be gentle, Martin, oh please be gentle.' And with that, she pushed his finger inside of her.

Martin's fears disappeared the split second he felt the exquisiteness of her: like nothing he'd ever experienced before. No one, *no one* had ever suggested it was going to be as absolutely amazing as this. She felt so smooth, so soft, so silky, so moist, *so* delicious. Now he knew why men drooled so much over women; this felt so good that surely there was no need to go any further.

She ushered a second of his fingers into her, pushing them deeper. She took her hand away altogether, and he could feel the soft silk of her pants on the back of his hand. For some reason this felt comforting to him – it was if her pants were protecting and guarding the naughtiness of what his fingers were up to from the rest of the world.

She now wriggled furiously against his hand, targeting on the fingers deep inside her. She seemed to want more, but surely he couldn't fit a third finger in there. Silly, he thought, when he considered the full implications of the act. Nonetheless, he felt it was better to leave things as they were. Hanna slowed down her movements against him; she slowed it right down to a gentle hypnotic rhythm.

'Oh that's gorgeous, Martin,' she sighed at the end of the longest kiss of their relationship, 'that's so beautiful what you're doing to me.'

Martin, God bless him, hadn't a clue what he was doing to her. Technically, *he* was in *her* hands. She unzipped his flies, and the minute her hand touched him he was gone, gone good and calling out her name simultaneously; a few seconds later she too was gone and calling out his name. He felt himself relax, and wondered if it had anything to do with the fact that he, in his new fulfilled state, was totally incapable of going any further.

How wrong he was about that point; 10 minutes later he was lying looking at her and her natural beauty, and she sensed he was interested again even before he knew it.

'Let's try something different,' she whispered, as she sank her head level with his waist. He couldn't believe it when she took him fully in her mouth and less than 3 minutes later he was again a spent force. If all of these experiments of theirs were so amazing, how was it humanly possible for it to be bettered by the act of making love? What must all that be about?

CHAPTER THIRTEEN

McClelland's
'Third Movement in C#'

Martin Dean and Hanna Hutchinson

The following Thursday, being the first Thursday of the month (August 1961 in fact), The Playboys from Castlemartin were back on the stage at the Dreamland Ballroom. The incident with Brendan had been all but forgotten, and everyone was in a great mood. Were they happy? You bet your life they were.

For his part, Martin was sure he would feel uncomfortable looking down at Hanna after all the experimenting they'd been doing, but if anything he felt the opposite. Something had clicked between them, and they were both aware of it.

Hanna was still insistent that neither of them acknowledge their relationship publicly. Martin didn't feel anything odd about that. They weren't your standard couple really, were they? He knew that Hanna absolutely loathed the idea of spending all her time planning things out. Her point was that married couples always seemed to be planning for some point in the future, which existed on paper but never actually arrived. She loved to live in the moment – very much in the moment – and she had proved this to Martin.

Dixie talked to her for quite a time during the Blues By Five set. Their singer, Paddy Shaw, created his own special moment when he performed an amazingly soulful version of Sam Cooke's 'You Send Me'. Martin was so distracted by Paddy's rendition that he unknowingly wandered into the middle of Dixie and Hanna.

'Are you going to do 'Still She Dances With You'?' he heard Hanna shout just above the din.

'Yes,' Dixie replied with a smile.

Hanna looked at Martin. 'Would you like a mineral?' she asked him, gesturing towards Dixie.

'Sorry, of course, head, can I get you a mineral?'

Martin was about to say no, but he spotted Hanna glaring at him. 'Yes… thanks, a pineappleade would be good.'

As Dixie went off in the direction of the mineral counter, Hanna moved closer to Martin. She was dressed in a stunning blue satin Nero-collared knee-length dress with matching blue high-heeled shoes. She was just beautiful, Martin decided – there were no other words to describe her.

'Are you okay?' Martin asked.

'I'm very okay, Martin, I'm very okay.'

'He's not hassling you about the engagement?'

'Martin, it's fine, honest. Dixie's got the rest of his life in order, he'd like a wife to complete the picture and he thinks I'd fit that picture. He'll eventually realise that we've absolutely nothing in common and he'll be after someone else with nobody being hurt or any the wiser.'

Martin saw Dixie approaching them out of the corner of his eye. Hanna caught him too. 'Will I see you at Old Man Hutchinson's hay shed after the dance?' she asked.

'What? Aren't you doing something already?' Martin asked, looking at Dixie who was struggling through the large capacity crowd.

'Dixie will walk me home; I'll give it a few minutes and then come and meet you. Please say you'll be there,' she whispered very close to his ear.

Martin nodded and she broke into a huge heart-warming smile.

'What are youse two grinning about?' Dixie asked as he handed over the drinks.

'Oh, we were just discussing what great fun it was when we were experimenting in our domestic science field trips. Weren't we, Martin?'

'Best fun I've ever had,' Martin replied. 'I'll leave you two to it and go backstage. See ya.'

'See you shortly, head,' Dixie smiled.

'See you, Martin,' Hanna said.

Dixie did his three-song dance with Hanna as usual. Martin sang 'Eyes', not *for* Hanna but *to* her, and he knew she was aware of it. And he sang 'Still She Dances With You', changing the words 'She still dances with him?' from a statement to an incredulous question: after all she's doing with me, she's not still dancing with him, is she? No one save two people in the ballroom noticed the subtle change.

The Playboys had a great night and a great payday. Brendan was totally made up when Dixie gave him his split in advance, 'Just to help you through, head.'

'First class, Dixie, first class. I appreciate that, I really do.'

Smiley was, as always, surrounded by his ever-growing fan club; Barry was happy because it was a home gig and he could rush straight home and enjoy his favourite occupation – sleeping. Dixie said his goodnights and left with Hanna. Robin, Mo and Davy were off to a late night drinking session somewhere. Brendan hadn't been seen since Dixie had paid him.

Gentleman Jim Mitchell loved to see his first and favourite ballroom full, and the only thing he loved more was to see it filled by the showband he managed. He left, supposedly to drive to Belfast for an overnight en route to Dublin, his Dreamland manager in charge of locking up.

Martin changed quickly out of The Playboys' blue suit, which would shortly be replaced by something more glamorous, or so Dixie promised. Martin chatted to the regular fans for a time. He noticed that The Playboys had two types of fan: the needy ones who wanted to boast about the fact that they knew and could talk to the band, and those who really listened to the music. As Smiley said, it didn't matter what type they were, they all bought tickets. It was important to be as civil to one as it was to the next – you made your own life easier by smiling, giving them the time of day and signing whatever bit of paper or picture they stuck in front of your face.

His fan duty complete, Martin made his way backstage to let the Blues By Five, particularly their lead singer Paddy Shaw and their excellent guitarist Vince McCusker, know how much he'd enjoyed their performance. Paddy and Vince tried to persuade Martin to write a song especially for them. Martin said he had one that might suit Paddy's voice, 'Three Spires', which wasn't really suitable for The Playboys. The three of them made plans to work on it together on Sunday afternoon.

One by one, everyone drifted out of the ballroom until there was only Martin, Paddy and Vince sitting on the lip of the stage. The Blues By Two invited Martin for a late night drink, but he declined, and soon they were off as well.

Martin was left sitting on the stage of an empty ballroom. It felt so quiet and peaceful. Less than an hour ago, The Playboys had been belting out a killer version of 'Jambalaya' and 2,100 pairs of feet were hammering out their own sympathetic rhythms –well, some had been more in time with Geronimo than with Mo of The Playboys. Martin imagined some of that energy was still reverberating around the walls of the Dreamland; it couldn't possibly have disappeared so quickly, could it? There was this incredible post-dance sadness, a feeling of resignation. Martin wondered if it was because so many relationships had moved in so many directions in the previous hours, you know, some new ones had been formed, some old ones resolved, some took but a single step forward, others a step or two back. Whatever the case, each would be suspended at that moment in time at the close of the dance. The thought gave Martin an idea for a lyric, but he was still floating it around, hoping for some special insight. Sometimes he felt so in tune with these feelings that he could put his finger right on them, but at others he felt inarticulate and so devoid of understanding anything that was happening around him.

That night, though, he felt great, he felt he was close to things, close to his thoughts, close to putting the sadness of the ghosts of the empty ballroom down on paper. He walked away from the ballroom with at least the title for his new song: 'Dreamland'.

Twenty minutes later he was waiting in the hay shed – his and Hanna's hay shed – with a mixture of fear and a sense of excitement. Not fear for her safety – in 1961, girls could walk alone at any time, day or night, in the quietest of countryside or the busiest of streets without fear of harassment or attack. No, his fear was a mixture of excitement and anticipation about what he and Hanna might *do*. The two were on a journey of discovery, a journey few of their contemporaries had taken. Martin would never have taken it without Hanna.

He knew their journey of discovery hadn't yet reached an end. Martin would gladly have admitted that, if it had been left to him, he would have been happy to continue to drink the pleasures they'd recently encountered. But he knew that something stronger than his will to resist was driving Hanna on. It wasn't recklessness on her part, rather her need to experience a natural high. Natural highs were definitely the only highs Hanna was after: she was an alcohol-free zone, and drugs were something they occasionally read about in the *Belfast Telegraph*. Some of the city showband heads had started talking about pills and the like and how they could give you a high or extra energy, but none of The Playboys was either brave enough or felt the need to try them.

Martin would have loved to have talked to her about their adventures on his couch and in the hay shed, to ask if she was as scared as he was, but doing so might somehow have ruined their *moment*. Don't forget, in all of this he had another agenda: he wanted to be with her. He wasn't confident they'd remain together if he wasn't up for their joint experimentation. She'd made it clear that she wasn't up for the traditional 'boy meets girl' scenario; she just wasn't going to become his girlfriend and live happily ever after. He was going to have to earn all and any of their shared moments. Perhaps he'd get a chance to discuss his feelings at a later date.

Martin, lost in thought, suddenly realised that Hanna was standing at the door of the shed looking at him. He didn't know how long she'd been there. She was smiling and still looked stunning in her high-collared blue dress. Sensibly, she'd replaced her high-heeled shoes with an old pair of gutties. She was carrying something under her arm, but in the half-light Martin couldn't quite make out what it was.

'That's one of your strengths, Martin,' she began as she walked over to him.

'Sorry?' he said, reaching out for her hands.

'You know, the fact that when you're alone you can occupy yourself happily with your own imagination. You were miles away when I arrived. I was standing there for ages and you weren't even aware of me.'

Martin just smiled as she took one of his hands and shoved a blanket in his gut with the other. 'I thought this might be useful tonight.' She broke away from him and gingerly made her way to their sheltered corner. She disappeared behind the wall of two high bales of hay and Martin could hear her busying herself.

Just as he was about to follow her, she said, 'Give me a minute to fix this up for us, Martin. A great crowd you had tonight – the dancers are starting to talk about your songs.'

'Really?'

'Yes, the ones around the front of the stage already remember some of your titles. Right, I'm ready, come in here now before you get a big head,' she ordered, breaking into a fit of the giggles.

Martin stumbled around until he found their corner. In the darkness he could barely make out her form. It looked like she had wrapped the blanket around her and, as he approached, she lifted the edge, gesturing for him to join her. And so he did. Martin gasped as his hands touched her bare skin. Hanna Hutchinson was certainly full of surprises.

'Martin McClelland, if you think you're going to crease and ruin my new dress you've got another think coming.'

A quick voyage of discovery and Martin realised he was enjoying one of his schoolboy fantasies: he was under a blanket with a girl, and she was dressed only in her bra and panties. The biggest thrill was that Hanna Hutchinson *was* the girl of his dreams, and it was she who was making his fantasy a reality.

They kissed.

And that's not all. But it's important in understanding this story, without wishing to indulge in voyeurism, that we see and experience at least some of the impact these two young people made upon each other. So here's what happened.

As they kissed, Martin undid her bra; his fingers didn't embarrass him this time. He was scared; we already know that because he'd already admitted it to us, but he was even more terrified because he felt something he hadn't felt before: this time he was more of an equal. She wasn't leading him any more. She'd led him to this stage, and now, on the third level of their discovery, he was more of a participant than an observer, which is exactly what scared him. He felt Hanna shiver in his arms as he took her nipple in his mouth.

He continued kissing, and gingerly moved his hand down to the top of her panties. This time, without their guide, his fingers were unsure and tentative. He felt her open her legs a little and he caressed the hair. He couldn't believe how soft and bushy it was. She had her arms around his head, lovingly pulling his face closer into her breasts. Eventually, he found that if he kept his fingers stationary for a moment she was happy to wriggle beneath him to position herself so she could be receptive to his fingers. Again, the touch, that magic touch, sent a shudder from his head to his toe. He wondered: was this what people meant when they said that beauty was on the inside? If so, he certainly would never ever disagree with them, whoever *they* might be.

Every now and then, she purred in his ear as his fingers continued to search for sensations. When they got lost, as occasionally they did, he would hold them still and she would wriggle and twist and moan to return them to their route.

'Ah, Martin, this is gorgeous, just gorgeous,' she whispered out of the blue.

For Martin, the funny thing was how much pleasure he was feeling doing these things to her. She wasn't touching him, apart from holding his head close to her breasts, and yet he was so turned on he couldn't believe it. He felt that he could easily get a release just from continuing to pleasure her. If anyone had told him of this possibility *before* these experiments, he truly would not have believed them.

They lay between her Black Watch tartan rug for about 10 minutes, and then her wriggles became less passive, her movements had more purpose and she ground into his hand three forceful times and pulled his head very tightly into her perfect breasts and gasped, crying out his name so loudly that he was happy they were miles from civilisation. She went totally limp and sank into the blanket, which sank further into the hay.

By this time, they were both covered in a film of sweat. She stroked the hair back from his sweaty brow and, without saying a word, she turned him from his side onto his back and undid his flies. She had trouble freeing him from the trousers and his under-garments, and so the moment, the very moment she took him in her mouth, he exploded. Totally exploded. He was worried, but she acted like it was the most natural thing in the world.

'Okay, now that you're no longer a danger to me,' she said, 'let's get these off.' She began to remove his shoes, socks, trousers and then his jumper, shirt and, to a little resistance, his underpants. She shivered, with excitement he hoped, as he in turn took off her white panties. By this time, their eyes had become a little more accustomed to the dark and they lay just looking at each other for some time.

He felt they were safe. He'd felt he'd never get an erection now that he was undressed in front of her. He was even uninhibited about letting her stroke him again – apart from anything else, it was too soon after the last time. He loved the way she gently feathered the spot just underneath his tip, which felt exquisite to her touch.

'Oh, I better be careful,' Hanna said, tightening her hand

'It's okay,' Martin replied, feeling he was ages away from a revival.

'Mind you,' she said, feeling his tip with her fingers, 'you'd never get inside me, it's too blunt.'

'Get me a penknife and I'll sharpen it up for you.'

'So you've considered it, then?' she continued, coaxing him onwards and upwards, as it were.

'And yourself?' Martin said, thinking that all he'd considered was how not to do it if the situation was ever presented.

She whispered something he didn't hear as she returned to the job in hand. He reached over to touch her again. It filled him with sheer joy that she was so responsive.

They continued this mutual caressing for a few minutes, and then she removed her hand from him, took his hand away from her midst and started to kiss him as passionately as she had since their Great Kiss, when he had felt her almost entering his body through her mouth. She kissed him with total abandon, her hands gripped on the back of his neck pulling him closer to her, pulling herself into him, he felt. They wriggled to get more comfortable, the lower part of their bodies finding each other. He touched her on the top of her thigh and she recoiled in shock, scared away by the charge. He'd have to be more careful, he thought. She was capable of being scared, and he didn't want to scare her for fear of what it would do to their relationship. Even when the lower part of her was doing a body swerve they were still locked in their kiss.

He positioned himself, nestling between her legs. She seemed more comfortable with that. He hadn't completely recovered, and found himself gently pushing between her legs. He imagined he was a few inches below her pleasure zone, so he didn't feel awkward about it. She returned his pressure but dropped a little, so it was his turn to feel a shock and pull back when he felt the softness of her hair around his fast-growing stiffness. Hanna seemed to be fine with it, and it did feel beautiful, and so, after a few more seconds of their kiss, he pushed back towards her. She responded in kind, and started to move very delicately along his length.

Hanna pushed down harder on Martin, and he could now feel some of her wetness through her soft, bushy hair. Martin was overwhelmed by the new sensations. She moved backwards and forwards, appearing to be careful not to pull back too far in case she reached his tip. Surely they were safe playing with each other this way, his revitalisation positioned away from her rather than into her.

She closed her legs slightly, tightening herself around him, trapping him, stopping him from moving. She kept him trapped between the triangle of her bush and upper thighs and then rolled onto her back, pulling him on top of her and all the time continuing their kiss. He lay on her, silent and still as she pushed up towards him with her hips, legs still closed. He felt her ever-growing wet-ness now along his complete length. She was breathing heavily and groaning and moaning through her kiss. It felt like she was using her tongue as an advance party to explore his body, preparing the way for her eventual invasion.

He reached down and grabbed either side of her bum, pull-ing her towards him as he pushed towards her. She responded by opening her legs, slowly at first, but then with total abandon as she hungrily wrapped them around him. He was still outside her. This must be what it's like to stand outside the gates of heaven: even on the outside, heaven was an exquisite experience to behold.

She broke from her kiss and, holding his head with her hands, pushed his face away from hers by about 6 inches so she could look deep into his eyes. Her look said everything to him; he would never forget it for as long as he lived. She did with her eyes what she'd being trying unsuccessfully to do with her kiss: she got inside of him. She was talking large breaths of air, but still held his stare. He knew he should have been thinking that she was about to say 'be careful'. But he wasn't thinking that. He was pushing against her still, with greater pressure. This time, though, she wasn't resisting; she continued to look deep into his eyes, deep into him. They were doing this as one body.

'Be gentle,' she whispered. And he knew she had said it not because she was scared or because she thought he would be anything but gentle with her, but they were both nervous at what the other was capable of. At that moment they couldn't hide anything, and neither would they want to. She had given him verbal confirmation of what they both had mentally agreed. They both wanted this; it was okay to do it. She was already deep inside of him when he entered her.

All the times Martin had dreamed about this moment it had featured Hanna. He'd had three fears: that of the physical unknown; that he wouldn't know how to enter her and would release all over her before their engagement; and finally that he would get her pregnant. Hanna had removed his physical fear. And Martin just knew he wouldn't get her pregnant. He didn't know how he knew, he just knew – they discussed it afterwards, and she also felt confident that she wouldn't be pregnant, not on that occasion.

His fear of entering her would be overcome by human instinct. In that split second, as they looked deep into each other's eyes, their bodies found the age-old way to facilitate the other and he instinctively found his way inside her. The thing that shocked him most was not how amazing it felt physically; that, perhaps, would have been the biggest understatement ever. No, what shocked him most was how absolutely amazing it felt spiritually. No one had even hinted at this in the schoolyards or the ballrooms. Every movement spilled on, creating ever-increasing circles of pleasure, as new ones were tripped off all around and about him and they too carried away together. Martin could tune into any one of them.

All the time Hanna held his head in her hands, and they both looked into each other's souls as they continued to make love. Just at the moment Martin felt he should hold back a bit, Hanna whispered in a hoarse voice, 'I'm ready, Martin.' And one joint thrust later they came, together.

They remained locked in position and started to kiss again, this time more gently, maybe even more lovingly, but still just as passionately; it was just a different kind of passion. They held each other tenderly, just the way that young lovers do.

It was one of those classic moments where we try to fool ourselves into thinking that if only we could remain in that position, in that state forever, life would be perfect – heaven in fact – and we'd live happily ever after. The reality, however, is that a combination of cramp, hygiene, hunger and stimulation – mental and physical – dictates that forever would last, oh, about 30 minutes. Then even the laziest or the most romantic of us would have to get up and dress and get on with our lives.

Soon – 38 minutes, to be precise – and one additional less complete and, perhaps consequently, less fulfilling experiment later, Hanna and Martin would do just that. They walked back into Castlemartin under the cover of darkness, saying their goodnights by the Pear Tree roundabout. They'd go to their separate beds – content and physically exhausted – and enjoy a deep sleep, which would rebuild their energies and prepare them for the rest of their lives; lives which, due to their adventures and discoveries in the hay shed, would never be the same again.

THE LAST DANCE
BOOK TWO

CHAPTER FOURTEEN

And there you have it, lads, the soils of victory

Brendan

We pick up our story of The Playboys again just over one year later in October 1962. It had been a busy year for the band, and a productive one for some of those involved.

In the wider world, Ireland's favourite third-generation son, President John F. Kennedy, had stood up to Khrushchev over Russian missile bases in Cuba *and* he hadn't blinked first. For once, the grey men behind the Iron Curtain didn't look quite so invincible. Back in late February of the same year, the IRA had announced the termination of the campaign of resistance to the British occupation, which had been launched in December 1956. Dixie's father and Martin's mother were very pleased with the announcement, if only because they now hoped their respective sons' frequent late night border crossings would be safer.

The Playboys had done a lot to consolidate their position in the showband hierarchy. That is to say, they hadn't moved any higher up but they were doing more solid business in the ballrooms. They'd even made their debut on the British mainland with a two-week jaunt to Scotland in early July. You'd have thought from the PR that their manager, Gentleman Jim Mitchell, had generated that it had been an all-conquering triumphant tour, but the truth was it'd been almost a complete waste of time. As is so often the case, it is the things you look forward to most in life which disappoint you the most.

The band had played four nights at a hotel in Inverness, and the locals couldn't have cared less who was up on stage. Some of the more vocal members of the audience had called The Playboys 'big Jessies', alluding to their brand spanking new suits. Dixie's tailor had played a blinder this time, creating smart chocolate jackets and yellow trousers trimmed with a chocolate stripe down each leg. Dixie had decided to push the Playboy angle, and had even got his tailor to run off a yellow cravat for each band member. They also had a reverse version with yellow jackets, chocolate trousers with yellow stripes and a chocolate cravat, which they were meant to change into halfway through the dance, but due to the hostility of the audience Dixie thought it best to save that party trick for home turf.

Some of the messers wandered into the band's dressing room after the dance. It was Brendan who proved he had the bottle to deal with them, physically removing the men from the room. Incredibly, this generated much respect and the three ended up being drinking buddies for the remainder of The Playboys' stay in Inverness.

Later in the tour, the band got to perform in the famous Barrowland Ballroom in Glasgow. Following the Inverness incident, and the general apathetic reaction they'd had, not to mention Glasgow's reputation for being a bit on the rough side, they were actually dreading the dance, fearful for the safety of their equipment and even their lives. But the Glaswegians were as good as gold, and were in fact very responsive.

Martin's songs in particular went down very well with the discerning audience, not that anyone in the audience knew they were his. After 'Still She Dances With You' attracted cheers and applause from certain female sections of the audience, Dixie decided to acknowledge it: 'Thank you kindly – that was one of our own.' Martin ignored the omission of the credit as he was thrilled enough with the audience's reaction. Brendan and Smiley glared so much at

Dixie he was convinced that they would burn a hole in the back of his new chocolate-coloured jacket.

The Barrowland owner introduced Martin to his son, who in turn introduced him to his girlfriend, Anne. She'd been told that Martin was the songwriter and, like the rest of the boys when they first met, she was in awe of him. Down in Liverpool, two lads by the name of John Lennon and Paul McCartney were causing quite a stir with the original songs they were writing for their band, The Beatles. Anne was a big fan of theirs, and she told Martin that getting to meet him – a songwriter – made her feel closer to her Liverpudlian heroes. They chatted for a while.

It was a good job he'd been polite to her: Anne turned out to be a journalist with the *Glasgow Herald*, and she filed the following review on July 12, 1962:

The Playboys Cruise into Scotland

The popular Glasgow Ballroom, the Barrowland, yesterday evening enjoyed the sweet music of an accomplished Ulster showband, The Playboys. The regular Saturday evening full house was enchanted by the rich, warm sounds produced by the excellent eight-piece band in their matching canary and brown suits.

They played a stunning version of Emile Ford's hit 'What Do You Want To Make Those Eyes At Me For'. Singer Martin Deen made the song his own, and his crooning had certain sections of the audience going weak at the knees. Martin, like the rest of the band, hails from Castlemartin, a wee village on the shores of Lough Neagh, and, even though he's from the countryside, he's actually composed a couple of his own songs. One of these songs, 'Still She Dances With You', was performed by The Playboys at the Barrowlands and it sounded as great as any other song they

---

performed yesterday evening. This journalist predicts that the infectious 'Still She Dances With You' could be a hit for one of the big boys like Elvis or Cliff, and that we'll be hearing a lot more of this young, well-mannered man's songwriting in the future. Also worth mentioning is guitarist Brendan, known to the entourage only as Brendan the guitarist.

Highlights of the evening were a cruising version of Hank Williams's classic 'Jambalaya', and a powerhouse treatment of Johnny Cash's magnificent 'Ring Of Fire'. The latter showed off to great effect The Playboys' outstanding musicianship, particularly their full-sounding four-piece brass section.

On a fashion note, their yellow cravats made them look more like dandies than Playboys, but apart from that I'd say after last night's performance it won't be long until The Playboys from Castlemartin are as popular in Scotland's premier venue, The Barrowland, as the best of the new wave of Irish showbands, The Royal Showband and The Freshmen.

– Anne Buchanan

The following day, The Playboys read and re-read that review as they drove to Dunfermline. Smiley seemed more upset than Martin about the misspelling of 'Dean'. Robin counted with amazement the number of times she'd managed to name-drop Barrowland. But these were all small points. They'd never actually been reviewed before, and this was in an international paper at that. Yes, they'd been mentioned in several of the Irish papers, but they'd never had anyone actually writing about how good they were for all the world to see. They all agreed that Gentleman Jim Mitchell was going to be really chuffed by that. Also agreed was the fact that the cravats had to go. Surprisingly enough, Dixie didn't put up even the slightest resistance.

Separately, Martin and Dixie had both gone to the trouble of discreetly sneaking off from the band to buy another copy of the paper. They had someone specifically in mind to whom they wanted to send it.

Six hours later, they bumped back down to earth and reality quickly when the village priest who was running the Dunfermline dance informed them that they were *too* loud, *too* expensive and they wouldn't be back in his establishment *too* often, well, in actual fact, never again. Brendan had to be restrained. He later told Martin he'd struggled to call forth the story about Jesus returning to his father's house and, on finding traders and money-lenders doing business, he threw the equivalent of a holy fit, overturning all the traders' tables. But Brendan couldn't quite get the simile to work for him, so he dropped it.

Speaking of fits, Martin reminded Brendan that the Reverend Ian Paisley had recently been arrested in Rome while demonstrating against the opening of the Second Vatican Council. Try as they might, they couldn't find a way of turning that to their advantage with the promoter priest either.

None of The Playboys liked working for promoter priests. This wasn't anything to do with religion; it's just that they generally paid the worst, demanded the most and had no clue what they were doing, betrayed by the fact that when things went wrong they'd look up to the heavens, clasp their hands and smile. Apart from which, when push came to shove the priests were not beyond using the pulpit to turn their congregation against rival ballrooms, and in some cases outright forbidding their flock from going to them. Yes, it might be a fund-raising exercise for good causes as far as the priests were concerned, but it was the Playboys' livelihood.

But before they got too hung up on priests as promoters, the following night, on a rare Monday night booking, The Playboys arrived at the Kerry Rooms in Grangemouth to be greeted by the promoter. 'Mr William Hartigan, my friends call me Bill,' he announced. They should have realised they were in for a sticky ride when he continued, 'but you can call me *Mr* Hartigan.' He shook only Dixie's hand, him being bandleader, saying 'And there you have it.'

Mr Bill Hartigan watched them unpack every bit of gear. When they appeared to finish, he looked around the stage at the instrument cases and their PA system. He went out to the van, and looked over Dixie's shoulder into the back of the Playboys' wagon. He went back into the hall, and looked around once more. 'Ah, lads, surely you've forgotten something?' he said.

'Look, sir,' Brendan began, 'we can assure you that we haven't murdered or kidnapped the priest from Dunfermline, tempting though the idea was.'

'What appears to be the problem?' Dixie asked, overhearing the end of the conversation as he returned to the ballroom from the van. Dixie made it his business to miss little, if anything.

'I'm just looking around your gear, lads, and I can't see your Binson echo unit,' the ballroom owner said very theatrically, his large hands arcing over their gear.

'That's because we don't have one, sir,' Dixie replied.

'Ah, come on now, lads – you can't play here without a Binson echo unit!'

'Are you their bleeding rep or something?' Brendan enquired, always the one with the shortest fuse.

'Now there's no need to get shirty with me, young man. My punters don't like bands that don't have the auld Binson.'

'So what happens now we don't have one?' Dixie asked, realising Hartigan was serious.

'Well there you have it,' the ballroom promoter replied, with an air of finality that shut everyone up. 'You can't play in my establishment.'

To cap it all, he produced the letter he'd sent to Reggie at the Central Agency, organisers of the Scottish tour. Right enough, there at the end of the letter was the line: 'The agent guarantees that The Playboys are an A-division band and use a Binson echo unit.'

So that was it – they were to be relegated to a B-division band if they didn't get hold of this mystical piece of equipment. Brendan had been on at Dixie for ages to buy a Binson, ever since he'd heard the Royal use one at the Cookstown Town Hall. The Miami used one, and they had the best sound in Ireland. Dixie had resisted Brendan's subtle hints. 'It'll make the auld harmonies first class, head.' He'd even resisted Brendan's less subtle hints, 'even the fecking Blueboys have one!' The Blueboys were a new showband from Magherafelt, and if The Playboys dropped below them, they were probably somewhere around the point where you'd start to forget about them.

Dixie and Martin left the boys to set up the gear in the Kerry Rooms. They drove around Grangemouth for the two hours, seeking out music shops and following up various local musicians' leads in search of the legendary Binson echo unit.

All this running around reminded Dixie of his days with The Teatime Orchestra when they would beg, borrow and steal equipment *and* musicians at the last moment. Sometimes they'd only make the dance by the skin of their teeth. Dixie remembered he'd always be in a panic, continually checking the time, watching the hour hand spin around on his watch like it had changed places with the second hand. He'd feel his insides churning like they were thrashing hay. He'd think of the fee for the dance, how desperately he needed those few pounds to keep the band going – to keep the band going so that he could spend his days running around like a madman trying to keep the band going.

But through all of it he never once felt like packing up with his band of misfits. He knew that some way, somehow, he could make a go of the music business – if he could just find that guitar amp, saxophone or accordion player, then he'd be okay. The funny thing was he would *always* find that vital piece of equipment and he'd *always* pick up that floating musician he needed to make up his numbers and his sound. Not to forget, however, those occasions when upon plugging in the amp they realised it didn't work and they'd have to strip it down and check as best they could for a disconnected wire or some such. Nor those moments when they were about to take to the stage and the accordion player would own up to his inability to read music. He could, he claimed, follow the guitarist's finger-work if he stood opposite him! Mind you, Dixie should have known better: wasn't his father always saying that the definition of a true gentleman was someone who could play the accordion, but never did so in public?

With The Playboys, however, Dixie had moved up a gear. Now he had a band of professional musicians working for him; professional in that they all earned a living from doing something that they loved. To a lot of musicians that was as good as it got, but those who believed in this alone were those not really making a living from music. When you'd met that ambition, the novelty soon wore off and you'd start to have other goals, like setting your targets on matching the successes of other bands.

Dixie wondered what it felt like to be in the Royal, to be a member of or, in Dixie's case, the bandleader of Ireland's premier showband. Now *they* looked like a contented bunch of musicians. The word out on them was that they certainly knew how to have a bit of fun. They really enjoyed each other's company and they behaved like a bunch of good schoolmates out on a wee adventure, while each night they got up on stage to continue the fun. Now where was the problem with that? As he drove around the deprived and grey back streets of Grangemouth, Dixie wondered what Michael Coppinger was feeling at that moment. Did he think he'd made it? Or had he set his sights on breaking England and being as big as Cliff & The Shadows, or could he even be eyeing up America and Elvis' throne? And while he was on the subject, what were Elvis' ambitions?

Sure, The Playboys had moved up the ladder a few steps from The Teatime Orchestra, but here was Dixie still running around at the last minute on a dance day trying to locate a missing piece of equipment. Surely someone else should be doing all this running around so he could spend his time on loftier things, like working out horn parts? However, he wasn't prepared to admit this to anybody; not out of humbleness, no, but because he felt his father would think ill of him for having such thoughts.

They arrived back at the hall, minus said piece of equipment, to be greeted by the ballroom owner.

'It doesn't look like you're going to be able to fulfill the contract with me, lads,' Bill Hartigan declared on seeing the two musicians return as empty-handed as they had left.

'We searched high and low, sir – no success.'

'That's a shame, I was expecting a good crowd tonight, saw you got a bit of a write up in the *Herald* – that should have worked wonders at the door.'

'Ah well,' Dixie sighed, 'they'll be fine. We can say it wasn't your fault, sir. We'll make an announcement.'

'The *only* announcement you're going to make on stage tonight, *sir*, is going to be one you make through a Binson echo unit.'

'We don't have one, sir, and we can't find one!'

'Well, there you have it,' the ballroom owner replied with a sigh.

'We better start to pack away the gear then,' Dixie said to Martin, hoping to bluff the owner into thinking they would really leave if he didn't stop with this stupidity.

'Aye, I suppose you'd better,' Hartigan replied, without the slightest concern in his voice. He had his hands in his pockets, and Dixie could hear him running coins through his fingers, perhaps implying his money was going to stay put tonight.

'Right then, we'll pack up and be off,' Dixie said.

'Right,' the owner said, 'and there you have it.'

Dixie and Martin made towards the door, but Hartigan stopped them before they could get to it. 'There is just one chance I might be able to find you a Binson at this late stage.'

'You could?' Dixie replied, turning on a sixpence, his shoe crunching on the gravel and the up-turned dust dulling its shine.

'Yes… you see my son's in a band.'

'He is?' Dixie replied.

'And they use the Binson echo unit.'

'They do?'

'It's a grand piece of equipment, lads. It comes all the way from Italy, you know.'

'It does?' Dixie hesitated for a split second. 'It did, sir, but of course it did.'

'And is there any chance your son's band is working tonight?' Martin asked.

'I don't think so,' the owner replied.

'Could you check?'

'Oh goodness, yes,' the owner replied with a knowing smile. He turned and shouted in the direction of the car park. 'Miles!' A ginger-haired nerd who looked like he was 14 at the most got out of a classic Rover. The reflections of the sun's rays were not distorted on the dirt-free, pristine vehicle; in fact it positively glowed amid the lesser transporters surrounding it. The lad scuffed his way across to the three of them.

'This is my son Miles, gentlemen.'

'Hello, Miles,' Martin and Dixie offered in unison.

'Miles, these gentlemen were inquiring about whether your band was working tonight.'

'No, dad, you know we're not.'

'And there you have it, lads, you're in luck. The boys are not working tonight, so I'm sure they'd be happy to hire their Binson echo unit to you. Miles, why don't you go to the back of the car and fetch the Binson and I'll work out some arrangements with the lads.'

'How much will it cost to hire the Binson, sir?' Dixie, as bandleader asked, putting his hand to his rear pocket where he kept his folded money.

'Oh, let's see,' the owner began expansively, 'shall we say £75?'

Dixie laughed, his hand stopping mid-arc. 'You've got to be kidding – £75? We're only getting £60 for the dance!'

'So you are, so you are. Well, let's see; let's see what we can do for you. I was thinking, one, it's short notice and, two, I'm quite prepared to accept that your agent, Reggie, might not have passed on the importance of this piece of equipment, and as you're finding yourselves so far away from home… I'll settle for £55.'

The boys argued and moaned and groaned, but there was no way out of it. They paid their £55 in advance, got the Binson and, because they didn't really know how to use it, The Playboys ended up sounding like they were playing in Dixie's bathroom. On top of which, only 57 people turned up. When Dixie went to get the fee from Hartigan, he was only prepared to pay him £35 owing to the fact there was such a bad crowd.

As expected, after the show Brendan fussed over the Binson as though it was his first-born child, getting Miles to talk him in great detail through the workings of the precious piece of equipment. Miles may only have recently entered his teenage years, but he knew his way around the echo unit. Brendan insisted on carrying it out to the car. As they passed the toilets, he excused himself for a call of nature. He carefully placed the echo unit on the floor and locked the door. Five minutes later, after some very serious grunting and groaning followed by a large sigh, Brendan deposited the Binson on the soft cream upholstery of the back seat of Hartigan's car, with Miles in the front seat, oblivious to his presence.

The Playboys set off back to their digs in Glasgow. They were all down in the dumps, depressed by their performance both on stage and at the box office.

'Tell me, lads,' Brendan, in a lighter mood than most, began. 'Isn't the Binson some relation to the buffalo?'

'I think so,' Smiley replied, in an effort to take their minds of the recent disaster.

'I don't think so,' Robin replied, 'you're talking about a *bison*.'

'No, I think it's a Binson,' Brendan said fit to burst. 'In fact, I'm positive it's a Binson.'

'What makes you so sure Brendan?' Dixie asked.

'Well here's my logic, lads,' Brendan began, leaning forward in his seat so that those in the front could hear. 'You see, I was thinking: if the cows around Castlemartin are anything to go by, then you'd have to think that the auld buffalo drops a *serious* number two. And from what I could make out, that auld Binson has just gone and done an extremely serious and very smoky number two on the backseat of Hartigan's precious Rover. So, the auld buffalo and the Binson must be connected, mustn't they?'

'You *didn't*, Brendan...!' Dixie squealed in sheer disbelief.

Brendan broke into an uncontrollable fit of the giggles, and one by one, as the band members twigged, they joined him in the hysterics. Eventually, through tears of laughter, Brendan said 'And there you have it lads – the soils of victory.'

CHAPTER FIFTEEN

Did you treat your Mary Ann to some dulse and Yellow Man?

John Henry 'The Carver' MacAuley

The Scottish trip was the prime reason why on October 5, 1962, Brendan, Martin and Dixie, with their PA system in tow, made their way down to Dublin to Dermot Hurley's music shop at the romantically named Crossgun's Bridge. Dermot was a famous man in showband circles because it was he who developed, built and sold the famous Crazy Box speaker cabinets that the majority of the big bands were using.

It's probably worth noting here just how a PA system works, and, therefore, why it is necessary in the first place. Okay, so you are in an empty ballroom, you stand at the back, the singer starts to sing and you can just about hear him. Now, you add in the drummer to keep the beat and rhythm of the song and you are going to struggle to hear your singer. Next, add in the bass guitar to lock the song solidly into the beat and layer the foundation. The singer is swallowed up even further into the song. Next, add the rhythm guitar and organ, which cements the top melody lines. Not only has your lead vocalist disappeared, but you probably find that the drums and bass guitar are drowning out your rhythm guitar, bits of your brass and most of your harmony vocals. Okay? Hold that thought and then imagine that the ballroom is filled with 2,000 people dancing, chatting and shuffling around you and you will probably only feel the unpleasant thud of the bassline in your chest.

The aim, therefore, is to allow each and every member of the audience to hear the band without having their heads blasted off. This balance of sound, and the band's ability to achieve it, was of paramount importance in a live format. Cut to the development of the PA system.

We start with a microphone. The singer sings into a microphone, a very sensitive membrane which translates the voice into an electronic signal via the pulses on said membrane. This signal in pluses and minuses is then transferred back via the microphone lead into an amplifier – in The Playboys' case a Philips 120-watt amplifier. The amp then enlarges this voice-generated electronic signal using valves, and in turn passes this new amplified signal, via leads, into a speaker cabinet. The speaker cabinet then translates the signal and reverses the process of the microphone. Each band has two speaker cabinets, one at each side of the stage. In the case of Hurley's famous Crazy Box, each cabinet would house six 10-inch Goodman speakers. The speakers in the cabinet translate the signals back into a louder reproduced version of the human voice, and transmit this new voice to the audience using the speaker cones. You can obviously use a microphone to repeat this process with the sounds made by the brass section.

Good so far? Now, this is where we should add the Binson echo unit into the equation. Instead of plugging the microphone directly into the amplifier, we divert it first through the Binson, and this enhances and enriches the original sound of the voice. The voice signal then goes back into the amplifier to follow the same route as above. The Binson echo unit was revolutionary in that it didn't use a looped piece of recording tape but a disc to create the echo, which was much more reliable and had a truer sound.

Dermot Hurley wore glasses which had the depth of two Coke-bottle bottoms, a less sophisticated version of Dixie's 'Derry American' style spectacles. Dermot's style, though, helped to make him look like a bit of a boffin. And boffin or not he was the man behind the showbands' sound. He set up a demonstration PA system using The Playboys' amplifier and mics and a brand new set of Crazy Box speakers, which Dixie had ordered to go along with their new Binson echo unit. The Binson set them back £250 and the pair of Crazy Boxes another £120, so he couldn't be persuaded to part with an additional £125 to upgrade his Skull Head microphone to the new snazzy Unidine pencil version. Nevertheless, old mic or not, the new system sounded amazing.

'First class,' Brendan and Dixie agreed in unison as Martin sat stunned and in shock at the cost of the microphone, which alone was more expensive than his first band's entire set of gear.

He smiled as he remembered The Chance's PA system, a Vortexion 50-watt amp with two 15-inch speakers in a separate rickety wooden box with holes cut in front, which acted as speaker cabinets. It was in such terrible condition that his mum had bought him three yards of Fablin, a sticky-back plastic material of various designs that could be used to hide wear and tear. Kathleen had chosen the simulated woodgrain finish, and Martin had spent an entire Saturday afternoon carefully covering the two boxes. He then attached a brass handle to the top. When he'd finished, the speaker cabinet looked brand new.

Martin's pride in his work was sent crashing down to earth when he plugged in the speakers and tested his microphone the following day at rehearsal. A dull and muffled sound could be heard: suddenly, he realised he had stuck the Fablin across the front of the speakers, restricting the sound. He removed the offending material with a penknife, and The Chance had their sound system primed and ready for action.

The first voice to be heard through The Playboys' new system was Dermot Hurley's, with the exact words: 'Sunday, Monday, Tuesday, Wednesday, Thursday, Friday, Saturday aaaaand Sunday.' He twiddled a few more knobs before adding, 'There you are now, lads, there's your Miami Sound.'

That week ending October 5, 1962, the first ever Irish singles chart was published. Elvis Presley held the top spot with 'She's Not You', out on RCA Records, while Ronnie Carroll earned the distinction of being the first Irish artist to have a record in the Irish charts with 'Roses Are Red' on Philips Records, showing at number seven that inaugural week. The Top Ten, compiled by Jimmy Magee, read:

1. Elvis Presley 'She's Not You' (RCA Records)
2. Ray Charles 'You Don't Know Me' (HMV Records)
3. Bobby Darin 'Things' (London Records)
4. Claude King 'Wolverton Mountain' (Columbia Records)
5. Mark Wynter 'Venus In Blue Jeans' (Pye Records)
6. Tommy Roe 'Sheila' (HMV Records)
7. Ronnie Carroll 'Roses Are Red' (Phillips Records)
8. Jim Reeves 'Adios Amigo' (Decca Records)
9. Jimmy Justice 'Spanish Harlem' (Pye Records)
10. Cliff Richard 'I'll Be Me' (Columbia Records)

Other singles which floated in and out of the chart between then and Christmas included Kenny Ball with 'So Do I' on Pye; Chubby Checker's 'Limbo Rock', also on Pye; Craig Douglas and his Decca hit 'Oh Lonesome Me' and Frank Ifield singing about the 'Lovesick Blues' on Columbia Records. Susan Maughan was telling anyone who'd listen (and there were quite a few listening) that she wanted to be 'Bobby's Girl', released by Philips Records, and to even things out Del Shannon was boasting about his 'Swiss Maid' on London Records. The Tornados were stepping out from the shadows with 'Telstar' on Decca Records, and Brenda Lee was seasonal and successful with 'Rockin' Around The Christmas Tree' on Brunswick Records.

Knowing their fans were going to be expecting them to attempt versions of most of these hits, Dixie bought the top six singles giving them, in theory at least, a head start on all the other Northern showbands.

For the remainder of 1962, Jim Mitchell went into overdrive in an attempt to push the band higher up the ladder. It might have been that he sensed that certain band members had started to feel a little restless. He printed up car stickers, new photographs and a new set of posters in Day-Glo orange, with black print proclaiming: 'The Playboys Are Coming!', which he ensured went up in every ballroom in which they were due to appear.

At the Quay Road Hall in Ballycastle, the efficient, friendly and hospitable ballroom manager, Mr Richard V. Greer, took them all out for fish and chips and dulse and yellowman, a local sweet-tooth treat of seaweed and honeycomb, before the gig. At Robert Ferris's Embassy in Derry, some local troublemakers actually risked electrocution by cutting through The Playboys' speaker leads with razor blades.

Castlemartin's finest also played at The Tempo, home of Mr Trumpet himself, Dave Glover. They did a disappointing Friday night at the Floral Hall in Belfast, but then to counter that they had an incredible Saturday in the Arcadia Cork, which had become one of the most important and pivotal gigs on the Irish circuit. The Freshmen had told Smiley that it had been one of their favourite venues, and with the enthusiastic audience and spot-on facilities, The Playboys could see why.

They rammed Trevor Kane's Orpheus and they had the smallest crowd for a big band in the Astor, a very poor 467 dancers. The Playboys had been to Danceland, Roseland, Romanos and Milanos, but they couldn't remember, without checking with their manager, where any of the venues were. They experienced their first taste of the stunning County Donegal countryside on their visit to the Borderland Ballroom in Muff.

On their way back from Muff, Dixie was driving and Smiley and Brendan were up front while the rest of the band slept in the back.

They were chatting about that evening's dance and life in general. The full moon was showing off the spectacular countryside to great effect, and the three lads were transfixed by the view. All of a sudden, a few miles past Draperstown, Smiley got a fit of the giggles. They were driving down a steep hill, which had a sharp right turn at the foot.

'What's got you?' Dixie asked, taking his eyes off the road for a moment.

'Don't you see?' Smiley said, pointing out through the front windscreen. They were all speechless as they spotted the object of Smiley's amusement – an amorous bull enjoying a moonlit liaison with a heifer. They felt the van shudder slightly as Dixie changed down a gear to slow it for the corner. 'God it was great for us too old boy!' Brendan shouted out of the window.

Suddenly, the van shook violently. They'd hit a large pothole in the road, and Dixie had lost control of the steering wheel.

'We're in trouble,' Smiley uttered, strangely continuing to laugh.

'Hold on to your horses!' Dixie screamed, the commotion waking up the lads in the back.

The next 10 yards seemed to pass by in slow motion as everyone shouted their instructions at Dixie. The most sensible order came from Barry, who obviously thought he was still mid-nightmare, 'Close your eyes, Dixie, for heaven's sake!'

But Dixie struggled on with the steering wheel.

'Drive shaft's gone,' the authoritative voice of Smiley shouted through his still uncontrollable laughter.

Dixie screamed, so loudly that everyone else immediately shut up. 'Everyone, jump over to my side of the wagon – NOW!'

And everyone did.

They still hit the hedge at the bottom of the hill. But shifting the weight in the wagon had managed to get a bit of a turn on it so that they'd risen up onto the bank, running along the verge and taking grass, nettles, dandelions, weeds and dirt with them. They came to a stop 6 inches short of a telegraph pole.

They were all in shock as they tumbled out of the wagon. Everyone was talking and muttering to themselves, but no one addressed any of their fellow musicians: rather they were thanking their various Gods for their good fortune.

One by one, the members of The Playboys regained their composure and they all piled into the field. They fanned out, eight silhouettes backlit by the moonlight, giving them the look of The Magnificent Seven hunting down a mystery man in the Badlands of Draperstown. Some doubled over like athletes trying to catch their breath, resting their hands on their knees, looking deep into the ground. Brendan was the first to communicate, yelping out in glee.

As they all congregated around him, Dixie said: 'Bejesus, that was close!'

'Ah,' Brendan said with a sigh of relief, 'sure we were always going to be okay.'

'And how did you figure that one out, Brendan?' Barry asked, his recent shock still evident in his quivering voice.

'Well, if we'd already made a record, that would have definitely been a different story,' Brendan said with a bit of a titter, 'but you can all thank your lucky stars that we've yet to make our first trip to the recording studio, 'cause you can bet your bottom dollar if we'd a few tunes down on that old magic black tape, we'd all be with our makers by now.'

The moon was making way for the sun before they got home that morning. First they had to go and wake up a local garage owner, who gave them the address of a mechanic. Then, when they woke him up and returned to the van, he insisted they take all the gear out before he'd agree to jack it up, check the axle and repair the drive shaft.

Yes, The Playboys were happy to return home safely from their first visit to Donegal. They were all still so charged with adrenalin that they didn't, as usual, fall into bed for a few hours. They felt the need to stay together. They didn't admit to the fact, but perhaps it was because they had narrowly escaped death and they didn't want to break that magic bond just yet. They all returned to Dixie's house, and dallied over a large breakfast, breaking up just before noon.

Something always seemed to happen when they played Donegal. Another episode started out as a wind-up, but ended up with them all in the Magherafelt nick. Here's how that one happened.

Davy had been learning to drive for ages, and he had eventually persuaded Dixie to let him do a few of the late night drives just so he could get some practice in. On one such occasion – a return trip from the Orchid Ballroom in Lifford – Davy had been at the wheel.

Now the thing about Davy and driving was that when you put him behind the steering wheel he talked on and on and on about everything under the sun. It might just have been his nervousness about driving, or maybe he figured that was a sure way to keep himself awake, but as well as driving everyone home, he was driving them all mad. On this particular night, he should have noticed that no one was getting agitated by his talking, in fact they all, if anything, seemed to be joining in with him. The other strange thing he should have noticed was that, uniquely, none of them were asleep in the van. All of them, including Barry, were wide awake. He didn't have time to work it out.

The two policemen walked up to The Playboys' vehicle very slowly, flashing their torchlights through the windscreen. 'Can I see your licence, sir?' the younger of the two asked Davy.

'Yes, of course,' Davy replied, presenting it proudly before the policeman had even reached the end of his sentence. The policeman studied it carefully in the beam of his lamp. He and his colleague, deep in conversation, walked around the vehicle before returning to the window.

'Could you step outside of the vehicle, sir,' the younger policeman said.

'What appears to be the problem, officer?' Davy asked.

The older policeman flashed his lamp back into the faces of the other band members, who had by this time fallen mysteriously sheepish. 'Two things, sir,' the younger policeman began. 'This licence of yours doesn't permit you to have more than two passengers in your vehicle. You're five over the limit from what I can gather.'

'Come on...!' Davy began.

'I'm sorry, sir?' the younger policeman replied immediately and slightly aggressively.

'Well, we're a band – we're The Playboys from Castlemartin! We're just returning from a dancehall up in Donegal.'

'I don't care, sir, if you're The Playboys of the Western World returning from a night on the tiles, you should not be driving a vehicle with more than two passengers.'

'Ah,' Davy laughed nervously, 'Ahm, I'm sorry... I didn't know.'

'Did you pick up all this gear in Donegal?' the older policeman asked, stepping into the conversation for the first time.

'No, it's our own,' Davy replied.

'You didn't smuggle it in from the Free State then, did you?' the older policeman continued.

'No, of course not!' Davy replied, now looking and acting every bit the smuggler.

'Of course, you'll have proof of all of this, won't you?'

'Somewhere I'm sure,' Davy replied, raising his voice in the hope of getting some backup from the van. None came.

'Good,' the older policeman smiled, 'in that case, let's check it.'

'Sorry?'

'Let's get all of the equipment out of the van and we'll check it off against your sales receipts.'

'Sales? Receipts?' Davy replied, each word coming as a question.

'Yes, sales receipts,' the policeman continued. 'When you take equipment into the Free State you need sales receipts to prove its point of purchase.'

'Dixie,' Davy shouted in desperation, 'do we have sales receipts for all the gear?'

'Of course we do, head,' Dixie replied, leaning his own head out of the window. Davy looked visibly relieved. 'When we bought it in Dublin we got proper receipts for everything.'

'Aye, Dublin was it?' the older policeman inquired, in a matter-of-fact manner.

'Aye, Dublin it was,' Dixie confirmed.

'And would that be the same Dublin that is the capital of the Free State?' the younger policeman returned.

'Oh yes, indeed it would, sir,' Robin, who knew his geography, confirmed immediately. Davy visibly recoiled as though another knife had been stuck in his heart.

'So in my book,' the older policeman said, removing his notebook and pencil from his tunic and addressing Davy again, 'as the official driver of this vehicle, that makes you a smuggler.'

'But...' Davy struggled for support as well as his voice.

'I'm afraid, sir, we're going to have to charge you.'

'But I was just driving the lads home... do you know Jim Mitchell? He owns the Dreamland Ballroom... he's very important in Castlemartin. . . '

'I hope you aren't going to suggest that he might give us some money, sir. Bribing a member of the police force is...'

At which point both policemen and the members of The Playboys, excepting Davy, erupted in giggles. Davy had been set up good and proper. The younger policeman was Samuel Watson, and the older one was Thomas Gilmour, both school friends of Dixie.

Davy didn't know whether to laugh or cry.

Three weeks later, with Davy again in the driving seat, although much quieter this time, The Playboys were returning from the Strand Ballroom in Portstewart when they were flagged down by another police vehicle. Once again, two policemen came up to Davy's window, but this time he knew exactly how to deal with them. No sooner had the police requested Davy's driving licence than he'd spat: 'Would youse pair of hairy bollocks ever go and feck off and catch some real criminals. I haven't time for any more of your tomfoolery!'

He put the van back into gear and drove off, shouting, 'And you can tell Watson and Gilmour that Davy from The Playboys said once bitten, twice shy and they can feck off as well!'

Thirty minutes later, with the aid of two further Morris Minor police vehicles and four more police constables, The Playboys from Castlemartin found themselves standing sheepishly before the desk sergeant in Magherafelt police barracks.

It took a lot of explaining from Dixie, a large donation to the Policeman's Ball and a promise of playing at the next one to ensure their release without charge. Luckily for Davy, the rest of the band saw the funny side of it. On top of which, it was another story that, over the months, would benefit from some serious embellishment and join the ever-growing list of tales that made all those hours cramped in their little van slightly more endurable.

During the remainder of that autumn The Playboys and their wagon, with its distinctive neon light and the Esso tail of the tiger dangling from the petrol cap, got to visit six of the fourteen ball-rooms on Albert Reynolds's circuit. Each and every one of these ballrooms had proper dressing rooms, and each and every one of their staff was anxious to take good care of both the dancers and the members of the band.

On the final night, it took a while for Gentleman Jim Mitchell to track down Albert Reynolds. He wanted to add the rest of Reynolds's circuit to his diary, and one minute he was over by the mineral stall; then he was off to the box office; then he could be seen sorting out a problem just outside the ballroom; next he was handing toilet rolls into the ladies' (this itself was quite a thing, since some of the lesser establishments were still cutting up magazines and such into four and stringing the pieces through the corner to hang them next to the toilet). However, towards the end of the night Reynolds eventually found a quiet moment to seek out Mitchell, and by the end of their meeting not only had he added 14 engagements to his ever-busy diary, but 28 – a double set in each venue. In the space of a 5-minute conversation, Mitchell had incredibly managed to fill one-tenth of the boys' 1963 diary.

CHAPTER SIXTEEN

Take off the glasses, Jackie

President John F. Kennedy

The car of the year in 1963 was the new Ford Zodiac. With its futuristic lines it quickly became *the* wagon to be seen in, and it came complete with a heater and demister, which were still considered to be so special that they were actually mentioned in the advertisements. And the cost of impressing the folks on your street with this new status symbol? A staggering £1,085!

On the political front, Lord Brookeborough resigned as Premier of Northern Ireland. He was succeeded by Captain Terence O'Neill, who was an ex-guardsman, an old Etonian and, according to Dixie's dad, the first liberal to hold the post. Blair senior added that as O'Neill could trace his lineage back to Niall of The Nine Hostages, one of the High Kings of Celtic Ireland, he had a far purer pedigree than the likes of de Valera in the south.

In entertainment, Gay Byrne won Jacob's inaugural Outstanding Personality Of The Year award. Ireland's position on the world music stage rose several notches when The Bachelors became the first Irish group to enter the UK Top Ten with 'Charmaine', which peaked at number six on January 26 (the best they could do in Ireland with the same song was number eight on March 25).

On the world's showbusiness stage, Ireland was very much in the spotlight in August that year when Grace Kelly – Princess Grace upon marrying Prince Rainier of Monaco – visited Carlton House in County Kildare. For most of the locals, the title 'Princess' was dropped in favour of Grace 'isn't she the one who flattened some patches of grass with Frank Sinatra?' Kelly.

The great news on the health front was that the TB sanatorium in Newcastle was closed in October due to 'lack of business'.

Gentleman Jim Mitchell was much amused by an advert that had appeared in *The Irish Times*. Apparently, a family in Ballybrack, County Dublin, had advertised for a cook-cum-housekeeper and, just to show how posh this particular couple were, they mentioned the fact that they already employed a nursemaid and a parlour-maid. The princely sum the new employee would receive was £5 per week, which on one hand was okay, but then maybe not when you considered the fact that the Irish National Stud had recently bought the horse Mitalgo for £85,000!

For The Playboys, the year 1963 proved to be their busiest yet, with 257 dates. They played every ballroom at least once, doing much better at the Floral Hall and the Astor second time around – and quite a few new venues besides. They were making so much money they couldn't believe it. They had money coming out of their ears… and noses… and mouths… and every pocket they could find about their persons, not to mention their mattresses. At the same time that cook down in Dublin was picking up £5 a week, members of The Playboys were averaging about £60 a week. Dixie and Martin, not to mention their manager, on double shares, were collecting £120 each, equivalent today to around £2,640!

But the new-found wealth was part of the showbands' problem. When they could make such great money on the Irish circuit for 48 weeks of the year, why would they have ambitions beyond that? The showband musicians were far richer than their British counterparts; why would they want to lose or invest part of their

Irish income, to try to break other territories, or even succeed with records or on television? The managers certainly weren't encouraging their cash cows to slow down or block out days in the diary for recording or promotional trips to England or Europe.

But The Freshmen and The Playboys had musical ambitions as well as financial ones. The non-stop series of one-nighters got in the way of songwriting. The road was exhausting, and you wanted your day off (Monday) as an actual day off, not a rehearsal day to learn new tunes, original or otherwise.

Equally, playing the same circuit continuously had started to lose its appeal once the initial buzz wore off. 'Oh, here we are again in the Clifftop Ballroom on the North Antrim coast and, sure, there's the owner, Black Hair.' Black Hair was so called because he had *no* body hair. As a child, his mother covered his head in boot polish so he wouldn't think he was any different from the other children. As an adult, he always wore a beret, which obviously saved on the boot polish, but he still insisted on painting black sideburns onto the side of his face. Black Hair was fun the first time, amusing the second time and downright sad from then onwards.

To combat the boredom, The Playboys made up games to amuse themselves in the van. One of their favourite pranks was to pick up some unsuspecting hitchhiker in one of the country towns. Each band member would know the game was 'on' when Dixie, who did most of the driving, asked one of the two members occupying the coveted front seat beside him to make way for their guest. A few miles down the road there'd be muttering in the back, and before you knew it a full-scale row would have developed, started by the culprit who'd left the front seat. The discussion was carried out in a hushed whisper, just audible enough so the stranger up in the front could hear it.

'Jeez, I'm getting fed up of giving up my seat to every Tom, Dick or Harriet we pick up.'

Brendan: 'Ah, come on now, Robin, sure it's only for a bit of fun, you know, *a bit of fun.*'

Robin: 'Yeah, it's okay for you, heads, but I prefer girls.'

Mo: 'Ah now, don't be selfish, Robin – we'd a girl two nights ago and wasn't that great craic? *For some of youse.*'

Smiley: 'If it isn't the old fecking moaning head again. He's doing my brains in with all his fecking moaning.'

Robin: 'I'd keep quiet if I were you, Smiley; you don't want to be drawing attention to yourself.'

Smiley: 'I don't know what you're on about – I'm the only one of youse who's faithful.'

Robin: 'Aye, to Gertrude – that's it, isn't it?'

Smiley (voice raised): 'Aye, and what's wrong with that?'

Dixie: 'Heads, heads, can we've a bit of peace and quiet from the back? Let's just enjoy the beautiful countryside.'

Dixie would then enter into a conversation with the stranger and Davy, who was alongside him in the front row of the van. Soon, the audible whispers from the back would start up again.

Robin: 'Gertrude, aye, I'd nearly forgotten about Gertrude.'

Smiley: 'Now, Robin, there's nothing wrong with having someone at home waiting for you. I'll tell you it's very comforting; it makes the long hours on the road all worthwhile.'

Robin: 'And how are you and Gertrude getting on, Smiley?'

Smiley: 'Oh, you know… we have our difficulties.'

Robin (laughing): 'That's no exaggeration, unless of course you use a crate.'

Smiley (in a loud voice): 'Robin! You promised you wouldn't discuss this!'

Robin: 'Oh, you started it, head, you started it.'

Smiley: 'Well, you were just about to ruin the lad's fun again.'

Robin: 'Tell me, have you ever met Gertrude's parents?'

Smiley: 'Robin, you're asking for one, you know they don't come from around these parts. Now whisht there.'

Robin (shouting): 'Whisht is it? I haven't even started. Tell me, heads, have any of you ever seen Gertrude?'

Smiley: 'Robin, I'm warning you.'

Robin: 'No, Smiley, it's okay, I'm just asking if any of the boys have ever seen the beautiful Gertrude you're always going on about.'

Robin would then lounge across the seat in the direction of Smiley, and there'd be a few minutes of screaming and shouting and fists flying and the rest of the band in the back trying to pull them apart.

Dixie (swerving the van back and forth over the road): 'Lads, for heaven's sake would you ever pull those two eejits apart before they force me into the ditch!'

It would appear as if Robin came out of the fight worst, and he'd hold a *staged* bloodied handkerchief up to his nose.

Robin (voice on the verge of cracking up): 'You bar steward you, you've only gone and bloodied my nose, and I have to get up on stage tonight.'

Smiley: 'I told you before, you've a big mouth.'

Robin: 'Well, you certainly know a big mouth, Smiley – sure, hasn't Gertrude only got the biggest mouth in Castlemartin?'

Smiley: 'I tell you what, Robin, if you don't shut that trap of yours once and for all I'll shut it for you!'

Robin: 'Would you indeed, big man... I wonder; would you be so big if the boys knew all about Gertrude?'

Smiley (roaring at the top of his voice): 'ROBIN!' A few of the lads would now be restraining Smiley in his seat.

Robin (regaining his composure): 'So tell me, lads, have any of you ever met Smiley's Gertrude?'

Various members: 'No.'

Robin: 'Really? That's surprising, she lives very close to you.'

Smiley: 'Please don't do this. You promised me you wouldn't tell people about her.'

Robin: 'Well, maybe if you hadn't bloodied my nose I might not have.'

Smiley: 'Please don't do this. I'll give you anything!'

Robin: 'Not interested. So, lads...'

Smiley: 'If you don't do this to me Robin I'll... I'll... I'll talk Gertrude into *looking after you*, just the once, mind you.'

Robin: 'Thanks but no thanks; she's *certainly* not my type, head.'

Smiley (close to tears): 'Ah, Robin, please!'

Robin: 'So none of you know where she lives, where Gertrude does her "looking after people?"'

Dixie: 'No, he's always kept schtum about her – I suppose she's a bit of a looker and he doesn't want any of us drooling around her.'

Robin: 'Perhaps, perhaps not. Lady Gertrude lives at the stables down on Station Road.'

Mo: 'Gee, Smiley, has she fallen on hard times then? It must be true love if you'd still go out with a girl from the other side of the tracks, you know – with your profile and all your money and all.'

Smiley starts crying and talking gibberish.

Robin: 'Good guess, Mo, but not right on this occasion. Can anyone else hazard a guess?'

Barry: 'What, she's hiding from someone? She's not hiding from the fecking Ra is she, head?'

Robin: 'No, I wouldn't exactly say she's hiding… you don't normally hide in your own home.'

Davy: 'Her own home? What are you on about, Smiley? Only animals live in stables.'

Robin: 'Warm, you're getting warm – very warm in fact.'

Dixie: 'What, Gertrude lives with the animals in the stables?'

Robin: 'Not exactly: Gertrude lives in the stables because she *is* an animal, she's a donkey in fact.'

Davy: 'A fecking DONKEY!'

Robin: 'Yes, but I do believe she's consenting.'

Silence would descend upon the van, then sniggers, led mostly by Robin, would give way to fits of laughter.

Smiley would struggle free and remove a revolver from under the seat, one that only he and his bandmates would know was a toy.

Smiley: 'Funny is it, Robin? See how funny this is.' He'd then fire off two rounds of caps, having tripled them to ensure an authentic bang. There'd be screaming and shouting as Dixie pulled the van up to a halt on the grass verge, dangerously close to the hedge.

Smiley (gun waving wildly): 'Right, any of the rest of you think that's funny?'

The wagon doors would fling open, and they'd scarper in all the directions of the compass, none faster than the hitchhiker who wouldn't be seen for dust. Such a caper would probably keep them laughing for the next three or four journeys.

They'd a few other routines to entertain themselves, but sometimes they'd travel in silence, each locked in their private thoughts. Martin spent much of this time thinking about his songwriting, and dreaming of turning some of his songs into records.

He never complained to Mitchell about the lack of recording — he certainly hadn't given up on his ambitions in that direction, but the reality was that on the recording front only The Royal Showband to date, with Tom Dunphy as the featured vocalist, had released a record in Ireland. The song 'Come Down From The Mountain Katie Daley' had been released by EMI Records in 1962. Martin figured that he and The Playboys were quite a bit down the pecking order when it came to thinking of a visit to the recording studios.

But if any of The Playboys fancied a moan about the lack of plans to get to a studio, they always remembered what it felt like in the back of the wagon when Dixie counted out the cash into their hands after each gig. And that pile of cash Dixie gave them seemed to grow and grow, month in and month out.

With his new-found wealth, Martin bought himself clothes (more English pop than Irish), another guitar (which he realised after 6 weeks he never used, preferring to write songs on his original), a reel-to-reel tape recorder for his bedroom (on which to record his songs) and a portable tape recorder for the road (to tape new tunes broadcast on the radio). With the aid of Martin's tape recorder, The Playboys could hear a new English single on the radio at 5 p.m., record it, listen to it in the van a few times as they travelled to their dance, and then, when they'd set up their equipment, work out their parts from the tape recorder. By 10.30 p.m. that night they'd be performing the new song on stage.

Apart from these small extravagances, and a little cash he kept for weekly pocket money, Martin gave every other penny to his mother. She took out a modest amount for housekeeping – she didn't need it, but Martin insisted – some she used to pay a token amount of taxes and the remainder she put into land and property, helped by her boss Jim Mitchell.

The band returned to Scotland, this time for a trip organised by the owner of Barrowland, where they played on three subsequent Saturday nights. Martin again met up with local journalist Anne Buchanan. He liked her: he could talk to her and she seemed to enjoy a very good relationship with her boyfriend, in that he didn't appear to be jealous of her spending a lot of time in coffee bars with the young Martin Dean. She wrote another review of The Playboys. This time she spelled Martin's name correctly, and she raved once more about his original songs. She also raved to him and Brendan non-stop about The Beatles and their fabulous songs.

On a night off, she took Martin, Brendan and Smiley to see the Belfast group Them, who were performing as part of a pop package at the Pavilion. Them were an exciting, if unpredictable, R&B band, and Martin was surprised when the lead singer seemed more interested in playing his saxophone all night. But they had a great time. In fact, it was a night to remember. But there would be one night they would remember above all others.

They were playing at the Dreamland Ballroom in Castlemartin. It wouldn't be memorable because it was a local gig, or because their manager owned the venue, or for the fact that they broke the box-office record that night, or even because it was the night Hanna Hutchinson reappeared on the scene. All four aforementioned facts are 100 per cent accurate. In fact, it was because on Friday, November 22, 1963, over 3,000 miles away in Dallas, Texas, President John F. Kennedy's life had come to an end, a mere split second after he had turned to his wife and said 'Take off the glasses, Jackie.'

As the saying goes, everyone can remember vividly what they were doing the night President Kennedy was assassinated.

For Martin it was particularly easy: he was on stage at the Dreamland playing to a capacity crowd. They were setting up their equipment, and there were a few people milling around the ballroom going through their pre-opening ritual; the girls getting out the boxes of Tayto Crisps, KitKats, Jacob's Orange chocolate-covered biscuits, and the two boys were lugging crates of minerals from the storeroom at the back of the mineral stall. The cleaners were having a final whish around the toilets, making sure everything was spotless before Jim Mitchell, on his way to the box office, did his final inspection. Martin's mother Kathleen was already in the box office, getting her change set up for the evening sales. It was 6s./6d. to see and hear The Playboys that evening – Dreamland's most expensive ticket, usually reserved for the likes of The Royal Showband, Freshmen, Miami, Cadets and The Capital – and the odd 6 pence made calculating the change difficult for Kathleen. Nonetheless, she, with the occasional help of Mitchell, managed to sell 2,357 tickets, which generated income of £768/15s.

Earlier, before the doors opened, the Blues By Five were hanging around the stage with their guitar cases, waiting to do their gear check. The ballroom staff were dressed in their uniforms, complete with pillbox hats, and were wandering around checking doors and windows simultaneously, getting up to date with each other's gossip. They worked in interchangeable groups of twos and threes

One of their number was late, a girl called Adel Scott from nearby Magherafelt. She caught Martin's attention only because he knew she was an old schoolmate of Hanna's, and he watched her from his vantage point at the microphone as she rushed to put on the remains of her uniform, busily whispering something to several of her fellow attendants. They in turn went to other groups and continued the whispers. One of their number wandered by the Blues By Five and said something to them. Martin still couldn't make out what was being said, but he was aware that something had happened. Jim Mitchell chose that moment to walk up to the Blues By Five. They all looked at him solemn faced and one of them, Martin wasn't sure which because three of them had their backs to him, said something to Mitchell, who in turn walked over to the stage to tell each of The Playboys the news: President Kennedy had been shot.

Martin remembered being in a daze, going out to his mum in the box office to see if she was okay and wandering around the ballroom in silence as the Blues By Five performed their usual set. He couldn't work out why he was feeling such a loss. Sure, the President had Irish roots, and he and his wife Jackie had endeared themselves to the Irish nation when they'd briefly visited the country that June. Sure, he was a *young* President. Sure, he seemed wise beyond his years and, sure, he'd proved that the Russians were not as powerful as everyone had thought they were. But why did Martin and the rest of the people in the ballroom feel a personal loss, akin to losing a member of their immediate family? Was it because everyone intuitively knew JFK's death marked the end of innocence, a signal that bad had won out over good?

The Dreamland filled up in slow motion for Martin. He was kind of aware of the people around him. He remembered thinking that it must have been the Russians who'd killed Kennedy, shot him down because he'd recently embarrassed them in front of the rest of the world. Martin didn't remember any of the rest of the Blues By Five set. He barely remembered The Playboys' own set.

Half an hour into the show, Dixie whispered in Martin's ear that he'd like Martin to say something about President Kennedy. This was unusual in that Dixie usually made all of the announcements. Martin didn't remember exactly what he said – something about a bright light going out and hoping that the world wouldn't be in the dark for too long. But he remembered the ballroom falling into a rare silence as each and every dancer turned and faced the stage to listen to him. Instead of calling a song of his own, he announced 'Adios Amigo'. Brendan nodded at Martin, and when Mo counted in the band, only the echo of a single drumstick hitting the rim of his snare-drum could be heard in the ballroom.

Brendan performed a perfect, understated version of the song, a recent Irish chart success for Jim Reeves, taken from the film

Carousel. He intuitively knew that the lyrics contained all the emotions necessary, and all he had to do was sing them. Tears started to appear in some of the girls' eyes, and then people started to sob gently. You could just about hear the sniffling of noses behind the sound of Brendan's heartfelt vocals. The audience openly cried at the end of the song. First there was nothing but silence, and then, very gradually, people started to applaud, a couple down at the back first, then a boy down to the left, then another couple on the right. Within 20 seconds, the entire ballroom was generating thunderous applause.

The Playboys performed 'Adios Amigo' another three times that night. From that moment on, whenever Martin heard the song on the radio or when Brendan sang it, he would always think of President Kennedy.

CHAPTER SEVENTEEN

So, what is it about my paintings that you don't like?

Martin Dean

Hanna Hutchinson was also in the Dreamland that evening, back home on one of her rare visits from Queen's University. It was a fact that went unnoticed by Martin, so distracted was he by the tragic Dallas incident. Dixie, however, had spotted her. He still carried a torch for Hanna, as the wee girls around the Dreamland had a habit of saying.

Uncharacteristically, perhaps even with encouragement from Martin, she had let Dixie down gently before leaving for Belfast. She'd said she didn't want to be engaged and settle into marriage at that time of her life, when she hadn't a clue what she even *wanted* out of her life. It would be wrong for her and it would be equally wrong for him. Might she consider him at some point in the future? Dixie would ask. She honestly didn't know, she would say, but she felt he would be better off thinking of it as totally out of the question. He should get on with his life, not hold out false hope for her coming back.

They spoke that night in the Dreamland, an awkward conversation with an even more awkward ending. Dixie thought it

strange that a girl he'd once considered marrying was now nothing more than an acquaintance, a neighbour you nodded to across
the street. Dixie asked her out again. She refused. He asked
if she'd met anyone else. She laughed that off – the time she
didn't spend studying or at lectures, she was asleep. Had *he* met
someone else? He very gracelessly said there was someone all
right, but if there was any chance of Hanna taking him back
he'd immediately end it with the other girl. On the positive side,
Dixie later felt very bad for betraying his new girlfriend, Adel
Scott, who worked at the ballroom, for someone who didn't even
want him.

Dixie's feelings towards Adel mirrored those of Hanna
towards him; namely that both he and Hanna had become
objects of their pursuer's affections, but they were marred with
guilt because of their inability to give that affection back. If he'd
had the courage to address this issue with Hanna, she'd have
confirmed his fears.

And if you think *that* was complicated, it was kindergarten com-
pared to the emotions flying between Martin and Hanna.

Following the night when they both lost their virginity, they'd
enjoyed similar, but infrequent, encounters. Every single time
was as earth shattering as the last: it was the one thing that didn't
change. But for the remainder of 1962, and up until Hanna left for
Belfast in April 1963 – she wanted to get away from Castlemartin,
for one to acclimatise herself to the city before she started at
Queen's University that September – they seemed to grow apart
mentally. They came together occasionally to service each other's bodies, but neither allowed the relationship to grow beyond
that. Martin didn't know how to, and even if he did he was on
a never-ending treadmill of dance hall engagements. Hanna, on
the other hand, was apathetic. In a perverse way, she thought it
was just too obvious, too predictable, to get into a 'normal' relationship. However, there was something which continued to draw
them back together. She didn't tell Martin, of course. Neither did

she tell him that he was still the only person with whom she had shared her most precious treasure.

Both had continued to be discreet to keep their relationship hidden from Dixie. Martin had secretly caught the bus down to Belfast on a couple of his days off, but for one reason or another they hadn't seen each other since the end of the summer. In fact, he hadn't known that Hanna would be in Castlemartin on that particular weekend. He didn't discover until, walking home alone after the dance, his mind still buried in thoughts of the loss of President Kennedy, someone called out from behind him.

'Hello, stranger.'

Martin recognised the voice immediately. 'God, Hanna,' Martin replied as he turned around. 'How great to see you!' He meant it. An overwhelming feeling of warmth towards her washed over him: she was there, just when he needed her most. It wasn't like he ran and hugged her or anything; neither of them was either confident of, or disposed to, such obvious signs of affection.

She took his hand, and they walked aimlessly about the streets for an hour, trying to come to terms with that dramatic day and catching up on other, less sombre news. Hanna had passed her driving test while in Belfast, and she had borrowed her dad's car. They decided to scoot out to the shores of Lough Neagh at Ballyroan, park up and walk to the stone pier just outside town. The moon was lighting up the Lough in an eerie kind of way, and they skimmed a token two or three stones along the water.

They sat down on the pier, facing each other. Martin looked at her as she stared across the water. He enjoyed the chance to steal this view, and was struck by her natural beauty. But he couldn't help but be confused: on the one hand, Hanna was the perfect package. She was stunning. If anything she grew better looking the more he got to know her, and she had the perfect body; he had absolutely no doubt about that. She was full-figured without being plump and her curves, to Martin's eye, were to die for. On top of that, she was willing to share the joys of her amazing body with him – maybe not frequently, but certainly regularly. On the other hand, she was what could loosely be described as troubled. Yes, she was certainly a troubled soul, and her need to question everything, to go against the grain continually and her desire not to be taken for granted were sometimes infuriating.

Really, what more did they need? They got on great; they shared all their secrets and knew how to pleasure each other. They were both young, healthy and presentable. He was making good money – no, he was making *fecking amazing* money – and she had set her sights on the university path. So why couldn't they just be happy with each other and get on with their lives – together?

Maybe their relationship wasn't much different to her dalliance with Dixie after all: if Dixie had been prepared to experiment with her, would they still be together, albeit in an *untogether* kind of way? However, unlike Dixie, Martin didn't want this to be over; he couldn't bring himself to file their relationship away as 'having been dealt with'. He chose not to; he was enjoying their encounters, and deep down he truly liked Hanna as a person. But her behaviour was stopping him from loving her. They had never used the 'L' word. Could Hanna simply be waiting for Mr Right to come along, and keeping Martin at arm's length to avoid the risk of him falling for her? It certainly seemed that way. Sometimes, he'd just like to have declared, 'Agh, for feck's sake, just go! Leave me alone, please, give me some peace!'

That was it, he thought: he wanted peace. He used to enjoy peace when he was writing his songs, but now when he sat down to write it would bring up all this stuff with Hanna and he'd wonder what the point was. It didn't help them, so what was the point of him getting up on stage and singing it to others? You know – shouldn't he get his own shit together before he started preaching to an audience?

As though reading his mind, Hanna turned to him and said: 'What's to become of us, Martin?'

God, he thought, we really are in trouble if she's asking me. 'What would you like to become of us?'

'Clever footwork, Martin,' she laughed. 'Okay, I'll tell you, but on condition you answer the same question to me truthfully.'

'But how will you know I'm being truthful? I might tailor my response to your answer.'

'Okay, good point, good point,' she said, pausing for thought. 'Right, here's what we'll do. How's about you write down your answer before I give mine – you hold it in your hand where I can see it, and then when I give my answer I can read yours.'

'Fine with me,' Martin replied eagerly, and took his ever-present spiral notebook out of the breast pocket of his denim jacket and started to write, extremely neatly, two lines on the page. He tore the page out, folded it in four and placed it in his hand.

'Okay, my turn. I'd like to see us grow old, still being friends and still doing the things we do.'

'You mean…'

'Yes, I mean…'

'But that would mean we'd have to live together…'

'No, Martin – we don't live together *now*.'

'But you mean we'd still live our other lives and now and then we'd meet up and make love?'

'Yes, Martin, make love and talk to each other – that would be nice.'

'Say one of us found someone else… what then?'

'Well, why would it change anything?' Hanna asked. Martin was struck by how sincere she sounded.

'Let's just say that there would be a third party involved on both sides and, you have to assume, they'd be making love to us, or at least one of us.'

'Yes, Martin, but no one will ever make love to me the way you do.'

'But you'd expect us to come together, and make love even though we were married to other people?'

'And why not? We'd still care for each other, and I'd have thought that still caring for each other was something to be more jealous of than making love, if we're considering the jealous type.'

'You mean, you'd be happy to make love to your husband and then come and meet up with me and make love to me?'

'Martin, I'm not like you in that respect. You and I make love; I don't need to make love to anyone else. I might want to have different types of friendships with other people, but for me, when I'm with you and we make love, it's perfect. I can't see it ever not being perfect. It's a gift we've been given to share with each other. It's not a God-given right, Martin; it's a God-given gift, the gift of taking pleasure from our bodies. In a small way, I suppose it's a bit like songwriting. Writing or catching songs is a God-given gift, not a right. And in the same way we can both share the love of a great song now. Take for instance 'Eyes' – we both enjoy that song, we could both sit down and enjoy it together, so do you mean to tell me in 5 years' time, when we're both with someone else, that just because of that we can't sit down together and enjoy that song?'

'Of course we could – that would be harmless.'

'And tell me, Martin Dean or Martin McClelland or whoever the feck you are these days, where is the harm in making love? Surely it's a beautiful thing, a wonderful thing?'

'Of course it is, but the point is that it's special, it's not something you share with everyone.'

'But *you're* not everyone, Martin. *I'm* not everyone. In fact, I can't see myself sharing this particular booty with anyone but you.'

'So you think I'm okay for making love, but there are other things I'm not so okay for?'

'I didn't say that.

'But you implied it, Hanna.'

'No, Martin,' Hanna said, letting her exasperation show, '*you* implied it. *I* said I might want different kinds of relationships with other people.'

'Thereby implying that you don't get all you need from me.'

'Not at all, Martin. Take your songs for instance; no one can write songs like you; your songs are uniquely yours and the fact that someone – say for instance me, babe – likes them doesn't mean they can't like the songs of another songwriter, or even like your, let's say, paintings. What I'm saying is, just because I like your songs it doesn't necessarily mean I'm going to like your paintings, and it equally doesn't mean that I shouldn't like someone else's paintings.'

'So what is it about my paintings you don't like?'

'I don't know; I haven't seen your paintings.'

'Exactly!' Martin shouted. 'My case rests, your honour.'

Hanna rolled her eyes. 'Now can I see *your* answer please?' she said, putting her outstretched palm in front of him.

'No. The *deal* was that when you gave me your answer, I would show you mine.'

'Okay, but I gave you my answer.'

'No, the question was "what do you *think* will become of us?"'

'And?'

'Well you said what you'd *like* to see become of us. There could of course be a difference.'

'Okay. Well, what I *think* will become of us is that we'll… we'll…' and she rose from her stony seat, took him by the hand, led him to the grassy verge by the water's edge and pulled him down on top of her, 'I think we're both going to turn blue from the cold if we don't hurry up and make love.'

Martin flung the torn page from his notebook towards the water as she raised her dress and guided his other hand to her treasure, her 'booty' as she had called it.

Later, when they were returning from Ballyroan to Castlemartin, she remembered the piece of paper with Martin's answer to her question. He explained that in the heat of their passion he must have dropped it. 'Okay, then *tell* me what you wrote would become of us.'

'Actually, I wrote that we'd probably christen your father's car.' She didn't believe him, but he fulfilled his prediction on the outskirts of town.

Afterwards, as she dropped him off and they said their good-byes, he stood on the pavement outside of his house. He was so lost in his thoughts – of what she thought was wrong with him and how he could fix it when he didn't even know what it was in the first place – that he didn't notice her avoiding the left turn, which would have taken her to her parents' house. Instead, she turned right, back in the direction from which they had just come.

CHAPTER EIGHTEEN

An audience would rather be confused than bored

Sean MacGee

When Martin Dean heard knocking on his door the following morning, he thought it was Hanna, and he actually considered pretending he wasn't in. He felt very guilty about his reaction, but the moment didn't last long, just long enough for him to be aware of it. He quickly buried the bad thought and went to the door. He was shocked when he opened it to find none other than Sean MacGee.

Sean, as usual, brushed past Martin and went straight to the kitchen, shouting back over his shoulder: 'I've got an idea for a song I've been thinking about all night, but I don't seem to be able to get a handle on it. I wondered if you'd like to work on it with me.'

Martin was delighted. He was going through a dry spell with his own songwriting, maybe because of the problems with Hanna. Or perhaps it was because The Playboys were now including six of his songs in their set, and when he wanted to add a new song Dixie insisted on him dropping an older one to make room. Dixie's point (which Martin agreed with to a certain degree) was that the dancers still considered them to be something of a human jukebox – they wanted to hear all their old favourites and the new pop hits as well. Roy Orbison's 'In Dreams' had been a popular choice at the dances since its release six months previously, but now Dixie wanted them to attempt the big O's newest hit, 'Blue Bayou', which had hit number one in Ireland at the beginning of November. Martin was fine with both these songs because they were perfect for his voice. He was, however, resisting doing 'Kiss Me Quick'.

'Kiss Me Quick' was The Royal Showband's first number one single in Ireland, and was the first of five consecutive number ones for the band and Brendan Bowyer, their lead vocalist (a record that still hasn't been broken in Ireland to this day!). All in all, the Royal enjoyed 20 chart entries over the years, including two further number ones, one with Tom Dunphy on lead vocals, and one with Charlie Matthews handling the vocal duties. Waterford's finest were happy to break the unwritten rule never to confuse your audience by changing your lead vocalist, particularly on records. It was important to convince your audience to accept one voice alone, making it the sound of your band. The Royal showed the strength of their musicianship by going three-deep on their lead vocalists.

Martin's reluctance to perform the song had nothing to do with the success the Royal were enjoying. He was extremely happy for them: he figured that the more success the big boys had, the sooner he'd be able to fulfil his own ambition and get one of his own songs out on record. Indeed, on the showband recording front, things were on the up, with Des Kelly & The Capitol being the first showband to record and release an album, *Introducing The Capitol*. No, in fact the reason Martin didn't want The Playboys to do a version of 'Kiss Me Quick' was that, quite simply, he thought it was a terrible song.

Sean MacGee disturbed Martin's thoughts by repeating his opening line. 'Why yes,' Martin replied, happy that he'd now be in a position to repay the favour. They went up to his bedroom and Martin got out his guitar. 'Okay, what have you got?'

'Well, not much, apart from the fact that it's about President Kennedy and I think it should be called "The Saddest Day".'

'Right,' Martin replied, a bit shocked by how little Sean had. For his part, he had a sad tune he'd been playing around with for several months. He loved the melody line so much that he had never tried to force a set of lyrics to it. He'd learned early on in his songwriting career that there were two kinds of songs: those that work and those that don't. Those that don't are generally best left alone.

Sean had read somewhere that one of President Kennedy's best qualities had been his ability to listen to other people and make his decisions by using this information expertly. This became the lyrical hook. They avoided a maudlin approach due to the fact that Sean was a total cynic and incapable of sentimentality.

Half an hour later, they had the structure to their song and about a quarter of the lyrics. Sean excused himself, and went down to the kitchen table with pen and paper. 20 minutes later, he returned with a perfectly crafted set of words, as only he could. 30 minutes after that, they were listening to the completed song on Martin's Philips reel-to-reel tape recorder. The best quality of the song was that it hid the fact that they were referring to JFK, and because of the beauty of the melody and its slower tempo, it could pass as a simple love song.

Martin felt something of a release of emotions from all the confusion he'd felt weighing down in the Dreamland Ballroom on that solemn Friday night, not to mention the mixed emotions he'd felt on the pier at Ballyroan. It was as if he'd drawn a line under something. He could tell that Sean had also wanted to get 'The Saddest Day' off his chest. That, he assumed, was part of the joy of being a songwriter – you could resolve issues for yourself by locking a set of images and thoughts into 3 minutes of music, where it would remain forever.

Kennedy would also forever remain in the hearts of the Irish, many households displaying a photograph or painting of the late President nestled within their particular holy trinity above the mantelpiece.

New song duly written, Sean and Martin enjoyed a cup of tea. Sean requested to hear several of Martin's new tunes, which he said were great. He liked 'Still She Dances With You' a lot, but he felt there was still work to be done on it. 'You always need to resolve the lyrics and the music. If you don't, Martin, you're not a real songwriter. Anyone can sit down, strum a few chords, hum a bit of a tune over the top and doodle away with a few words, but that's not songwriting, Martin – that's like one of Dixie's dad's favourite jazz greats having a blow and improvising, not the same thing as playing music under the discipline of a structure. It would be the same as me just talking away to you now for ages without making a point. To me, writing a song is similar to writing a good book or making a good movie. In all three you need to have an arresting start: you must grab the attention of your audience right from the word go. Then you need to keep the audience with you as you develop the theme of your verse, book or film. Next, just when the listener or audience thinks they've got you sussed, and you, songwriter or filmmaker, are in danger of losing them, you need to stick in a twist, in the case of a book and a movie, or a chorus, if it's a song. But the twist, or chorus, serves the same function, and that is to prod your audience, push or pull them in a different direction. Then you return to the verse again to advance the story, then straight into the middle eight of a song or the middle of the movie or book. This is the place where you realise that if your audience have come with you that far, they're going to stay with you for the remainder of the song or movie or book, so you can take the space to allow them to reflect on what's happened so far. Then it's another twist or chorus, and then straight to the final verse, where you tidy everything up, maybe even throw in a curveball to send them away with a feel-good factor or leave them deep in thought about the outcome.

'The only difference between a song on one hand and a movie or a book on the other is that you're only allowed three minutes to get your point across.'

Martin had never really thought about it that way, but he warmed to the approach: 'Yeah, you might just have something there... and your instrumentation could cover the same ground as the scenery or description.'

'Maybe, but I tend to think of the instruments as the characters and the melodies as the scenery,' Sean replied.

Although he was extremely generous with his praise of Martin's songs, he also tried to encourage Martin not to be scared of trying to write lyrics with weightier themes. They discussed the virtues of songwriting versus entertainment. Martin claimed that a great songwriter could do both; they could entertain their audience while at the same time making their point, Bob Dylan being the perfect example. 'To some degree you have to give the audience what they think they want to hear,' Martin said.

'Ah, the auld showband philosophy,' Sean said, mocking him something rotten, 'keep the punters happy. Glad to see you're walking in step.'

'It's not as simple as that, Sean,' Martin said, taking it all in good humour. 'We're there to entertain the audience; we don't want to confuse them – we want them to come back again.'

'An audience would rather be confused than bored.'

Martin thought about that one for a bit. Although he tended to agree, he didn't admit it to Sean, who continued: 'Martin, the biggest illusion the showbands are working under is that the dancers come to see them.'

'Of course they come to see the showbands!'

'Wrong, Martin: they come to dance, they come to meet people.'

'What kind of people go to places just to meet people?' Martin asked, deadpan.

'They come because they instinctively know that girls will be there or that boys will be there *because* the girls are there. They think they might get lucky, or they innocently think they may meet someone nice who, perhaps, they might spend the rest of their lives with. Yes, they get to know the different bands' gimmicks, you know like Dixie dancing the first three songs with a member of the audience, or The Clippers with their Jukebox Saturday Night entertainment selection with the Laurel and Hardy impression, or Brendan Bowyer leaping over the bass player and guitarist, or The Cadets' snazzy uniforms or Joe Dolan sweatin' a lot, or whatever… but, at the end of the day, the wee girls who hang around the cafés in Castlemartin are still going to go to their regular dance at the Dreamland Ballroom. They are *not* going to go to the Cookstown Town Hall just because The Royal are on there, they are not going to traipse down to Ballymena to the Flamingo just to sample The Freshmen – not to mention Sammy Barr's famous hotdogs,' Sean said, still managing to keep it light-hearted despite the obvious undertones.

'You're wrong, Sean. People *will* travel to see The Freshmen.'

'Yes, Martin, granted – people like you and Brendan and people like me and other wannabe musicians, but not the dancers. The Freshmen play Dreamland at least three times a year, so the eager fans aren't going to have to wait very long to see them, are they?' Sean looked like he'd finished until he added: 'And you know what else? I think real dancers get annoyed when The Freshmen or The Royal are in town.'

'Oh come on, Sean, please,' Martin said, now finding it was his turn to wear the cynical cloak.

'No, seriously… when The Freshmen play in Castlemartin, all the musicians like you and me and whoever else will go and we'll *stand* and *watch*, and dancers hate that because it encourages other people to stand around and watch to see what the 'standers and watchers' are watching, and pretty soon there's no room to dance – there's no room to pick a new girl every three songs, or to be picked by a new boy every three songs, and before you know it the dancers are cheesed off because their night is ruined. Like the boy who's spent his hard-earned five bob so he can search for that wee girl with the white bobby socks pulled up over her knees, the one he's probably been eyeing up for ages and trying for weeks to pluck up the courage to ask for a dance, but she'll be nowhere to be found.'

Martin laughed as he considered the implications of this. Did Sean have a point?

Sean pressed on. 'You know, all you showband *heads* are some day going to wake up and realise that instead of all these seven-hour journeys cramped up in the back of your wagons spending fortunes on petrol, Tayto crisps, lemonade and Jacob's Kimberley biscuits, you'd all be better off staying in your own town and playing in your own local ballrooms. That way you'd have no need to enlist the help of Esso to put a tiger in your tank.'

For all his negativity, Martin enjoyed his chats with Sean. One of the main reasons he liked Sean was because Sean was one of those people who felt the need to tell the truth about absolutely everything. He was refreshing while at the same time brutal, but at least you always knew where you stood with him. That morning, Sean convinced Martin that he was a good singer; the sting in the tail was that he felt Martin would have trouble becoming a great singer as long as he stayed with The Playboys. He also told him that his songwriting was only safe for as long as he didn't start writing his songs for the showband.

'I hear you've given 'Three Spires' to the Blues By Five. That's a great idea, Martin – Paddy Shaw is a great soul singer, he'll do an amazing version of it. You should keep your attention on finding other outlets for your songs. Don't always write for the auld showbands; just write songs and don't be scared of writing big songs.'

'But Sean, you can't consciously write a big song.'

'Aye, but you can consciously *try* not to write a big song, that's all I'm saying.'

'The Saddest Day' marked the first day in a while that Martin had completed a new song. It also marked the day Martin and Sean resumed their songwriting partnership.

Martin was happy to see and hear his friend in control of his senses and back in action. However, later in the afternoon, as The Playboys' wagon was leaving Castlemartin, Martin was sure he saw Sean stumble and fall on the pavement outside Brady's public house. Yes, it could have been an accident, and yes, it could have been a coincidence that the 'accident' happened outside a public house, but sadly, somehow Martin didn't believe it.

CHAPTER NINETEEN

There's nothing beats a nice, handy week; a well-routed, good-paying, five-day jaunt

Gentleman Jim Mitchell

March 1964 saw The Playboys go off on what Jim Mitchell called 'a nice handy week; a well-routed,' even though he did say so himself, 'good-paying, five-day jaunt.' Apart from their two trips to Scotland, this was the first time they'd stayed in hotels, and it was certainly their first overnight in Ireland.

By the time The Playboys were parked outside Barry's house, waiting, as usual, for him to emerge, Gentleman Jim Mitchell had already been on the road for four hours – so crucial was the success of this mini tour that he was acting as the advance party. He drove non-stop to Galway in his pristine Vauxhall VX490, and went straight to the Seapoint Ballroom. He met the manager, who treated him to a grand, if somewhat too liquid (especially on the ballroom manager's part), lunch. On his return to the ballroom, he pinned up several new Day-Glo green 'The Playboys Are Coming Tonight!' posters in the foyer and then headed into town, sticking them in newsagents, a record store, a couple of hotels and an electrical store, which also sold a limited supply of musical instruments.

Mitchell then made his way to their hotel: the Atlantic View, a little outside Galway. The prim and proper hotel manageress managed to squeeze in a lecture that she didn't want any bother or 'carryings on' from The Playboys that night. Mitchell gave the necessary assurances and ordered tea in advance for the lads, who were due to arrive around 6 p.m. He also left instructions that he wanted several rounds of sandwiches and five pints of milk to be left out for the boys to enjoy when they returned to the hotel early the following morning. The milk order seemed to hit the right spot with the manageress – Mitchell could see the gears of her mind working: 'Well, if they're planning to come back here and drink nothing but milk, then surely they won't get up to any devilment…'

Meanwhile, back in Castlemartin, the boys were sitting restlessly in the back of the wagon as Dixie plodded up to Barry's door for the third time. His mother came out, wiping her hands on a kitchen towel, and shouted up the stairs in a voice so loud that everyone in the housing site must have heard her: 'Barry, it's time to get up, it's Wednesday!' proving to all in the neighbourhood, and maybe some in the nearby graveyard too, that Barry's reputation as half man, half mattress was merited.

Barry waddled down the stairs five minutes later, out to the wagon, climbed into the back seat, lay his head against the window and dropped off again before Dixie even had a chance to start up the van. Sleeping was no problem to him; he could literally have slept leaning against a fence.

In fact, on one occasion Barry had suddenly woken up, sat bolt upright, and said to Dixie: 'Can you drop me off first, head?' Dixie was used to such requests, the drop-off procedure sometimes adding an extra 20 or 30 minutes to the journey at the end of the night. But this time he replied in amazement: 'Barry, we haven't even been to play the fecking gig yet, for heaven's sake.'

The rest of the band were in stitches, which Dixie eventually put to rest by saying, 'Ah whisht, will you, and let him get back to sleep.'

For the band members, these long trips could be an educational journey. The conversations would usually start within 10 miles, when the novelty of the journey had worn off and the musicians had begun to discard the thoughts, conversations or domestics they'd been involved in immediately prior to being picked up. They'd start discussing something, anything under the sun really, and investigate it thoroughly during the course of the journey.

On this particular morning, the topic was pigeons and pigeon racing. Mo and his father kept pigeons in a green-and-white striped pigeon-loft at the end of their garden. The boys in the band were fascinated at how you could put pigeons in a basket and take them as far as several hundred miles away, releasing them in a strange land, and yet they would still manage to find their way home, at well over a 1,000 yards a minute. Mo explained that no one really knew how the pigeons managed this amazing feat, but that didn't stop everyone in the wagon coming up with their own theory. Robin, who knew about absolutely everything, reckoned that pigeons were telepathic, and as they flew through an area the pigeons down below would pass on a progress report to their brethren flying overhead. The fascination was sufficient that the boys from the band had, one by one, visited Mo and his dad to be shown around the loft and introduced to the birds in question.

The conversations would sometimes link seamlessly from one specialist subject to another. For instance, Mo would tell the lads how, during the Second World War, pigeons were invaluable, taking messages home to base from behind enemy lines. This in turn sparked off a Second World War conversation, with Brendan in the hot seat, regaling the group with the tales of his father's wartime exploits and how he'd won his medals in particular. On such days, the journeys would positively fly by.

Today, before they knew it they were pulling up behind Mitchell's green car with the white flash outside the Atlantic View Hotel.

Ten minutes later, after they'd checked into their rooms –
Brendan and Martin sharing one, Dixie, Mo and Barry in another
and Robin, Davy and Smiley in the third – they were sitting down
with Mitchell to enjoy four fish suppers and five steak and chips
between them. Mitchell washed his down with his regular drink, a
'kit', or whiskey chased with a half of lager.

Mitchell had an unwritten rule: that they never discuss band
business during these meals. In fact, he was unaware of anything
in this world that it was worth spoiling a meal over, so mealtime
conversations fell into two groups: music, and what was happening
in Ireland and the world, at least according to the newspapers or
the radio.

On the day of the Galway show, in late March 1964, they could
have discussed the new Jim Reeves song, 'I Love You Because',
which had just reached the top spot in the Irish charts and which
they were planning to perform for the first time that night. At that
time, Jim Reeves was probably more popular than Guinness in
Ireland and he was a must on showband set lists across the land.
Other subjects on the music side might have been that The Miami,
with lead singer Dickie Rock, had just emulated The Royal's chart
success by taking their first single, 'There's Always Me', to number
one. The Bachelors had bettered their 1963 UK chart position by
climbing the whole way to the top spot in the UK and Ireland with
'Diane' early in 1964. Despite The Beatles beginning to dominate
the international scene, The Playboys were still split on their virtues.
The majority actually favoured The Dave Clark Five, with their two
stomping hits, 'Glad All Over' and 'Bits And Pieces', both songs
currently in The Playboys' set and very popular with the dancers
since they were sure floor-fillers, and Mo because it was exactly
the same drum part for each tune. Martin, however, was sure that
The Beatles' songs were strong – particularly their new one, 'Can't
Buy Me Love', which was flying up the charts – and that they'd
be around for a long time. Apparently, two members of the band,
John Lennon and George Harrison, were currently on holiday at
the Dromoland Castle luxury hotel, which was setting them back a

staggering £77 a week – each! George, allegedly the most money-conscious of the band, would surely have been very concerned about such an extortionate price.

The Clancy Brothers, with Tommy Maken, had just returned from America for a quick tour. Their unique selling point, apart from their Aran sweaters, was that they were fabulously successful Stateside. Robin was wary: how did the Irish public know for sure that the Brothers and their Strabane friend were so successful, when no one aside from the band had been to America? Not even the press, who were faithfully carrying the stories of their success, had been there. Mitchell commented that although the Clancys' album had just entered the American charts, a huge feat in itself, the press could definitely be very effective in spinning a story, regardless of its validity.

The non-music topics might have included the author Brendan Behan's death on March 20, aged just 41; or that a southern gentleman by the name of Charles Haughey had introduced a complicated one-way system in Dublin on March 18, on the same day that it became mandatory for members of the Free State to take a driving test to secure a licence. (The driving Playboys, Dixie and Smiley – who'd both had to pass driving tests in the Wee North – were very pleased at this news, having been more than a little concerned at the driving ability of some of the southerners.)

They would certainly have discussed that Badley Limited, of Donegal Place, Belfast, had announced that they were just about to stock some topless frocks. There was a lot of banter about this, with the majority of the boys in the band looking forward to the exposure. Smiley, for his part, wasn't so sure: 'Frocks don't care who wears them, and there are some sorry sights out there that believe you me are better covered up, if only to protect your appetite for food, not to mention your appetite for women.'

On a more serious note, they might have discussed that, in faraway South Africa, Nelson Mandela had just been sentenced to life imprisonment. Then, on their own doorstep, according to a recent census, 94.9 per cent of Eire's population were Catholics against 3.7 per cent Church of Ireland; 0.7 per cent Presbyterians; 0.2 per cent Methodists; 0.1 per cent Jews and 0.2 per cent 'others'. Hard though they tried, they couldn't come up with who might have been included in the 0.2 per cent.

One subject that didn't put Gentleman Jim Mitchell off his food was horse racing, and so, over his fish supper and Fanta, he'd probably have been very enthusiastic about Arkle and how his legend had been set in motion, with the magnificent horse recently winning the Cheltenham Gold Cup, ridden by Pat Taaffe, and trained by Tom Dreaper. Arkle had already won the Irish Grand National at Fairyhouse, and the Cheltenham Gold Cup was the first of three years where the horse, and Mitchell, with more than a few bob on the nose, won consistently.

Dinner and chat over, The Playboys headed down to the Seapoint Ballroom to set up their equipment for the evening's dance. Smiley, being Smiley, had come up with a theory that his time at the end of the dance was more valuable than his time before. So, on certain nights, he'd offer to carry in all of the equipment on the condition that he didn't have to hang around afterwards to see it back out. The lazy members of the band, namely Davy and Robin, thought this was a grand idea. All they had to do was come up with an excuse for the not-carrying-the-equipment-out part of the bargain.

Brendan and Martin were the fussiest about the gear and the proper setting up of the sound system. They'd usually be the ones testing it, with one on stage either playing a guitar or talking into the microphone, and the other wandering around the various parts of the ballroom to see how good or bad it sounded in those foreign parts.

The whole issue of sound was a funny one. Both Martin and Brendan knew better than the other members of the band that the sound they created on stage during their equipment-check in an empty ballroom was completely different to that of a few hours later when the ballroom would be filled with dancers. However, if they could get it right beforehand, it would (hopefully) become only slightly worse. Starting off with a bad sound would surely only lead to total disaster.

Ballroom managers had their own version of good and bad sound: too loud was bad and everything else was good. Some even walked around the ballroom brandishing two torches – one with a red bulb and one with a white. If you saw the red one flashed up at the stage, you were too loud; if you got the white, all was fine. Some ballroom managers never failed to amaze the band with their self-confessed knowledge of *how* the art of performing worked, while having no conceivable talent for performing themselves. In one strange case, the ballroom owner in Fermoy often asked the bass player to tighten his strings up, as they were making too much of a racket being 'loose'.

Equipment set up to Brendan and Martin's satisfaction, the relief group or, as they were known in the posh ballrooms, the 'show' group, would then carry their bits and pieces up onto the stage and start to assemble their own gear. As Galway was too far away for the Blues By Five – not to mention the fact that the support money of £1/10s. wouldn't even have come close to covering their costs – a relief group from nearby Limerick, working under the unusual name of Granny's Intentions, had been booked; their unique pop-orientated country style kept the audience confused rather than bored, thereby proving Sean MacGee's theory correct.

The Playboys used the time off between 7.30 p.m. and 11 p.m. in a variety of ways. Naturally, Barry went back to the hotel for a kip. Mo went off to scout out the town, especially all the knick-knack shops. He'd have limited time during the following morning before they headed off to their next stop so, if he mapped out a route to the interesting-looking stores that evening, he'd save himself a lot of work. It has to be said that, of all The Playboys, Mo was the one who made the most out of their tours visiting the various cities, towns and villages. He loved spending time getting to know the different places, talking with as many people as would speak with him. Unlike Smiley, though, he wasn't a conversation instigator – he was happy to respond, but always felt a little weird just coming out with something to a complete stranger. He was very friendly, if a little shy, and he'd usually find himself being invited back to someone's house for a cup of tea to see their paintings, collections of bric-a-brac, records, souvenir spoons, stamps, Marvel comics, pigeons or anything relevant to his many other interests.

Smiley had a theory: he thought Mo collected things – anything, it seemed – because he was scared of dealing with girls. Mo kept his council on the matter, but he knew better; the girls he met in a ballroom were not the type he'd take home to meet his mother. That wasn't to say that all ballroom girls were the same, but those who made it their business to meet the band would definitely not go down well at home.

But there was one occasion that changed his mind.

The ballroom in question was St John's Hall in Magherafelt. Mo wasn't playing that night, but was dancing to The Breakaways. He liked The Breakaways, particularly their lead singer Brendan Quinn, who had the best Jim Reeves voice this side of the Atlantic. He went to see them as often as he could.

Anyway, that night Mo had experienced the luxury of being picked during a ladies' choice. Once the set was through, the girl had invited him to join her at the mineral stall. It was there she informed him that he was too old to be living at home. How did she know he still lived at home? She knew, she said, because his nails were spotlessly clean; married men who came to the ballrooms looking for girls always had dirty fingernails with a clean, white band of skin on their ring finger. Girls learned to spot these things early on, she said; some to take advantage of the information, and others using it to steer clear.

Mo liked this girl. Her name was Angela Convery, and she wore black-framed Buddy-Holly-type glasses and had shoulder-length, jet black hair, parted with a knife-edge line on the top of her crown. He discovered straightaway that her eyesight was appalling, when a boy (with dirty fingernails, I might add) bumped into her, causing her glasses to fly off. Mo got down on his hands and knees and kept everyone away from the area until he located the precious item. It was no doubt this chivalrous gesture that prompted her to accept his offer of a date. He was stunned; she was so beautiful.

That was the previous November. Since then, they'd been out several times, a fact that he'd kept hidden from Smiley and the others when they ribbed him about his apparent nervousness around girls.

For his part, Martin Dean used his time off to go back to his room with his guitar and play a bit, read a bit and try to write a bit more, before going downstairs to the lobby where he met with Brendan and Smiley to enjoy a cup of tea and a bit of craic.

Davy and Robin, on the other hand, teamed up to go searching for the girls' pre-dance rendezvous, usually a café or a coffee shop in town. This at least gave them a head start over Smiley with the girls.

In a way, Davy and Robin were perfect partners. Robin thought he knew everything and Davy, while admittedly slow on the uptake, wanted to learn from him.

Dixie, meanwhile, would remain at the ballroom all evening for a bit of networking with Mitchell. He knew from his own days as a manager just how important this small talk could be. Mitchell agreed, highlighting those bands who were pretty average, yet secured regular gigs – and money – in the big ballrooms.

Teddy Bee and The Bubble Band were one such group. Everybody knew that Teddy couldn't carry a note, even in his imagination, yet he was always first to the ballroom – chatting happily to the caretaker, the cleaner, the owner, the manager and then the dancers – and he'd always make himself available for photos and autographs after a gig. If there was one Billy Bunter left at 3 a.m., Teddy would still be talking to them. He was never patronising, rather very generous and gracious and, first and foremost, a gentleman.

'Someday, someday soon, please God,' Dixie would repeatedly say, 'he'll go into politics. No harm to him, but he's wild bad for business – he makes the dancers think that anyone can do this, and we know that's not true.'

But Mitchell knew that a great musical band with the same approach to public relations as Teddy could go far.

So the two of them would go about their work, Mitchell striking up friendly banter with the girls working in the ballroom. 'If you're a good girl, I'll take you to Dreamland some day,' he'd quip, a bit of harmless fun that would see the young lass responding: 'Oh, don't be cheeky, you – you're old enough to be me mam's ex!'

In fact, nobody had ever seen Gentleman Jim Mitchell intoxicated by feminine charms. There had been a wee bit of chat about a woman down in Dublin – or was it Belfast? – which was all very mysterious, but he didn't exactly go out of his way to put anybody, particularly his musicians, straight on the matter.

For his part, since Dixie had lost Hanna Hutchinson and dropped Adel Scott, he'd taken up with a Castledawson girl called Colette Curtis, a blonde, blue-eyed beauty who was being all the things to him that Hanna hadn't been. You guessed it – this is the same Colette that Martin had left sucking air behind the school bike-shed several years before. Colette, showing a little more restraint than she had in her encounter with Martin, had kissed Dixie, which had been more than enough for him. Without delay, he proposed. Her answer was that he should ask again in 6 months when it was decent, but that she wouldn't disappoint him.

Dixie still wondered why Hanna had disappointed him though. Her signals had confused him; in fact, he thought it was all going to be so much simpler. Boy meets girl, boy likes girl, girl (appears) to like boy, so boy and girl get it together. But it hadn't happened that way. Why? He'd never been able to figure it out. Because of Hanna, he'd been expecting Colette to shoot him down, so he was amazed at her response. As far as Dixie was concerned, Colette and Hanna were as different as chalk and cheese. But that was only on the surface. In reality, they were quite similar deep down and that's why

Dixie had felt an immediate attraction to Colette. But she wasn't exactly settling for less than she had dreamed of; no, rather she felt that dreams, like movies, didn't just appear out of thin air and a lot of hard work had to go in to making them happen.

For the first time, free from the strains of his relationship with Hanna, Dixie was allowing himself to enjoy The Playboys' success. In fact, nothing could be better than the mini tour they had embarked on. His dad had thought as much, too: 'Don't forget to enjoy yourself, that's the important part in all of this,' he advised his son before he left. 'Have fun, enjoy yourself.'

Having someone at home who cared about him, aside from his parents, made everything easier and somehow more worthwhile. And he knew that his manager cared about him too. It was uplifting, someone so genuine being so committed to him and his band's music.

At the same time, you could forgive Dixie for forgetting that Mitchell had made it a condition of his management that Martin Dean would be a member of The Playboys.

The same Playboys started off that evening's entertainment in the usual manner: Dixie jumping down from the stage and inviting three lucky (some would say) ladies to dance. Dixie had devised a very cool way of remounting the podium: he'd place a folding chair by the lip of the stage, and as he stepped up onto it and then up to the stage, he'd cock his other foot under the back of the chair and smoothly hoist it up onto the stage after him. Sometimes it looked like he would miss or collapse back onto the dance floor, but he always accomplished this feat with perfect timing, never appearing even to break a sweat. The dancers were still a mix of girls in their late twenties to early thirties, dressed in sturdy court heels or slingbacks, both of which were practical for dancing. Only the girls with great legs would wear stilettos. The older girls would put great care into the preparation of their bouffant-type beehive hairstyles with assistance from Bel Air lacquer, which they could buy in most chemists' shops for 2s./6d. (12½p). This was the same price as Max Factor's Sheer Genius make-up, also popular with the girls and generally found along with other girly necessities in their short-strapped handbags. The centrepiece of the look would be an A-line dress ending just above the knees, with lots of full petticoats to make the skirt stand out. This they would layer with a cardigan or a jacket of a contrasting colour, completing the outfit with a string of pearls, matching earrings and a bracelet.

The younger girls favoured brightly coloured blouses, mini-skirts, maxi patent-leather belts and kitten heels, or a variation on the fashions on show each week on *Top Of The Pops*, although their variations were more Mary Quaint than Mary Quant.

In the mid-sixties, the boys were still smartly dressed in dark-coloured suits, white shirts and dark ties. The younger lads tended to dance without their suit jackets. Their hairstyles varied from the Tony Curtis DA, through to the American-styled crew cut and the Irish countryside-styled AOTP, short for 'all over the place' – wild manes which were occasionally tidied by a quick run of the fingers through them. Their shoes were still traditional leather, although the tips had started to get more pointed, some to the extent that they looked like they might pierce skin.

Following Dixie's dance set, the band thumped into an up-tempo line-up which usually started with the Dave Clark Five hit 'Glad All Over'. Most good ballrooms had a sprung floor, where the boards below the audience would give by as much as 3 inches. During a song like 'Glad All Over', with Mo really crack-ing out a solid beat on his snare and bass drums, the audience would appear to frantically bob up and down. With 2,000 danc-ers bouncing at any one time, you could be forgiven for thinking it dangerous. There'd never been any tales of collapsing floors, though.

Mitchell was more concerned about the floors' slippiness, which dancers adored because of the freedom of movement they afforded. The best slip was achieved through a combination of var-nishing and polishing, before layering a liberal sprinkling of flour on top. An even cheaper way to achieve a slippery dance floor was to use a combination of candle wax and paraffin, turning the ball-rooms into potential fire hazards. Again, just because a disaster had been averted up to this point, it didn't mean this would always be the case.

After 'Glad All Over', Mo counted 'a one, a two, a one, two, three, four' and they were straight into the infectious 'Still She Dances With You'. Barry's Vox Continental organ took over from Mo's cheerleading on this one. It went down a storm with the Galway audience; so well, in fact, that the audience begged to hear it again half an hour later and then once more in the second-to-last set.

The last dance was *always* a slow dance, allowing the (mostly male) punters to get out their final chat-up lines before the end of the night. A slow waltz was a perfect chance to practise this per-suasive skill. But the days of proper waltzing were officially over. The new approach was to grab hold of your partner and mooch around the ballroom as unobtrusively as possible, both to the other couples and your partner's modesty, since girls allowed only for contact at the shoulders. Sometimes a head on the shoulder or an arm around the waist was acceptable, but middles would have to remain at least 18 inches apart, a space apparently big enough for the Holy Ghost to nestle in. From the stage, this tended to make the couples look like a camp of Native American tepees on the move.

For Martin, one of the joys of being on stage was watching the dancers. People-watching was one of his favourite pastimes, and he found that he could still do it while singing. He scanned a sea of different scenarios: the unadulterated look of sheer joy on a young girl's face as the boy of her dreams walked towards her, turning to devastating sadness in a split second as he picked the girl beside her. Boys risked painful humiliation, some taking the time to study their prey from afar before pouncing. Martin would smile to himself as some boys moved in confidently, while others meekly slithered up, hoping to catch a girl unawares.

He was always amused at how quickly the activity on the dance floor picked up as the clock ran ever nearer to the last dance, particularly when he called the ladies' choice, which gave the girls a chance to make their mark. Let's remember; girls could (and would) turn down boys, but boys never ever turned down a ladies' choice. It was as simple as that. Cruel, but as Mr Bill Hartigan from Grangemouth in Scotland would have said: 'And there you have it!'

The ladies' choice also afforded the girls the chance to redeem any lost opportunities. If a girl had previously turned down one boy in favour of another, who'd chosen a different girl altogether, it gave them an opportunity to eat humble pie. A feeble excuse along the lines of 'I promised my mate I'd make up a foursome with her boyfriend's mate but I've just danced with him and... well, if your offer still holds, I'd enjoy having the last dance with you' usually saved face. The point was to hold out as long as possible in the hope that the boy of your dreams would request the last dance, otherwise you'd be left with the dregs. On the positive side, if your tactics failed and you ended the night alone, at least you'd be first in the queue at the cloakroom.

The responsibility for the timing of the ladies' set fell on Dixie's shoulders: call it too early in the dance and a girl still had no idea where she stood; too late and even her second choice could be gone.

From his vantage point, this and all the other dramas of the ballroom played out perfectly in front of Martin. Cupid could be very careful in aiming his arrows, and the dancers were very careful to be seen to take what were considered the correct steps, moving off gently onto the dance floor of life.

Surprisingly, one of the most popular songs that evening was 'The Ballad Of Jed Clampett', taken from the popular television series *The Beverly Hillbillies*, with Brendan taking up the banjo and the audience repeating the end of the chorus lines.

The Playboys received polite applause before they commenced the National Anthem, quite a thing considering applause was not a big thing in the ballrooms. By the end of the night, the dancers had other priorities on their mind. It didn't matter, though – the only approval the showbands really needed was ticket sales, and in Galway, they had played to a very respectable 1,174 paying customers.

The night's work completed, Smiley headed off into town with a couple of girls. The rest of the band packed away the gear and chatted to the stragglers. Mitchell didn't interfere with Dixie's usual procedure of picking up the flat fee of £400 for the night. Out of politeness to the venue manager, he accompanied Dixie to the pick-up. All in all, it had been a happy and very successful evening.

For the manager and the majority of his band, the evening ended with sandwiches and milk back at the Atlantic View. The following morning, however, one band member's bed was still unused, the sheets and pillowcase still as fresh as they had been the previous day…

CHAPTER TWENTY

A leopard never changes his spots and a priest never changes a fiver

Gentleman Jim Mitchell

As he had on the previous day, Jim Mitchell set off before The Playboys. This time he was on his way to Thurles. The Thursday evening dance was scheduled for the Red House Ballroom, not a terribly original name but maybe more realistic than calling a Belfast ballroom Romanos. It was intriguing in the same way that the names Oxford Circus or Piccadilly Circus were to those who'd never been to far-away London. Was London really *so* big that it actually had two permanent circuses, and so close together at that? Every time London was mentioned on the television news they'd show you a map of the West End and there they'd be, the two circuses signposted for all to see. Likewise, was the Red House in Thurles really so big that it had its own public ballroom? No. Just like you were disappointed when you learned that London's two circuses were mere roundabouts, The Playboys were equally disappointed to learn that Thurles's premier venue got its name from being an extension on the side of a red house – a very small red house at that.

The Red House was a priest-run venue, one of the better ones in fact, although when Father Pat met with Mitchell, all he could talk about was how well The Dixies did for him and how amazing The Freshmen were: 'Sure didn't everyone in the venue stop in their tracks when Billy Brown sang 'Cara Mia'? Didn't he only bring the blessed house down? Sure, you would have thought you were in the Gaiety Theatre in Dublin listening to Joseph Locke.' He'd then go on about how wonderful The Plattermen were and how amazing their new bus was – sure, wasn't it bigger than some of CIE's buses? And how great was their manager Jim Aiken? Didn't he only go and give them back a lucky penny even though the house was sold out?' Showbands were expected to give the ballroom owner a lucky penny – a small percentage of their fee – when they were paid at the end of the night, but some didn't. 'Aye, Jim Aiken is a truepenny to be sure.' Father Pat said all this not *to* Mitchell, but *at* him. Sure, if you were to believe Father Pat, The Plattermen could have sold out the Red House for a week at least!

Meanwhile, back in Galway, The Playboys were preparing for some en-route entertainment. Today's anti-boredom device was 'The Trial'. This rather too frequent game would occur when one in their midst was charged with some offence or other. Today, the accused was Smiley. The charge? Taking advantage of not one but two girls. Truth be told, his biggest crime was actually that he wasn't prepared to share his spoils with one of his fellow band members.

Brendan was to be the judge, and he carefully arranged it so that Smiley found himself not only in the dock but also in the driver's seat, his logic being that people found it hard to tell lies when they were preoccupied with something else at the same time.

As always, Robin was for the prosecution; Smiley requested Martin be for the defence; and Barry, as ever, was for slumber land. This left Dixie, Mo and Davy to serve on the jury. Many people would say a three-man jury was unfair, but (a) it was all their numbers allowed, and (b) it meant that you'd always get a verdict one way or the other.

Brendan, as the judge, read out the charge: 'That on or about a certain Wednesday in March 1964, Smiley, the trumpet player with the popular entertainment showband know as The Playboys, just back from a very successful tour of Scotland...'

'M'lud,' Robin interjected, 'with the greatest respect, I think you need to restrict yourself to reading only the charge.'

'Oh, on what grounds, sir?' Brendan bellowed.

'On the grounds that if you make this man out to be associated with such a great big band, then perhaps the jury might be swayed in his favour.'

'Pray tell, are there any cases you wish to cite?' Brendan asked, again going with the flow, as Smiley continued to drive and... smile.

'Yes, The Drifters versus Joe Dolan in the Mobile Wagon Court, June 1962.'

'Yes, I know the case, remind me of the details please.'

'Well, basically the members of The Drifters showband claimed that Joe Dolan sweated too much on stage.'

'Yes, yes I see where you're going with this, but in that case it was slightly different. Didn't Joseph Dolan assert that as he was the leader of the band, they could either like it or lump it and the case was thrown out of court?'

'Yes, but...'

'No, no we've wasted enough time on this,' Brendan interrupted. 'The charge is that on that certain Wednesday night in the townland of Galway, he was a stop-out and acquired information on two girls...'

'No, sir, I think you mean had knowledge of...' Now it was Robin's turn to interrupt.

'Yes, that's what I said, had knowledge of two girls, names unknown.'

'Oh, I knew their names all right,' Smiley admitted, 'the blonde was Maeve and the brunette was Carmel.'

'Silence in court, sir. You'll have your turn to speak in time. We'll hear the case for the prosecution first, I think.'

'Thank you m'lud,' Robin responded, and then in a whisper, 'that would be fitting with tradition.'

'What's that you said?!' Brendan bellowed.

'I said that knitting is a great tradition, sir.'

'Quite, yes, yes.'

'I'd first like to call Davy as a witness.'

'My lord, I object,' Martin said, making his first interruption.

'On what grounds do you wish to object, sir?' Brendan the judge asked.

'Well, sir, it's highly unusual to call a member of the jury as a witness,' Martin replied.

'Pray bear with me, m'lud, you'll see where I'm going with this.' Robin said smugly.

'Okay, but be careful, I'll be watching you. The defence has a point, and I don't want any appeals on this case.'

'Thank you, m'lud,' Robin replied to the judge, and then addressed Davy, 'Tell me, do you share a room with Smiley?'

'I do, aye.'

'And do you know where he was last night?'

'Objection!' Martin offered. 'What this man thought Smiley did yesterday evening is pure conjecture Your Honour.'

'Objection upheld.'

'Okay Davy, could you tell me if Smiley slept in his room yesterday evening?'

'No, he did not.'

'That's all with this witness, m'lud,' Robin said, concluding his first round of questioning.

'Tell me,' Martin said, beginning his cross-examination of Davy, 'how do you know Smiley didn't sleep in his bed last night? Were you awake all night?'

'No I wasn't, but when I woke up this morning, his bed was still freshly made.'

'But if you weren't awake all night, how do you know that Smiley didn't come into the room late, fall asleep, wake up before you and make his bed?'

'Actually I don't, sir,' Davy replied sheepishly.

'That's all at this time with this witness.'

'I'd like to call Brendan,' Robin announced next.

'Objection, you can't possibly call a judge in a case he's presiding over,' Martin protested.

'Overruled,' Brendan said, 'needs must.'

'Brendan, were you on stage yesterday evening with Smiley?'

'Yes, I was.'

'And did you see him leave with two young girls, one blonde and one brunette, at the end of the night?'

'Yes, I did in fact, greedy bar steward; both of them had cally jupaley.'

'Excuse me Your Honour, but the young girls' cally jupaley, sorry, I mean beautiful bottoms of course, and the fact they were cally jupaley doesn't have anything whatsoever to do with this case,' Martin interrupted.

'I think they do and I'm the judge.'

'No, you're the witness.'

'Sorry, yes of course, but my point as a witness would be that it was the girls' cally jupaley that led Smiley astray.'

'The prosecution rests, Your Honour,' Robin offered hopelessly.

'The defence calls Smiley.'

'Yes, I'm here,' Smiley offered hopefully.

'Can you tell me, Smiley,' Martin asked expansively, 'did you once say that all girls believe that boys are only after one thing?'

'Yes.'

'And did you also tell me that the secret of success was to make them think that it was only *their* one thing that you were after?'

'Yes?' Smiley replied, sounding like he was being hung out to dry.

'Well, don't you think it would be impossible to be with two girls at the same time and make them both think that it was *only* their one thing that you were after?'

'You might have a point there, I've never thought about it that way.'

'My case rests, Your Honour,' Martin declared proudly.

'Mine doesn't,' Smiley said while searching for a gap on the left-hand side of the road. 'I'd like to call Maeve and Carmel as witnesses.'

'But they're long gone,' Robin protested.

'No, they're not. They live up here on the left, somewhere … it was dark, let's see… ah yes, here it is, my Aunty Nuala's house. Maeve and Carmel are her daughters – my cousins. I stayed here last night *and* they've invited us all back for a late breakfast.'

'Aye, sound, first class,' Brendan said. 'Case dismissed of course.'

In they went, and they all ate a hearty meal which they thoroughly enjoyed because, apart from Jim Mitchell, they had all missed the breakfast that was included in their room rate at the hotel. Although they were each making a lot of money, none of them liked spending it unless they had to. They were all fast developing the showband member's traditional short limbs and deep pockets. Stopping off with various relations along their many routes had become a popular pastime to break up the journey, enjoy some homespun hospitality and save some money into the bargain.

The dance that evening was good, if not great. As we've already discussed, the priests answered to a higher power than a bank manager or to the softness of their mattress. This attitude is also evident as much in their dealing with the audience as with the musicians.

Dancers will go into a ballroom as individuals, but once inside they will react to circumstances and the music as a body of people; they don't know how not to. So if there is, shall we say, not a particularly pleasant atmosphere in the ballroom, they will react accordingly. Mitchell had already sussed this when he opened his first ballroom, the Dreamland, and he made it his business that his staff made it *their* business to look after both the audience and the band. Mitchell insisted that his employees made both the dancers and the band feel equally welcome in his establishment. In doing so, he claimed, there was a pretty good chance that both band and audience would enjoy their evening and wish to return.

There was no support group in Thurles, so The Playboys were on stage from 9 p.m. until 1 a.m., or 'Nine o'clock to eternity' as Robin claimed.

At 10.45 p.m., four musicians left the stage for their 15-minute break. This left Martin on guitar and vocals, Barry on bass, Dixie on keyboards and Robin on drums. Martin quite enjoyed these infrequent sets; with everyone on strange instruments, they produced a different kind of energy. He always stuck a couple of Dean Martin songs into the set and, before you knew it, Brendan would be back on guitar, Mo on drums, Davy on bass and Smiley on keyboards and vocals, all suitably refreshed and decked out in reversed suits (that is, changing from chocolate jackets and banana trousers to chocolate trousers and banana jackets). Brendan's four-piece section of the band specialised purely in country songs, and was very popular in the rural ballrooms. After 15 minutes, they were back to full strength and off with a sprint to the end of the set and the end of the night.

Gear packed up, they were all back in the hotel tucking into their tea and sandwiches by 2.15 a.m., only this time none of the troops were missing so there'd be no need for a court martial on the following day's journey. Doubtless they would find some other novel way to entertain themselves.

CHAPTER TWENTY-ONE

Money doesn't grow on trees.
It's much simpler than that:
they just print the fecking stuff

Johnny McIvor

The following Friday night found the boys in the Ponderosa, Clonakilty, on the south coast of Ireland about 26 miles to the south-west of Cork. This gig was what was known as 'a sweet one', in that Mitchell had negotiated them a fabulous fee of £750. The reason was that the ballroom was reopening that very night and the owner, a local publican, had spent a lot of money doing the place up, but hadn't managed to get any of the 'A' list bands.

The Playboys from Castlemartin were pretty high up the 'B' list, and available on this prime Friday night just before Lent. Truth be told, Mitchell had been trying to get the big fee – the grand – but hadn't quite made it, nor could he persuade the publican, Johnny McIvor, to give him a percentage. McIvor reckoned with the money he was spending on promotion he was going to have a big crowd no matter who was playing. In terms of the volume of promotion, he was as good as his word. The minute that Mitchell hit the town of Clonakilty, he spotted posters for The Playboys all over. And there was yet more: Johnny McIvor had stretched banners from telegraph pole to telegraph pole across the street in the town centre, proclaiming that 'Yes, The Playboys are coming, but this time they are coming to the Ponderosa!' Mitchell spied four such banners. In every shop window he passed he saw Playboys posters, and an announcement that on the opening night all girls would get in free before 8 p.m. The support band, Halfdeck, was also well covered in the promotion.

Johnny McIvor greeted Mitchell like a long-lost friend and proudly showed him around the ballroom, pointing out the various refurbishments as they went along.

'Look up there' McIvor said, pointing above them. 'I had to replace the entire ceiling.'

'Wow, was it damp or something?' Mitchell asked.

McIvor turned his head from side to side, signalling 'no', but at the same time checking that there was nobody nearby listening in. 'Come 'ere, hi, and I'll tell you,' the publican eventually said, leading Mitchell back through the dressing rooms and into his office.

By the way that the dressing rooms has been done out, Mitchell could immediately tell that McIvor cared about his bands. Not a penny had been spared in helping the visiting musicians to while away the time. He had installed a bar, a pool table, a darts board and a card table in one corner. The walls of his office, which joined the ballroom to his pub, were lined from floor to ceiling with LP sleeves. Every artist you could think of from the forties through to the present, from jazz to folk to blues to pop, from the Clancy Brothers to The Royal Showband via The Beatles and John Lee Hooker.

'Hi, would yer like a KitKat?' he asked, taking a seat and tossing one from a full 48-bar box that was just behind his desk.

It wasn't the fact that Johnny McIvor had so many bars of his favourite food that betrayed his sweet tooth; no, it was the fervour with which he removed the wrapping and the enthusiasm with which he bit into the first finger of the chocolate-coated biscuit, showing just how badly he needed the fix of cocoa. Sugar now running freely through his veins, he seemed to relax a little as he leaned back in his chair and said reflectively, 'The things I could tell you about this place.'

'The roof for instance?' Mitchell replied, as he, not quite so enthusiastically, munched on his KitKat.

'Hi aye, exactly,' Johnny said, stalling until he could scoff down the remaining three fingers of chocolate. He'd a habit of addressing someone as 'Hi' instead of their name. 'Right, hi. There's been a building on this site for ages. I think it was a barn or something first off and then a store. Then the store began deteriorating so much that it was a danger to everyone, but I couldn't get the feckers to sell it to me for what I knew was the right price. Next thing I knew, they sold to this out-of-town man, a man from Fermoy, the son of a rich farmer, hi, a lad by the name of McKee, a good lad but too much money too young. Anyway, sure didn't he have these great plans and it was all going well and then he was disappearing up to Dublin and they said he began losing a lot of money on the gee-gees, hi. It didn't take long before he got in over his head with some bookie, and then the ballroom really started to go downhill because he wasn't paying attention to it. I knew he was doing badly because when he was having a great night we'd be packed to the rafters in the pub, and when he wasn't, my barman's face was as long as an undertaker's top coat.

'Then the word around town was that the bookie was leaning on McKee. This is all true, hi. One night, two of the bookie's men came down and tried to beat McKee up and, when he still wouldn't cough up, you won't believe this, hi, but they took him for a walk up in the attic. They could tell it was flimsy at best and they made him walk across. He fell through of course. Great scam, isn't it? Just like in the movies – a good way to kill someone but make it look like an accident. You always get a better class of crooks in New York though, don't you? When these two Dublin heads made him go for a walk and he fell through the ceiling, instead of clearing off and leaving him to die of his injuries, didn't they only come into my pub to have a drink, and after a few drinks didn't my barman only pick up the drift of their conversation, so he came and told me, I told the sergeant, and when I visited next door there was McKee lying on the floor like one of my daughter's discarded dolls. I tell her that dolls don't grow on trees, and she, the cheeky skitter, hi, do you know what she said back to me?'

Mitchell didn't know, but he did notice that McIvor used the pause to open two cans of Fanta and another KitKat. Mitchell accepted the former but refused the latter.

'She's only 5 years old and she says, she says to me, "Aye, daddy, I know dolls don't grow on trees, but money does, and we could use that money to buy more dolls, couldn't we?" The wee skitter. She gets that from her mother. She's a wee dote though. So I phoned for an ambulance. There was blood everywhere, hi. He looked to me like he was a goner, but he managed to pull through. Anyway, auld man McKee took care of things when he found out. He put the boy back on the straight and narrow again and sold the ballroom to me for a song, hi. You know, because I'd looked after his son and all. I think he thought I'd saved his life. It's perfect for me, I love the auld bands and it's right next door to the pub, so it's just the ticket really. I was able to spend a lot of money on the place, but I tell you what, you'll never get me up into that roof space. Who wants to walk the plank for not paying your bills? Now isn't that the most stupid thing you've ever heard? Pay your bills and you'll sleep easy, nothing should come between a man and his sleep. It's not even as difficult as my daughter says, that the money grows on trees. It's much easier than that; sure, don't they just print the fecking stuff?'

Mitchell and McIvor discussed the ballroom and showband scene in great detail for the next hour or so, and Mitchell thoroughly enjoyed the conversation, not to mention another Fanta, a cup of tea, a packet of Tayto crisps and an egg sandwich, in that order. They talked about the possibility of Mitchell booking the Ponderosa as part of his own circuit, thereby getting McIvor the better bands, not to mention the keener deals. Mitchell was up for it too. Another venue under his wing would give him all the more clout on the circuit. They agreed to discuss it further following the dance.

Mitchell had booked The Playboys into Brown's hotel, so named, he felt, because of the brown sheets on every bed in the house, and situated just outside the village on the Cork side. By the time The Playboys arrived at 5.30 p.m., everything was set up for them to go straight to their rooms, drop off their stuff, freshen up and join Mitchell in the dining room for an early tea, their traditional five steaks and four fish suppers.

The Playboys' night at the Ponderosa was an amazing one. Thanks to Johnny McIvor's thorough groundwork, and the extensive local promotion, the 'House Full' sign went up at 8.45 p.m. – 1,680 dancers had purchased tickets, which was on top of the 220 female dancers who had taken advantage of McIvor's free offer. McIvor had charged 7s., which Mitchell thought was a bit on the high side for The Playboys, but McIvor claimed, 'Hi, I only want the better class of clientele in my establishment, on top of which, I have to pick up the cost of the free tickets from somewhere.'

The Freshmen were playing the Arcadia in Cork that night, and McIvor, who knew The Freshmen's trombone player, Sean Mahon, persuaded him to bring a few of the boys down after their show. 'Hi, as many as you can would be great. We'll look after you well, we're having a bit of a party, don't worry how late you are.'

They didn't worry about how late they were; they arrived in the company of Father Brian D'Arcy, *the* showband priest, at 2.45 a.m., 75 minutes after The Playboys had played 'Jambalaya' to a storming reception. McIvor, decked out in bow tie and formal black suit, just like Sammy Barr every night at the Flamingo in Ballymena, was the perfect host and the perfect ballroom manager. Nothing was too much trouble, and everything that needed sorting out was attended to immediately.

Martin Dean in particular was nervous about meeting the great Billy Brown. He couldn't believe how much presence the man had, even when he was off the bandstand. Brown was very friendly; his philosophy seemed to be that he smoked, drank and spent his money because people who did not do any of those things always seemed to be miserable as sin. He was very gracious about Martin's compliments, and said he was also hearing great things about The Playboys. The band's work done for the night, both groups and assorted Ponderosa people retired to McIvor's bar to continue the celebrations. None of The Playboys were prolific drinkers, but a certain clear liquid from Russia found little resistance as it slipped down a few throats that evening. Martin stuck to a couple of Fantas and the showband priest stuck to orange juice. Johnny McIvor had met the famous showband priest, Father Brian, a few times over the years, and he still looked young, very young. McIvor said, 'Hi, are you sure you don't have a painting up in your attic ageing away?'

Inevitably, the conversation wound around to showband stories. The funniest Martin could remember was about a band from the south. They had got so into the show aspect that they would plan amazing grand entrances. On one occasion, in a ballroom near a riding school, the lead singer came up with the idea to come on stage on horseback to start the evening off. He had a plan: the band would take their places behind the closed curtains and at the last moment the horse, a beautiful snow-white stallion, would be led on and positioned between the bass amp and the drum kit. When the horse was in position, the singer would mount his trusted steed with the assistance of a stepladder and nod to his manager and, hey presto, the curtains would open.

The band members took their positions, the horse was led on. The audience on the other side of the curtain were obviously intrigued by all the behind-the-curtain noises. As planned, the singer climbed up the ladder and mounted the horse. The manager took the ladder away, rushed to the side of the stage and, receiving the signal from his singer, opened the curtains. The introduction to their opening song of the evening was 'Champion The Wonder Horse'. The audience, totally transfixed by the marvellous opening, burst into applause and started screaming and shouting. The horse, scared out of its wits by all the pandemonium, started to pee, the liquid flowing into the back of the bass amp, which electrocuted the horse, whose response was to drop a rather large number two. He then reared up on his hind legs, throwing the singer halfway across the stage in the process. Quick as a flash, the manager closed the curtains again and the band and audience collapsed into fits of laughter.

The other great Bin Liners' entrance story had to do with a gig they were playing at the Galtymore in London's Cricklewood. The band arrived to set up their gear, only to find that they were to be the second band. On top of which, they discovered that the venue had a revolving stage just like the one The Royal Showband proudly stood on at the end of their performance on *Sunday Night At The London Palladium*. The singer thought this was great, and decided to set up their gear facing the back of the stage. They would start to play as the stage revolved, revealing them to their audience during the first song. Coming on second, they didn't have a chance to rehearse their entrance, but it all looked secure. The drummer counted the band in – the signal for the stage to start turning. For the first 5 seconds everything seemed to be going grand, then, as the band came into view, no one could hear them; it looked as though they were all miming. They'd only gone and left the speaker cabinets on the static part of the stage, and the leads connecting the speakers to the amplifier were snatched out as they revolved round, thus shooting another of the Bin Liners' great entrances down in flames.

Apparently, the same singer was also desperate to have his band be the first band in Ireland to go on stage wearing black leather trousers, which at the time were very popular in America. The manager nearly dropped dead when he found out the price of the trousers, so he came up with a clever plan: he persuaded his band to wear black bin-liners, stapled up the back of the leg to make them look like tight leather trousers. This was fine for the first set of dances, but by the third set, when they started to warm up a bit, the boys found the bin-liner leggings so hot that the sweat was literally spilling into their shoes by the cupful. Hence, The Playboys christened them 'The Bin Liners'.

You'd wonder how bands like this continued to exist, wouldn't you? They always seemed to go from mishap to mishap. On another occasion, they were due to go to England. The majority of the band flew into London, but Mickey the drummer and Fergie the singer hated flying. It wasn't the fear of being so high in the sky that worried them; they were more worried about the speed at which they'd hit the ground if the engine failed. So they both decided to cross by ferry, along with the equipment. They arrived in Belfast with plenty of time to spare, went and checked their wagon onto the Heysham ferry and went back into Belfast for a few pints. They came out of the pub a bit worse for wear, wandered back down to the docks and climbed on board. The following morning, they woke up with very sore heads and searched the ferry high and low and in between, but couldn't find their wagon anywhere. Eventually, they realised their mistake. In their stupor they had boarded the Liverpool ferry and not the Heysham one. At the same time, their wagon was creating havoc on the Heysham Ferry because there was no one to drive it off, so it was blocking the exit for all the other vehicles.

Martin loved the passion with which The Freshmen told these tales, and even though they had obviously heard them on many occasions before, the members of The Freshmen were laughing just as much and as heartily as the members of The Playboys. Stories like the one about the Bin Liners' singer. He was, apparently, the most quick-witted, and possibly the worst, singer on the circuit. After one of their appearances down in the country, where they managed to struggle through an entire set without any mishaps, the ballroom owner came up to him and said, 'I have to say that without a shadow of doubt you are *the* worst chanter I've ever had in here.' The singer, quick as a flash, replied, 'Do you think if I was a good singer, I'd be playing in a dive like this?'

Not to be outdone in the story stakes, Brendan told his favourite Smiley tale. Apparently, on one of The Playboys' nights off, he and

Smiley went to a dance in Cookstown Town Hall. They arrived late, which meant that most of the real talent had already been spoken for. Smiley, never a man to be put off by outward appearances, always believed that there was great beauty lurking on the inside if only you took the time to discover it, especially if you could remove any clothes in the process. He spotted this girl, well more of a woman really, in her early thirties with black, curly hair. She'd obviously been left sitting all night. Smiley went up to her and said: 'Could I have the pleasure of this dance please?'

'And sure wouldn't the pleasure be all mine,' Esther, for that was her name, replied.

Smiley and Esther did several laps of the Cookstown Town Hall. Apart from anything else, dancing around the floor, especially from Smiley's high vantage point, gives you a chance to view the other talent in the ballroom.

'Esther, has anyone ever told you that you are, without doubt, the most beautiful woman in this ballroom?'

'Well actually, no – no one has said that, but it's very kind of you to say so.' Esther was so excited that her voice had gone up an octave. A few laps later, the three songs of that particular dance set completed, Smiley politely bid Esther goodbye.

He repaired to the mineral stall, and then decided to return to Esther, who had just sat out the last three dances. Smiley ignored this and made a fuss about inviting her out for another dance. Esther was over the moon and beaming from ear to ear as she and Smiley took to the dance floor, this time with a lot more confidence. After four laps of the ballroom, Smiley said: 'You know, Esther, I'd have to say you are the most beautiful woman here, just look at you with your curly hair and your gorgeous dress, sure aren't I the luckiest man in Cookstown Town Hall tonight? Tell me, Esther, has anyone ever told you that you look like Elizabeth Taylor?'

'Well, no, Smiley, actually they haven't.'

They danced another couple of laps.

'Tell me, Esther,' Smiley continued in full flow, 'would there be any chance, any chance at all, you'd save the last dance for me?'

'Sure aren't you the perfect gentleman, Smiley, and I'd be delighted,' she demurely replied, clocking his pioneer pin (worn proudly by the men who were off the drink). Such men were in great demand in the ballrooms, and Esther continued with genuine enthusiasm, 'The pleasure would be all mine.'

Two dances later and they're lapping the dance floor again, and this time it's the last dance and Smiley says: 'Esther, I hope you don't think that I'm being forward or anything, but would there be any chance I could walk you home?'

Esther, God bless her, is in seventh heaven, but then she appears troubled. 'Smiley, er… the only problem is that I live miles away on my father's farm and you can't drive a car up our lane, you have to walk.'

'It would be my pleasure to walk you home, my pleasure, Esther.'

Fifty-five minutes later, and Smiley is out in the wilds of the countryside, walking up the lane arm in arm with Esther. About halfway along, Smiley said, 'And this is all your father's property, Esther?'

'This and the whole way down the other side of the hill,' Esther replied proudly. Another few steps and Smiley decided to make his move: 'It's a great farm, Esther; I've never seen one so big. Tell me, Esther, would there be any chance at all that I could have a kiss?'

Esther allowed an appropriately decent amount of time to pass before replying, 'That would be very pleasant, I'm sure.' So they kiss passionately, very passionately, and soon both their faces have a red glow.

'Goodness that was beautiful, Esther, would there be any chance I could have another one?' No sooner said than done, and this time even more passionately. Smiley decided to push it a stage further.

'Ah, Esther, you don't know what you're doing to me. Look, I hope this is not too forward, but you are so beautiful and you kiss great… is there any chance I could have a grope of your magnificent breasts?'

Esther mutters something under her breath and obliges, unbuttoning the top of her dress and guiding Smiley's large hands through the maze of straps, frills and what have you onto her breasts. During all of this, Smiley is filling the time by looking all around him and going on and on to Esther about her father's farm.

Then it was back to the business in hand, as it were. Both became quite carried away at this point and Smiley, ever the gentleman, soon had another request. 'Gosh, Esther, that's just brilliant, I was wondering was there any chance I could have a fe… a fe… a fe… ' Smiley gasps. He's now so excited that he can't quite get his tongue around the polite word for a grope.

'A *field*!' Esther gasped, misunderstanding him, and now so excited herself that her voice has slipped into an even higher octave. 'You want to know if you could have a field, Smiley? For goodness' sake, man, you can have the whole fecking farm when my father dies.'

As the stories continued, it transpired that another northern showband, The Plattermen, were truly wild on the road. After a gig, they'd follow the usual procedure of divvying up their fee. They'd put the money in the lid of a biscuit tin before gathering around it. Next, a lighter would be presented and, incredibly, they'd ignite the notes. The first musician to lose his nerve and extinguish the flames lost his share of the pot. That band also had a drummer who was game for everything and would do absolutely anything for a bet. He once agreed to nurse a dead rabbit – complete with all its maggots – that they'd pick up at the side of the road if everyone would give him a fiver (£35 being the equivalent of £420 today). He arrived at the gig covered in maggots, and hid the rabbit behind his drum kit. During the dance, he lobbed it over the heads of the band and into the dancers, with the result of total pandemonium.

Then there were other tales of how some of the big showbands went through their money like it was water. For instance, before the days of remote controls, one of the members of The Clipper Carlton spent an absolute fortune having the local television engineer come around to his house and dismantle the control unit of his television set, connect up a multi-core cable to the various exposed leads and then lay said cable across the floor of his room over to the arm of his armchair, where he had him re-assemble the control unit of the television into the arm of the chair, just so that he could operate his television without getting up. That led on to other Clipper Carlton stories, like the one where the band dumped their music stands to become a showband. The original leader and piano player was quite old and not really up to it any more, but they were a loyal lot and, rather than get rid of him, they stuffed newspapers down between the hammers and the strings of the piano, and with the new, louder racket the band was making, you could no longer hear him.

The Playboys all listened in disbelief when someone in the company told a story about several members of one big showband going to see another. The next day, a couple of the lads were discussing the show's merits.

'I thought they were great,' said one of the chaps, the newest member of the visiting band.

'So did I,' said the other.

To get to the point of this tale, let's say Jimmy, for example, was the name of a third, and very important, member of the visiting band.

'Do you know what Jimmy thought?' the new boy asked.

'Yeah, I think he liked them musically,' replied the other, 'but I know for certain he fancied the saxophone player.'

The new boy thought for a minute. 'I don't remember seeing any female members in the band?'

'*Exactly*,' replied the other, winking, 'there wasn't!' And then, as the realisation set in, he added, 'Don't look so shocked.'

Afterwards, Davy, The Playboys' bass player, had Robin explain this story in detail to him.

The Playboys headed off to their (individual) beds that morning at 5.40 a.m. Before Mitchell left, he'd finalised a deal with Johnny McIvor that gave him exclusive booking rights of McIvor's Ponderosa Ballroom. In the good-hearted negotiations, Mitchell had asked for 5 per cent. McIvor had claimed that he wanted the Dreamland boss to be making enough money out of the deal to pay good attention to the Ponderosa, so he suggested 7.5 per cent and they shook hands on it, with Mitchell extending an invitation to see his ballroom in action. It wasn't that Mitchell thought Johnny McIvor had anything to learn, for he hadn't, he just wanted to return some of his fine hospitality, and if they both knew each other's environments they could enjoy a much better working relationship.

Martin Dean couldn't sleep when he went to bed; he and Brendan continued a conversation across the darkness of their room for another hour, until dawn in fact. Even after that, Martin lay awake, thinking. He'd been happy to discover that Billy Brown, the great showband legend, was equally great as a man, very down to earth, with a great sense of humour and, if anything, quite an introvert. Martin thought it was interesting that after chatting with some-one famous, when you eventually got to reflect on the words they somehow took on a greater significance, as if they forming into an anecdote that you'd perhaps be able to tell your children one day.

Martin eventually drifted off to sleep a very contented man. He made two resolutions that evening: one concerning his career and the other concerning Hanna Hutchinson.

CHAPTER TWENTY-TWO

And when love breaks,
it's broken for good

Martin McClelland

The fourth day, the Saturday, saw a very tired bunch of Playboys and their manager arrive in convoy in Naas, County Kildare, to play, and stay, at Reid's Hotel. This was to be yet another night to remember, this time for a completely different reason.

To start with, everything was perfect: the facilities, both in the hotel and the ballroom, were excellent, and the equipment check went well. There was a wedding reception in the afternoon, so The Playboys retired to their rooms to catch up on some sleep. They drew a great crowd, just under a thousand, which covered their £400 fee (hotel accommodation was thrown in), and the dance seemed to be going well.

No one could really tell how the trouble started. Dixie remembered hearing some kind of shouting out in the entrance hall as he was announcing their sixth set of the evening. He put it down to high spirits and didn't worry too much. Martin was singing one of his own songs, which was called, inappropriately enough for what was to follow, 'Broken For Good', when he was sure that he saw this girl fly through the air and land on some lad's back. Again, his first reaction was to think that it was all a bit of high-spirited fun. The girl looked like she was either the bride or the bridesmaid from the wedding. Either that, or she was a dancer out looking for a husband to marry on the spot. Then the affray moved closer to the stage. Martin could see that the girl was using her stiletto to try and punch a hole in a man's skull.

Suddenly, some other lad got behind the couple and tried to prise the fighting girl off the boy's back. By this point, the front of her dress was stained crimson with his blood. No sooner had the second boy come to the rescue than two other girls tore into him with their shoes. Then an older man came into it and did something Martin had never seen a man do before; he raised his right hand high and swung it down towards the two new girls, hitting them with such force with the back of his hand that he quite literally sent them flying across the dance floor. The dancers opened up, like Moses' parting of the Red Sea, to make way for the flying girls. In the melee, another older gent chinned the first, whereupon a woman removed his coat and the two men tore into each other. The first girl continued drilling for brains with her shoe in the man's skull.

All hell broke loose, and within three minutes the entire ballroom was at it. The Playboys looked on in shock. They could hear grunts, groans and bones cracking from men and women, boys and girls alike. Unlike in the movies, when these things were perfectly scripted and choreographed for the cameras, this was an undignified and ugly affair. It was a real eye-opener for Martin, who couldn't believe how vicious some of the girls were, and they weren't always saving their most violent behaviour for the opposite sex.

The girls' favourite weapons appeared to be their shoes, although Brendan had to repel one girl, who seemed to have taken a fancy to the steel microphone stand, to use, he assumed, to the same end. The Gardaí, about six of them, arrived ten minutes later, but they merely stood around the door. The Playboys had given up any pretence of performing at this point, and moved most of their equipment to the safety of the back of the stage. Brendan said that the Gardaí were being clever. 'You never rush into the middle of a hurricane to stop it,' he advised his fellow band members, 'you let it burn itself out. That's what they're doing, they're waiting until the worst of this is over and then they'll jump in to pick up the pieces.'

Several minutes later, that's exactly what happened. But guess what the biggest surprise of the night for the band was? Barely 20 minutes after the police stepped in, The Playboys were back on the bandstand performing to a full house, well almost, who danced away as though they'd done nothing else all night. Yes, there were a few bruised faces, bloody noses and ruined hairstyles in view, and that was just the boys. Actually no, that's not strictly true, because most of the boys wore so much Brylcreem that they could have ventured out into a hurricane without a single hair being blown out of place. The girls' beehives were another matter altogether, though. They looked quite attractive in a Calamity Jane kind of way, with strands of hair falling down around the front of their faces, and their Sunday-best clothes torn here and there. Boys and girls, men and women alike all shared an even greater number of bruised egos but, to all intents and purposes, it was back to business as usual; the business of attracting or catching a member of the opposite sex. If anything, The Playboys noticed that during the smoochy sets that evening, the dancers were much closer than usual; that is, there was no space for the Holy Ghost between their bodies, and when it came to the ladies' choice, well, the gay abandon with which they tore across that dance floor was something to behold.

Afterwards, the Gardaí sergeant told the band that the trouble that had erupted on the dance floor had been brewing for quite some time, a good few years in fact. It had all started, believe it or not, in the twenties — according to the sergeant, who was enjoying a hot toddy as The Playboys were tucking into their late-night sandwiches and milk — when a local girl, Kathleen O'Neill, a rich farmer's daughter, fell in love with a local poor boy, Sean Bradley, who worked for her father. That should have been that, you'd have thought, and they should have lived happily ever after – were it not for the fact that Sean, although flattered by Kathleen's attentions, was not himself in love with her. No, he was in love with another, a young lady of humble roots by the name of Jane Foye. To add insult to injury, Jane had been Kathleen's best friend at school. Jane and Sean were wed, and lived happily ever after. Kathleen and her second choice, Billy O'Neill (no relation – at least none that could be traced in the previous ten generations), were married and lived unhappily ever after. Fast forward 40 years and what do you know? Jane and Sean's first born, Connor, and Kathleen and Billy's first born, Lizabeth, meet each other, fall in love and eventually marry that afternoon in Reid's Hotel.

If Kathleen had never forgiven Sean, then Kathleen's second daughter, Dolores, had forgiven him even less. When, on the wedding day, Dolores had come across Connor, apparently with another girl, she'd thrown a fit and was soon up on Connor's back, walloping him around the head with her high heel!

It transpires, as it tends to, that the girl Connor had been caught talking to was not in fact the *other* girl, but his long-lost cousin, home from England. All of this should have been completely innocent enough, but it still proved to be the perfect excuse to vent 40 years worth of anger. It would have been perfect fodder for Martin to write a song around, if only he could find a way of fitting all of the above into four verses, two choruses and three minutes.

At one point during the fight, Martin was terrified. Not for his own safety, though – he could see the look in people's eyes. It was this that worried him more than the violence. Down in the audience, the violence seemed to be contagious. It was a look that said that, although most of the crowd hadn't a clue what they were fighting about, there was some invisible thing connecting them, something very infectious, which willed all of them beyond their own comprehension and consciousness to become embroiled in the melee. It was almost tribal, as far as Martin could make out.

The last time that he had felt that power overcome an audience had been when he'd seen The Freshmen perform. That, however, had been a much more positive kind of energy, where the crowd, of which he had been a member, had been overcome by the power of Billy Brown's performance on stage and they'd all, at first individually and then collectively, connected into his magic, becoming overwhelmed by it.

For the second consecutive night, Martin found himself falling asleep thinking about Hanna Hutchinson. And then, after what felt like five minutes, Brendan was waking him up, warning him that it was just after midday, they were due to check out of their hotel and to be in the wagon in half an hour.

The Playboys' final stop on the mini-tour was Granard, in County Longford, to play at the Pride of West Meath ballroom. Yes, you read that correctly. The ballroom owner obviously had a great sense of humour, and thought it was a great hoot that you'd have to travel into the adjoining County Longford just to enjoy the best ballroom in West Meath!

In the bigger towns, Saturdays were the biggest dance nights, whereas in the country, Sundays were by far the best. Mitchell thought that this had a lot to do with how much more city folk worried about Monday mornings than country folk did.

The Pride of West Meath was packed, which was encouraging, as it was The Playboys' first appearance there. Following their experiences the previous night, the boys were ready for anything. It was a great dance, with the girls all lined up along the left side of the ballroom and the boys on the right. The minute that Dixie called the first dance, there was an almighty stampede. Every single dancer in the ballroom had been partnered off before the band had a chance to hit the first note of the first song, and moreover not a single person sat out the last dance, which was a first for The Playboys. The girls seemed friendly and the boys willing – a perfect dance crowd.

And it didn't end there either. The female friendliness wasn't focused exclusively on the locals: three of the band scored that night. And wasn't it typical that the nights you were away from home with a bed to spare, there was never anyone to share it with, yet on the one night of the trip when you didn't have a bed, there were girls virtually falling out of trees. In actual fact, The Playboys stood a better chance of talking the girls into the trees than into hotel rooms. Trees didn't tell stories – gossipy hotel staff did.

Apart from Smiley, the two others who scored that evening were the rhythm section, so they had a great night, on and off stage. Smiley hooked up with an absolute beauty who'd been dancing with the same boy all night. She took Smiley for a walk in the country, and 20 minutes later he returned with an even wider smile on his face. The two other couples went to opposite sides of a hedge, and both band members could hear the other trying to convince their respective dates to remove their garments. It was a dead heat – the chatting stopped on both sides of the hedge at just the same moment. Two minutes later, the boys were talking again, this time through the hedge to each other, and with a noticeable lack of enthusiasm for their female accomplices in their voices.

In all of this, it has to be said that sex was the legal tender of the ballroom scene. Alcohol was a distraction, indulged rather than embraced; drugs were practically unheard of, let alone used. Some of the city musicians, who were using showbands as stepping-stones to pop groups, might have been starting to experiment for the first time – with tabs of LSD to help distract them on the long journeys, and purple hearts (amphetamines) for an energy boost – but that was by no means the norm. Sexual attraction was *the* addiction. This fact was confirmed, if confirmation was needed, by the substantial prevalence of sexually transmitted diseases.

In winter or summer, it didn't matter, the aim was to talk the girls out of their clothes. A lot of the boys hadn't a clue what to do when they'd accomplished this amazing feat. Sometimes the girls had to guide them. There would be a lot of fumbling, cold sweats and 'Really?' then gentle cries of pain, then masculine cries of pleasure, then physical *and* mental relief. *Then* the boys knew how to go about things next time. Sure, what was all the fuss about; wasn't it as easy as taking a spin on a bike?

The most common phrase used by the girls who allowed the musicians to walk them as far, but no further, than their street corner was, 'Now promise you won't tell anyone?' Smiley's lips were forever sealed, so well sealed in fact that the next time the same girl met up with him, she'd question *him* on whether they did or didn't do the wild thing last time they met. The rhythm section, on the other hand, with their continual schoolboy-type giggling, gave their particular game away to one and all. However, that was only within the confines of their wagon; *the* golden rule in the showband world was that everything had to be concealed from wives, girlfriends and parents. No matter how much one musician may fall out with another, *no* tales of life on the road were ever relayed.

Dixie knew that his band, like every other band in the country, depended on this secrecy to thrive. He had advised the boys that disclosure of this type of information would not be tolerated. Anyone telling tales, true or false, would immediately be fired and branded a liar by all the remaining members. Gentleman Jim Mitchell, in turn, lectured them all individually on protection, personal hygiene and on the dangers of furious boyfriends, angry fathers and ugly brothers.

'Don't forget,' he would always say in conclusion, 'that within six months, God willing, we're going to be back playing in every town again. So whatever you do out there, whomever you're doing it with, for God's sake be careful.' Dixie repeated the warning to the band members, Smiley and the rhythm section in particular. Despite the distractions on the road though, once again, Martin Dean found himself thinking about Hanna.

On the way home, didn't they come across one of the strangest sights any of them had ever witnessed? Just outside of Monaghan, Dixie pointed out to them what looked like The Freshmen's van parked along the side of the road. Around the very next corner, he said, 'God, and there they are, hitching a lift, all neatly decked out in the matching pink suits.'

'I hate to break this to you, head,' said Robin, who was hogging the front window seat as usual, 'but they're not matching pink suits!' Dixie was so flabbergasted that he nearly drove the wagon into the ditch.

'All I can say,' he said, when he'd regained his composure, 'is that I'm glad the tiger was in the tank and didn't have to witness that sight for sore eyes.'

'Right, Dixie,' Brendan said, 'shove that pedal to the metal. They'll be after us, they're famous for it.'

With their superior van, The Freshmen caught up with The Playboys on the other side of Monaghan, pasted The Playboys' wagon, and their tiger's tail, with eggs and flour and drove off into the distance, mooning at them through the windows of their plush van. Not familiar with mooning? Well, what's large and round, you know, like the moon? On second thoughts... I'm fairly sure there's no hair on the moon!

At 6.43 on that Monday morning, driving down the steep hill into Castlemartin, Smiley, Dixie and Martin (each being awake) experienced one of the most wondrous views in the world. The sun was rising, and over to the left you could see its reflection, a crystal clear crimson on the waters of Lough Neagh, and there, in the foreground, was Castlemartin, rising out of the green trees and surrounding fields. All of this was set against the spectacular background of the Sperrin Mountains reaching up to a deep blue sky. It was an awe-inspiring view, perhaps made all the more special because it was the beginning of a new day, and no one in the village, apart from the trio of musicians, was around to experience it. Dixie and Smiley wound down their windows. The air smelled so fresh, so new, so clean. In a way it was a shame that they were all going to waste most of this beautiful day by sleeping through it.

CHAPTER TWENTY-THREE

Sure, the producer's Aran sweater gives his preference away

Gentleman Jim Mitchell

As 1964 progressed, Dickie Rock had two more number one hit singles, 'I'm Yours' and 'Candy Store'; Eileen Reid & The Cadets, in their snazzy uniforms, had a number one with 'Fallen Star'; as did Brendan Bowyer & The Royal Showband with 'Bless You' and Butch Moore & The Capitol with 'Down Came The Rain'. Joe Dolan & The Drifters reached number four with 'Answer To Everything'; Sean Fagan & The Pacific had 'She Wears My Ring' (number three) and 'Distant Drums' (number five); and Brendan O'Brien & The Dixies had two chart entries – 'I'm Counting On You' (number six), and the follow-up, 'It's Only Make Believe', bettered that to claim number four.

So that was The Royal Showband, The Dixies, The Cadets, The Miami, The Drifters, The Pacific and The Capitol all holding their own in the Irish charts, even though the likes of The Beatles (three Irish numbers ones), Peter & Gordon (who had a number one with the infectious Lennon and McCartney song 'World Without Love'), Dave Clark Five (two number ones), The Searchers (two number ones), Roy Orbison (three number ones) and Jim Reeves (two number ones) were all extremely popular.

The Rolling Stones, who could never escape their runner-up position behind The Beatles, had yet to get into their stride as far as the Irish charts were concerned (they scored three Top 5 entries in 1964 but had yet to clinch that first elusive number one). They did, however, cause a bit of a commotion with their first visit to Belfast. The headlines the next day detailed how disgusting and outrageous they were, but when it got down to it, it was merely that several girls had fainted and, as they were dragged up onto the stage to recover, their underwear became visible.

It's interesting to note that, on that same visit, the Stones' appearance at Sammy Barr's very professionally run Flamingo Ballroom in Ballymena went off without a hitch. And, on reflection, the Stones' Belfast 'riot' appeared relatively innocuous in comparison to The Beatles' visit to the Adelphi Cinema in Dublin the previous year, which saw twelve arrests, cars overturned outside the cinema and numerous fans treated in hospital for broken bones and minor injuries.

That same year, the English charts testified to the fact that pop music's old guard was changing. Cliff Richard & The Shadows, Frank Ifield, Matt Monro, Billy Fury, The Tornados, Frankie Vaughan and the like were making way for The Beatles, Bob Dylan, The Rolling Stones, The Kinks, The Animals, The Hollies and Manfred Mann. Yes, it would take a little time for the trend to infiltrate Irish shores, but the showbands, with their ears to the ground and their eyes open, were already starting to adjust their sets, dropping a lot of the old favourites in favour of the young and the new. The Playboys had even gone so far as to learn a little comedy number called 'Call Up The Groups', which had been a hit single for The Barron Knights.

The band discovered that keyboardist Barry had a keen ear for voices on the long journeys (that was, if they managed to keep him awake for long enough). His impressions included lippy Elvis, rubbery Mick Jagger, wholesome Cliff Richard and classic

Frank Sinatra. One day, while checking equipment before a dance, Brendan, Davy and Mo spontaneously broke into 'Call Up The Groups' and, for a laugh, Barry left his keyboard, took the microphone and immediately had everyone in stitches with his Jagger, Lennon, Freddie Garrity and Gerry Marsden impressions. At first, Dixie and the boys thought the skit would be too much of an 'in' joke, but they tried it one night at the audience-friendly Dreamland and it went down an absolute storm.

Television was growing in popularity by the second, and if the reaction to Barry's impressions in the Dreamland Ballroom that night was anything to go by, every single home in the area had one; it appeared that everyone immediately knew the characters he was lampooning. The Playboys were persuaded to perform the song a further three times that first evening. It amused Martin that mixing the traditional showband 'show' with a parody of the latest and hippest English groups worked so well. It proved that old show-business adage, as if it needed proving again, that no matter how cool and hip people were, or thought they were, they still wanted to be entertained.

Martin took the 'Call Up The Groups' idea a step further by working up a song based on the Irish showbands. He called it 'Bring The Boys Back On Again'. Borrowing the tune from 'Down From The Mountain Kitty Daley', he had Barry mimicking lads from the ballroom circuit: Brendan Bowyer, Joe Dolan, Dickie Rock, Joe MacCarthy (The Dixies' drummer and the zaniest man on the ballroom circuit) and, just to make it totally current, Val Doonican – Waterford's answer to Jim Reeves, who'd just topped the English charts with 'Walk Tall'.

'Bring The Boys Back On Again' became the talk of the circuit, and it led to The Playboys' first television appearance – a two-and-a-half minute slot on Ulster Television's *Teatime With Tommy*.

Overnight, The Playboys experienced first-hand the power of television. Before the spot, they were doing good business; after the spot, they went through a run of 17 consecutive sold-out dances. There was talk of releasing the song as a single, but as it was based on other people's songs, the record company, a wee label in Belfast called Seven Inch Records, was concerned about copyright. But as far as Martin was concerned, it at least nudged Jim Mitchell into talks with the label.

The song also won the boys their first mention in the showband bible, *New Spotlight* magazine. Father Brian D'Arcy, the showband priest, was also very complimentary about them in the Ponderosa Ballroom.

And there was more.

After the television appearance, Mitchell got a call. Being as we're talking about the sixties here, it wasn't a direct call. No, that would have been too easy – and it wasn't how things were done. One morning he was on the phone to Sammy Barr, who was keen to stick The Playboys in on a few more dates at the Flamingo. Towards the end of the conversation, he happened to mention a great opportunity, almost as an afterthought. 'Oh yes,' he said, 'I was speaking to Trevor at BBC Radio in Belfast the other week and he said he'd like to have the boys on the show.'

As it transpired, Trevor *was* interested in putting the boys on the radio. Mitchell was somewhat frustrated by the roundabout way of doing things: what if Sammy Barr had forgotten to tell him, or it turned out to be too late and they'd missed their chance? This was the only thing that still niggled him about the showband circuit. Yes, you had all these amazing ballrooms and bands, which were generating incredible amounts of money (there was even a rumour doing the rounds that The Royal had taken away a staggering fee of £3,000 for an appearance in the Kings Hall in Belfast. Three thousand fecking pounds! That's about £34,000 in today's money.), but despite this phenomenal success, the scene was still run in a fairly amateurish fashion.

If Trevor from the BBC was so interested in them, why couldn't he have made it his business to contact The Playboys direct? The simple answer was that he was Trevor, he was from the BBC and it was 1964. All Jim Mitchell could do was to resolve to follow the example of the other band managers – Sammy Barr, Jim Aiken, Albert Reynolds, Peter Demsey, Oliver Barry and, the leader of the pack, T.J. Byrne – and behave as professionally as possible so that eventually the amateur behaviour would be eradicated.

The Playboys and their equipment showed up at the BBC studios in Ormeau Road on the last Monday of October 1964, the very week that Roy Orbison reached the top of the Irish charts with 'Oh, Pretty Woman', his third chart-topper of the year. To reinforce how current The Playboys were, they performed the song as one of six they recorded for their 25 minute slot. They also included 'Hippy Hippy Shake', 'I Won't Forget You', 'Bring The Boys Back On Again', and two Martin McClelland originals, 'Broken For Good' and 'Still She Dances With You'.

The producer, impressed by the band's professionalism and eagerness, was keen to speak with the band's resident songwriter and his manager after the show's recording. He wanted to do another programme, this time with Martin and his songs alone. Martin was happy to do it, on one condition: he wanted the boys with him; after all, it was The Playboys' arrangements of his songs that was responsible for the admiration they received.

It was the first and last time they heard about the one-off show. It was Mitchell's belief that the producer had been keen to create Ulster's answer to Donovan or Bob Dylan. However, Martin's display of loyalty to his bandmates wasn't part of the producer's vision. 'Sure, didn't the producer's Aran sweater give his preference away?' he'd offered, by way of explanation. Whatever the reason, Martin's show of loyalty had given his manager a warm flush of pride.

After the recording, Mitchell headed to Dublin for talks concerning another radio idea he was working on. The Playboys returned to Castlemartin, minus Martin, who'd decided to stay in Belfast to check out the record stores and catch a movie. Or so he claimed; the reality was that he'd arranged to meet Hanna Hutchinson, who'd promised to take a day off from university to hang out with him.

Martin left The Playboys in Ormeau Road at 2.20 p.m., and by 3.05 p.m. he was in bed in a flat in Malone Road – Hanna's bed. If anything, their hunger for each other had intensified to a degree that shocked them both. For her part, Hanna was surprised by the warmth and tenderness she felt towards Martin after they made love. Maybe it had something to do with having the comfort of a bed in the warmth of a house for the first time. The hay shed had been so cold that they could actually see each other's breath and the steam rising from each other's bodies as they climaxed together. No sooner had they finished than they'd be rushing to put their clothes on. Instead of reacting against this new feeling of affection and cosiness, Hanna allowed herself to bask in it for a time.

Martin thought that Hanna's body was more beautiful than ever. Perhaps it had something to do with the few pounds that a student lifestyle was sure to shed for you. She looked perfect to Martin. As he drifted into a light sleep, Hanna's head seemingly content in the nook of his shoulder, he was surprised by how blissfully happy he felt. In all their previous sessions, he'd always wanted this secret pleasure, the pleasure of the afterglow. For the first time he actually allowed himself to feel confident about their relationship; despite Hanna's vocal misgivings, her body and her spirit were subconsciously voicing that she was happy and safe here, with Martin. For the first time, he detected a sense of vulnerability in Hanna, and, if he were being honest, he was enjoying his new role of protector.

About 15 minutes later, Martin was awakened from his snooze by Hanna trying to coax him back to life under the blankets. No coaxing was necessary; Hanna mounted him, controlling both their movements from above, taking extra care not to 'get' him too soon. Martin had to cheat slightly and close his eyes – if he'd continued to look at Hanna in all her beauty, twisting and writhing above him, with her hair thrashing from side to side, he'd have been helpless to resist. When he started to feel the beginnings of her convulsions, he bucked against her twice quite forcefully and they both peaked in the most exhilarating orgasm they'd ever experienced.

The intensity was a welcome surprise for Martin, who felt that, by this stage, they would be starting to lose interest in each other's bodies, their sexual drive for each other on the wane. In fact, the opposite appeared to be true. Once more, Hanna seemed happy to fall into his protective custody, lying on top of him.

And so it was.

She took him to her favourite restaurant, and watched in hysterics as he tried to master the art of eating pasta. They talked for hours over the meal and several cups of coffee, about music, her course, the books she was reading, poetry, about how fulfilled she now felt in life, doing what she wanted. She declared how much her views on life had changed now she had a purpose; a purpose, she admitted, she never thought she'd have. Then they talked at length about films and about Martin's songs. In fact, they covered everything under the sun, everything, that is, apart from their relationship. They returned to her flat in the early evening and made love one more time just before Martin left to hitch a lift back home.

As Martin thumbed a ride back to Castlemartin, two very significant things were happening. The first was that Gentleman Jim Mitchell was in Dublin meeting the Radio Caroline people. Radio Caroline was the highly successful pirate radio station, moored in the North Sea just off the English coast. The station's owner was the charismatic Dubliner Ronan O'Rahilly, who had recently set up a company seeking Irish-based advertisers. Mitchell had worked out a deal that, for £45 a week, The Playboys would have their own fifteen-minute show on the station. It didn't mean that they would be paid £45 every week, rather that *they* would have to pay £45 every week for the privilege of doing three songs which, with adverts, would fill the time slot. In truth, at least on paper, it was a fabulous deal for The Playboys. Mitchell only succeeding in pulling off the coup because none of the other showbands were, up to that point, taking Radio Caroline seriously. Mitchell had used this to his advantage; if the deal worked out for The Playboys, then, he predicted, 'all the other big boys would be jumping on the bandwagon.'

Mitchell, however, was faced with a problem: how would they record the weekly batch of material for the show? Radio Caroline didn't have an onshore studio. Mitchell, content with his day's work, addressed this problem over a fine dinner at the Gresham Hotel. The relevant hotel bills do not record whether Gentleman Jim Mitchell dined alone or not.

The second simultaneous occurrence saw Hanna Hutchinson lounging in bed and writing the following letter:

Martin,

You've literally just left my bed.

I loved to watch you dress and I thank you for insisting I stay in bed and not walk you up to your thumbing point, even though I still feel I should have gone with you. I hope it didn't take long to pick up a lift. Now you've been on telly you probably had a queue of people wanting to take you in their cars. Sorry, sorry, sorry, I know you hate all that.

I've suddenly realised I've never written to you before, which is surprising when you consider how long we're apart and how much we talk when we meet.

Martin, I just loved our day together. You'll never really fully appreciate how much it meant to me. It was just the perfect day. I need you to understand how wonderful it is for me when we don't spend our time discussing 'us', where we're going or if we're even going anywhere. I think you know I need to just do stuff and not spend forever talking about it. I hope you enjoyed our time too, Martin. We're so good together and I know you feel that too. I know you'd never say that.

Heck, I've never admitted it before. Why am I admitting it now? I really don't believe it could be possible for two people to feel more than what we feel when we're together. We're an odd couple, aren't we? Sometimes I don't know whether that's all me and you just go with the flow, because you want us to be together.

I love it the way you never push, you never get confrontational and threaten that if we aren't this, or if we aren't that, then we're not going to do any of this again. Martin, I don't know what we have, but I do know that I would not have missed the feelings I've experienced with you all day (in and out of bed, by the way) for anything in the world. Sometimes, I feel I don't give enough.

I still experience that lost feeling, Martin. I don't want to scare you, but I feel I should admit to you that I feel closer to you than I do to either of my parents. I still don't feel like I'm their daughter. I know how weird that is, but for me the weirder thing is that, if anything, I'm now more convinced. When I was younger, I used to think I would grow out of these feelings but now, as I say, I am even more convinced.

As I appear to be in a confessional mood, I'm also going to admit to you here that I haven't been out with any other boys here in Belfast. It's not that I feel it would be really wrong to date other boys, because, as I mentioned to you before, I will never be as close to anyone as I am to you. It's so special when we're together. There's no need for anyone else and, in a way, I feel I would be being disrespectful to you if I dated anyone else, even socially. I've come to realise that it's not important what I would think about it, but it is vitally important what you would think of it. I'm not saying this because there are lots of suitors calling at my door — there aren't — and I'm not saying it because I want you to reciprocate — although I will admit that while considering that possibility I find myself feeling that I would be hurt if you did! I know I shouldn't, but that's what I find myself thinking and so that's what I feel I should admit to you — but that honestly wasn't the reason to tell you that… I'm struggling for my words here, Martin. I suppose what I'm trying to say is that I feel that there is magic between us and I should in some way honour and respect that.

I've never felt so close to anyone as I felt to you today, Martin, and I don't even really know what that means, but the big thing is that this feeling doesn't scare me the way I thought it would. Now the moment has passed because I think (I hope) I've said what I started out to say, and I am left wondering how much further you are on your journey.

Me,

Hanna

P.S. On reflection, that's not all I was thinking as I was writing. I am also hoping that maybe you won't get a lift and you'll come back, knock on my door and we'll get to spend our first night together!

CHAPTER TWENTY-FOUR

Conquering is not just the hero's sport

Gentleman Jim Mitchell

The trouble with people who appear enigmatic is that there is always the danger that they are, in reality, just boring and shallow. They are aware of this inadequacy, and so hide behind a mysterious and inscrutable cloak. Hanna, on the other hand, wanted to be transparent, so that people wouldn't even bother to notice her when they looked in her direction in the first place.

Then you had Elizabeth Taylor. She and Richard Burton came to Dublin in January 1965. Richard was starring in the film *The Spy Who Came In From The Cold*, which was being made primarily in Ardmore with location shots in part of Dublin, apparently because it could easily be disguised to resemble parts of East Berlin. At the same time, on the other side of Dublin, house prices were shooting through the roof, with a new record price of £27,750 being paid for a house on Burlington Road.

Several of The Playboys were now spending their free Monday nights in Dublin, mostly at the Television Club in Harcourt Street. Their logic was that if, as happened on January 14, Sean Lemass could take the trouble to travel up to Stormont to see O'Neill – the first meeting between Northern and Southern Prime Ministers since December 1925 – then surely the least The Playboys could do would be to take the trip down to meet their own opposite numbers in Dublin for a bit of a night out.

The Television Club was fast becoming *the* meeting point for all the showband heads on their traditional Monday nights off. That January, February and March, there is no doubt that the conversation would have, eventually, returned to the showband craze currently sweeping the country and The Royal Showband's monster hit, 'The Hucklebuck'.

It has to be said, their timing was perfect. You take a movement, a very strong movement like the Irish showbands. You reach the stage where that movement has its own media outlets: radio, television and press. All the main bands would regularly appear on television and radio, north and south of the border. The press in general was always up for the wee plugs. On top of all of that, like any successful movement, the showband phase had a magazine dedicated exclusively to them. *New Spotlight* had no fear in hitching its wagon to the showbands – and by this point, the groups were travelling in absolute luxury: £5,000 coaches, which were being gutted and their insides personalised and customised to accommodate the musicians' every whim. Some say the petrol tanks of the big wagons had enough space for three tiger tails.

The more successful the showbands became, the more readers *New Spotlight* added to its circulation. It's always the same with movements, whether political, musical, sporting or showbusiness: the bigger the movement, the bigger and more successful the journals that dedicate themselves to them become.

So, we've got our fabulously successful movement. Then, the biggest band in the land launch their own dance, 'The Hucklebuck'. Next, they release a catchy record, also called 'The Hucklebuck', and what do you have? You have The Royal's third consecutive number one single, one of the biggest-selling Irish singles ever, and even more dancers flocking to the ballrooms. Everyone, but everyone, was talking about 'The Hucklebuck' and The Royal Showband. And to think that the Royal's recording of the song, which became synonymous with the band, nearly didn't happen at all.

The Royal, like The Beatles, recorded mostly at Abbey Road studios in London. With 20 minutes of recording time left at one session, the producer asked if they had anything they wanted to put down. It just so happened that they did have a song, a very special song as it turned out. 'The Hucklebuck', with lyrics by Roy Alfred and music by Andy Gibson, had been a Top 5 hit in America in 1949 for Tommy Dorsey, had been recorded by Frank Sinatra and was also Chubby Checker's follow-up to 'The Twist', which had initiated a worldwide dance craze at the start of the sixties.

'The Hucklebuck' came to the attention of The Royal Showband when, one night, Charlie Matthews heard The Clipper Carlton perform it. Charlie was so taken with the tune that he introduced it to the rest of the band. By the time the Royal found themselves with 20 minutes of valuable studio time to fill, they had been performing the song at dances to a great response for a few months. The definitive recording was put down with seconds to spare. It started out as a B-side to 'I Ran All The Way Home', but soon, after that song reached number one in the Irish charts in fact, popular opinion forced them to flip it and make 'The Hucklebuck' the A-side, where it continued to hold the top spot. Not only that, but the single was a number one hit in Australia, Hong Kong and even Singapore. The band were also awarded the honour of an appearance on the biggest UK television show at the time, *Sunday Night At The London Palladium*. On top of, and despite, all of this, we've mentioned it before but it's worth mentioning again, the Royal were a great bunch of fun-loving chaps.

Smiley and Brendan had met up with Michael Coppinger, The Royal's affable bandleader and saxophonist, in the Television Club, and he was a great hoot. He recounted an incident that occurred on April 2, 1962, and although it hadn't appeared significant at the time, in hindsight it proved to be quite a historic occasion.

On that particular spring night, The Royal Showband had performed at the Pavilion Theatre in Liverpool as part of their UK tour. Their opening act for the Liverpool show had been none other than The Beatles, who had played a lunchtime session at the Cavern earlier that day and had recently been added to The Royal Showband's bill to try to help sell tickets. The Royal had been billed as 'Ireland's Pride' to 'Liverpool's Joy' The Beatles. The show didn't do very well in the end, in fact, it was the worst night of the tour, as Michael informed the ever-attentive Smiley and Brendan. You see, the Pavilion, or 'the Privvy', as it was known to locals, was in fact Liverpool's premier striptease theatre. Well, the local Irish immigrants and second-generation Irish dancers couldn't risk being seen at such an establishment!

Michael said that The Beatles seemed like fine boys one and all, and that they'd had a bit of a chat. About the virtues of writing their own songs? No. Wanting to be as big as Elvis? No. Getting a number one hit record? No. The thing that intrigued The Beatles most was the Royal's wagon. Michael took John and Paul on to the bus for a look-see and the boys, who were to become the most famous songwriting partnership in the world, couldn't believe how luxurious it was – it even had its own built-in wardrobe!

Here we were, almost three years later, and both The Royal Showband and The Beatles had made tremendous progress.

Showbands ruled the land during the first half of 1965. Well, ruled it apart from a little interference from 'Liverpool's Joy', who started off the first two weeks of the year at number one in Ireland with 'I Feel Fine'. This was knocked off the top spot by 'The Hucklebuck / I Ran All The Way Home', which stayed at number one for seven weeks, and was in turn replaced by Butch Moore & The Capitol Showband with 'Born To Be With You'. The Royal Showband returned to number one for a further two weeks, this time with Tom Dunphy singing 'If I Didn't Have A Dime'. This in turn was followed by Butch Moore & The Capitol, who had released their follow-up, Ireland's first Eurovision Song Contest entry, 'Walking The Streets In The Rain'. That single enjoyed the following three weeks at number one, before being knocked off the top spot by The Beatles and their new single 'Ticket To Ride'. The Beatles enjoyed four weeks at the summit before being replaced by Dickie Rock & The Miami Showband with 'Every Step Of The Way'. Dickie was to hog the coveted top spot for the next four weeks, taking us through to the middle of the 1965. Both Brendan Bowyer and Dickie Rock were each to enjoy another number one single later in the year; Brendan with 'Don't Lose Your Hucklebuck Shoes' and Dickie with 'Wishing It Was You'.

Meanwhile, back in Belfast, ex-showband head George Ivan Morrison, who had started off his career playing tenor saxophone in The Monarchs Showband, had started to enjoy some mainland success with his rhythm-and-blues band from Belfast, Them. The band, who Martin had enjoyed seeing in Glasgow, became the first real Irish group to make the UK Top Ten, thanks mainly to the fact that Them's recording was adopted as the theme song for a UK television show dedicated to pop music called *Discs A Go–Go*.

In January, 'Baby Please Don't Go' made it to number ten in the UK chart. Their follow-up, 'Here Comes The Night', made it all the way up to number two in both Ireland and the UK that March. The same May, Them climbed into the elusive and mysterious American market when 'Here Comes The Night' peaked at number 23 on their Hot One Hundred. The previous week, on May 22, two Irish artists had debuted in the American charts: Ian Whitcomb's 'You Turn Me On' went on to reach number eight, and the aforementioned Them's classic and oft-covered 'Gloria' enjoyed a week at number 93 before giving way to 'Here Comes The Night'. Martin thought that 'Here Comes The Night' was the perfect pop song. There was just something about it that connected to his subconscious the first time he heard it. Every time he heard the song thereafter, it made the same connection, which was so unlike the majority of pop songs, whose novelty started to wear off a bit more after each listen. The new pop songs, in fact, sounded better and better.

Martin had long been examining what made these songs work so well in the hope of trying to repeat the formula. His favourites and most admired were The Beatles' version of 'Twist And Shout', 'Hang On Sloopy' by The McCoys, 'When You Walk In A Room' by The Searchers, the aforementioned 'Here Comes The Night' by Them and The Kinks' classic 'You Really Got Me'. It wasn't that these were Martin's favourite songs; it was more that he, and the majority of Irish dancers, found them totally irresistible. There was something unfathomable in the way all of them had something unique, something which involved the listener, demanded their attention. But more importantly, the big pay-off was that, having demanded and got your attention, these songs then repeatedly delivered a totally rewarding experience.

Martin kept listening, hoping to unlock the secret, and he continued to try and write his perfect pop song. He wondered whether any of his favourite writers had themselves recognised that they had written the perfect pop song. How would they have felt? Would they have been exhilarated and driven to try and repeat it, or even better it? Or would it tempt them to rest on their laurels? Perhaps the secret of many a perfect pop record wasn't so much the song itself, Martin thought, as it was its recording and production. For example, 'Twist And Shout' was recorded by the writers, The Isley Brothers, to a much lesser degree of success. Similarly, 'Here Comes The Night' had previously been covered by Scottish lass Lulu, who simply hadn't sung the lyrics as thought she meant them.

At the same time, all these groups in general, and the Irish showbands in particular, were enjoying chart success. The Playboys had managed a couple of appearances in *New Spotlight*'s poll; they were the number three 'Northern band' (The Freshmen were first and The Plattermen second), and Martin Dean was voted fifth most eligible male after Brendan Bowyer, Brendan O'Brien, Tom Dunphy and Billy Brown. Still, they were yet to receive any news on the recording front.

The Playboys recorded their Radio Caroline sessions down in Belfast at Lloyd's Studios on Cromac Square. 'Studios' is probably too palatial a word to describe the accommodation they found on the fourth floor of the building. Lloyd's was equipped with a Revox recorder, five microphones and the good intentions of the owner. On top of which, the studio was above a solicitor's office, which meant that recording could never start until the suits had finished for the day. The Playboys had to haul their equipment up four flights of stairs. Smiley counted the 72 steps every time they ascended to the fourth floor. After each trip, he sought replenishment from his current favourite bar of chocolate: a Mars. This brought lots of sniggers from the rest of The Playboys, plus the odd 'Smiley you sure are *faithful* to the old Mars bar' comment.

But the Playboys, never afraid of hard work, were soon set up and ready to launch the next part of their career. They learned quickly that the quieter they played, the better the quality of the recording. Martin found himself being distracted by his own voice. Generally, at the dances, what with all the racket, he could hardly hear what he was singing. But in the studio he could hear himself perfectly. It took him a few takes to overcome the distraction, but overcome it he did. He was not as in love with his voice as some of the other band members and the dancers were, seeing it merely as a part of their overall sound. He had always been more intent on serving the song well than trying to come across as a great singer. He figured that no one who'd ever heard Billy Brown could harbour such illusions.

As with the BBC radio recordings, The Playboys managed to contain their awe at finally being in a recording studio, and they were happy to get stuck in to getting the best results possible in the circumstances. They recorded enough material on the first night for six shows. In fact, it ended up being enough songs for eight shows, Radio Caroline being so delighted with the results that they edited two additional shows incorporating the best material.

Despite this success, Mitchell's Radio Caroline promo ideas didn't exactly bear fruit. The problem was that, with it being a pirate station, the radio reception in Ireland was pretty poor. The signs were there, if Jim had only paid attention to them. No matter how many listeners the station claimed, all you had to do was look at the poor record sales in Ireland of David McWilliams, who was managed by the station's owner and was being advertised off the air. Ballymena's McWilliams was a great songwriter – just how great a songwriter was to be proven later when other artists successfully covered his tunes. Unfortunately, though, the production on his own records always seemed to get in the way of the songs. At least, that was the view of a certain Martin Dean, who noted what he thought were the mistakes in the hope that he wouldn't fall into the same trap.

Mitchell, being the gentleman he was, paid for his mistake himself and halted the project after three months. In fact, he decided to call it a day when, on one occasion, he couldn't even tune in to the station to hear his band.

Despite this, he was still convinced his idea was a good one, and he entered into talks with Radio Luxembourg. The Radio Luxembourg people were very friendly and very realistic and they recommended that Mitchell first secure a record deal for his charges before committing to a similar campaign with them. If The Playboys had something to sell, the deal the radio station could offer was a fifteen-minute show once a week for £100. Mitchell was disappointed, not by the price – he could make that work easily, it was, at best, half a per cent of The Playboys' weekly income. What disappointed him was that he believed the best way to get a good record deal was to make the record companies sit up and pay attention to them in advance. The Playboys were a popular band, people knew them and recognised their name, but they had got themselves stuck in a bit of a rut, and sadly this had occurred before they'd reached the 'A' division of bands. Radio Luxembourg listened to a couple of the band's sessions for Radio Caroline, and, although the recordings were terrible in quality, they were impressed with the singer and his original material.

They suggested that Jim Mitchell contact Mr Thomas Boyle, who ran City Records. In fact, they rang up Boyle on the spot, building Mitchell up and adding that they were in negotiations to present a weekly radio show with The Playboys. They and all the girls in the office loved the band's original songs and, although there were several record companies already expressing interest in The Playboys, they hadn't yet signed a deal. 'Could Mr Mitchell come over and see him immediately?' came the answer down the phone.

'I think he's just about to head to Belfast, just give me a moment and I'll see if I can persuade him to change his plans,' Mitchell's new best friend had said. She put her hand over the mouthpiece, smiled at Mitchell and then removed her hand. 'Sorry for taking so long but he was literally on his way out of the office, but the good news is he'll be able to change his plans. I can send him over now if you can see him immediately.'

Sheila, the young lady in question, explained that the best way to deal with record companies was to make it seem like you were doing them a favour, offering them something that everyone else wanted. She further advised: 'If you just went to Mr Boyle cold, he'd be thinking, "Why have none of my competitors taken this?" and so you'd immediately be off to a bad start. We do quite a bit of work with him, so now he thinks we're grateful for the business he's given us and we're passing something special on to him, which of course we are. So you see, no one is losing out. It's the way it works.'

Arrangements made, Mitchell said he didn't know how to thank Sheila enough. 'Oh that's fine,' she said, 'if you get your record deal perhaps you can fix me up on a dinner date with young Martin Dean?'

Mitchell looked at the beautiful young lady. Once again, he wasn't sure who'd be doing whom the favour. Apart from which, even if the record company talks materialised to nought, she had, in one short conversation, got The Playboys further than Mitchell had in his two years of trying. 'Deal or no deal, young lady, you can count on it.'

The next hour spent at City Records was equally astonishing for Mitchell. Until recently, the label had been called Dublin Records, 'after the famous London Records,' Thomas Boyle explained. 'The only problem was that we were finding we couldn't sell a record in anger in the wee North, so I was forced to change the name to City Records.'

Mitchell had expected to be making a pitch to the owner, just like he'd done with other labels before now. But thanks to Sheila, he found himself in the position of the record company making a pitch to *him*, before he'd even played the songs to Boyle. Once he did, the label boss flipped. He wanted to sign a deal with Mitchell. Boyle hurriedly called his employees into his office: this was something they all had to hear. Tape reel rolling, they sat in silence as 'There's Always A Song On The End of A Teardrop', 'Broken For Good' and 'Still She Dances With You' played. All were convinced that the latter was a hit single. 'And not just in Ireland,' Boyle boasted.

The deal was this: The Playboys would pay for the recording and City Records would release the record, promote it and pay them a negligible royalty rate of 4 per cent. Gentleman Jim Mitchell, like the good manager he was, would consider the offer and get back to Boyle in a couple of days, despite bursting to say otherwise. In truth, there wasn't really a lot of consideration necessary. Mitchell knew it was as good as any of the other deals being offered around town.

So that was how, three weeks later on May 15, 1965, The Playboys were setting up their equipment for the first time in the Eamon Andrews Recording Studios in Harcourt Street, Dublin, for their first proper recording session. In a six-hour session they recorded 'Bring The Boys Back On Again', which City Records were prepared to risk as a B-side; 'Still She Dances With You', which they definitely wanted for the first single; 'Broken For Good' and 'I Should Have Known Better', a Lennon and McCartney song which The Playboys had recently discovered on *A Hard Day's Night* and had successfully included in their live set. Martin absolutely loved The Beatles' gem, and pushed for The Playboys to record it more than he pushed for either of his own compositions. Martin couldn't sing this song and not think of Hanna.

> *I should have known better with a girl like you*
> *That I would love everything that you do*
> *And I do, hey hey, and I do* .

As they started recording, he was reminded of their BBC session in Belfast, but it was the aftermath he remembered most fondly, particularly the letter he'd received two days later. He treasured that letter with all his heart. It was the only encouragement Hanna had ever given him, if indeed it was encouragement and not an explanation. He forced himself to put all thoughts of Hanna out of his head as he was about to make a record, even though deep down he couldn't conceal the fact that he was making the record for her.

The band set up their equipment on the bandstand in the TV Club, part of the same building. Martin was happy with that. He figured that setting up just like they were at a dance meant that the boys would be more relaxed while performing. He'd read that Billy Brown had said in an interview that musicians should ignore the studio staff and play to each other. The microphone was the ear of the entire world, according to the recording engineer; a comforting (if expensive, at £28 an hour) thought. There was no producer present on that first recording session, nor was one necessary, because they essentially recorded live and all they needed was an expert engineer. Martin remembered Billy Brown's important lesson regarding the recording process: 'It doesn't matter how talented you are, and it doesn't matter how brilliant your songs are, believe you me your records are going to sound like shite unless you have a brilliant engineer.' When the session was first booked, Martin had Mitchell check out the studio's best man for the job and they had booked their session around his availability. The engineer was enthusiastic and helpful, if a little weary – the studio was so busy recording showbands that he was currently working 24-hour shifts.

They didn't have a lot of time for duff takes, but that is what was great about The Playboys: no matter how varied their personalities were off stage, on stage each was wholly committed to making great music. They were lucky enough not to have any messers or bluffers in their midst. Bluffers could get away with their shortcomings at dances; what with the excitement and the noise of the crowd and the fact that everyone was preoccupied with their own parts.

But in the studio, the minute you 'put a song down', everyone had a chance to listen to the playback and dissect each part in detail. That's when the cracks, if there are any, begin to show. For their part, The Playboys worked together surprisingly well in the studio, which certainly wasn't the case with every band. The engineer had some horror stories about several band members being sent around the corner to the nearest bar, leaving the more competent musicians to try to repair the mistakes. He was discreet enough not to mention names, but the lads had a good bit of fun trying to guess. Martin had earlier worried that Dixie or Brendan might try to take over the session, but neither did, and they in fact made their music in a very convivial atmosphere.

The control room was packed as the band crowded in to listen to the first playback. Martin was completely happy with it in that nothing got in the way of the song; the playing and the arrangement were so flawless that you were immediately drawn into the tune's subtleties. Martin had to admit that he felt a real charge hearing his efforts committed to tape.

Of the four songs they recorded that first session, the one that suffered the most under the live conditions was 'Broken For Good'. Thomas Doyle, in the studio for support, wasn't unduly concerned. He was extremely happy with the two tracks chosen for their first single: 'Still She Dances With You' and 'Bring The Boys Back On Again'.

The Playboys had four months to wait before their single was released. In the meantime, on July 21, 1965, Jim Reeves died in a plane crash. The kids on the ballroom scene had loved Mr Reeves, and although he had always done fabulous business for the owners, it was his fans who counted him as a hero. In fact, some owners found him 'trou-blesome', his demand for perfection being legendary. He'd played two or three ballrooms a night, breaking house records everywhere. Playing piano, he refused to use an un-tuned instrument. Over time, Mr Reeves and the venue owners developed a very healthy distaste for each other and, allegedly, he would announce from the stage, 'If you feel this show is of an inferior quality, it's because the piano I've been supplied with is a piece of shite.'

The Irish fans, on the other hand, took to Jim Reeves in a big way, buying his records by the truckload and flocking to see him at every available opportunity. His death left a gaping hole in many people's lives, and Leitrim's very own Larry Cunningham and his band The Mighty Avons set about trying to fill that gap. Larry became the Irish Jim Reeves, the main difference being that he and his extremely professional band would arrive at all engagements with their own set of reliable equipment, giving the venue owners a much easier life.

As Ireland was coming to terms with the untimely death of Jim Reeves – Nat King Cole (a personal favourite of Martin's), T.S. Eliot and Winston Churchill having also died in the first half of the year – Martin Dean waited impatiently for copies of his single to arrive. He'd waited five years to release a record, but this final month nearly drove him mad. He knew it was vain of him, but he dreamed of that single every night for the four weeks leading up to that magic release date, September 1. He couldn't wait to get his hands on the single, with its Dean Martin influenced front cover shot, taken from below with the camera looking up at the boys standing in a 'V' formation, Martin and Dixie sharing the foreground and the Castlemartin hills rising up in the background.

Martin worried that something was bound to go wrong before he actually got the single in his hand. Then, one morning while he was enjoying a lie-in, he heard a car pull up outside their house. His mum opened the door downstairs, followed by a familiar bass voice. It seemed like ages later – he wasn't exactly sure of how long – his mother called up the stairs to say he had a visitor. He threw on his jeans and a jumper, combed his hair and went downstairs in his bare feet to be greeted by the smiling face of Gentleman Jim Mitchell. He had just returned from an overnight to Dublin and was carrying a box of The Playboys' single, 'Still She Dances With You'. Martin felt like roaring with excitement, although outwardly he retained his usual calm demeanour.

He raced back upstairs and placed a copy on his record player, turning it up to full volume. Mitchell and his mother were standing on either side of his bedroom door, listening and watching. Tears of pride were rolling down Kathleen McClelland's face. Then the neighbour invited herself in – she'd heard the music through the window and insisted Martin play the song again, but first she wanted to go and get her children. Others began to arrive, wondering what the fuss was all about. Within 20 minutes, Martin had played the song six times, and soon the neighbours were spilling down the stairs and out into the garden. Kathleen heeded the request to open the bedroom windows so that those down below could hear it. Within one hour, similar playing parties were occurring in eight other local households as Jim Mitchell continued his journey to deliver the single to the other band members.

True story: by 1 p.m., all of Castlemartin had heard, some several times, the Playboys' debut single. And sure, wasn't Martin a grand lad for being able to write *and* sing a song. The Playboys' single was a nine-day wonder in Castlemartin. By the time it reached Tone Sounds, the local record shop, the following Friday there was a queue outside the door. Toner, the owner, boasted that neither the mighty Royal Showband nor the 'Fab Four' had ever caused a queue outside his shop! He sold four boxes of singles that first morning – 100 copies in total – and he claimed he'd never ever done that before, not even for religious records. Toner *personally* drove down to the distributors in Belfast that very afternoon to pick up another 200 copies of 'Still She Dances With You'. He knew that he'd be inundated with requests once the village filled up with the country folk who only came into town on Saturdays. By the time he returned to Castlemartin in the late afternoon, there were still people mingling around his shop front and, inside, his harassed assistant already had orders for 186 of the 200 copies he'd brought up from Belfast. The remaining 14 were sold out to the crowd as quickly as the 6s./8d. per copy could change hands. Toner, waiting on the distributor's doorstep before they opened the next morning, took another 250 copies. In fact, it was the last of the Belfast distributor's stock – he in turn was trying to get more copies from Dublin.

As Toner continued to sell the single, Martin continued to examine the record. He read and re-read every single word on the jacket and centre disc several times. There, underneath the song title, secure in brackets, was the legend 'Martin McClelland', in the same position as Lennon and McCartney, Bob Dylan and Ray Davies (the Kinks' leader, and a particular favourite songwriter of Martin's). This finally made it real for Martin. Yes, he'd been writing songs for several years now, and yes, The Playboys had been playing a couple of them most nights on ballroom stages around Ireland, but until that moment, and that credit on The Playboys' first record, it had all been a dream. That credit made it legit. He knew his thoughts were generated from vanity, but he didn't care a fig – he was going to enjoy his moment, Billy Brown having told him that he would never, ever enjoy it as much again.

The B-side was credited as 'arranged by McClelland/Brendan/Barry', the record company listing the guitarist's and organist's first names because that was how they were always referred to. The Playboys, in showing the extent of their gratitude to Mitchell, had listed the producer credit as 'Produced by James Mitchell'. The pleasure Mitchell took from the gesture is not recorded anywhere, apart from the fact that Martin's mother said that she had never seen her boss so moved.

A strange thing occurred on the following Monday: Toner, confident that he'd satisfied the initial local demand for The Playboys' single, closed the shop on Saturday night with 45 copies left in stock. However, by lunchtime on Monday it started all over again. This time, though, people were asking for 'Bring The Boys Back On Again' and, after the first couple of requests, Toner started to recognise the faces of those he was convinced had already bought a copy. 'Sure, haven't you already got the single, Donny?' Toner said on the fifth occurrence.

'Aye,' replied Donny, prouder than a rooster at a hen's party, 'I've got 'Still She Dances With You', but my mate Patsy got the other one, 'Bring The Boys Back On Again', and sure that's great craic altogether, I'd love a copy of that too.'

And so Toner had to show Donny, and several of his mates, that if you turned over the copy of your single and played the second side you got this other song for free. Toner knew he was turning away business, but he was feeling very generous, having just enjoyed his highest takings since he'd opened the record department six years previously. Toner predicted the single was going to do very well in the following week's charts. When Mitchell called in to see how Toner was doing mid-week he was greeted with the news, 'You've outsold everything else 100 to one!'

The week of The Playboys' release, The Beatles were number one in the Irish charts with 'Help' and The Royal were number two with 'Don't Lose Your Hucklebuck Shoes'. The following week, those positions were reversed and The Playboys, thanks mainly to sales in Ballymena, Portrush, Belfast, Cork, Magherafelt, Cookstown, Derry and a late surge in the Queen's University district of Belfast, stormed into the charts at number 23. Due mainly to shops running out of stock and their owners not being as resourceful as Castlemartin's Toner, the single dropped the following week to number 31. Or that was what Thomas Boyle concluded to Mitchell. Mitchell wasn't sure if this was the case or if Boyle was putting a spin on the actual state of play. Which was true? One would never know, because the charts were only tabulated down to number 30.

Either way, it didn't really matter. The Playboys were enjoying their moment of glory: their first single had been released, they'd been in the charts and people had sat up and noticed them. The whole episode had more than served its purpose. On top of which, he now had 'product' which he could send out to ballroom owners and music industry insiders in Scotland, England, America, Canada and Australia. From what Mitchell could establish from City Records, a big smash hit in Ireland would sell a maximum of 20,000 copies, and an average single sold around 5,000 copies, while The Playboys' single, within three months of release, had sold 1,684 copies. This was the reality, but as Mitchell had learnt from Sheila at Radio Luxembourg, you had to talk the talk differently.

Martin readily agreed to the promised dinner date with Sheila. 'Thanks for being so understanding,' Mitchell said, because he meant it. On the one hand, he really did want to repay his debt to Sheila, but on the other he felt a little guilty for agreeing to it on Martin's behalf.

'I think it's very honest of you to admit how important a part she played in us getting a deal,' Martin replied, sitting lightly in his favourite basketwork seat in Mitchell's office. The fuss of the single was subsiding a little, and Mitchell was squaring things away in his head. 'I'm sure other managers would have taken all the credit for themselves.'

'Ah now, conquering is not just the hero's sport, Martin,' Mitchell said, and then continued shaking his head to clear his thoughts for something else. 'If, when you meet her, you don't think it would be... ah... pleasant, then don't worry about it – it'll be okay, we'll make some excuse and all go out together instead or something.'

Martin wouldn't hear of it. Sheila had been of great assistance to The Playboys, and he had no qualms whatsoever about repaying the favour. He'd prefer it not to be a blind date though; instead, he'd try to find an excuse to meet her and then *he'd* ask *her* out to dinner, making no reference to the earlier agreement. Mitchell was impressed by how Martin seemed to be developing into a real gentleman at such a young age.

On their first meeting, Martin Dean was 20 years old and Sheila McGinley was 26. He was a country boy and she was a city girl. It's hard to say who made the biggest impression on whom, but suffice it to say that on the following day Radio Luxembourg made 'Still She Dances With You' their power play (most frequently spun record) for the following week. Martin sent her flowers, and a note saying how much he'd enjoyed the evening.

And he had; he'd really enjoyed the evening. He'd enjoyed it in the same way he enjoyed being with Hanna Hutchinson and journalist Anne Buchanan, in that all three were very easy to talk to, had a great sense of humour and wanted more than the mundane in their lives. Unlike Anne Buchanan, though, Sheila McGinley didn't have a boyfriend. Could they really just be friends? With a boyfriend there, his relationship with Anne was clear cut. That's not to lessen the intensity of their relationship; he'd only met her twice so far but she'd made such an impression on him that she was never far from his thoughts. Sheila, though, was different; her being single meant only one thing: their relationship would either be romantic, or nothing at all. He hoped, in this case, it would be the former; this was one girl he really wanted to get to know.

CHAPTER TWENTY-FIVE

I'm not going to sleep with him just because we've run out of other ways to amuse ourselves

Anne Buchanan

Flush from their recent Irish record success, The Playboys started to broaden their horizons. There were reports in the press of trips to England, Canada and even as far afield as Australia in the works. In the meantime, they made a return trip to Scotland that August. Dixie and Mo made the fatal mistake of having their respective girlfriends over for a long weekend. It wasn't that Colette Curtis (Dixie's girl) or Angela Conroy (Mo's girl) were anything other than good people, it was just, well, showband life was all about mucking in and having a laugh together; if you managed to achieve that, then a bit of that same spirit came across on stage. When you didn't, well it was more of a tiresome job, wasn't it?

Believe it or not, it really was part of the lads' job to chat to the girls afterwards. Mostly it was innocent and harmless, and when it wasn't and you got lucky, well, the last thing you were expected to be was innocent. But with Colette and Angela there, the rest of the band didn't want to be seen chatting to the girls, innocent or not, just in case the girlfriends got the wrong end of the stick about their boyfriends. Such doubt could ruin a relationship, and it became an unwritten rule that while girlfriends were on tour, the band remained 'innocent'. Both Dixie and Mo, however, fell at the first hurdle, owning up to this mistake in the dressing room the second night the girls were over. Dixie even went as far as to fine himself and his bandmate for their failure, the fine being a tenner each (although it's believed that Dixie paid both fines in this instance). His logic was that a hit where it hurts most – in the pocket – would prevent the other lads from making the same mistake.

He needn't have worried. It was a rule that was never broken again. Colette and Angela benefited from the trip too, returning to Castlemartin firm friends and confident that their boys were behaving themselves on the road.

Martin enjoyed his usual coffee breaks with Anne Buchanan, and he even confided in her about Hanna. She encouraged him to be quite candid, and he felt such relief. He had never spoken to anyone about his bizarre relationship before, apart that was from the very oblique conversation he'd had with Smiley a few years before.

'But where would you like the relationship to go?' Anne asked him during their second chat.

'Well, you see that's the thing; I don't really know,' Martin admitted.

'But you must have some dreams for it, for the two of you?' she pushed without appearing to push, a secret many good journalists have mastered.

'Well, I'm on the road a lot, so I'm not sure that there's really much more of a relationship we can have. I'd hate to be someone who was always wishing to be somewhere else, or with someone else. I don't know what you would do next. I mean, on one level we have a relationship that is so intense it's probably better that we do spend time apart.'

'But wouldn't you like to just come home sometimes and find her there waiting for you?'

'Goodness, no!' Martin laughed. 'You don't know Hanna. That would drive her nuts, living her life sitting around waiting for someone to come home. She wants to *live* her life. She really doesn't want to waste a moment of it. I mean, I see her point. I don't see the point of being a couple in that way, you know, her sitting around waiting and caring for him and he in turn becoming dependent on her so that by the time he gets to 30, he can't do a single thing for himself.'

'Oh come on, Martin, I can't believe that you are so naïve. It isn't like that. You create a home together; your life together adds to your own life, it doesn't take away from it. Don't you ever feel you just want to go home to Hanna and be in a cosy, warm, safe place you've created together? You know, a nice home like you had when you were growing up?'

'There was always just my mother and me when I was growing up,' Martin said, matter-of-factly.

'I'm so sorry, Martin, I forgot.'

'Oh, there's nothing to be sorry about. I mean, I never felt that I was missing anything by not having a father about the house. The reality would have been that he was off to work before I went to school and I'd have been in bed before he got home. That would just leave Sundays, so I figured that all I was missing out on was Sundays – that seemed to be the only thing my mates had that I didn't have. Then of course you also realise from your mates that it always seems to be the father who lifts the strap. My mum has never hit me in my life.'

'Isn't that view a little simplistic?' Anne offered.

Martin hesitated. He felt that Anne was disappointed in him, and he didn't want that. Yet, at the same time, he was just approaching the point in his life where he was starting not to worry so much that the other person had a difference of opinion. But with Anne, just there, in that split second... well, he felt he was letting her down by having an inferior view on something. The feeling wouldn't leave him.

'Well, you know,' he started, not really sure of where he was going, 'it's like, I can imagine what it's like having what is accepted as a normal family, but I can never experience it. I'm never going to meet my dad now, and to be quite honest, I've no desire to.'

'But for your own life, would you not like to be to your children what your father never was to you?' Anne asked.

'That all seems so far away to me. It seems like I need to do something, to go somewhere, to learn something, to even get to the stage of being able to think about any of that.'

Anne sighed.

Martin continued: 'Sometimes I feel that Hanna and I met at a time when we just weren't ready for each other, and now we're struggling, trying to hold on until we reach a time when we will be ready for each other.'

'Yeah, I can see that; that makes sense.'

'It's like, I keep thinking that I can't mess up, and if I mess up just once, make just one mistake, I'll have blown our chance.'

'Do you expect the same from Hanna, you know, that she's not even allowed to make one mistake?'

'No, it's not like that, it's not that kind of a mistake,' Martin said, appearing to struggle to get his words out fast enough before they disappeared. 'I'm not saying that she is sitting there in judgement, waiting for me to make a mistake, and when I make it she'll dump me; it's more like neither of us are in charge of this, something greater than us is in control. But the heartening thing is, you know, with her letter, Hanna seems to be as desperate to cling on to this – to whatever it is that we might one day have – as I am.'

'I think Brian and I have stopped struggling to hold on,' Anne said more in a whisper.

'No? I thought you were all set to be an old couple together?'

'So did I,' Anne sighed, 'but it has now reached the stage where we've got to go somewhere else with the relationship or drop it, and that's no basis for a relationship now, is it?'

Martin looked at her. He smiled and hoped it came across as a sympathetic smile. He didn't know what else to do or to say.

'I'm not going to sleep with him just because we've run out of other ways to amuse ourselves.'

'So this is all about doing the wild thing?'

'No it's not, Martin,' she said, the thickness of her Scottish accent coming through fully as she bit his head off, 'it's not an issue for me. It never has been. At the same time, it's not a card I want to play in a game. You know, you have to save your card and then play it at the appropriate time to win the pot. Sex is not a prize, Martin, and if it becomes one, aren't we just becoming prostitutes?'

Martin thought about this for a time, and after a few seconds Anne continued: 'You see the main difference between you and Hanna and me and Brian is that we're the ones who are dating, who are only meant to be *going steady*, while you and Hanna are the ones who have made the connection, and yet neither of you have made any commitment to each other. Something greater is pulling you together, refusing to allow you to lose each other, and we're kinda going along enjoying the scenery, you know? "Oh, shall we go to the movies? Shall we go out for dinner? Shall we go to the Barrowland? Oh, what shall we do to occupy ourselves? Shall we do," what is it you call it, "the wild thing"?'

'Well, I don't know about you, Anne,' Martin laughed, looking at his watch, 'but I am going to the Barrowland and I need to be there in five minutes or I'll be fined.'

The gig that night at the Barrowland was a sell-out; it was the first time The Playboys had completely sold out, to the extent that they were actually turning people away. The entire Scottish tour was an outstanding success, and each and every night The Playboys' version of 'I Should Have Known Better' went down an absolute storm. They returned to Glasgow two Saturdays later for the last night of the tour, again a smash sell-out, and they had to repeat the song five times during the course of the evening. Anne told the boys that people had been ringing up the venue non-stop for the past fortnight, asking when they could buy a copy of the single.

The first record had not been available in Scotland, although it had received a very positive write-up in the *Glasgow Herald*, thanks to one Miss Buchanan. For the second single, though, the Barrowland management – who were now successfully organising The Playboys' Scottish tours – worked out a deal with City Records in Dublin and a local Scottish distributor, Glen Discs, to have the record released in Scotland the same week that it was released in Ireland. That is how on November 8, 1965, 'I Should Have Known Better', written by Lennon and McCartney and recorded by The Playboys, entered the Irish charts at number 18 and the Scottish charts at a phenomenal number seven. The same week, Chris Andrews was number one in the Irish charts with 'Yesterday Man'. (Mr Andrews' follow-up single, 'To Whom It Concerns', despite not faring as well as his first – reaching number nine in the charts – was the song that he would come to be more associated with, as it was to be adopted as the theme song for Gay Byrne's very popular and long-running RTÉ series, *The Late Late Show*.) The B-side of The Playboys' single was a Martin McClelland original, an old song, one of his earliest songs in fact: 'No Time To Say Goodbye'. Martin was proud of the song about the 1953 sea disaster where 128 people had lost their lives when the MV *Princess Victoria* sank at the entrance to Belfast Lough, but he knew it would never be a single, not like 'Broken For Good', if they could only get it recorded properly.

On advice from Thomas Boyle at City Records, Mitchell registered Martin's songs for the publishing rights. Rather than go with an established publisher, and it has to be noted that at that stage, none were exactly beating Martin's door down to sign him up, Martin formed his own publishing company. He chose the name Southern Songs, and Mitchell did the rest. As Martin's publishing income, should there ever be any, was outside The Playboys' agreement, after consulting his mother, he decided that he should pay Mitchell commission on these funds. Mitchell was amenable to this, and they agreed on a rate of 20 per cent.

The following week, 'I Should Have Known Better' jumped to number four in Scotland and, thanks to Radio Luxembourg's support, it nudged into the Irish Top Ten at number eleven. The following week, they stayed at number four in Scotland and dropped to number seventeen in Ireland. The week after that, they gave up their precious Monday and Tuesday and flew to Scotland for two dances and two more full houses in the Barrowland. In the meantime, Glen Discs had imported copies of 'Still She Dances With You', and on the Wednesday morning, as The Playboys flew back to Aldergrove, they heard that 'I Should Have Known Better' had crept up to number three and 'Still She Dances With You' had entered the Scottish charts at number twelve.

From that Wednesday until the first Sunday in January, The Playboys, to use an old showband term, 'couldn't see a bare floorboard on the ballroom floor'. 'I Should Have Known Better' sold 4,300 copies in Ireland – creeping up towards that mythical 5,000 sales of the average Irish single. Although, position-wise at least, it did much better in the Scottish charts, it still only managed to sell 1,487 copies there. Dixie pointed out that this put them over the average Irish sales figure, and, sure, wasn't Scotland really a province of Ireland?

CHAPTER TWENTY-SIX

Life's a beach, and then the tide comes in

Martin Dean

After their new-found success, The Playboys took a two-week break, during which time Colette Curtis became Mrs Dixie Blair. That was on the first weekend. The following Saturday, Angela Convery married Maurice the drummer. For Castlemartin and the other towns of Mid-Ulster, it was the showbusiness double wedding of the century, making front-page news in the *Mid-Ulster Mail* and the *Coleraine Chronicle*. It even made page seven of the *Belfast Telegraph*. It was relegated to the middle pages of the *News Letter*. Guess where they went on their honeymoons? Correct, Scotland! It rained the whole time, though none of the four were heard to utter a word of complaint.

It was the 50th anniversary of the 1916 uprising. The celebrations in the Free State included Nelson's Column in O'Connell Street, Dublin, being demolished. The population increased for the first time since the famine, and on January 7, Sea Quest, a 7,000-ton oil rig – a rig that the Japanese claimed couldn't be built – was successfully, but cautiously, launched in the Belfast Lough.

Martin went down to Belfast, purportedly to see the *Alfie*, with Michael Caine at his prime. Indeed, Martin and Hanna Hutchinson did make the 3 p.m. matinee and then, in the evening, at Hanna's insistence, he took her to see Derrick & The Sounds at the Orpheus. Martin had wanted to see the band ever since the members of the Blues By Five had told him of this great group of excellent musicians, one of the few big bands to treat the relief groups well. They enjoyed themselves, both at the dance *and* during their long-awaited first overnight stay together.

Their relationship had neither progressed nor regressed by the morning. Because he'd nothing else to do, Martin hung around Belfast the following day, amused by how the university students had a certain kind of look, halfway between beatniks and English pop stars – long hair being the common factor. Martin and Hanna met up after her lectures and went straight back to her flat and to bed. Hanna got up at 8 p.m. and cooked him some pasta; he tried some of her wine but couldn't manage more than a sip. They talked mostly about her current favourite books, namely William Trevor's *The Boarding House* and Brian Moore's *The Emperor of Ice-Cream*. They talked about Bob Dylan and how the visions he was prepared to share with one and all were such a *complete* joy. They talked about Martin's songwriting and his work with The Playboys. Hanna felt, though she didn't present it in a negative way, that as long as Martin was with The Playboys, his songwriting would suffer. They talked about her and her ambitions. She still didn't know exactly what she wanted to do, but she thought that she was on the correct track with her literature course. She felt, and Martin agreed, that going to university was the best thing she had done; unknowingly, she had given her life the focus it obviously needed so much.

Eventually, they noticed that it was 1.30 a.m. Hanna wanted to keep on talking, but knew she'd suffer for it at lectures the following day. She tried to persuade Martin to stay for another day, but he couldn't – he had stuff to do up in Castlemartin. They retired to bed again and fell asleep, this time immediately making up for the previous night's sleep deprivation. They made love first and second thing in the morning though, and before he left she had a present for him: an envelope, which she made him promise not to open until he was on his way home.

Martin returned to Castlemartin, catching a direct lift with the second car to pick him up. On reaching home, he tried to work on a song he'd an idea about called 'The Perfect Day'. It was about Hanna and their first day together in Belfast. Suddenly, he remembered the envelope and reached into his back pocket. He felt it closely between his finger and thumb and felt something solid, metallic maybe, like a coin. He opened the blue envelope and removed the note contained therein. As he was removing the blue note, something dropped out and fell to the floor. Martin stooped and picked up a brand new and shiny key for a Yale lock.

Martin,

I wanted to give you this, and not just so you could open the door to my flat.

My present is to show you that you are welcome any time, day or night, and that you can come and go as you please. I want you to know you can use this place as your own.

I suddenly realised on the first night you stayed with me that the reason (though I couldn't figure it out at the time) that I didn't take up any of the other girls' offers to share accommodation and to split the rent was because I had to save my space to share it with you.

I suppose, in another way, it is also to show you that there is nothing I have that I want to hide from you.

Me,

Hanna

Martin stared at the letter in shock. It seemed like they were having two different kinds of relationships, actually, three now: the physical, which Martin felt was also spiritual, but that didn't qualify as one alone because surely spiritual was a sub-division of the physical; the conversational, which meant they could talk to each other until the cows came home, and left again; and now, a relationship of letters was developing.

He returned to work on 'The Perfect Day', but couldn't get any further on it, so he packed up, wandered around the house for 30 minutes or so feeling lost and alone, went upstairs, packed his guitar into its case and, although it was raining, hitched back down to Belfast again, letting himself into Hanna's flat with his own personal key. Martin was sitting on her sofa, strumming away on his trusted guitar, making progress with 'The Perfect Day', when Hanna returned from lectures.

She was delighted to see him, in fact, she would have been disappointed if he hadn't been there. She made coffee, they talked as he casually strummed the guitar and, before you knew it, it was the following morning and she was returning to Queen's and he had resumed work on his song. She came home at just after five and they picked up where they'd left off as if she'd only been gone for a minute.

The following Monday morning, he hitched a ride home and they got back to their individual lives, but for the first time it was easier for them to imagine what the other was doing when they were apart.

Martin met up with Sean MacGee, who looked like he was on the sauce again, only this time in a big way. Sean seemed to be blown away by 'The Perfect Day'. Sean took Martin's guitar to play his latest songwriting offerings, but he was so out of it that he couldn't get his fingers to follow his brain's instructions. Sean was flustered. He ran out of Martin's house, muttering 'You don't understand.' Who didn't understand? And what didn't they understand? Martin wondered what Sean's problem was. Should he chase after him? Should he give him money?

Martin was confused. As far as he was concerned, songs and writing songs were one and the same as having a conversation with someone, maybe Hanna in this instance, about what was troubling you. As a songwriter, at least some of the time, you were trying to deal with an emotionally charged issue. You were trying to find a way, through your song, to resolve what was troubling you. You could then pass the song on to other people, in the hope that they find it useful or comforting. Martin wondered if Sean had wanted to write songs in order to get to the bottom of what was troubling him. Did the fact that Sean had said '*you* don't understand' mean that *he* himself now did understand? And had he run off because it was too big a problem to explain or to deal with? Martin focused on the one thing that might be the basis of Sean's malaise: he wondered if Sean felt guilty about his brother's untimely death. As the older brother, Sean perhaps felt he was meant to look out for his younger sibling. If this was the case, Martin knew that it would be fruitless to explain to Sean that it would have been impossible to be with his brother all day, every day. Apart from anything else, his brother would have hated being smothered so. This was something Sean had to work his way through, Martin thought – kind words of support from your best friend would never do it alone. The next few occasions that Martin saw Sean, he was completely out of his tree and seemed to grow worse by the day.

Martin decided it was time to help. He went to Sean's house, not knowing what he would find. In fact, for once, Sean wasn't out of it, but he was the worse for wear and Martin was very worried that there seemed to be no one to care for him. He decided he had to find Sean's mum, who he thought would be at the Dreamland Ballroom. She wasn't there. He was getting more and more concerned, so he turned to his manager. Mitchell said that the sad thing in all of these situations, in treating people like Sean MacGee, was that for anyone's help to be effective, the person had to first ask for help. Mitchell claimed that if and when MacGee realised he needed help, then he'd already have started the process of recovery. It didn't mean that he was going to make it through, but at that point at least he had a chance.

He decided that both of them should return to Sean's house. Martin was surprised by Mitchell's reaction: he was so shocked at what he found that he wanted to take Sean immediately to the nearby Mid-Ulster Hospital in Magherafelt. MacGee laughed that off, claiming he'd be fine by lunchtime, adding something about the hair of the dog. Mitchell made MacGee some soup and cajoled him into eating it. Martin had to admit, after the piping hot soup had found its way into MacGee's system, he looked like he'd gained at least a week's reprieve from the grim reaper's visit.

At one point during the morning, though, Martin was convinced that MacGee wasn't going to make it. Like Martin, MacGee had just turned 20, yet his skin was grey and loose around his face; the bum fluff that covered his chin looked dirty and matted. MacGee had started to let his hair grow, but it was curling in all the wrong places and was a complete mess, looking and smelling like it hadn't been washed in over a week. Martin found himself considering MacGee physically for the first time in his life. You kind of accept the shape and look of your friends, don't you? But that morning, Martin suddenly realised that MacGee looked dangerously thin. He also looked like he had lost a tooth or two.

The Playboy and his manager stayed with MacGee that afternoon. Mitchell forced him to have a bath and a shave and put on some clean clothes. Martin was impressed by the way that Mitchell handled MacGee. He didn't adopt the usual school-teacher formula for whipping someone into shape, but exuded more of a look-for-heaven's-sake-get-a-grip-you-look-disgraceful-and-you-don't-have-to kind of vibe, saying: 'Look. You might have to drink, but you don't have to look so dirty.'

Martin winced at this. He fully expected Sean to throw one of his wobblers. But no, he rose from the sofa, went to the mirror, looked into it, rubbed the stubble on his chin and, without a word, went out of the room. A few minutes later, Martin and Mitchell heard water running in the bathroom. Mitchell took Martin and the cleanly shaven Sean into Bradley's in Magherafelt and they all feasted on fish suppers with baked beans, two rounds of buttered bread and a can of Fanta each.

'Two meals in the one day,' Sean said, half joking, and half serious. A bit of colour had reappeared in his cheeks, but Martin was truly worried about his weight. Mitchell suddenly said: 'Look, Sean, I don't know what this is all about, and I don't really need to know. This will mean nothing to you, but you really should think about it: you really need to get a grip on this situation, and fast.' Mitchell then turned to Martin. He looked like he was considering what to say next. 'Look, it's not my call and it's not entirely Martin's either, but pretty soon, if a plan I have up my sleeve takes off, The Playboys are going to need someone to drive them and look after the equipment. Sean, for the love of God, please give Martin and myself an excuse to go to the lads and convince them that the person should be you.'

'Brilliant idea! Sean, it's a great craic on the road with the lads, we've great fun,' Martin said, hoping the nervousness he felt wasn't apparent in his voice. He was thinking, but not saying, that The Playboys as a group of people worked fine together on the road, and adding another person into that mix, particularly someone as potentially volatile as Sean MacGee, could be destructive. He wasn't sure that he wanted to be the one convincing the band to take Sean on board as a driver. He figured that Mitchell probably thought someone like Sean would never take a job with a showband, but by making this offer it might just be the encouragement MacGee needed to get his life back on track.

And what trick did Mitchell have up the sleeve of that fancy coat of his? This was the first mention Martin had heard about anything 'special' in the offing. There must be something though, he thought. Mitchell was not the type of man who liked to spin a yarn for the sake of it. Were any of the other Playboys aware of this special something, which would necessitate them needing an extra person to help out on the road?

Martin was still lost in thought when Mitchell, as he took his wallet out of the inside pocket of his camel-hair coat, said, 'In the meantime, Sean, you can come and work for me at Dreamland. I need someone to troubleshoot between all my ballrooms so I'd like you to come in and learn the ropes and, if it works out, travel around the other ballrooms too. At the same time, you'll be gaining valuable experience for when you do eventually go and work with the boys.'

Sean surprised Martin by looking quite taken aback by the offer; he was speechless, in fact. 'Aren't you going to give me a lecture about drinking?' Sean said, spoiling the moment somewhat as far as Martin was concerned.

'Listen, Sean, I don't need to threaten you with things you already know; you're not a kid. I'm offering you this chance because this is what I need; good staff are hard to find. If you work out, it's great for me and it's great for The Playboys, because you'll know the ropes if you go and work with them and, sadly, if it doesn't work out, I did say good staff are hard to find, but I didn't say they were impossible to find.'

And with that, Mitchell got up, paid Mrs Bradley and was out. Sean and Martin looked at each other. Eventually, Sean rose from his seat. 'Who was that masked man?' he spluttered, as he ran outside to catch up with Mitchell just as he was opening the door to his extremely clean Vauxhall.

'Look,' he said, 'ah, thanks for that. Um… I'll really try, okay?'

'That is all we need, Sean. See you in the morning, 9 a.m. sharp, eh?'

'Yeah,' Sean agreed, as Mitchell got into his car and drove off.

As Sean returned to their table, he said, 'God, Martin, I was never expecting any of that. Maybe the fish supper, but none of the other stuff.'

'Yeah,' Martin agreed and adopted a Jimmy Stewart accent, 'Life's a beach,' he paused, rolling his chin around to form the next words, 'ugh, and then the tide comes in.'

THE LAST DANCE
BOOK THREE

CHAPTER TWENTY-SEVEN

Put a tiger in your tank!

Esso promotional campaign

I n 1966, Dickie Rock was Ireland's entry in the Eurovision Song Contest and, like Butch Moore the year before, it increased his media profile enormously. That same year, The Beatles played their final paid show, at Shea Stadium in San Francisco, and they breathed a collective sigh of relief, having escaped with their sanity. Free from the chains of the road, The Beatles released not one but two classic albums: *Rubber Soul* and *Revolver*. The Beach Boys reached their own artistic peak with *Pet Sounds*. The Royal Showband spent hours at rehearsal learning 'God Only Knows', and were quite chuffed with their efforts, at least they were until they heard The Freshmen's version of the Brian Wilson classic. They decided to leave the Beach Boys material to the best (bar none, including the original). Martin Dean was very pleased to see a member of the Rat Pack return to the charts with 'Strangers In The Night', which turned out to be one of the biggest singles of the year. Phil Spector produced the classic 'River Deep – Mountain High' for Ike & Tina Turner, resulting in an artistic high that neither artist nor producer would attain again.

In Ireland, all the top showbands featured prominently in the Irish charts; in fact, 1966 would prove to be a vintage showband year. The Playboys worked as hard as the rest, chalking up umpteen miles on the country roads. They frequently met up with other bands and exchanged stories in late-night pit stops, such as Dirty Dick's in Limerick. The best tale they heard from around that time was of a guitarist with one of the big bands. He was a brilliant musician by the name of Edward, and he was aptly nicknamed 'Tiger'. One night, outside the Pallidrome Ballroom in Strabane, one of his fellow band members came across this wee girl wandering around, 'waiting for her mate to give her a lift home'. The mate, it turned out, was in the back of her car with the aforementioned Tiger. The stray girl explained to the showband musician that she was worried about her mate, who was making no signs of emerging from her Mini – 'the one with all the windows steamed up'.

'I hope she's okay?' the girl pleaded.

'Oh believe you me, she's *very* okay,' the musician replied with a knowing smile, 'she's got a Tiger in her tank.' The members of The Playboys were never able to look at the Esso Tiger's tail on their wagon again without breaking into hysterics.

1966 was also the year that the Moors Murderers – 28-year-old Ian Brady and 23-year-old Myra Hindley – were both sentenced to life imprisonment. Their evil shocked both England and Ireland so much that both populations collectively crossed themselves and hoped that life imprisonment meant exactly that.

Ian Paisley was also back in the news again. This time he announced his intentions to become an MP at a rally in Belfast Ulster Hall. A thousand people turned up, and Paisley was later arrested because he had refused to be bound over on charges of unlawful assembly arising from disturbances in Belfast on June 6.

In the little town of Castlemartin, Sean MacGee, sadly, fell off the wagon in a big way – you could have heard the thud three villages away. He also fell out of favour with his two supporters, Mitchell and Martin.

Mo and Angela announced that they were expecting their first child in the first week of September, and Castlemartin's villagers counted off the months on their fingers, the more charitable among them reaching the fourth finger of their second hand. Mr and Mrs Blair moved into a new house that Dixie had built for them by the Lough shore, close to the Dreamland Ballroom.

Now that The Playboys were on the radio, everyone knew them. Even people who didn't go to dances knew them – and that included people from Randalstown to Ramelton; from Tobermore to Tipperary; from Maghera to Moy and from Castlemartin to Cork. If RTÉ Radio, the only station in the country, played your single, then everyone in Ireland heard you!

The band's third single was released that summer. It was a double A-side, coupling a Martin McClelland original, 'There's Always A Song At The End Of A Teardrop', with The Playboys' version of 'What Do You Want To Make Those Eyes At Me For?', the song that had proved to be so popular at dances. Martin insisted that Brendan sing lead vocals on 'Teardrop'. The song was best served in a country setting, and he therefore thought it much more suited to Brendan's voice. Brendan, for his part, was very happy with the decision and accepted graciously. Dixie thought that if The Royal could have more than one lead singer, then so could The Playboys. Mitchell was happy with the arrangement because Martin was happy, as in ecstatic, to be the songwriter and let others perform his self-penned tunes.

Once again, it was the cover that received the majority of the airplay, and Martin Dean and The Playboys did what Emile Ford & The Checkmates had failed to do, namely take the song 'What Do You Want To Make Those Eyes At Me For?' into the Irish Top Ten – it peaked at number six. It was their third hit in a row in Ireland. In Scotland, the single sold moderately well, the fans opting for the McClelland original, which just made the Top Ten (number nine, in fact).

So, in a way, you'd have to suppose that Gentleman Jim Mitchell could have been forgiven for doing what every other manager in the country would have done in his place: bask in the glory of his new-found success. And there were certainly enough outward signs of positive movement to confirm this to be true. Things like better ballrooms, larger crowds, bigger fees and, of course, higher wages; more media coverage, including the front cover of *New Spotlight* magazine (a colour shot of Martin Dean, which both Hanna Hutchinson and Kathleen McClelland had framed and hung in their respective homes). *New Spotlight* was now also basking in the glory of a claimed 35,000 circulation.

Mitchell had discovered early on that the secret to securing the front page of the showband bible was not so much about making progress on the circuit as it was about paying for a few adverts within its pages. But Mitchell, driven by some indeterminable thing, decided to bide his time, waiting to make his move when the band picked up momentum; something as much to do with physics as showbusiness.

He had a plan, and he summoned all the members of band to his office on one Monday in August 1966. He was convinced that he had an idea that would secure the future of The Playboys, and catapult them into the rare air hitherto occupied only by The Royal Showband, The Miami, The Freshmen, The Drifters and The Dixies.

CHAPTER TWENTY-EIGHT

Who's Brian Epstein – a solicitor?

Davy

The Playboys from Castlemartin knew that there must be something big in the offing when they were called for the meeting on that fine Monday in August. It was the same week, in fact, that the future number one hit single by The Johnstons, 'The Travelling People', entered the Irish charts. The Johnstons' place in Irish music circles was secured, albeit through the folk back door, by the fact that, in one of the later line-ups, they introduced to the music world Paul Brady, a young lad from Strabane and a successful musician later in life.

Normally, Playboy matters would be discussed by Dixie and Mitchell, and once they'd near enough made up their minds about how best to go about their business, Dixie would bring it up with the boys. These conversations would start off in one of two ways: good news would always be delivered on an outward journey on the way to a dance with: 'Listen, heads, I was thinking that maybe we should...'; bad news was delivered the minute that Lough Neagh came into view and just as they coasted down the steep hill into Castlemartin: 'Bit of bad news for you, heads, Jimitch has just informed me that...' (It was too early to tell if The Playboys' new nickname for their manager would stick. One thing was sure; it would certainly never be used in his company.)

Unusually, Dixie was late for the meeting, and suggestions were made that Colette had taken to handcuffing him to the bedpost and probably forgotten to unlock him before she went to work that morning. Dixie had gone to great pains to explain to Colette that she didn't have to work, but she ignored him; she wanted and needed to do *something* while he was away on the road. So she had kept her job, and her mates, at the Burns's shirt factory in nearby Magherafelt.

Rather than waste valuable time until Dixie decided to show up, Mitchell left the leaderless band in his office with their coffees, teas and KitKats and went about his business in other parts of the ballroom. The band was happy to catch up on Smiley's recent adventures. 'So, head,' Brendan began, 'how did you and the Lone Ranger and Tonto get on last night?'

Robin and Davy had recently been nicknamed after the masked one and his trusted companion because they were always off on romantic adventures – *together.* They also, supposedly on a dare, had both dyed their hair black. As both of them had been dark in the first place, the only difference it seemed to make was that they now looked as though they had permanently dirty necks. On a less acceptable level to the married men in the band, they both appeared to have become preoccupied with hanging around Agnew's Café in Magherafelt so they could ogle all the college girls with their short skirts and white bobby-socks pulled up over their knees. Smiley said they'd grow out of it. Martin wasn't sure if he was referring to the girls or to Robin and Davy.

On this particular occasion, following the previous night's dance in Belfast, they, along with Smiley, had set off into the night insisting that they'd make their own way home, which was usually a sure sign that they'd either scored or *thought* they'd scored. There had been two girls who ran the mineral stall; one, Tessie, generous in proportion, and the other, Twinkie (that's what she swore her name was – mind you, she swore about quite a few other things as well), who was smaller and, unlike her friend, totally stunning. Although Smiley was too much of a gentleman to admit this, last night's adventure, or at least the opening chapters of it, was a textbook display of his modus operandi in that he didn't always go after the most obvious girl as his first choice. That didn't, of course, mean that they didn't frequently chase *him*, but that was another adventure. So, whereas he was happy to chat up Tessie, unchallenged I might add, Robin and Davy were fighting off competition for her friend, Twinkie. Smiley's girl wasn't going to risk losing her catch; she had a quiet word with Twinkie, who then announced it would be okay if Robin and Davy joined her and her mate, and Smiley of course, 'back at our house for a cup of tea and sandwiches'.

'Back at *our* house' was code for 'we don't live with our parents'. Even Davy could tell that they weren't sisters. For The Playboys' terrible trio, this meant that as far as the other band members were concerned, 'We're okay, we'll find our own way home tonight thank you very much, lads.'

The five of them piled into a taxi, the driver charging them a premium because 'it's illegal to carry five'. Apparently that didn't matter, as long as the passengers paid 50 per cent over the odds. 20 minutes later, they all arrived at a small, terraced house in the back of beyond. A small, terraced house that three years later they wouldn't dare to have visited because of The Troubles, even if Brigitte Bardot was inviting them home.

The minute they walked through the front door, a bit of a pong wafted around five sets of nostrils. In the living room, there were two large plates in the centre of the table, one with egg and onion sandwiches and the other empty. The boys glanced at each other knowingly, and the girls went off to make some tea. The boys, still hungry from their work on stage, and the chores they predicted lay ahead for them during the night, tore into the sandwiches. They tasted okay, but eventually one by one they detected something didn't smell quite right. Robin knowingly excused it with, 'You know, just girls living together', and winked at Smiley and Davy, who nodded in agreement. On they went, tearing into another round.

Next thing they knew, there were footsteps coming down the stairs. They were convinced that they hadn't heard either of the girls go up the stairs, so by a process of elimination they assumed it must be a husband or, at the very least, a boyfriend coming down to see what all the racket was. Intuitively, Davy and Robin, sandwiches still in hands, ran behind Smiley. Now Smiley, as we know, was so thin and gangly that a decent gust of wind would have blown him over, and maybe Robin and Davy were hoping that the old adage 'surely you'd never hit a man with glasses?' or maybe more appropriately in Smiley's case, 'surely you'd never hit a matchstick man?' would help their cause. But whatever the reason, they obviously felt safer behind Smiley, so that was where they stayed as they heard the creaking of the last stair and then the flip-flopping of bare feet against the oil cloth.

'Oh Jesus, Mary and St Joseph,' Davy whispered, 'we're all going to get murdered. I can see it now on the front page of next week's fecking *New Spotlight* and that awfully nice showband priest, Father D'Arcy, saying, "Of course they were sinners, but they didn't deserve to die so young".' The door to the living room creaked open agonisingly slowly, inch by inch, as the boys' lives flashed before their eyes.

'Ma, she's thrown my dish out in the garden,' a wee black-haired boy cried. He froze when he saw the lads from The Playboys, and turned on his heels only to run straight into Tessie's midriff, which didn't cause him any pain due to the fact that it acted as a very soft cushion.

'What are you doing up so late?' Tessie asked, appearing to ignore her more instinctive aggressive demeanour.

'Ma, she's thrown my dish out the back.'

'Oh, we'll get it in the morning,' Tessie said, trying to comfort him, 'now off to bed with you.'

'Nagh,' the wee boy bawled at the top of his lungs, waking the entire neighbourhood Smiley was sure. 'I want my dish; me da gave me that dish. I want my dish.'

And that is how, five minutes later, Tessie, Twinkie, a wee boy and his sleepy sister were out in a very small garden, sharing three torches and searching for a dish, Smiley, Davy and Robin, for something else. Smiley thought the dish surely would be broken if it had been flung out into the stony garden. He wondered why the boy would have grown so attached to a dish in the first place, perhaps a valuable piece of Clarice Cliff? At least that would make some kind of sense.

Ten minutes later, Tessie grew impatient with the search and left the wee boy and his sister out in the garden with the torches: 'Two of you with three torches will see just as much as seven of us and three torches'. Obviously she was working on some variation of the five loaves and two fishes tale, Smiley thought, not realising just how close he was; correct tail, wrong miracle.

They left the children to it, retiring to the living room to the sandwiches and the other game in hand. Every now and again they were distracted by the giant shadows on the window blinds that the children created with their torches. Some of the images were eerie and some comical. The tea was scorching and the sandwiches, even though they smelled a bit off, went down a treat, thanks to the tea. Twinkie was interviewing both Davy and Robin about a potential horizontal opportunity while Smiley and Tessie were on a sofa by themselves. They were just about to make their own sweet music when there was a bit of commotion outside the window.

'I've found it,' the wee boy screeched. 'I've found my dish!' They all turned to look at the window and, even though they couldn't see clearly, they could make out the elongated shadow of the wee boy bending down and then rising up again, holding between his thumb and forefinger not a *dish*, but a *fish*.

The Playboys trio looked to one another as the wee boy ran into the room and plonked a rainbow trout on the empty plate beside the sandwiches. The wee girl kept her distance at the living-room door and cried, 'I can't believe you're still allowing him to keep that thing, our da caught it for him over a week ago!'

The following day, Dixie walked into Mitchell's office just as Smiley was concluding telling this story to the rest of the band, who thought it was hysterical. Dixie, whose face was flushed, seemed relieved that he was able to slip into the room under the cloak of laugher and he helped himself to a mug of tea and a KitKat. Half a minute later, Mitchell returned to his office and took his seat behind his desk. Dixie made his apologies, and Mitchell announced that he was sure that the band would excuse him and understand his new-found marital responsibilities.

'Colette home early for lunch, then?' asked the not-quite-so dis-creet Robin. A few more titters followed.

Mitchell cleared his throat. 'Okay, I wanted to see you all today because I wanted to discuss what I think The Playboys should do next.' No one spoke. 'I'll assume you want me to continue,' Mitchell said, openly amused by their silence. 'I think we should enter The Playboys as Ireland's next representative at the Eurovision Song Contest.'

'Wow!' said Robin, the trombonist.

'Gear,' said Brendan, the guitarist.

'God,' said Barry, the organist.

'Fab,' said Davy, the bassist.

'Out of sight,' said Mo, the drummer.

'Hold on, I'm coming,' said Smiley, the trumpet player, and everyone enjoyed another laugh. Neither Dixie nor Martin offered any comment.

'Okay. The way I see it,' Mitchell continued with his semi-pre-pared speech, 'the big boys seem to be happy running around in circles.'

'But *what* circles,' Robin said, in genuine awe.

'Yes, but it can't last forever,' Mitchell said.

'I hear T.J. Byrne has a two-year waiting list for The Royal; that's not bad, head.' Brendan said.

'No, it's not,' Mitchell agreed, 'but there's only one Royal and they are starting to spend half their year in Vegas, so obviously their time in Ireland is at a premium. But I've seen this kind of thing before. You can't keep going to the well and drawing out water. No matter how deep the well was to start with, it will eventually run low.

Only a fool will let the well run dry before they start looking for another source to sustain them.'

'So, you think the Eurovision Song Contest would be a good alternative source for us?' Dixie asked.

'One of them,' Mitchell, replied. 'Obviously, it's not one we can run to continually; once will be all, in fact. But you just have to look at the crowds who turned up at the airport to welcome Butch Moore back home from Naples.'

'Aye, but then it all went pear-shaped when the papers jumped all over him for being married,' Brendan said.

'Yes, but that's only because he was trying to hide the fact that he was married. Everyone knows the married men in our band and you've got nothing to hide, Martin, have you?'

'Not a thing,' Martin replied immediately, and then chastised himself under his breath as he thought about the relationship he was secretly conducting with Hanna.

'And look at Dickie Rock,' Mitchell continued, 'and The Miami's number one Irish single earlier this year with their Eurovision entry, "Come Back To Stay".'

'But The Capitol died off,' Dixie offered, 'how do you explain that?'

'Well, as I said, there was all that hoo-ha in the papers with Butch and the wife he told no one about. That sort of press does no one any favours. As I say, it's a great platform, a grand opportunity, but you have to use it wisely. '65 was The Capitol's year, but this year they seem to have lost it. The big mistake made by both Butch and The Capitol and Dickie and The Miami was that they couldn't see beyond Ireland. They only beat their drum about their success here. The Eurovision Song Contest will be broadcast in seventeen countries next year; what we should do is look to promote ourselves in some of those territories, or in England at least.

'We've enjoyed two chart successes in Scotland, that proves we've got legs beyond Ireland. Why not use Scotland on the one hand and the Eurovision Song Contest on the other to attack England in the same way we've attacked Ireland? Then, you know what? We'll be so busy in England we won't get a chance to tour Ireland nonstop, so the Irish dancers will be desperate for us when we do get a chance to tour Ireland.'

'Oh, I wouldn't want to give up the ballrooms,' Brendan said, quick as a flash.

'Me neither,' Davy immediately agreed.

'And I'm not asking you to; I'm asking you to help me develop other countries so we can *secure* Ireland,' Mitchell pleaded.

'But I heard you tell Jim Aiken at the dance in Belfast last night that we don't have a free night for fifteen months,' Robin said, proving once again that nothing missed his large and floppy ears.

'Yes, and when a girl tells Smiley she won't kiss him, it makes him want to kiss her all the more, doesn't it?' Mitchell said.

'And that's a fact,' Smiley agreed, as the rest of them laughed

'But I'd be totally up for the Eurovision as long as it means we wouldn't be deserting Ireland,' Brendan chipped in, offering the first sign of a positive response from the band.

As usual, Davy, Barry and Robin toed the party line. Smiley said that he would go with the flow. Mo agreed to nothing that would keep him away from Angela, but he was happy to go with the lads' decision because he could always report back to his wife that it was for the good of the band. He also chose this moment to advise the band that they too wanted to build a house, and they were going to need one more room than Dixie and Colette had built.

'Dixie?' Mitchell started, now he had a bit of wind in his sail, 'what's your view on this?'

'Well, my dad agrees with you. He's also saying that we need to seriously consider our future. He thinks the bubble will eventually burst too, and he feels we should make as much hay as we can while the sun is still shining.'

'Without getting sunburned, of course,' Mitchell couldn't resist adding. 'Look, lads, The Playboys are a good, well-respected band, no doubt about it. But the difference between being remembered and not being remembered is *greatness*.'

'Yes,' Dixie added, 'but if you and my dad both agree that the bubble is going to burst, what's the point of wasting time trying to break into other places when we can still continue to rake it in here in Ireland? Surely trips to the UK and Europe merely distract us from our maximum earning potential here?'

'Tell that to Brian Epstein.'

'Who's Brian Epstein – a solicitor?' Davy asked.

'No, you fool, he's the manager of The Beatles,' Robin chipped in.

'But we're not The Beatles,' Smiley said, with a hint of sadness in his voice.

'No, agreed, and that's fine – there's only room for one group like The Beatles. My point wasn't to say that we should try to be The Beatles; my point was that if Brian Epstein took your approach, Dixie, he'd have had the band playing in the Cavern in Liverpool forever. But his plan was to make his band the biggest in Liverpool, and then move out from that success and become the biggest band in Northern England, and then the whole of England and then onwards and upwards to Europe and America…'

'… and as of today, the world,' Brendan agreed.

'*Exactly*,' Mitchell replied, raising his voice a little, 'and so now they're in a position whereby they've made enough money to last them and their heirs for generations to come. But do you see them stopping? No, of course not, because they've got goals, musical goals, and the reason why they are being so successful is because they are chasing those goals more feverishly than anyone else around.'

'And they've got great songs,' Martin added.

'And The Playboys have great songs,' Mitchell stated positively.

'Yes we do, head,' Brendan said, leading where the others would follow.

'Would you see us doing one of Martin's songs in the Eurovision Song Contest?' Dixie asked.

'Why, yes, of course – his songs set us apart from the rest of the bands,' Mitchell replied.

'It's not just the songs, it's the band's arrangements,' Martin added, looking directly at Dixie.

'Of course,' Mitchell agreed, 'it's Martin's songs and the band's sound that makes The Playboys unique.'

'The Capitol had a lot of assistance from Phil Coulter for their Eurovision song,' Robin chipped in.

'Who's Phil Coulter?' Davy asked and – thinking of Epstein – added quickly, 'Their manager?'

'No, he's a young songwriter from Derry and he wrote their first two songs and arranged "I'm Walking The Streets In The Rain",' Robin replied, in his role as the accepted voice of knowledge in the band.

'Who actually wrote "I'm Walking The Streets In The Rain?"' Dixie asked. Robin seemed to think it was Fred Astaire.

'No, I don't think it was,' Martin said, correcting him politely. 'Being the Irish entry it had to be by an Irish writer; I believe a young Kildare woman called Teresa Conlon wrote it.'

'Do you have any suitable songs, Martin?' Brendan asked. Martin looked to Dixie, acknowledging the unwritten chain of command and not saying a word.

Dixie immediately picked up on Martin's etiquette and said: 'I don't suppose you have any Eurovision Song Contest winners up your sleeve for us, Martin?'

CHAPTER TWENTY-NINE

I hear all the fish up in the Moyola River have been dying of vinyl poisoning

Anonymous

On reflection, Jim Mitchell was more than a little disappointed by Martin's initial reply. Whereas the manager had been expecting a very positive response, The Playboys' in-house songwriter promised he would look through his songs when he got home and see what he could come up with.

But then, as the boys were drifting off to set up their gear for a rehearsal, Martin hung back in the office. 'You didn't seem so sure you'd have a suitable tune for this auld contest?' Mitchell said, at a volume he knew only Martin would hear.

'No, I'm sure I'll have one. I just didn't want any of the boys pushing me for titles yet. I need to review all the songs and see which one would be most suitable for the contest,' Martin replied, stepping back into the office again.

'Surely your best song will stand the best chance?' Mitchell said, hoping that he wasn't putting pressure on the young writer.

'Not necessarily so,' Martin continued, proving he'd been giving the matter some serious thought. 'For instance, "Still She Dances With You" is great for the ballrooms, but I'm not sure it would be so good as a Eurovision entry. Television requires you to make a different kind of connection. With the dancers, it's simply a matter of getting the tapping of feet to open the door to your song; for television, however, from what I can work out, you need a bigger melody more likely than not, and it needs to have a beautiful chorus and a smooth, arresting instrumental break. A song like The Beatles' 'If I Fell', for instance, would be perfect for the Eurovision Song Contest.'

'Okay,' Mitchell said, noticeably relieved. 'So do you think you can look through your songs and come up with one by the end of the week?'

'Yeah, if there's one there, I'll definitely be able to let you know by the end of the week.'

'But do you think there might be?' Mitchell pushed.

'I think there might be,' Martin agreed. The Playboys were starting to crank up the volume on stage, so Martin made his excuses and went off to join them.

Mitchell was left in his office, still not exactly sure how the meeting had gone, but semi-content in that he felt he had the band's blessing to approach the Eurovision project. He was surprised by how unsupportive Dixie appeared, and belatedly congratulated himself on not initially addressing the matter with Dixie alone, as had been his usual method.

Now that he had the band's mandate, sort of, what should be his next move? How would the Irish entry be selected? Which came first, the singer or the song?

The oracle on these matters, Sammy Barr, his friend in Ballymena, thought that the big boys, the managers of the top ten Irish showbands, had a committee, and that each year they got together and selected the artist. The Flamingo owner didn't really know how they selected the song.

Okay, Mitchell thought, at least that's a starting point. He knew all the members of that particular exclusive group because he dealt with most of them on a weekly basis. What if he lobbied them for The Playboys to be the 1967 entry? What kind of response might he expect? Could he expect a better kind of response if he offered them all an extra 5 or 10 per cent of the box office the next time their bands appeared on his circuit? Or would some of them be perhaps a little more agreeable if Mitchell booked their new unproven acts for his circuit?

But then, he thought, wasn't that just a little corrupt? Hell, maybe even a lot corrupt. Mitchell knew that in all big-money businesses there was a certain amount of corruption, and *acceptable* corruption at that, in that it was seen as the norm within certain quarters of the ever-growing showband industry. For instance, a lot of the show-bands bought their own singles, inflating their chart positions. The penny hadn't even dropped when Sammy Barr claimed that after The Playboys' 'Still She Dances With You' entered the Irish charts, someone had told him, 'I hear all the fish up in the Moyola River have been dying of vinyl poisoning.'

Mitchell and The Playboys only found out about this 'chart-hyping' when the wee girls who gathered around the stage after the dances started asking for free singles, 'just like so-and-so give us. So-and-so give us four and five copies of their new single to every-one that asked.' The more Mitchell looked into the chart-hyping, the more seedy undertones he discovered. There was a famous inci-dent with The Cadets, where their most famous single, 'I Gave My Wedding Dress Away', was reported to be outselling everything else in Ireland in October 1964 by at least two to one, and yet the high-est position the single could make in the charts was number four. Mitchell thought that their singer, Eileen Reid, must have been sick as a dog for having to dress up in that wedding dress each night to plug the single, only to find herself *allegedly* beaten to the top by sleight of hand.

Other reported forms of corruption, if you could call them that, were bands buying hundreds of copies of *New Spotlight* around poll time and voting for themselves – hardly an imprisonable offence, mind you. The Playboys, of course, had also found it easier to secure their first front page after they'd spent a few bob advertising in the same magazine. But that was hardly corruption, more like what was to become standard business practice. There was also talk of some showbands being sued for money laundering, but Mitchell could never get to the bottom of that one. And then there was the cash issue. The showband world was cash, all cash, lots of cash. This meant that the taxman had a harder time, but then the cash issue wasn't exclusive to the showband world, far from it in fact.

Mitchell thought about The Playboys and their association with him. What effect would it have on them should he have chosen the blatantly corrupt route? Say, for instance, he had bought off the top ten managers with an extra percentage for their bands, in order that The Playboys secured the Eurovision nomination – assuming of course they'd accept it, which they just might not. People, in this case musicians, go about their work in whatever way they choose. They may be straight, they may be bent, and if they are not bent, they may see others do dishonest things and feel superior to them. But what if some of those others, Mitchell himself for instance, in doing something that was bent or dishonest, actually benefited the musicians in question? What would the musicians then feel? Would they still feel superior?

But that had never been Mitchell's way. He was an honourable man. Sometimes stories would go around the town about this deal and about that deal. These stories usually originated from people who'd not been able to take advantage. But Mitchell's philosophy, borrowed from Plato, was that when people speak ill of you, live your life to prove them wrong. This had always been his approach, even though he knew the words of Spurgeon to be equally true: 'A lie travels around the world while the truth is still putting its shoes on.'

That August day in his office – as The Playboys practised The Kinks' recent Irish number one hit, 'Sunny Afternoon', below him

– Mitchell wondered if he was actually considering doing something he knew to be corrupt, or whether it was the fact that he *wouldn't* do it, even though it could prove to be very beneficial to Martin and The Playboys. He came to the conclusion that the thought process was exactly the same for both, but was that a way to justify doing something corrupt?

Suddenly, the phone rang.

It was Thomas Boyle, the owner of City Records in Dublin. Mitchell had already told Boyle of his plans, and Boyle, for his part, had done a bit of research of his own in Dublin. The good news, no, the *great* news, was that the showband managers had nothing whatsoever to do with picking the Eurovision entry. Apparently, according to Boyle, you sent your songs into Radio Éireann (even though Eire's national radio station had changed its name to Radio Telefís Éireann, or RTÉ for short, earlier that year in February, everyone, especially those in the wee North, still referred to it as Radio Éireann) and *they* consider the entries along with the singer.

'Does young Martin have a song?' Thomas Boyle asked.

'Does he have a song?' the overjoyed Mitchell sang back down the extremely crackly line. People in America were dreaming about putting a man on the moon, and yet Mitchell couldn't enjoy a clear-line telephone conversation with a colleague 150 miles down the road.

'I think he might have the first, second and third entries,' Mitchell boasted through the static.

'Fabulous,' Boyle replied, refusing to use the shorter, hipper version of the word. 'The song contest is in March, so we need to get the single released in Ireland and Scotland by early February at the latest.'

Before Mitchell had time to register the obvious complaint, Boyle continued: 'The minute we have it recorded, you and I will play it to a friend of mine, John Woods. John runs Pye Records very successfully. I'd like to play it to him with a view to getting it released in England the week before the song contest. We're hoping to do a few projects with John, and I've already mentioned Martin to him.'

'The Playboys you mean, of course?' Mitchell cut in.

The static filled the space between them for a good ten seconds.

'Jim, this is a bigger conversation that we need to have at a later date.' Now it was Mitchell's turn to hesitate.

'Okay, Thomas. I'm in Dublin tomorrow,' Mitchell lied, 'why don't we meet up and we can talk about this in more detail? I really do need to pick your brains on this Eurovision issue.'

'Okay, that's fine, lunch or dinner?'

'Dinner's good,' Mitchell said, knowing he'd have limited time, not to mention attention, over lunch, as Thomas hated being out of his office during working hours. 'I'll meet you in the Shelbourne at 7.30 p.m.'

'See you then,' Boyle returned before disconnecting.

CHAPTER THIRTY

*Spotting your own band, a
band no one else had spotted,
and making that work... well
that's just like beating the
odds in gambling*

Gentleman Jim Mitchell

eanwhile, back on stage at the other end of the Dreamland
Ballroom, The Playboys were also discussing the merits of the
Eurovision Song Contest as they sat facing each other in a circle, noodling away quietly on their instruments.

'You were a bit quiet up there, Dixie. Don't you think it's a good idea?' Brendan was the first to draw the conversation back towards the meeting.

'I suppose it was a bit of a shock, that's all, a lot to take in,' Dixie said hesitantly.

'But you do think it's a good idea?' Davy asked, for he really wanted to know.

'I don't think it's as cut and dried as that,' Dixie replied, still feeling his way.

'Dixie,' Brendan began, exasperated, slipping into the Ben Lang language he was so frustrated, 'you're our legeader, for Jegesus' sake, tell us what's on your megind?'

'Well, as well as having a lot to gain, I also think we have a lot to lose. We're not The Capitol…'

'Aye, we're a lot better,' Robin said, 'and that's a fact.'

'Yes, but they're a lot bigger than us and they only came sixth,' Dixie continued. 'No wonder their career has all but disappeared. Sixth is no victory, sure it's a disaster!'

'But they were number one in Ireland with it?' Barry offered.

'But they'd already achieved number one twice before 'Walking The Streets In The Rain' and they've barely made the Top Ten with their three singles since,' Robin, who knew everything, added.

'But what about Dickie?' Brendan asked.

'Well, it certainly doesn't seem to have done him any harm, but then The Miami were a lot bigger than The Capitol in the first place, so I'm surprised they even entered it,' Dixie conceded.

'But then Dickie always knew all the correct moves, didn't he?' Robin said, and broke into a fit of laughter. 'What was that famous quote of his? "Brendan Bowyer jumps around the stage, Joe Dolan slides around the stage, but I *move* around the stage."'

'Aye, a bit of a mover, and maybe he and Butch know something we don't,' Brendan said, and played a few chords before he continued, 'maybe Jimitch knows something we don't as well!' Jimitch had now definitely become the accepted nickname for their manager.

'Well, I think we need to be cautious,' Dixie said solemnly. 'Just because Jimitch says it's a good idea doesn't mean that it automatically is.'

'Equally, just because he says that it's a good idea doesn't automatically mean that it isn't,' Martin interrupted, probably shooting way above most of the heads' heads.

'He certainly seems to have known what he's been doing so far,' Davy said.

'Yeah, that's a good point, Davy,' Brendan said, 'I mean, I take on board what you're saying, Dixie, and if we were as big as The

Royal or The Miami maybe we should be scared and protective of our position, but really we don't have a lot to lose.'

'Well, on the plus side,' Dixie conceded, 'there is the fact that there will be a tremendous amount of publicity if we manage to make the cut. On top of which, I suppose in a way if we did become the Irish entry then you'd have to say that we'd be up there with The Capitol and The Miami immediately.'

'We'd draw better crowds, we'd get a bigger split on the percentage and we all take home even more money,' Davy declared confidently.

'Which would mean, Dixie,' Robin added, 'that we'd have a bigger cushion if the bubble ever bursts.'

'But not if we're working Europe,' Dixie added.

'Dixie, I don't know about you,' Brendan chipped in again, 'but I'm making lots of money. I've even paid off my debts. I've a right few bob left over as well, and I'm certainly not hurting. But you know what, head? I wouldn't mind seeing a bit of Europe.'

There was then a bit of general discussion about Europe for a few minutes before Dixie, finally turning with the tide, said: 'Well, I suppose you're right. Maybe we should give it a stab, just as long as we keep an eye on things and Jimitch doesn't put us into Europe unless we all agree.' Now they'd reached this point, Davy and Barry started to grow quite excited about the prospect.

It was Martin's turn to be the voice of reason: 'You know, heads, there's more to this than us agreeing to do it: we still have to get into the contest,' he said, choosing that moment to remove his comb from his back pocket and give his hair the once over.

'Oh yes,' Robin agreed, 'but that's outside of our control, isn't it? That's down to you and your songs.' Martin was worried that they all just might have figured that one out.

'Have you got a winner for us, Martin?' Brendan asked, trying to contain his excitement. Martin's reply to the band was a lot more modest than Gentleman Jim Mitchell's had been to Thomas Boyle.

Mitchell and Martin had a chance to compare notes at 7 p.m., when the manager surprised the songwriter by picking him up on the outskirts of Castlemartin as he hitched in the direction of Belfast. Martin actually spotted Mitchell coming down the road in his trademark highly polished Vauxhall VX490, and hoped his manager would pass him. He was supposed to be trawling through his batch of songs in search of the Eurovision Song Contest winner. Martin knew exactly which song he wanted to use, but there were some aspects of it he wanted to work on before he presented it to manager and band.

'And where are you off to?' Mitchell asked as he opened the door.

'Down into Belfast for the night,' Martin replied, as he threw his guitar onto the back seat.

'Tell me,' Mitchell said, as he put the car into gear and moved off, 'would Belfast be the big attraction, or would it be an old schoolmate?'

Martin didn't know if Mitchell meant Sean MacGee, which he hoped was the case, or Hanna Hutchinson. He didn't like to lie, so he didn't. 'Ah sure, there'd be a bit more excitement in the city wouldn't there? And yourself, where're you heading?'

'Aye, I'm on my way to Dublin for a couple of meetings.'

'What, the song contest stuff?'

'Aye, that and other,' Mitchell replied, 'I just want to get a bit more background, and then City Records are going to have a few ideas to throw in the pot as well. Do you want to come on down for the spin?'

'Nah,' Martin sighed, 'not this time. Perhaps another though.'

Martin had a good, long chat with Mitchell. They talked mostly about showbusiness, songwriting, ballrooms, showbands and family. Well, Martin's family.

'Did you ever get to meet your father?' Mitchell asked.

'No, never. It's always just been me and my mother,' Martin replied immediately.

'Did you ever want to get to know him?'

'No. It's always been me and my mam, and she's been great and that's all I've ever needed. My father for some reason decided that he didn't want to be with me and my mam, and so off he went. It can't have been easy for her, but, you know, I never ever felt I was missing out on things. I mean, thanks to you of course, she's always earned good money and, how does she put it, she's "always enjoyed flexible hours".'

'Now, it's been a two-way thing, believe you me. My organisation would have ground to a halt if it hadn't been for your mother.'

'So what about yourself?' Martin asked, turning the tables. Mitchell looked a little disappointed, maybe not so much at Martin's question but more at the questions he didn't have the chance to ask.

'What about myself?'

'Well, you know, have you ever been married? Do you have any children? Do you have brothers and sisters? Are your parents still alive?' Martin reeled off his list of questions, the list often discussed by The Playboys.

'I've never been married. I was an only child. My parents are dead.'

'I'm sorry… sir,' Martin said, not knowing what else to call him.

'Jim, Martin, I keep telling you that my name is Jim; it's perfectly fine to use that.'

'Did your parents die when you were young, Jim?'

'Aye, my parents died when I was very young. My mother died during childbirth in fact, and my father died of a broken heart three years later. My aunt Terry, my father's sister who was living in the Cotswolds, brought me up. My uncle Terence was a bookie, and I learned a lot about horses from him. When I was 21, I inherited my father's estate, and out of that I bought some land around Castlemartin. My grandfather was from here, and I don't know why I did it really, I just came up here once to have a look around the Lough shore and I felt some kind of connection, and so I bought some land, and believe it or not I got into the ballrooms through horses.'

'Really?'

'Yes, a lot of the ballroom people are big gamblers. In fact, a lot of them will tell you that is what they are doing when they run a dance – gambling on the fact that such-and-such a band will draw a certain number of people. That's why we derive such pleasure from unknown bands. I mean, it's no big achievement to make money with The Royal, now really, is it?'

'No, I suppose not,' Martin agreed.

'But spotting your own band, a band that no one else had spotted, and making that work… well that's just like beating the odds in gambling.'

'I suppose,' Martin said. 'The thing that amazes me is that there are just so many bands, there seems to be no end to them.'

'Well, every time a new ballroom springs up in a rural area, if it's a good ballroom, not only will it give dancers an opportunity, but it will also encourage local talent, and so the cream of that crop will be introduced to the circuit. And then you also have to remember that some of these managers have connections to the ballroom chains, some are even involved in consortiums which own the chains, so they are always on the lookout for new bands, new talent to feed their very hungry ballroom machine.'

'So, some managers will manage more than one band?' Martin asked. It wasn't that he was surprised by the news, it was just that he'd never thought about it before.

'Of course, that's how some of these bands, you know, the ones you were wondering about, get their break: riding on the coat-tails of one of the bigger bands. The Clippers used to go around the ballroom circuit plugging The Capitol Showband at the end of their dances, and the following week the same places would be packed for The Capitol.'

'Really?' Martin continued, warming greatly to Mitchell's background stories.

'Yes. The first time that The Capitol played the Arcadia in Cork, they drew 3,000 people. First time in, and 3,000 people showed! Amazing, particularly when you think that all of those 3,000 people were there because The Clippers had given them such a fabulous plug the previous week,' Mitchell said, and then smiled. 'By all accounts, The Capitol were brutal, and that is why they didn't get back into Cork for over eight months! Then, when The Capitol got their act together, and broke into the big time, you had to confirm three engagements with The Miami before you'd be allowed one night with The Capitol.'

'I didn't know any of that stuff.'

'It's business Martin, it's *show* business, but it's still a business. Take for instance The Freshmen, hugely successful, full date-sheet, they couldn't take on any more engagements, so they form their own splinter showband called The *New*men to play some of the dances they couldn't do. The Newmen are actually managed by a couple of members of The Freshmen.'

'I suppose it makes sense once it's pointed out,' Martin said, twisting around in his seat. Do you enjoy it, sir... sorry, I mean Jim?'

'I do,' Mitchell replied, 'I enjoy the characters immensely, I enjoy the gamble, I enjoy the craic.'

'Do you enjoy the music?'

'I don't know a lot about music, Martin. I like The Beatles, but I'm not so fond of The Stones. I like The Kinks, but mostly it's the older stuff I like the best. I do like The Freshmen, I think they are one of the best bands we have in the Dreamland.'

'I'd say they're easily *the* best band in Ireland,' Martin announced proudly.

'But they need to be careful, Martin,' Mitchell cautioned.

'Why?'

'Well, if they're not careful and everyone keeps referring to them as geniuses, the dancers will begin to think that they're above their heads and start to give them a miss.'

'But I've been to some of their dances and the crowds *really* love them; they go down a bomb every night.'

'Martin, you'll get no arguments from me about how good they are. I just think they should be careful about what they do next. A nice, big, commercial hit would do them the world of good. Their first record wasn't exactly great, was it? 'La Yenka'. I think it barely managed to make the Top Ten when it was in the charts at the end of last year. For such a big draw, that single should have done a lot better, that's all I'm saying.'

'I think they'll be fine. With 'La Yenka', I think they were just trying too hard to ape the success of The Royal's "Hucklebuck".'

At which point they'd reached Queen's University in Belfast, and Martin said he was happy to hoof it from there. He was happier still not to have Mitchell drop him off at Hanna's and have her name enter the conversation.

Just as Martin was beginning to congratulate himself, Mitchell said, by way of a farewell, 'See you Wednesday. Oh, and by the way, give my regards to Hanna, won't you?'

Martin knew of only two people who were aware of the relationship he and Hanna had, and even they were totally in the dark about what exactly was going on. As he walked to Hanna's flat, he realised that one of the two people he was thinking about wouldn't have any communication with Gentleman Jim Mitchell, and so there was only one person who could have blabbed.

CHAPTER THIRTY-ONE

Hey love, you forgot your glove!

George Ivan Morrison

E ven though Martin had a key to Hanna's flat, he always rang the doorbell when he came around. Hanna just laughed at him and accused him of being an old-fashioned gentleman. He was now regularly coming down to see her after the weekend, and would have stayed on following last night's dance in Belfast were it not for the fact that Jimitch had called the Dreamland meeting earlier that day.

Hanna talked him straight to bed, saying 'more for me than for you'. He was continuously amazed by the fact that they both wanted each other so much and that it was always, at the very least, a mind-blowing experience.

Twenty minutes later and they were up and in the kitchen. Hanna said it was her favourite thing when Martin strummed and played his guitar as she cooked for them. Martin brought Hanna up to speed on the Eurovision plans.

'Isn't that a wee bit twee for you and your songs?' she asked.

'Possibly,' Martin agreed, 'I suppose I was kind of hoping Dixie would object and I wouldn't have to voice an opinion.'

'But he didn't?' Hanna said, mixing the ingredients for one of her magic omelettes.

'No, he didn't.'

'Why would Dixie *not* want his band winning Eurovision? Like you and Jim, he's got two shares, so he'd benefit doubly?' Hanna asked.

'I don't know, I couldn't figure it out. I mean, he was late for the meeting and maybe that threw him. Usually he and Jim Mitchell discuss things together before mentioning it to the band, but this time Jimitch talked to all of us about it at the same time. I've never really seen Dixie behave in that way before, he looked as if he wasn't really saying what was on his mind.'

'So what about you, Martin? It's your song they're talking about – what do you think?'

'Jim Mitchell is very keen on it, and says it could be the perfect way to launch The Playboys outside Ireland.'

'Yes, that makes sense, Martin, I understand that but what do *you* think?'

'Well, I think it could be to the band's advantage, so I'd be wrong to hold them back by not agreeing to it.'

'Yes, I agree with you on that, too' Hanna said, 'but what about *you*, would it be to *your* advantage?'

'Well, I suppose if it's a great enough song, it will draw attention to my songwriting, and that certainly won't do me any harm, no matter what I'm going to do. It's the songwriting that I derive the most pleasure in my life from,' Martin said.

Hanna flashed him a coy look and raised her eyebrows into a 'really?' arch. 'Well no, maybe not the *most* pleasure. Anyway, moving swiftly along, Billy Brown told me an amusing story about The Beach Boys and their songwriter, Brian Wilson, whom Billy Brown positively raves about. He's so into songwriting and recording that he now sends The Beach Boys out to do concerts without him and he stays at home, writing and recording.'

Hanna looked like she had a question, so Martin stopped talking to encourage her to ask it. When she did, it turned out to be the most asked question of the day: 'Have you got a song in mind, Martin?'

'I have,' Martin replied.

'That sounded very much like, "I have *but*..." to me, Martin.'

'Well, I think it might work...'

'Which song is it?'

'It's called, "Did She Say Anything To You?"'

'And can I hear it?' Hanna pleaded in her best 'pretty please' voice. With that, Martin continued with the chord sequence he'd been strumming quietly for a few minutes. He gave them a bit more weight and purpose, and started to sing. Quietly at first, until he closed his eyes, and then he started to sing the song full-voiced.

When he completed a verse and a chorus, Hanna said quietly: 'God, Martin, that's gorgeous, it's absolutely beautiful.' Martin opened his eyes and smiled at Hanna, and then closed his eyes again before slipping back into the second verse.

Hanna was right; it was a beautiful song, a song that owed more to 'The Mountains Of Mourne' than it did to the current crop of pop songs. It hinted slightly at Martin's Irish roots, just enough to hook the listener into the song immediately. Hanna made him sing the song to her three more times, and then she was so overwhelmed by the glimpse of the soul she was being allowed to have she took him back to bed, saying, 'This time is more for you than me. Well that's my excuse, and I'm sticking to it.'

Their relationship, if that's what it was, was strong, if on something of an unmarked road. Martin knew that Hanna didn't want either to know, or to discuss, where they were going, if in fact they were going anywhere. Instead of it making Martin feel insecure about their future, he found himself excited by the unknown. Instead of feeling what was often discussed in the back of the wagon – namely that familiarity breeds flaccidity – he felt excited about and by her, because each time with her felt new and a gift, as opposed to a chore.

Thirty-five minutes later, they were back in the kitchen, and she would agree to complete cooking his meal only if he'd sing her 'Did

She Say Anything To You?' again. He had to repeat it another three times before the meal was ready.

In the midst of all this, he realised exactly why he had been so desperate to get down to Belfast that evening. He wanted her to be the first person to hear the song he was considering putting forward to the Irish panel for the Eurovision Song Contest. She was so excited and enthusiastic about his song that Martin didn't tell her about the one little niggle he had.

CHAPTER THIRTY-TWO

Aye, meanwhile, down in Dublin City...

Andy Charles

The Shelbourne was perhaps Jim Mitchell's favourite hotel. A lot of the showband-manager fraternity preferred the Gresham, but there was just something more old world, old money, about the Shelbourne that made it more comfortable to Mitchell. To him, it was a home away from home. When an overnight was required in Dublin, The Playboys stayed in the Atlantic, where they could swap their on-the-road stories with members of the various other showbands certain to be staying there.

Mitchell arrived in Dublin just after midnight. A ten-bob note in the right palm ensured that he received some tea and fresh scrambled-egg sandwiches before retiring. He spent the majority of the following day, Tuesday, doing more research on the selection process for Eurovision, and he was 'starving and fit to eat a horse' by the time he met Thomas Boyle, the owner of City Records, at 7 p.m. They went straight through to the hotel restaurant rather than loosening up in the bar first.

Thomas Boyle was a man of ample proportions, more Friar Tuck than Billy Bunter. Mitchell was always taken with how Boyle would eat with such dignity, not to mention grace. It wasn't that he expected a stout man to absolutely wolf his food down, but neither did he expect one so rotund to be so dainty an eater.

They chit-chatted their way through the starter and main course, and then made their way to the residents' lounge for coffee. Once they settled comfortably in Mitchell's favourite far-right-hand corner, they got round to the topic on both their minds.

'Okay, Jim,' Boyle began, 'this is rather a delicate matter, which is why I preferred not to discuss it on the phone. Basically, we're going to have to drop The Playboys' name for this Eurovision enterprise.'

Mitchell avoided all the usual staged huffing and puffing. He knew this was difficult for Boyle and, if anything, he welcomed his frankness. For Mitchell, this was a quality to be applauded, as the majority of the people he seemed to come into contact with as The Playboys' representative seemed only ever to tell you what they thought you wanted to hear.

Boyle, sensing the green light to proceed with the conversation, continued: 'I know for sure that Radio Éireann only consider a solo artist's name just like they did with Butch and with Dickie. The emphasis is on a singer, not on a band, because it's a song contest, so the spotlight is on the writer and the singer. In your case, obviously, they are one and the same.'

He paused for a sip of his coffee, but from his mannerisms it was clear that he had more to say, so Mitchell didn't challenge for the floor. A few seconds later, Boyle continued: 'But that's not the main issue here, Jim. It's to do with England and how serious you are about your ambitions over there. None of the Irish showbands are ever going to break England and shall I tell you why?'

Mitchell's eyes said yes, so Boyle went on.

'Okay, the reason Irish showbands will never break England is because of the word *Irish* in their title…'

'Oh come on, Thomas,' Mitchell interrupted.

'You may well sneer at me, Jim, but it's a fact. Val Doonican has had a few hits over there, but he doesn't work under an 'Irish' label or as part of an 'Irish' showband. Belfast's Them are considered a pop group, but not an 'Irish' pop group. The same applies with The Bachelors. But look at everyone else: Phil Solomon has nearly gone bankrupt trying to break Irish showbands, particularly The Capitol, in the UK. Before The Beatles came along, he and a few other influential people in London were saying that Irish showbands were the next big thing in England. That was thanks mainly to The Royal Showband. Phil manages The Bachelors and Them, among others, and it was he who secured The Capitol that fabulous spot on *Sunday Night At The London Palladium*. He has the clout to score a few more of those, too.

'But I know for a fact that he's wasting his time. You know why?' Boyle said, leaning in closer to Mitchell in a 'hush hush' manner. Mitchell, in turn, leaned closer. 'Because, there's a few friends of the girls who work at City Records, working in a record shop over in Camden Town. Now they've been told, in no uncertain terms, not to stock the showband records. And the reason? It appears the powers that be don't want Irish showbands breaking into the scene over there.'

'Ah come on, away with ye,' Mitchell sighed, leaning back into the comfort of his chair again.

'Listen to me, Jim. I can tell you that there are still guest houses in London with notices on their doors or in their windows saying "No dogs, Blacks or Paddies!" and that's a fact.'

'So, we might as well give up and just continue playing the ballroom circuit in Ireland, because if what you're saying is true, that's all we're ever going to have.'

'Well, it's not exactly true. First off, the Americans are the total opposite. They welcome anything Irish with open arms; The Royal seem to be carving out quite a nice little career for themselves over there. Let's not forget Scotland, that's there for The Playboys for the taking. But let's get back to Martin Dean. Martin's a lovely young man and he's got a talent for songwriting. Now, I'm sure even you'll admit, he's not a singer who's most comfortable singing in a showband. Don't get me wrong, he does a great job; they all do, but you never get the impression he's totally comfortable working within the showband format, and their obvious restrictions.

'Take Brendan Bowyer for instance. One of the secrets of Brendan's success is that he looks like he's been plucked directly from the audience. He looks good, but at the same time he has an awkwardness about him that makes him look like he'd be equally happy dancing in the audience or back working behind the counter of the local baker's shop, chatting and gossiping with the customers as he served them, or sitting on the back of a Massey Ferguson tractor ploughing his dad's land with a bit of straw sticking out of his mouth. Brendan is successful with the dancers because he looks and acts like he's one of them.

'Martin Dean is something else entirely, which is perfectly fine too. But it's our responsibility to help him to realise his full potential, Jim, and I have a sneaky suspicion that this Eurovision Song Contest thing could very well be the perfect tool to do that.'

'What about The Playboys?' Mitchell asked, betraying his loyalties.

'Well, there are two issues here as far as I can see. In the short term, none of us have a choice. If you're going to be the Irish entry for next year's Eurovision Song Contest, then it's to be under Martin Dean's name. You have no say in the matter. So that's the first thing, and we can prevent that from becoming a problem. The boys in the band will see from the last two years that, although neither The Capitol nor The Miami were mentioned, or even performed, at the contest, they certainly reaped the rewards in Ireland. We can rightly say that it's nothing to do with us, it's Radio Éireann's, sorry I mean RTÉ, it's RTÉ's call.

'The second issue is more difficult. I think I can persuade Pye to release the record in England under the The Playboys' name, but I can tell you now, as an Irish showband, it's guaranteed to do little or nothing. So far, two Irish showbands have made it into the UK charts. One was Larry Cunningham's "Tribute To Jim Reeves". Now that was bought by Jim Reeves fans, and I think a lot of shops stocked it as an actual Jim Reeves record. Don't forget, at the point when he died you could have released a record of Jim Reeves complaining about how bad his piano was up in Donegal, and it would have sold in its millions. The other Irish showband to reach the UK charts was The Cadets, and those copies were probably bought by the RAF…'

Mitchell looked at Boyle in disbelief. 'No, just kidding. That was on Pye Records. They worked so hard and spent such an awful lot of money on it, and it still only managed to reach number 42, which was a shame because anything below number 30, as far as the majority of people are concerned, doesn't really exist. The band and Pye were very disappointed. I have to believe they were victims of what the wee girls in the record shop in Camden were talking about.

'So, as I say, we can release the single under The Playboys' name if you insist, but I think we'll be wasting our time. I think we should release this record under Martin Dean's name, and use the Eurovision platform to launch his singing and writing career. I know what you're going to ask me again, "What about The Playboys?"'

'Exactly, that's exactly what I was about to say, *again*. What about The Playboys?'

'Well, as we know, they're all lovely men. I suppose you could just replace Martin. For instance, Brendan the guitarist is a fair old chanter…'

'Yeah, he used to be the lead vocalist,' Mitchell added, appearing to warm to the notion.

'And they could continue on the ballroom circuit. I'm sure with you behind them they wouldn't ever be short of work…' Boyle left it hanging in the air.

'But…?' Mitchell prompted Boyle.

'But Martin's going to need a band, maybe some of them, maybe even all of them. He knows them; he'd be comfortable with them.'

'In other words, just keep things as they are?' Mitchell asked in disbelief.

'Well yes, apart that is from dropping the name,' Boyle suggested.

'It would be a nightmare, a recipe for a disaster and that's a fact,' Mitchell sighed, depressed even thinking about this possibility, 'apart from which, Dixie would *never* agree to it.'

'I know. Let him go, let him keep The Playboys' name. Believe me, that's going to be a lot easier than putting a new band together.'

'I think if we are to consider this seriously, Martin's got to make a clean break. If he nicked the band, there would still be a certain amount of resentment...'

'Even if the individual members of the band were making more money?' Boyle asked.

'Believe me, *particularly* if they were making more money because of Martin's success. He'd no longer be one of them. I'm telling you, it would lead to so much trouble on the road. At the minute it's all for one and one for all and it works beautifully.'

'Aye, if only things could continue forever,' Boyle said with a large sigh.

Mitchell returned to his room just before midnight to find a note from reception under his door, advising him that Sammy Barr had rung at 11.23 p.m. and needed to talk to him urgently.

'Hello there, Jim, thanks for ringing back. Look, sorry, I'm in a bit of a hurry, I've got someone who wants to take a load of these prams off my hands, but in the meantime what are the boys doing on December 26?'

'Boxing Day?'

'Well, yes, that's part of the problem,' Sammy replied.

'Sorry?'

'Well, up here it's Boxing Day, but down in the Free State where you are they call it St Stephen's day, and one of the eejits in a rather large band's office – I won't tell you which one – didn't realise that Boxing Day and St Stephen's Day were one and the same, so he's only gone and double-booked his band with me for Boxing Day and down in the Ritz in Carlow for St Stephen's day.'

Mitchell couldn't help but catch a fit of the giggles down the phone. Sammy joined in, obviously forgetting about his pram sale for a while

'Save me, Jim lad,' he continued when they'd regained their composure. 'Now, he says he'll try and sort me out with another band, but I'd much prefer The Playboys, so how are the boys fixed?' It so happened that Mitchell had kept Boxing night clear, in the hope of a good pay-day.

'Well, Sammy, as you know, two of the lads got married this year and I think they were kind of hoping to have this Christmas Day and Boxing Day off. Hey, maybe I'll even give them St Stephen's Day off as well.'

'How about a grand, against 60 per cent of the door?'

'Done!' Mitchell replied immediately.

'Aye, I know I have been. But not to worry. Thanks, Jim. Listen, I'll look after the boys, lots of hot dogs, you know, the works.'

No contracts were issued or necessary. That was all it took; that was their deal done. Their word was their bond, and in showband circles that was more watertight than any legal document could ever be. 'What about your prams? How are you managing with getting rid of them?' Mitchell asked. Sammy Barr was famous for his side deals. He could never refuse what he thought was a bargain, and someone had sold him a job lot of prams that had been cluttering up the storeroom behind the Flamingo Ballroom ever since.

'Slow, Jim, very slow.'

'Any ideas?' Mitchell asked.

'Well, none of my own, but I had lots of suggestions from some of the boys in the bands. I'll tell you what, though, I think The Capitol's idea was the best so far. They suggested that I should go around Ballymena some Friday lunchtime and buy up all the condoms in the town. That way, they reckoned in about nine months' time there'd be a rush on prams and I'd get rid of all of them. Listen, I better go, my caretaker has told me about this woman who's about to have twins, so I'm off to see if I can get her to take a couple off me hands. Thanks for sorting out Boxing Night for me, Jim.'

'And thank you for St Stephen's night, Sammy.' They were both chuckling as they sat their respective telephones down.

After the information that Mitchell had been forced to process by The Playboys' record company boss, he was happy for the day to end on a lighter note. He smiled as he thought about how he could always depend on Sammy Barr to bring a bit of humour into the world of showbands.

CHAPTER THIRTY-THREE

Martin Dean the singer, and Martin McClelland the songwriter, are one and the same

Sheila McGinley

T he first Eurovision Song Contest was held in 1956. It was the result of a committtcc set up by the European Broadcasting Union in the mid-fifties. The idea was to encourage some of the European territories to collaborate on some kind of trans-European light-entertainment programme. The chairman of the committee, Marcel Bezençon, Director-General of Swiss Television, came up with the idea of a song contest; a spin-off, no doubt, from the extremely successful Italian San Remo Song Festival. Marcel's pet project was christened the 'Eurovision Grand Prix', but a certain Jackie Stewart's enthusiasm was thwarted when he found that the only tuning required was for musical instruments and not his single-seater racing car. There were ten countries registered for the inaugural year, but three entries (Austria, Denmark and the UK) were immediately disqualified and withdrawn *due to irregularities*; the entry forms from the three offending countries were deemed to have been submitted after the deadline. The first year, the contest was staged in Mr Bezençon's home turf and the winner was – yes, you've guessed correctly – Switzerland! The song was called 'Refrain', and was written by Émile Gardaz and Géo Voumard and interpreted (that's 'sung', to you and me) by Lys Assia.

Ireland entered the Eurovision Grand Prix for the first time in 1965, by which time eighteen countries were taking part. Butch Moore *interpreted* Teresa Conlon's song, 'I'm Walking The Streets In The Rain' for Ireland, and the song finished sixth. In 1966, it was Dickie Rock who stood up to the Eurovision microphone to sing 'Come Back To Stay', which had been written by Soper-King. Ireland, Dickie Rock and Soper-King finished fourth that year. Fourth position was, you know, okay, but Mitchell thought that everybody had been just a wee bit too happy about it. If they had won the competition, or maybe even finished second, well yes that was certainly an excuse to break open the shampoo, but fourth – not to mention last year's sixth – didn't really give any cause for celebration, did it? Mind you, Mitchell admitted to himself, it would take the pressure off The Playboys somewhat if they were lucky enough to be the next representatives. Fourth shouldn't really be a difficult position to beat, whereas if Dickie had won, well then, only winning the following year would have been satisfactory.

On a Wednesday morning in August 1966, Jim Mitchell, undeterred by the previous evening's conversation, contacted RTÉ to find out the procedure for entering a song. Mitchell had heard that a gentleman by the name of Tom McGrath, an RTÉ producer, was responsible for Ireland's side of things in the competition. Mitchell spoke to McGrath's office and discovered that, yes indeed, there was still time to submit an entry. As long as it was in by the end of August, it would be considered.

If there was one thing that Mitchell had learned in his short time in showbusiness, it was that it wasn't so much what you knew as who you knew. He was canny enough to appreciate the fact that just submitting a Martin McClelland song cold wouldn't pass the muster, so he rang someone up who would know a certain someone or, worst case scenario, *they* would know someone who knew the certain someone. He was about to phone, but he decided the personal approach would work best, so, ten minutes later, after checking out of the hotel and en route to Castlemartin, he turned up at the Dublin office of Radio Luxembourg to see the extremely delicious and well-connected Miss Sheila McGinley.

The Playboys' Radio Luxembourg shows had been a moderate success. Successful enough to encourage both Jim Mitchell and the station to continue with the project, and he and Sheila had remained in contact. They had met up a few times since, and seemed to get on well. Sheila, for her part, thought it was encouraging that a man would be interested in something other than her body, although she would admit to Mitchell that a bit of interest in that direction would have been very welcome too.

As ever, Sheila made Mitchell feel very at home, and had one of the girls pour him a cup of tea while she was on the phone to a friend who worked at RTÉ. The news was good. The national radio station had received very little interest for next year's contest. As far as Sheila's contacts were aware, there were only about half a dozen entries and Oliver Barry had, the previous week, been checking out the possibility of one of his clients, Sean Dunphy, being the official representative for the following year. They hadn't heard a song yet but, obviously because of Oliver's involvement, they were interested to hear it.

Sheila did her bit for Martin, telling her friend that she was trying to persuade an incredible songwriter to enter one of his songs. Her friend obviously admitted that she had heard The Playboys' single because Sheila responded: 'Yes, you're absolutely correct, The Beatles did write "I Should Have Known Better", but this writer, Martin McClelland, wrote The Playboys' other hit, "Still She Dances With You".' Then there was a pause, while Sheila listened to her friend.

'Yes, I did send you a copy of both... and I preferred "Still She Dances With You", too... No, you're absolutely spot on with that as well. The lead singer did write the song.' Another, longer pause.

'Let me explain. Martin Dean is the lead singer with The Playboys. Martin McClelland wrote "Still She Dances With You", and the connection is that Martin Dean is Martin McClelland's stage name. Martin Dean the singer, and Martin McClelland the song-writer, are one and the same. He writes all his songs under the name of Martin McClelland.' Another pause.

'Well, look, if I can persuade him to enter, I'll have him send in his song and have him mention both Martin Dean and Martin McClelland… You'll look out for it? Great, I appreciate it. Now, how is that bog man of yours behaving? … He's not? Brilliant! Tell me exactly how he's misbehaving?' From that point on, there were lots of girly giggles and even a few, 'Oh, you didn't!'

Just before she hung up, Sheila said, 'Look, are there any entry forms or contracts or suchlike for this Song Contest thingy?' Pause.

'Okay. Tell you what. Send everything you've got to me and I'll pass it on.' Pause. 'No! He's not my mystery man. That would be extremely unprofessional, wouldn't it, Roisin?' Pause. 'Just forget how cute he is, Roisin, and promise me you'll give the song a good listen to?' Pause. Fits of laughter from Sheila and then: 'Okay… okay… fine… look forward to it… byeeeeee!'

'Sheila, what would we do without you? How can I thank you?' Mitchell asked as he finished off his coffee.

'You can give me a job when Martin wins the Eurovision Song Contest, that's what you can do, Jim Mitchell.'

Sheila's words were ringing around Mitchell's head as he headed out past the airport on his way home to Castlemartin. He honed in on the fact that Sheila McGinley, who wasn't ever a girl for flannel, had said, '*when* Martin wins', not '*if*'. That very positive thought carried Jim Mitchell up as far as Armagh.

CHAPTER THIRTY-FOUR

You can't call death a bed of roses

Sean MacGee

Martin knew that his manager was on his way back from Dublin. He also knew that his manager would be expecting him to have a song for Eurovision. Martin had made up his mind what he wanted to do, and he'd even executed the first part of his plan. The second part was not going to be so pleasant, and in truth he was dreading it – truly dreading it.

He called around first to the Dreamland Ballroom to see his mother. He had a long chat with her. He didn't get into details; he just enjoyed the soothing effect she had on him. Well and truly soothed, he then went around to Sean MacGee's.

At first there was no answer. Martin knew that it was now or never, so he banged on the door heavily until he eventually heard mutterings from within. 'Who's there?', a voice shouted.

'Sean, it's me, Martin. I need to talk to you.' Martin didn't hear any more movement or noise from within. 'Sean, Sean,' Martin persisted, banging on the door again. A bit of grumbling was heard on the other side of the door, and slowly it opened.

'Oh, it's a fecking Playboy; well I don't want to play with your fecking gang,' Sean offered, with an alcohol-induced slur to every word. Not even noon, and he was sloshed already. No wonder Mitchell had to fire him from the Dreamland if this was the condition he was in when he turned up for work each day.

'You might be a Prayboy, ye wee fecker, but you're definitely not a Playboy.'

'Sean?'

'In fact, I've never seen a less likely bunch of fecking Playboys in my life.'

'Right, Sean, there's something I need to talk to you about…'

'There's feck all I need to talk to you about.'

'Sean…'

'You had your chance to talk to me. You could have talked to me when Jimitch fired me; you could have talked up for me then, Martin, hey? Where were you then?'

'Sean, it had nothing to do with me. I helped you get a job, but at the end of the day Jim Mitchell hires and fires his own, it's nothing to do with me. He gave you a chance.'

'I didn't need a fecking chance; I needed a fecking drink.'

'That was the problem, Sean.'

'That wasn't the problem, Martin, that's the solution,' MacGee said, as he staggered into the kitchen of his mother's house in search of some more liquid solution. He found a bottle of cider, opened the top and took a large swig before turning around to Martin. 'Are ye still here, ye fecker? Where were you when I needed you?'

MacGee took a few threatening steps towards Martin, but stumbled over his own feet and landed in a heap on the floor, spilling the cider all over himself in the process. Martin tried to help him back onto his feet, but MacGee lashed out at him.

'Look, Sean, I've important things I need to talk to you about. Let me make you some coffee, come on, man.'

'Oh aye, you're here to help me now, when *you* need *me* for something, but where were you when *I* needed *you*…?'

'Sean…'

'You could have hired me as a driver for The Playboys after Mitchell fired me. That would have gotten me through.'

Martin looked at him in disbelief. 'A driver, Sean?' Martin replied in sheer disbelief. 'The only place you would have driven us would have been to our deaths.'

'Deaths?' MacGee said, slurring his words so much it was hard to understand what he was saying. 'Deaths, Martin, what do you know about death? You can't call death a bed of roses.' MacGee stumbled to his feet again, and took another swing at Martin, this time missing his chin by a couple of inches before he collapsed into a heap on the floor. He continued muttering to himself, and then seemed to fall asleep.

Martin rolled him onto his side, and propped him up with cushions so that he wouldn't roll onto his back and choke if he was sick. Martin McClelland then made an important decision, one of the most important decisions of his career, if not his life. He walked away, leaving his old friend, Sean MacGee, to his own personal hell.

CHAPTER THIRTY-FIVE

And so what can a poor boy do?

Smiley

The Playboys played dances that Wednesday, Thursday, Friday, Saturday and Sunday. There was major excitement in the back of the wagon on the Wednesday as they drove up to Portrush for their last dance of the summer at the Arcadia Ballroom. Martin told the boys, when asked, that he had come up with a song for the Eurovision Song Contest. This, he knew, would be the hardest test of all.

Telling Hanna had been easy. Martin knew that if she hadn't liked it she would have been very honest but equally polite about it. Martin had been round to the Dreamland Ballroom already that morning to tell Mitchell, who had immediately requested a preview, which was exactly why Martin had brought his guitar with him.

'Martin,' Mitchell said, the very second that Martin had strummed the final chord, 'I have to tell you that not only will you win the selection to be the Irish entry but you will win the whole fecking contest.'

'Gegod!' Martin Ben Langed.

'That's just such a perfect song. Where have you been hiding that one?'

'Well, I, er… I have a bunch of songs in varying stages of completion.' Mitchell had Martin play the song to him twice more before Martin had to pack up his guitar and head off to the band meeting.

He unpacked the same guitar in the back of the wagon. Martin knew that if the boys didn't like it they'd let him know, saying something like, 'Haven't you got anything else you could play us?' That would be the biggest put down. Martin started to sing. He was no more than one minute into the song when Brendan interrupted him:

'Bejesus, head, what an incredibly beautiful melody.'

'Whisht, Brendan, let him finish,' Barry said quietly. As Dixie drove the van along the bumpy roads, Martin strummed away on his guitar and sang his song, 'Did She Say Anything To You?' He was flabbergasted by the band's reaction. They broke into a spontaneous and very enthusiastic round of applause, a reaction that made Martin feel a bit overcome.

'Jeez, Martin, I swear to you, Lennon and McCartney would be proud to put their names to that song,' Brendan said, leading the praise.

'When did you come up with that gem?' Robin asked.

'It was the second song I ever wrote. We did a version of it in The Chance, but it didn't really work out.'

Brendan, who'd been watching Martin's fingers on the fretboard of the guitar, did his trademark thing and grabbed the back of his right wrist with his left hand and immediately started to ape the chord sequence with his fingers of his left hand.

'So it's C to D, to G, and back to C?' Brendan said, as he figured the chords out.

'That's it,' Martin replied.

'That's all?' Barry said in disbelief.

'It's what he's doing with the melody line that's deceptive,' Brendan said, addressing Barry. Robin asked Martin to play the song again, and he happily obliged.

Martin played it twice more, and then Brendan asked for the guitar and once again aped Martin's chord sequence, this time on an instrument. 'That's just brill, head, pure brill. The bridge looks awkward, but in effect it's not, and it's the perfect connection to the rest of the song. How long is it, Martin?'

'2 minutes and 20 seconds, head.'

'It can't be, not with all those verses?' Mo cut in.

'No, he's probably right, it's very deceptive. You see, he doesn't repeat himself and only uses the chorus three times. He doesn't need to use it any more than that because it's so fecking brilliant you remember it immediately,' Brendan explained, as Smiley continued to beam from ear to ear.

To prove his point, Brendan sang the chorus in full over his own playing. He sang it again, and then asked Martin for the rest of the lyrics. Martin obliged and, within ten minutes, Brendan was able to perform the song in his gentle, distinctive, country-influenced tones. To Martin, that was the first big test for his song. He knew that great songs could stand up to any treatment. 'Did She Say Anything To You?' obviously suited Martin's more pop-orientated voice, as it should, seeing as he wrote it. But Brendan had just, unwittingly, done a pure country-music interpretation of the song, and that worked just as well.

At the end of one of Brendan's passes, Davy said: 'Yep, 2 minutes 25 seconds, I've just timed it!'

'Wasn't it George Martin who reckoned that was the perfect length for a pop song?' Smiley asked.

'Who's George Martin – another songwriter from Derry?' Davy asked.

'No, Davy, he's The Beatles' record producer,' Robin replied, rolling his eyes.

'The Beatles and just about anyone else who has made it to the top in the UK,' Martin added, 'and yes, I think he did say something like that.'

'Dixie, you're a bit quiet up there,' Brendan said, 'what did you think of the song?'

'Brendan, I'm trying to keep the wagon out of the ditch, which is quite difficult as you seem to want to take the back of my head off with Martin's guitar,' Dixie replied, putting a bit of a dampener on things, but then he added, 'but I think the song is first class. Let's see what kind of an arrangement we can work up for it when we get to the Port.'

The band was still excited about Martin's new song when they reached Portrush a couple of hours later. The equipment was set up in record time, and they were all keen as mustard to get stuck into working up a treatment for the tune.

Martin and Brendan taught Mo, Davy and Barry the basis of the song. Meanwhile, Dixie with his tenor saxophone, Robin with his trombone and Smiley with his trumpet all retired to the dressing room, 'to work on some dots'.

Twenty minutes later, they all reconvened on the stage and, on the first play through, Martin thought the brass part sounded a bit feeble, really just amplifying what Barry was doing on the organ, if slightly sweeter.

'Okay,' Dixie ordered, once everyone was confident with their parts, 'let's try it once with Barry doing a bit more of what Brendan is doing on guitar. We cover his part with the brass. Brendan, I'd like you to try and ape one of Martin's melody lines' – here Dixie paused to demonstrate which melody line he meant on the sax – 'and let's use that as an intro. Martin, you let him do that for one pass before you come in with the vocal and push up the tempo just a little. I think the song will benefit from being just a tad faster. Brendan, after Martin starts to sing I'd like you to pick this line' – and again Dixie paused to demonstrate – 'under the first two verses, and then use the line from your intro to take us in and out of each chorus, and then improvise something powerful but subtle to complement Martin's voice on the last verse.' And that was it.

By the time they'd performed it three times, Martin was dumb-struck; Dixie had transformed his song into a classic. To Martin's extremely discerning ears, 'Did She Say Anything To You?' now sounded like the perfect pop classic in the same vein as 'Here Comes The Night', 'When You Walk In The Room', 'Hang On Sloopy' and 'You Really Got Me'.

When Jim Mitchell arrived at the ballroom, the band had already finished their rehearsal, but Brendan insisted that they return to the stage to perform 'Did She Say Anything To You?' one more time for the manager, who looked beside himself with joy. Martin did note, however, that Dixie appeared very uncomfortable when they were discussing the song contest for the band, although he looked totally happy when he was playing the music.

Mitchell made a quiet note to himself to see exactly what odds he could get for the most unusual treble of his gambling career. He'd lost a few bob recently on the horses, but he'd found a way, he was convinced, to win it all back plus a lot more besides. He planned to bet on 'Did She Say Anything To You?' (a) winning the nomination as the Irish entry for the Eurovision Song Contest, (b) reaching the top of the Irish pop charts and (c) winning the Eurovision Song Contest outright.

The Portrush show went well. The ballroom manager posted the 'house full' sign just before 10 p.m. The other highlight of the night for Martin, apart from hearing 'Did She Say Anything To You?' fleshed out and taking shape, was to hear the relief group, the Blues by Five, do an amazing version of 'Three Spires'. Sean MacGee had been right: Paddy Shaw did have a beautiful take on the vocal. He sang it like he'd written it. Martin had to wonder whether Paddy, who had a reputation for being a bit of a ladies' man, knew Hanna. Apart from anything else, it was great hearing one of his songs in the middle of the Blues By Five's set. Their set was mostly made up from songs taken from the *Them Again* album and Otis Blue and Wilson Pickett's 'In The Midnight Hour'. They even did an incredible version of Dylan's classic 'It's All Over Now, Baby Blue'. Being Portrush, the Blues by Five had quite a few fans of their own in the ballroom, all up around the front of the stage and all watching Paddy as he pulled nervously at the scraggy moustache he was forever trying to grow, waiting for the band to start up the next number.

After the dance, the Blues by Five's guitarist congratulated Martin on 'Did She Say Anything To You?'. He also asked him if he had any other spare songs that might be suitable for his band. Martin suggested the JFK song he'd co-written with Sean MacGee, 'The Saddest Day'. They agreed to meet up on the following Monday at Martin's place so that he could pass the song on.

The rest of that weekend's gigs went ahead without incident. Without incident, that is, apart from Smiley, who'd been off on one of his adventures, which he colourfully recounted for the band on the way home from their Friday night dance in Kilkenny to their Saturday night dance in Dublin. Friday night was the only night that week when they were staying in a hotel, and that was really why Smiley had gotten into trouble.

Smiley had taken the opportunity of an overnight stop-off to be responsive to a beautiful, if somewhat strange, girl who'd been giving him the eye all evening. 'How did you know she was giving you the eye?' Davy asked innocently. 'I saw her and she was looking at me and Martin too. So, how did you know she was giving *you* the eye? What was she doing exactly?'

'Davy,' Smiley began expansively, looking slightly annoyed by the early interruption, 'my man, these are things you just learn. You see a girl looking at you, you look back at her, you smile and then she smiles back. Now the friendly contact's been made. Socially, that's all that's meant to happen, and that's all perfectly innocent and acceptable, okay?'

'Okay,' Davy replied, still sounding unsure.

'So, I continue looking at her, keep smiling at her and if she doesn't look away, that's the second level of contact established. Now, in 98 times out of 100, that's when she is most likely to look away, but if she keeps looking at you, or more importantly, if she briefly looks away and then looks back at you to see if you are still looking at her, then that's another level of contact again. If this happens several times, or if she continues smiling at you then you know she's giving you the eye.'

'But,' Davy replied, exasperated, 'how do you manage to read all these signals and at the same time concentrate on playing the music?'

'Whisht, head,' Brendan said, 'let the head tell his story of legove.'

'Thank you, Brendan,' Smiley sighed and continued. 'So, I go out into the crowd at the end of the night, and I'm chatting away generally to the punters. It's important, you see, not to go straight up to her, you know, you might scare her away. You have to let her do her dance, move around you discreetly, hear you talk to people, hear how you respond to other people, smell you…'

'Smell you?!'

'Davy!' Brendan said, raising his voice this time, 'we're only going as far as Dublin. We'll never hear the end of this story.'

'Sorry.'

'Naturally,' Smiley said, responding to Davy's question, 'girls like to get the scent of a man. Most of the time, they don't even know that they're doing it. Then they suss you out. All the time I'm signing autographs, this girl is making a beeline for me. Eventually, she gives me a copy of 'I Should Have Known Better' to sign, so I figure she's a real fan, so I feel comfortable. We start to chat, and I find that not only is she beautiful but she's also intelligent, and not only is she intelligent but she's also available, and not only is she available but she's interested in me. So what can a poor boy do? At this point, and only at this point,' Smiley now stared intensely at Davy, the way a teacher would at a pupil when trying to make a point without interrupting the flow of his lecture to the remainder of the class, 'do I begin my dance around her. I gently move in on her. I pretend to ignore the fact that I'm aware she has already set her sights on me and I start to woo her; I start to chat her up. I lean against the stage and turn towards her, thereby separating us from the rest of the fans. She allows me to do this, showing that she is willing to be my partner in this dance.'

'But wouldn't you feel awkward being the only two dancing, you know, with the dance already over, the lights no longer dimmed, the band having stopped playing and all of that?'

'Dixie, stop the bus and let this megoron out!' Brendan said, turning his head away from Davy but keeping his eyes on him. 'He's talking about a metaphorical dance, head.'

'I know, I know, of course I know,' Davy replied proudly. 'Tell me, Smiley, the metaphorical dance... now would that be an old-time waltz or is it a slow foxtrot?'

'Davy!'

'It's okay, head,' Smiley laughed, and smiled as only he could do, 'at least he didn't ask me what key it was in. Where was I? Oh yes, so Maggie is being responsive to my moves and we've been talking for a while and I casually ask her is there somewhere we could go for a cup of coffee or something. Obviously everywhere is closed,' Smiley says, beating Davy to his question, 'so Maggie says we could go back to her place for a coffee. As we're walking back, she's telling me that she doesn't know many people from town, she's just moved down from Dublin. She went very quiet at this stage and starts to tell me about her boyfriend in Dublin, and how they'd been together and then, when she wasn't looking, he scarpered with her best mate. That was never going to happen again, she declared. The next time she found her man she was going to keep him. She can't tell me what she works at, so I assume it's for the government and I don't push.

'We get into the centre of town, and she's got this cute little two-bedroom flat above the baker's, and she makes a whole palaver about letting herself in – and that should have been my first clue, all the locks she had on the front door. She made some noises about how much security she needed in the centre of town, about the bread attracting thieves. Which I thought was a joke, but she was being serious. When we get inside, she repeats the locking thing, and I still don't twig anything is wrong, and so we have a coffee and one thing leads to another and... I'll spare you the details but, well, you know...'

'Oh, please don't spare us the details, head?' Robin pleads.

'Anyway, we kinda lie around in the afterglow for a while, as you do; a gentleman never dresses immediately. But after half an hour it's getting late, and we're chatting about this and that, and she's asking me strange questions at this stage, like do I have anyone at home waiting for me? Is there someone who'll miss me? We'll have such a great time together, it's going to be great, all that. I don't bother to tell her that The Playboys have no plans to come back to Kilkenny on a weekly basis. I tell her I've really enjoyed the evening, and start to put on my clothes…'

'You'd your clothes off as well?' Davy said in clear disgust.

'She starts to grow a little upset, visibly,' Smiley continues, completely ignoring Davy's remark, 'and I tell her that I'm sorry but I need to leave. The word "leave" seems to trigger something, and she starts to say I can't leave. Of course I can leave. I'm dressed by this point, and bid my goodbye and head down the stairs, but the door had been double locked from the inside and it's some weird kind of lock and I'm futtering around with it and making no progress whatsoever, and then this laugh from behind me totally freaks me out, scares the shit out of me. "Oh," she says, sitting on the stairs behind me. She'd obviously crept down the stairs in her birthday suit and was just sitting there watching me. "Oh", she says, "you're mine now, Smiley, you're never going to get away from me. I told you I wasn't going to lose another boy, this time I've made sure you can't get away."

'Okay, now I'm scared! She's freaking me out. I ask her for a key, she says there's no key, there's just a combination and to come back to bed. She says it's brilliant in the morning – the baker arrives at 5.30 a.m., and when he starts to bake the smells are absolutely wonderful. I tell her the only thing I want to smell at that time is my pillowcase. I rush past her, up the stairs and I try all the windows. They're all fecking locked as well, the place is an absolute firetrap. I hear her coming back up the stairs, and all the time she's laughing this insane laugh and so I rush into the bathroom. And there's a window in there and she hasn't bothered to lock that because it's so small. So small that only someone as small as a child could get out through it…'

'Or someone as thin as Smiley?' Brendan asks.

'Exactly!' Smiley shouts, reliving the relief he felt the previous evening. 'Exactly, so I lock the bathroom door from the inside, and open the window and carefully squeeze my way out through it. There's a bit of a drop down to a flat roof, obviously the extension at the back of the bakers. I climb down over some dustbins into some back alley and I hightail it out of there.'

'Jeez, Smiley, you do get yourself into corners,' Barry said. Even though Smiley had obviously escaped – he was with them in the van – there was such a sense of relief from all the members of the band when Smiley had told them of how he'd done it.

Smiley did lead a charmed life. It was really incredible how he always seemed to land on his feet, as it were. He was always getting into spots and then finding some way out of them. There was another famous occasion: again, the boys were staying in a hotel, this time just outside Galway, in Salthill, where there are several similar small hotels, all along the seafront. Again, Smiley had been enticed back to a young girl's dwelling – this time a caravan not far from the hotel. Anyway, it was an altogether more pleasant experience than the one with Maggie above the bakers had been. And he'd fallen asleep. He woke up in the dead of the night not really knowing what time it was, but knowing that he needed to get back to his own hotel because the band were leaving for a recording session in Dublin first thing in the morning. So, still half asleep, he dressed and made his way into the night.

He woke the night porter, who was himself half asleep and none too pleased. To add insult to injury, he needed letting into his room because Robin had the key. Smiley didn't dwell on it too much when he was up on the landing as the porter let him in; he'd thought that his room should have been on the other side of the corridor, but he knew it was the correct room number and he quietly tiptoed in, whispering his thanks, and 'you'll never see what I'll get you for Christmas' to the night porter. Smiley was so exhausted by this stage that he threw off his clothes and crawled into the nearest bed. He was just getting snug when he sensed another presence in the bed. Shit, he thought, I'm in Robin's bed, I'll never live this down with the band. He put his hand out to feel not the rough form of a man but the gentle form of a woman. The woman woke up with a jolt, turned around and switched on the light. She was in her forties and Smiley's permanent smile immediately defused the situation. She nodded to the other side of the bed and made a shush sound. There was another man there, obviously her husband. Smiley put on his best Sherlock Holmes manner.

'I'm frightfully sorry,' Smiley whispered, 'I must be in the wrong bed.'

'I'd say more like the wrong room,' the lady whispered, a wicked grin spreading across her face, 'but now that you're here...' she giggled as she turned off the light.

In his tiredness, Smiley had remembered the right room number but the wrong hotel, the one next to his own in fact. Now, any of the other members of the band, in similar circumstances, would have ended up in a riot, with the police being called. Well, didn't our Smiley only go and land on his feet once more? Well, not so much on his feet, but on his back!

CHAPTER THIRTY-SIX

And the perfect day is the day with you

Martin McClelland

The recording session that Smiley had been rushing back to make was none other than the session at the Eamon Andrews Studios in Harcourt Street, where they recorded 'Did She Say Anything To You?'. They also recorded 'The Perfect Day', which Martin had worked hard to finish in time for the session. He was very happy with the completed effort, in that he managed to get across the sentiment that the perfect day was only so because it was a day that the narrator (Martin) had spent with his lover (Hanna).

The Playboys' recording system was the same as before, but this time Dixie wanted the credit for 'Did She Say Anything To You?' to be 'produced by Blair & Dean'. He explained that Martin had written it and he had arranged it. Everybody was happy with the quality of the song, and everybody was happy with the music arrangement, so everyone agreed.

Brendan, though, looked and acted a bit put out, and Martin felt very awkward about it. He felt that it was just like putting titles where titles hadn't existed before. Why hadn't Dixie discussed the issue with him before? If he had discussed it with him privately, he would have told Dixie that he didn't feel comfortable about it. Did Dixie know this? Is that why he hadn't come to him first? Surely Dixie hadn't mentioned it to Jim Mitchell? No, not possible. He felt 100 per cent confident that if he had, Mitchell would either have mentioned it to Martin or dismissed the idea entirely.

Was this Dixie's token way of continuing to assert that The Playboys were still his band? Martin wondered if it would upset the creative mix. Had it anything to do with Eurovision? He assumed that this must be the case, because Dixie had not requested a similar credit on 'The Perfect Day'. To Martin, The Playboys worked because everyone was happy to muck in and do what was required to make good music. A bit like the four musketeers. Well... more like two sets of four musketeers: eight for one and one for all. But Martin wondered if Dixie's newly requested producer credit might upset the artistic flow of the band. One thing was sure, it certainly wouldn't upset anyone's share of record sales.

Everyone knew in reality that was a bit of a joke, because each single was costing them between £500 and £1,000 to record and market. They all knew it was worth it, however, because the promotional benefits of having a single release were invaluable. That outlay would be more than covered in the extra business they did at the box office the week after the single was released. Obviously, if they ever cracked it, and had a big single like The Royal's 'Hucklebuck', or Larry Cunningham's 'Tribute To Jim Reeves', there would be record royalties and, small though they were, they would amount to something. In the meantime, they were all happy with the fringe benefit and were not unduly concerned by Dixie and Martin's production credit.

Martin couldn't help but feel sorry for Brendan, but he didn't say anything. He wondered if this was because, in his own way, he was as selfish as Dixie appeared and was trying to protect his Eurovision chances. He was stunned by his own actions, or lack of them. Was this the start of his ego inflating to unbearable levels? His mother had often warned him about this. Martin hated all these new and mixed emotions that he was experiencing. Given the choice, he'd like to have turned back the clock and have things continue as they were before Mitchell had raised the issue of the Eurovision Song Contest.

The problem with someone rocking the boat, and the same someone not being stopped immediately, was that the next time they rocked the boat, you'd find yourself merely holding on to the edge a bit tighter. Before you knew it, the previously still waters would become so troubled that anyone who then objected would simply ensure that the boat capsized and all the occupants would end up in the water. Whereas, Martin thought, if you stop the fool the first time and call him a fool, as you should, that would tend to nip the problem in the bud and steady the vessel. Martin wondered how much more Dixie would be allowed to rock the boat before anyone objected. He didn't have to wait too long to find out.

Martin took a copy of his completed song to Jim Mitchell's office in the Dreamland the following morning. Mitchell was desperate to hear the song before they sent it off to RTÉ, so manager and artist went to Martin's house so he could play it on his tape recorder. Kathleen seemed very surprised and a little put out to see Mitchell in her house. Martin put it down to the fact that she took care in her appearance as well as being house-proud, and hadn't had a chance to do either up.

Neither prevented Mitchell from loving the recording, and they returned to Dreamland where he presented Martin with some forms and documents to sign. Martin checked his name, address and age, all of which Mitchell had already filled in, and then signed at the relevant 'X' on the page. On the song details page, he filled in the name 'Southern Songs' as the publisher, the name 'Dixie Blair' as the arranger, and then wrote 'Martin' in the full name(s) of composer section and paused.

'Do you forget how to spell your own name, Martin?' Mitchell asked.

'No, no,' Martin laughed, feeling a bit flustered, 'I was consciously stopping myself from writing 'Dean' instead of 'McClelland'. It's surprising how easy the auld stage name rolls off the pen these days.'

'I've never really thought about it before, but I suppose it must become very confusing. Okay, all done?'

'Yep, that's it,' Martin replied. 'What happens next?'

'I take the song and these forms straight to RTÉ, just to be sure they don't go astray in the post and miss the deadline. And then we wait.'

Martin didn't find waiting easy. In a bizarre way it was like waiting for exam results or like waiting, in the early days, to see if Hanna would contact him again. He considered how disappointed he'd feel if his song was rejected. He was sure he would deal with it. He wondered if that was because he and Hanna were together and enjoying some kind of a relationship. Now that they seemed to be making progress, he found himself underwhelmed by everything else.

A week of waiting turned into a month. During that month, he went down to Belfast to see Hanna every Monday and Tuesday and on one of the Wednesdays. On the week that Martin had all three days off, he and Hanna went down to Dublin and, on the recommendation from Sheila at Radio Luxembourg, they went to see Johnny McEvoy at the Embankment. McEvoy was incredible, just incredible – a lot more than just 'the Irish Bob Dylan' that he was being billed as. Like Dylan, he stood up on stage alone with just his guitar and harmonica. Unlike Dylan, his songs were set not in the land of the free and the home of the brave of America, but in the land of the green and the home of the romantic of Ireland. The songs that stood out were 'Will You Miss Me?', 'Boston Strangler' and 'Mursheen Durkin', which would reach number one in the Irish charts before the end of November.

From the genuine, unbridled enthusiasm of the audience, Martin could sense the changing of the guard. People had come to this club in Dublin for no other reason than to listen to the words and music of Johnny McEvoy. On top of which, Hanna thought the troubadour was very cute with his Beatle-bob hairstyle. Martin wasn't sure that he would ever have the bottle to get up on stage and bare his soul like that. He was fine to write songs, and he was fine doing them on the bandstand, where the majority of the audience manoeuvred and cajoled their way around the ballroom, concentrating more on being at the right position at the right time to chat or be chatted up.

Apparently, according to a guy who tried to chat Hanna up when she went off to get their drinks, McEvoy had also started sharing the bill with some of the bigger bands in the ballrooms and, taking a leaf out of Jim Reeves' book, squeezed in two and sometimes even three appearances a night. Sheila McGinley and her mate, the girl from RTÉ, joined Hanna and Martin for a chat at the end of the performance. The RTÉ girl informed Martin (unofficially, of course) that the powers that be at RTÉ loved 'Did She Say Anything To You?' and believed that, when it would be put to the country, Martin's song would be selected as Ireland's entry for the 1967 Eurovision Song Contest. After the performance that Martin had just witnessed from Johnny McEvoy, this felt like a hollow victory.

During a quiet moment, Sheila informed Martin that (officially) she thought everything about Hanna was amazing and that now she understood the inspiration behind his songs. Martin felt that there seemed to be a little regret in her voice, but at the same time she seemed very happy for him. 'Martin, if you *ever* do anything to blow this relationship of yours, not only will I never forgive you, but believe you me, you will never forgive yourself.'

When Martin told Hanna this on the way back to their hotel, where they'd taken two rooms rather than face the inevitably embarrassing moment with the desk clerk, she merely hugged him closer and said: 'Well, in that case we'll have to make sure you don't.'

They talked into the middle of the night, mainly about songwriting and how passionately Martin wished that all songs could be written not to compete with each other, but as forms of expression to bring comfort and solace to both the performer and the audience. Martin told Hanna a story about the last time The Playboys were in London. They'd met this guy, a young guy who had just emigrated to London from Magherafelt. He knew someone who knew Dixie, and he was a nice enough guy. Martin and Brendan thought he was a little sad, and asked him if there was anything they could maybe do to help.

'Nah,' the lad replied, 'I just realised that I'd much prefer to be in the warmth and comfort of my parents' house than over here by myself eating beans on toast in a cold, dingy flat. Before I came here I felt so strongly that London was the place to be, but recently I'm starting to realise the place to be is with your family.'

'Why don't you just go home then?' Brendan asked.

'Nah, I can't,' the lad replied.

'Why not? Brendan persisted. 'We'll give you some funds if you need them.'

'Nah, it's not just that. I can't go back now, even though I know my mother and father would love me to. The thing is, if I do go back, then I'll have failed. I have to stay here now and make a go of it. I made such a fuss about coming over here and was given such a send-off. I just can't go back until I don't need to go back.'

The boy's plight was exactly the kind of story Martin would like to weave into a song. He wanted his new lyrics to be of some use, and sure, losing-or-winning-at-love songs are fine and well, and good for the comfort they give. But equally, Martin felt, if he could find a way of putting this boy's story into a song, perhaps people like that young immigrant and the family he left behind would take comfort from it. He'd like to try and find a way to let the immigrant and family understand each other a little better. The only person Martin knew who managed such things in a song was Bob Dylan.

Martin and Hanna resolved to go somewhere, anywhere, it didn't matter where, to see the great man perform.

CHAPTER THIRTY-SEVEN

*And it's no use in turning
on the light, babe I'm on the
dark side of the road*

Bob Dylan

etting to see Dylan was actually quite simple. Martin rang up Anne Buchanan in Glasgow; as she was a journalist, he figured she'd know exactly where and when he was playing. And she didn't disappoint. Dylan was playing Glasgow in three weeks' time, on a Thursday and, unusually for The Playboys, that particular Thursday was a night off. When he found out about Dylan, Martin went to Mitchell at the Dreamland Ballroom and, for the first time in his life, asked him for a favour.

Mitchell said he'd no problem marking the appropriate date down as a day off. He comforted Martin by telling him that it probably wasn't going to be filled anyway, as some of the second-division ballrooms had started to cut back to three nights a week. Dixie would not have taken the same comfort from these words that Martin had.

By this point, Mitchell had heard officially that Martin's song, along with four others, was to be presented to the country to decide which song should go through as the Irish selection for the Eurovision Song Contest or, to give it its official title, the Grand Prix Eurovision 1967. Mitchell's inside information (from Sheila's RTÉ mate) was that it was down to either Martin Dean or Sean Dunphy. Dunphy and his band, The Hoedowners, had very recently climbed to number two in the Irish charts with 'Showball Crazy' on Pye Records. They were kept off the top spot, in succession, by The Beatles with 'Paperback Writer' and then The Kinks with their first Irish number one record, 'Sunny Afternoon'.

Popularity-wise, the Hoedowners had a bit of an edge on The Playboys but, as Mitchell pointed out, in the form of Martin Dean The Playboys had more than an edge in the songwriting department.

The decision would be made by the end of October, which meant that, either way, it would be released as a single in time for the lucrative Christmas market. Martin tried to look pleased and enthusiastic for Mitchell. He left him taking a phone call from Dixie and went off to make his own travel arrangements to Glasgow to see the one and only Bob Dylan.

'How's Colette?' Mitchell asked Dixie, by way of pleasantries.

'Fine, just fine. Listen, sir, I need to talk to you about this song thing…' Dixie started off hesitantly.

'Yes, it's great news, isn't it?' Mitchell enthused.

'Well, maybe yes, and maybe no,' Dixie continued, sounding like he was growing madder by the second.

'Oh?'

'Yes, I've just been listening to RTÉ,' Dixie began, and Mitchell left him a gap to continue, 'and I've just heard that Martin Dean and 'Did She Say Anything To You?' is one of the songs in the contest to seek nomination as the official Irish entry.'

'Yes, great news, isn't it? But I'd already told you that, Dixie. I told you last Friday when I found out.'

'NO! You did not tell me that, you told me that "we" were up for nomination.'

'Yeah? And we are.'

'No *we* are not, *Martin Dean* is,' Dixie spat down the phone. '*We* are The Playboys, *we* are *not* Martin Dean, comprende?'

'Sorry, you've lost me,' Mitchell replied.

'Okay, in that case I'll spell it out for you, sir. The RTÉ presenter said, and I'll quote, "Martin Dean and 'Did She Say Anything To You?' and blah blah are the nominations for next year's entry to the Eurovision Song Contest." The presenter made *no* reference whatsoever to The Playboys.'

'Dixie, Dixie, lighten up, man, for goodness' sake. First off, this is a song contest, not a showband contest, okay? Secondly, the previous Irish entries had been Butch Moore and Dickie Rock. Okay? That's not Butch Moore & The Capitol Showband or Dickie Rock & The Miami Showband. For this competition, it's simply the singer who's listed.'

'Yes, yes, that's fine and dandy with both those bands,' Dixie said, cutting off his manager mid-flow, 'because Dickie *is* bigger than The Miami and Butch *is* bigger than The Capitol but Martin is *not* bigger than The Playboys.'

'Dixie, this is not about who is bigger than whom. RTÉ make their own rules, *they* call the shots.'

'So, will RTÉ be insisting that the next single be released as Martin Dean & The Playboys or even as *just* Martin Dean?'

Mitchell hesitated just a split second too long. He realised what he was doing: did his hesitation come from considering the pause or from Dixie's shot hitting directly on target, he wondered?

'I thought so!' Dixie fumed down the phone. 'Do yourself and me a favour, Mr Mitchell: fix this, before I have to fix it. And I'll tell you this for nothing; if I have to fix it, no one is going to be very happy. Comprende?'

And he was gone, leaving Mr Mitchell holding the phone and experiencing the same horrible feeling he used to have when a horse he'd put a lot of money on – usually the favourite – had tripped and fallen at the first fence.

'I could be doing with staying in Belfast and doing some revision,' Hanna said to Martin as they flew over the North Channel between

Belfast and Edinburgh, 'but there's something happening here and you don't know what it is, do you, Mr Dean?' Martin laughed at her Dylan quote. 'No, seriously, Martin, I feel this is very important to you. It feels like something magical is going to happen and it feels good that we're going to experience it together.' Martin squeezed her hand.

Anne Buchanan met them at the airport. 'Well, you look nothing like a showband singer,' she proclaimed, clocking his denim jeans, Beatle boots, dark blue roll-neck sweater and battered, brown leather jacket. She kissed him on the cheek. Martin reacted awkwardly, not so much out of embarrassment as a lack of sophistication.

His journalist friend, totally unfazed, continued, taking and shaking Hanna's hand. 'And you look every inch the kind of girl who would knock this boy for six. Pleased to meet you. Very pleased to meet you.'

'And you too,' Hanna replied, 'I've heard all about you.' Fifteen-all, Martin thought, but didn't say. What was it about girls that they could immediately get on so well with other girls? Boys took a lot longer to warm up with boys. Girls didn't seem to mind investing time with those they could become friends with, whereas boys seemed to save their energy for getting to know girls, envious of what might be waiting for them at the end of the line.

Three hours later, after the Bob Dylan concert at Green's Playhouse, they were one and all still reeling and speechless. When Dylan first walked onto the bare stage in a single beam of white light that followed his every move, he looked small, frail and so white-skinned under his crash-helmet-shaped curly hair that Martin was convinced he must be ill. However, when he started to sing, he grew in stature and strength to the giant they knew from the Columbia albums.

Where Johnny McEvoy had been entertaining and engaging, Dylan was challenging and aggressive. He cajoled them this way and that with line after line of perfectly crafted lyrics. Martin felt that each line was the thought behind, and the basis for, another song.

His imagery was vivid and disturbing, but at other times gentle and comforting. Martin had never known an experience like it in his life. By the end of the performance, he realised just how hard he and Hanna had been unconsciously squeezing each other's hands throughout the concert.

Martin had an overwhelming feeling of being in the presence of greatness, and he didn't feel inferior; he simply felt thoroughly invigorated having been able to see and hear such sheer perfectly paced poetry in such beautiful motion. In his own words, Dylan was a song and dance man; perhaps even the ultimate song and dance man.

Hanna and Martin couldn't wait to get back to their hotel room and *be* with each other. In their lovemaking, they felt an intensity they'd never experienced before. It took Hanna to put it into words: 'I've never been so excited by a performance in my life, Martin. The evening was made so perfect by the fact that we were there together to enjoy it. I looked at you during the concert and I felt... I felt this thing... you and me was so right. Whatever else we do from now, we will do with each other. If this is love, then so be it.' She didn't wait for Martin to affirm his feelings to her, for she already knew.

CHAPTER THIRTY-EIGHT

And the lumps are going to be big, Jim, very big I can tell you

Sheila McGinley

Martin and Hanna returned to Castlemartin at lunchtime the following day. That evening, The Playboys were performing at the Dreamland Ballroom. The first sign that something was wrong was when the Blues By Five made a big thing about announcing 'Three Spires' as being an original Martin McClelland song.

Dixie was at the mineral stall with his wife, Colette, and Martin was talking to Hanna. Dixie knew nothing about Martin and Hanna; no one did really, apart from Martin's mum, Sean MacGee and Jim Mitchell. Martin knew they'd have had no need to share this information with anyone else.

Martin and Hanna hadn't meant to be holding hands, but they just were. They weren't consciously doing it. They'd been lovers for several months by now, and even though their brains might have been telling them that they were in public, their bodies were telling each other that they were in close proximity to the people who gave them the most pleasure. Dixie and Colette walked over to them. At first, Dixie was convinced that Martin and Hanna must have met by accident at the local dance, on one of the rare occasions Hanna was back in Castlemartin.

Dixie said, 'Ah, the Lennon and McCartney of Castlemar...' He stopped mid-sentence as his eyes settled on Martin and Hanna's interlocked hands. Colette looked uncomfortable. 'You're holding hands!' Dixie said in disbelief, clearly not in control of his words. Colette squeezed her husband's arm, trying hard to shake him back to reality without being too obvious about it.

'Oh, we're doing a *lot* more than holding hands, Dixie,' Hanna boasted coyly. Afterwards, she told Martin that she couldn't help but say that. She knew it was unnecessary, even bordering on childish, but the fact that Dixie had tried to put Martin down with the Lennon and McCartney remark just brought out the worst in her.

Colette led her husband away, shocked by how visibly shaken he was. During the dance, the ballroom seemed to be buzzing about RTÉ and the Eurovision Song Contest. Dixie announced 'Did She Say Anything To You?' and made a big meal of saying it was *The Playboys'* Eurovision entry. He did not mention that Martin had written the song on any of the four times The Playboys had to perform it.

Martin, for his part, sang his heart out, especially on 'I Should Have Known Better', 'What Do You Want To Make Those Eyes At Me For?', 'Somebody Help Me' and 'The Perfect Day'. But he had to admit that, after witnessing Dylan the previous evening in Glasgow, he found his performance, apart from those Hanna-inspired songs, pretty shallow and very unrewarding. He found himself tuning in to Brendan's effortless singing and enjoying that far more than his own.

After the dance, Dixie tried to excuse his earlier behaviour by saying that Martin should be more careful; he was the heartthrob of the band, and as such shouldn't really be seen in a ballroom holding any particular girl's hand. He packed his saxophone away and disappeared quickly in search of Mitchell and the band's fee.

Once again, Dixie reiterated to Mitchell that he'd better sort out the RTÉ situation or he'd do it himself. Mitchell explained once more that it was outside of his control; RTÉ called the shots, made the tapes and threw their shapes.

Hanna returned to Belfast first thing on Saturday morning, but not before securing a promise from Martin that he would come down to see her on Monday, sealing the deal with one of the most passionate kisses ever seen about the streets of Castlemartin. The Playboys played Caproni's in Bangor on Saturday and the Fiesta in Letterkenny on the Sunday. Both dances were sold out, and both drew great performances from the band. The only incident worth noting from either dance was on the way back from Letterkenny. It was an incident that nearly sent The Playboys to join Jim Reeves on his current divine circuit.

Smiley was riding shotgun up front with Robin, and Dixie was in his favourite position, behind the wheel. Martin had recently twigged that it wasn't so much that Dixie liked to drive, but more that while driving he was able to remain detached from the band but still tune into what was going on between the other musicians. From his hours on the road, Smiley had become a bit of an expert on the mechanical side of the van. He'd hear a noise and say: 'Dixie, I think the exhaust is getting a bit loose; you better have it seen to.' Dixie would take the vehicle into the garage the following day, and lo and behold, wouldn't Smiley only have been right. The amazing thing was that he was 100 per cent correct each and every time. So much so, the boys in the band took great comfort from his qualities.

They'd just passed Newtowncunningham when there was a bit of disturbance at the rear of the wagon. Smiley announced: 'I'd say the rear wheel, driver's side, has worked itself loose.'

'Jeez, you're amazing, head,' said Robin, who, if truth be told, was very envious of Smiley's mechanical insights, 'you're able to work all that out just from a bit of a rumble at the back of the van.'

'No,' Smiley said, somewhere between a laugh and a cry, 'the fecking wheel's just passed us by and is scooting on up the road.'

Luckily enough, their Sunday ended up fine. They were going up a hill, so Dixie hadn't much trouble bringing the vehicle to a stop. If they'd been on the other side of the hill, well, it didn't bear thinking about.

Nothing much happened on Monday, apart from the van being given a complete service. Martin hitched down to Belfast where he remained until Wednesday morning.

Around the same time that Martin would have been returning to Castlemartin for the pick-up for that evening's dance in the Silver Slipper, Strandhill in Sligo, Jim Mitchell received quite a disturbing phone call from Dublin. It went something like this:

'Jim, it's Sheila McGinley here.'

'Hi, Sheila, good to hear from you.'

'You may not think so, after what I'm about to tell you.'

'Oh, that sounds ominous.'

'Jim, this afternoon RTÉ got a call, "from a Northerner," was all they'd say.'

'Oh?'

'This person claimed that Martin Dean did not write "Did She Say Anything To You?"'

'Really?' Mitchell replied, going into damage control and recalling Dixie's threat at the same time.

'They say they have proof that this song was in fact written by someone else... a Sean MacGee. Do you know a Sean MacGee, Jim?'

'Why, yes,' Mitchell admitted, 'he lives around here, he used to be in a band with Martin, and he used to write the odd wee song with him.'

'Oh, I see,' Shelia said, a little aggressively.

'You don't honestly think...'

'Jim, it's not down to what I think. The damage has been done.'

'What do you mean, "the damage has been done"?'

'Well, RTÉ are obviously very disturbed by the allegation.'

'Yes, but we can prove it's not true,' Mitchell said, hoping the desperation wasn't showing in his voice.

'Good. I was hoping you'd say that, Jim,' Sheila admitted. 'How do you plan on doing that?'

Mitchell thought for a moment. 'Okay, here's what I'll do. I'll go round to MacGee's house immediately, sober him up and drive him straight to RTÉ to set the record straight.'

'Good man yourself. That is exactly the reaction I wanted, Jim. I can get my mate to keep a lid on this until close of business today. After that, I'm afraid it will be out of her hands, which means it will be out of my hands. If this gets out, Jim, it doesn't matter whether it's true or false. If it gets out, it will destroy the band... and Martin.'

'I know, Sheila; I appreciate what you're doing for us on this.'

'Until the end of the day, Jim, that's as long as I can help you.'

Mitchell left for MacGee's house. He wasn't there. His mother didn't know or care where he was. She reckoned it had been a few days since she'd last seen him, but she wasn't sure. Then Mitchell went to check out every pub in Castlemartin, just in case MacGee had his own private back-door key. No joy there either. Next he went to Magherafelt, then Maghera, then Ballyronan, then Tobermore. Then he realised it was 4 p.m. and that he couldn't possibly make it down to Dublin now by the end of the day.

He knew that RTÉ wouldn't accept a voice down a phone line. At least if he could find MacGee, he could drive overnight and have him at RTÉ first thing in the morning. But where was the drunk? No one had seen him for ages.

He could not even ask Martin Dean, who had arrived back late from Belfast and had jumped straight into The Playboys' wagon, which left immediately for the Embassy Ballroom in Derry. Mitchell had two choices: one, he could locate MacGee, or two, he could get Dixie to admit that it was he who had made the call. But then, such an admission would equally wreck the band.

He rang Sheila at 5.55 p.m. He hadn't been able to track down MacGee, but he would keep looking.

'It's no use, Jim, you're too late,' Sheila said. He could tell by her voice that she'd also suffered a very traumatic day as well. It had probably been even worse than his day.

The RTÉ person was Sheila's friend, to whom she'd made the first call regarding Martin's entry. The friend had then passed it on up the line, and soon it was all going to come falling back in the opposite direction, only this time, the smell wasn't going to be quite so pleasant or, as Sheila put it: 'The cow crap will hit the fan first thing in the morning and the lumps are going to be big, Jim, very big, I can tell you. I'm sorry. Tell Martin I'm really sorry. Tell him there was nothing else I could do to help him.' Mitchell still felt that, if only he could find MacGee before daybreak, before any of the RTÉ bods had a chance to do anything, he'd still have a chance to save the situation. He had a sudden thought. Being a drunk, MacGee would have been hiding from the sun all day. Now it was sundown, surely that was the time all the creepy crawlies came out again.

The Playboys' frantic manager did another round of everywhere, this time enlisting the help of the only person he could trust, Kathleen McClelland. He disclosed to his bookkeeper only that he was looking for MacGee, that he was desperate to find him in fact. He never let on why and she didn't ask.

Gentleman Jim Mitchell dropped his bookkeeper off at her house at 3.45 a.m. She sat in silence with him for a short time. She asked him if he'd like a tea. He gently caressed the scar on her upper cheek, just below her right eye, and thanked her, but said that there was something he needed to do.

An hour and three quarters later, when the moonless night was at its darkest, Dixie Blair was shocked to find his manager parked in the drive outside his new house, waiting for him. Dixie waited in the wagon, its 'Playboys From Castlemartin' neon light turned off long enough to have cooled down. Usually, he turned off the sign the minute that they crested the hill, which brought Lough Neagh and Castlemartin into view below them.

The manager wasn't moving, so Dixie, exhausted by his drive back from Sligo, stepped out of his wagon and went up to the pristine Vauxhall and rapped on the window.

Mitchell wound the window down very slowly. The reality was that he wanted to get out of the car and beat the man to a pulp, but there would be people who would be disappointed in him if he did that.

'Mr Mitchell, I know why you're here,' Dixie started off, the nervousness very evident in his voice, 'but before you do anything hasty, can I just ask you to give me five minutes.'

'Okay,' Mitchell replied, still not sure where his calmness was coming from or for how long it would last.

The bandleader, followed by his manager, walked up to his front door and let both of them in. Dixie hadn't said a word since his request outside Mitchell's car. He walked into the sitting room and switched on the light, causing Mitchell to blink quite a bit, so accustomed had he become to the darkness over the previous two hours. Dixie crossed the new plush carpet to a cabinet, which he slowly and quietly opened. He searched around in the back left shelf and eventually, slowly, produced a piece of paper and handed it to Mitchell.

Mitchell squinted his eyes a few more times before he focused on the hand-written page of lyrics. The lyrics were written in a neat and precise handwriting. It wasn't the lyrics or the handwriting that Mitchell recognised, but he did freeze in on the legend, 'Did She Say Anything To You?'. He continued reading the words coming off the page as though in slow motion. On the next line, 'written by', and on the line after that, 'Martin McClelland and Sean MacGee'.

Mitchell found himself staring at the 'and' that joined the names McClelland and MacGee as partners in crime in this sorry little drama. In a split second, it all made sense. He remembered the moment's hesitation when Martin was filling in the writer credit for the song for the RTÉ documents. Mitchell had asked him if he'd forgotten how to spell his name and Martin had fobbed him off with the plausible excuse of not being sure whether to write 'Dean' or 'McClelland'. At least, Mitchell thought, in that moment's hesitation Martin had the decency to feel guilty about his deception.

Either way, it didn't change the fact that Martin Dean had tried to claim something that was not entirely his. He had tried to steal part of someone else's song. It didn't matter how Dixie had come into possession of the set of lyrics. It didn't even matter that Dixie had probably even stolen them. Mitchell was not disappointed in Dixie, because he had never expected anything from him in the first place.

He could hear Dixie going on in the background about how it was better for the band. Martin entering Eurovision would surely have split the band up. The bigger Martin would become the more The Playboys would need him. The more they would depend on him, the more of a disaster it would be to them when and if he left. Surely Mitchell could see this, Dixie pleaded, they were both making good money out of The Playboys, and now, with the Eurovision thing out the window, they could continue to rake it in for as long as they wanted.

Mitchell could hear Dixie blabbering on and on in the background, but he didn't really care about what he was saying. The manager could only focus on the fact that Martin McClelland had tried to take credit for someone else's part of a song.

He walked out of Dixie's house and didn't say a word. He went to his car, took out his keys and started to open the door. He stopped dead in his tracks as if he thought he had forgotten something. He returned to Dixie's house, and rang the doorbell. Dixie answered. Ten seconds later and Mitchell said: 'Sorry, Dixie, I forgot something.'

Before Dixie had a chance to ask what, Mitchell delivered his best knuckle sandwich. It might not have been forceful enough to send Dixie into the middle of next week, but it was certainly forceful enough to send him into the middle of the next room, where he landed in a heap on the floor, his bloody nose leaking rich crimson on Mrs Blair's nice, lush, wall-to-wall, freshly fitted carpet.

CHAPTER THIRTY-NINE

... now there's something Robin didn't know!

Smiley

Things happened fast the next morning. Jim Mitchell went straight home after dropping Dixie Blair. He had a shower, a shave and forced himself to eat some porridge before going to his office at the Dreamland Ballroom.

At 8 p.m. he rang Sheila McGinley at home to tell her that he hadn't succeeded in finding Sean MacGee. He felt he owed her more, but he knew he couldn't tell her any more because she, in turn, would feel she owed the same information to her mate at RTÉ.

And what was there to tell anyway? That Martin McClelland had been caught red-handed trying to cheat? Why on earth would someone as honest as Martin have wanted to cheat his friend out of his share of a song? It's wasn't as though he had a great incentive, you know, having made a grand from the publishing of one of his already recorded songs. No matter how Mitchell considered it, it just didn't make sense. Martin was cash-rich beyond his wildest dreams, so what difference would an extra £100, £300, £500 or even £1,000 make to him? Absolutely no difference. Well, at least no difference that Mitchell could work out.

Or was this all about ego? About being broadcast on television over all of Europe and standing up not only as the singer of the song but also the sole writer? Surely it couldn't be either? Sure, hadn't Martin been happy for Dixie not to ever mention him as the author of the songs they performed in the dance halls? And that would have been more of a reality to Martin than a television audience. In the ballrooms up and down the country, he saw these people over 200 nights of the year. They were real to him. He was real to them.

No. Mitchell just couldn't get a handle on it. As far as he was concerned, he felt that Martin drew more pride from the writing of the song than from being known as the person who wrote it.

The Dreamland owner and Playboys' manager sat in his office early that morning wondering why he fought so hard to find a reason to absolve Martin. When he swung for Dixie on the previous night, should it not have been Martin he was swinging for? By hitting Dixie, was he really relieving the anger he felt towards Martin? He'd never hit anyone before, and he was taken aback by how much damage you actually did to yourself. His knuckles were still stinging, a stinging that had removed any chance of sleep earlier that morning.

He thought of Kathleen McClelland. She had complete faith in her son. He was convinced that even if Kathleen had known Martin had done something wrong, no matter how wrong, she would still support him unconditionally.

The thing was that he liked Martin, and even though Martin's actions were causing him a lot of grief, and would cost him a lot of money, he still found himself liking him. The young singer-song-writer *was* likeable, likeable in that you wanted him to do well and to get on.

But still Mitchell kept returning to the plain and simple fact: Martin had done something very wrong. He found himself thinking back to the incident where Brendan the guitarist had a run-in with Dixie over money. Brendan claimed that Dixie had been in the wrong because he had spent some of Brendan's money without his permission. From Brendan's point of view, as far as Mitchell was concerned, he was right. In theory he had been wrong, but in practice Dixie had been in the right when he'd wronged Brendan, simply because he had the power to do as he saw fit. Mitchell decided that he didn't really want to go down that road in case he'd end up justifying what Martin did as right; right maybe because Martin, unlike MacGee, wasn't a mess, right because Martin, unlike MacGee, would go out there actively working at a career up to 60 hours a week, right because he, like Dixie, had spotted his opportunity and he'd taken it. Right because he could justify what he was doing.

No, Mitchell didn't want to go down that road, because he knew there *was* a right and there *was* a wrong and Martin McClelland by his actions had committed a sin and was guilty of a serious wrong.

At 9.10 a.m. Mitchell got the first of the calls, the endless stream of calls that would let him know exactly of how monumental a crime Martin Dean was guilty. 'Jim,' a ballroom owner and one of his so-called friends said, 'no offence against you personally, but I'm going to have to pull my Playboy dates.'

'Why?' Mitchell asked. He was on automatic, he didn't have the heart for this and his so-called friend could hear this in his voice.

'You know why, Jim, and I'll tell you this for nothing – if I were you, I'd drop them like a hot potato or your core business will suffer.' Mitchell knew what the ballroom owner meant; if there was to be a complete ban on The Playboys, ballroom owners, who also managed bands, would need to feel that they weren't going to lose bookings on their own bands (on Mitchell's circuit) when they rang up to cancel The Playboys.

He thought of fighting it. He knew he could have nipped the whole thing in the bud if he'd said to the first ballroom owner who rang up to cancel, 'Okay, that's fine, I accept that, but let me tell you what's going to happen. I'll ring up all the showband managers whose bands play my circuit and I'll tell them that if they play for you in your poxy little ballroom again, they'll never work for me in my circuit again.'

Mitchell knew it was easy to take a stand, but ballroom owners would take a stand against The Playboys only if it wasn't going to hurt them directly, that is to say in their pocket. People's principles tend to disappear when it was going to cost them money.

On the other hand, there were people like Sammy Barr, who were on the phone within the next half an hour offering support and saying, 'Ah sure, don't worry, this will all blow over. It'll be a storm in a teacup. The only people who'll be talking about this will be the people in the business. Now they've got something to gossip about, but that'll stop when they find the next thing to gossip about. The dancers will never hear about it; it won't concern them. Keep your head down for a couple of months and this will all blow over, it'll become history.'

At 10 p.m. an announcement was made on RTÉ: "'Did She Say Anything To You?", the Martin McClelland song seeking the nomination as the Irish entry for the Eurovision Song Contest, has been withdrawn due to irregularities.'

And that was it. Not even 30 words. That was the sum total of all the grief that had been caused. Sammy Barr had been right. How many people in Ireland knew that Martin Dean's real name was Martin McClelland? How many people in Ireland knew that Martin McClelland had anything whatsoever to do with The Playboys' Showband from Castlemartin?

Mitchell bet that Dixie was happy *now* that RTÉ had used Martin's name and not the name of The Playboys. He spoke on the phone to Thomas Boyle, who was also surprisingly supportive: 'I don't know what went on, and I don't want to know what went on, but I'll tell you this, *whoever* wrote that song is a brilliant songwriter and has a great career ahead of them. Maybe this was the best thing that could have happened to them. Really, Jim, it solves the problem of Martin working without the showband in one fell swoop. I still want to put out the record, and I want to put it out under Martin's name. I've sent it to my man at Pye and they're up for it too, big time, as long as it's not by a showband. When you've sorted out your publishing problems give me a shout and we'll do a deal.'

Before they disconnected, Jim Mitchell brought up one other piece of business with Thomas Boyle. The surprising thing was that nobody was asking him what the 'irregularities' were, so he assumed everyone knew. For all of that, no one had questioned if Martin really had tried to steal part of the song, and equally, no one had asked Mitchell *why* he had tried to steal part of the song.

Between the phone calls, Mitchell had asked himself the same questions all morning. The only conclusion he could reach was that Martin probably felt that MacGee was in no fit state to sign the documents, nor was it likely he would have signed them even if he were in a state to. Martin had probably tried, only to be met by drunken resistance. Gentleman Jim Mitchell had watched how Martin worked up close. He'd seen how he dealt with Sheila McGinley; he'd seen how he'd defused the situation when the band was accusing Dixie of spending their money without their permission; he'd seen how Martin and Hanna had kept their relationship under wraps, he assumed, to save Dixie any embarrassment; he'd seen Martin seek and accept his mother's advice in certain matters. These were not the actions of a boy who'd try and cheat his oldest friend out of the shared songwriting credit and half the songwriting royalties. Hell, Martin hadn't even seemed all that interested in Eurovision in the first place. Mitchell felt that no matter what the credits were, Martin would still have paid MacGee his dues. He pulled it all together very neatly and tidily. But he was sure it was not Martin's natural instinct to be deceptive; he *hoped* it was not Martin's natural instinct to be deceptive.

It's time to call The Playboys in, Mitchell thought. This wasn't going to be pleasant. He sent Scotty Connelly, complete in his Bob Dylan haircut, white T-shirt, blue pants and PVC jacket, to do the rounds of The Playboys and advise them of an 11 p.m. meeting at the Dreamland Ballroom. He sent Mickey to get everyone, bar Dixie and Martin. Mitchell planned to get both of them himself.

When Mitchell knocked on Dixie's door, Colette answered. She looked drained and tired, but still had time to give Mitchell a sympathetic moment. She even had the decency to ask after Martin. Mitchell wondered if she'd just realised what a shit the man she married was. She said that she would ensure that her husband was at Dreamland in time for the meeting.

Kathleen McClelland opened the door at Martin's house and immediately invited him in. 'You look awful,' she said, as she led him through to the kitchen and started to make some coffee.

'It's a sorry state of affairs, isn't it? Is he up yet?'

'He's gone, Jim…' Mitchell was about to interrupt, but she continued, 'This is not the way it looks, Jim.'

'How is it then, Kathleen?'

'I don't know. Martin reassured me that everything would be okay. He said that nothing untoward had happened, and something I didn't understand about Sean being in a very delicate stage just now. He told me to tell you that he was sorry for any trouble he was causing. He hadn't meant to cause anyone any trouble. He told me that circumstances had just taken over a certain situation as they very often do. He said that Hanna had always been telling him that when circumstances conspire against you, not to waste your energy fighting them. Someone or something bigger than you is telling you to change, so you should change.'

'Sorry?' Mitchell was now confused, very confused. Circumstances and conspiracies, what was this all about? 'When will he be back?'

'He said he wasn't sure.'

'Where was he going?'

'He said he didn't know.'

'Jeez, Kathleen,' Mitchell said, gratefully taking a large swig of his piping hot coffee, 'you know what it looks like, don't you? Everyone is going to think he's guilty as hell and couldn't stay around to face the music.'

'Jim,' Kathleen said, her voice very quiet and very calm, 'it doesn't matter what people think, it only matters what *we* think. Martin said he was sorry, very sorry, but there was no other way to do this. He said he was sad about the way things had turned out, but equally that he was happy for the other opportunities which were arising out of it.'

'Kathleen, I don't mean to hurt you, but do *you* think Martin tried to cut Sean out of the Eurovision song credit?'

'All I know, Jim, is that Martin is a good lad and I know that he would never intentionally do anything bad, or that he would never do anything, no matter how it looked, without good reason.'

'Aren't you beside yourself with worry about where he's gone, about where he's going to stay, about what he's going to do… about when you'll see him again?'

'Jim, he's a grown man,' Kathleen replied, with a gentle smile on her face. 'He's just left home; he had to do it one day. It's not such a big deal. He's ready for the big, bad world. It breaks my heart to see him go; it breaks every mother's heart to see their child go, but we have to let them go.

'When Martin was born, I couldn't believe how much he changed my life. I couldn't believe how strongly I was connected to him. I don't just mean by blood, but spiritually as well. I remember when he was younger, he was always on at me to take him to the swing boats at the Fairhill in Magherafelt, and I told him that I would take him when he was eleven. I told him that when he was 11 years old he'd be old enough to go.'

Kathleen looked out through her kitchen window. She had her coffee cup in hand, but she wasn't drinking from it. She was using it to warm her hands. Having gained the required heat, she took a gulp of her coffee and continued: 'So, when he was eleven he made me take him there and they put him in the swing boat by himself. The boat looked beautiful, painted in yellow, blue and red. He looked so small in the big boat all by himself. He was hanging on to the rope for dear life, and the man was pushing him, and every time he went up, I swear to you, I felt in the pit of my stomach like

I was there with him going up as well, and I was also struggling to catch my breath the way I knew he was. My heart was racing and I was getting butterflies in the pit of my stomach.'

'But does that feeling,' Mitchell started struggling for words, 'does that not make it all the more difficult to let go, particularly in these circumstances?'

'I'm not worried about any of that,' Kathleen said firmly, 'and you know what? I've been learning how to let him go for 22 years. Sometimes it's a very physical thing, learning to let someone go. I remember the time when he was learning to ride a bike. He was finding it very difficult, so I said I would walk him to Magherafelt with his bike because I didn't know any other way to do it. And so, the whole way there and the whole way back, I walked behind the bike, steadying him up and balancing him by holding on to the back of the saddle. I had to run down the hills behind him. When I returned home that evening, my arms were killing me and my legs were killing me and you know what, no matter how much I wanted to, I couldn't teach him to ride the bike.

'About three months later, he was out in the back garden sitting in the nook of the bars on my much bigger bike, and he was going up and down the garden path, powering the bike by pushing his legs along the ground and then, as I quietly watched him through the kitchen window, suddenly he was paddling along as fast as his wee legs would push the wheels round, and then he lifted both his feet off the ground and some way, somehow he found his balance and rode the bike the whole way down the garden. The look of joy on his face was magic.

'But you see, the point in telling you this is that it was not something I could teach him. It was something he had to learn to do by himself. When I left him to it, he was fine, he taught himself how to ride the bike.'

Kathleen was about to continue, but she paused, either searching for her words or searching for the strength to say them. 'Now it's time for him to go out and fend for himself in the big, bad world.'

Mitchell knew that Martin's mother was close to tears. He rose from his chair and patted her gently on the back. 'Oh,' she said, picking herself up, 'I almost forgot, he asked me to tell you that he's not sure what it is he wants to do yet, but if it's music, and he's not sure it is, he wants you to be his manager – if you'd still want to after all of this?'

Mitchell's look told Kathleen that even if he wanted to, he could never say no to such a request.

If Jim Mitchell was 50 per cent successful in rounding up the two members of The Playboys that he'd gone after, then Scotty Connelly was 100 per cent successful in rounding up the six members he'd set out to find. So, at 11.05 p.m., Jim Mitchell, Dixie Blair, Brendan the guitarist, Mo the drummer, Davy the bass player, Smiley the trumpet player, Barry the organist and saxophonist and Robin the trombonist all sat down in Mitchell's office at the Dreamland Ballroom for their meeting.

'Hey, head,' Robin started, addressing Dixie, 'what happened to your eye? Colette wallop you one at last?'

'Ah no,' Dixie replied sheepishly, 'I walked into a door.'

'Okay, lads,' Mitchell said, bringing the meeting to some kind of order. He had been surprised that the room wasn't abuzz with the RTÉ story, and then he remembered that they'd all probably just been woken from their slumber. 'Let me tell you what's been happening over the last day or so.' He paused to make sure that he had everyone's undivided attention and, when he did, he continued: 'Somebody has rung RTÉ and advised them that Martin stole the song 'Did She Say Anything To You?', or at the very least that he hadn't written it entirely by himself. RTÉ have consequently withdrawn our song, due, they say, "to irregularities".'

'It's over,' sang Brendan to Roy Orbison's melody.

'Feck!' said Mo.

'Agh no,' said Smiley.

'The wee skitter,' said Davy.

'I knew it,' said Robin.

'Mmmm,' said Barry, who was still trying to wake up.

And Dixie said nothing.

'Where's Martin?' asked Brendan.

'Who'd do such a thing?' asked Smiley.

'One of the other acts?' suggested Davy.

'How would they know?' asked Mo.

'Exactly!' said Robin, looking at Dixie.

'Mmmm,' said Barry.

And Dixie said nothing.

'Is Martin okay?' asked Brendan.

'Did he really steal it?' asked Davy.

'Of course not,' said Smiley.

'I bet he did,' said Robin.

'Why's he not here?' asked Mo.

'Mmmm,' said Barry.

'Exactly!' said Robin.

And Dixie said nothing.

'Dixie, have you anything you'd like to say to the lads?' Mitchell asked, bringing back a hush to the table.

'Dixie, *you* didn't ring RTÉ?' asked Brendan, and laughed.

'You never liked him,' said Davy, and sneered.

'You wouldn't, Dixie?' said Smiley, and unsmiled.

'You couldn't, Dixie?' said Mo.

'Mmmm,' said Barry and yawned.

'Fecking *exactly*,' said Robin, and took a swing at Dixie across the table.

This finally woke Barry up, and he restrained Robin by pulling him back down into his seat. Whatever else Mitchell felt about Dixie, he had to admire his courage for showing up. Martin, on the other hand, had chosen not to turn up and face his colleagues. His issues, whatever they were, shouldn't have come into it. He should still have turned up and faced his fellow band members to put them in the picture.

'Look, lads, I'm not going to beat about the bush on this...' Dixie began.

'I *fecking* knew it,' Robin said loudly.

'Okay,' Mitchell announced, anticipating the furore that was about to erupt, 'let's hear him out.'

'Okay,' said Dixie, 'no matter how much you may or may not want to hear this, Martin Dean didn't write the song by himself, if at all. I have proof of this,' Dixie started. He was very shaky, and his voice was close to breaking up. He dug into the inside pocket of his jacket and produced a sheet of paper, which he unfolded and passed around the table.

'This shows that, at the very least, the lyrics were written by Sean MacGee,' Dixie continued.

'How does it show that?' Davy asked.

'Well, because it says at the top, 'written by Martin McClelland & Sean MacGee,' Robin said begrudgingly.

'Apart from which, it's in Sean's handwriting,' Dixie announced

'How did you get this copy of the lyrics?' Brendan asked, focusing in like everyone else on the 'written-by' line.

'I don't feel that's important,' Dixie said, immediately going on the defensive.

'I think it is,' Brendan pushed.

'I *don't* feel that it is,' Dixie replied, climbing onto his high horse again. Mitchell wondered if the man would never learn. Just because he thinks he's regained a little of the moral high ground, he's pushing that 'I'm the bandleader' crap again.

'Just tell us, Dixie,' Robin ordered.

'All that's important here is that Martin Dean was trying to deceive us, RTÉ and the Irish dancers by pretending that he wrote that song,' Dixie said, with an air of finality.

'I'll tell you what, Dixie, I don't know where this is all going, and I don't know how it's going to end up,' Smiley began, a tremor noticeable in his voice, 'but I can tell you this, though: unless you tell me how you got that set of lyrics, I'm out of here and I'm never coming back.'

'And I'm with him,' said Brendan.

'I found it in Martin's guitar case,' Dixie started, obviously deciding to cut off the attack at the pass.

'What? In the dressing room?' Davy asked.

'Not exactly,' Dixie admitted.

'Exactly how then?' Brendan pushed.

'In the van,' Dixie admitted.

'What? You went through Martin's guitar case while it was meant to be packed away in the safety of our wagon?' Robin spat out the words like the rat-a-tat of a military drum.

'Tell me, Dixie,' Brendan asked, mocking Ironside, 'did you ever go through *my* guitar case while it was in your custody?'

'Listen, I think we're getting things way out of proportion here,' Dixie protested, 'we are here because Martin Dean tried to steal a song.'

'No,' Smiley protested, 'as far as I can make out we are here today because you rang RTÉ like a snitch and grassed on a member of this band.'

'Dixie, did you discuss any of this with Martin or with the manager?' Mo asked, nodding in Mitchell's direction but not daring to look him in the eye.

'No,' Dixie replied indignantly.

'Did you ever discuss it with Sean MacGee?' Robin asked, picking up quickly on Mo's theme.

'No,' Dixie replied, as if the thought of such a possibility made him scundered to his bones.

'So how do you know that Martin was trying to steal the song?' Brendan asked.

'Because he claimed he wrote it by himself,' Dixie replied.

Mitchell was beginning to feel sorry for Dixie – at least in a court of law he would only face the one inquisitor.

'So wouldn't it have saved everyone a lot of pain and trouble if you'd taken your problem to Martin and Mr Mitchell and said, "Look, I think there's been a wee mistake made here, let's correct it immediately", and we would still have had time to fix things?' Brendan continued relentlessly.

'But that wasn't the only issue,' Dixie protested, 'don't you see we're better off out of Eurovision?'

'How do you work that one out, Dixie?' Brendan asked.

'RTÉ only wanted *Martin Dean*. They didn't want *The Playboys*. If Martin had won, we'd have lost him and that would have been the end of The Playboys. Don't you see? I was saving the band!' Dixie pleaded.

'What? Saving the band by shopping Martin?' Robin asked, still fuming.

'Well, now he won't be going to Eurovision and England, he'll be staying with us. The Playboys can continue as usual, everything will be fine,' Dixie replied, perhaps the realisation of what he had actually done sinking in for the first time.

'Jeez, Dixie, you're one fecking eejit,' Brendan said, letting out a very large sigh.

'Believe me, head, it was for our own good,' Dixie continued.

'Ehm, excuse me, Dixie, but do you see Martin Dean sitting around this table?' Brendan inquired, shaking his head from side to side in disgust.

'Don't worry; he'll be back,' Dixie said, looking from musician to musician and finding no support from anyone.

'Martin Dean left Castlemartin this morning, lads,' Mitchell started, 'and he won't be back, at least not for a long time. And if he ever does return, it will not be as Martin Dean.'

'Then we'll replace him,' Dixie said defiantly.

'Not with me as manager.'

'Nor me as guitarist,' said Brendan.

'Nor me,' said Davy and Smiley in unison.

'Count me out,' said Mo.

'And me,' said Barry.

'And never, ever come knocking on my door, Dixie, or I'll fecking clock you,' Robin added.

'I'll put another band together. It was my band in the first place,' Dixie said proudly.

'Didn't we fecking know it, Dixie?' Brendan said, 'Didn't we fecking know it?'

'You blew it, Dixie, you blew it big time.' Now it was Smiley's turn, 'you had one of the best sets of players in the country – outside of The Freshmen that is. On a good night, there was no one bar Billy Brown's men who could touch us, and you went and blew it.'

'Dixie,' Mitchell began, 'you can go now, you have no further business in my ballroom; please do me the kindness of never setting foot in this establishment again.'

Dixie got up to leave. He saw that the offending lyric-sheet was in Mitchell's hand. He made moves to retrieve it, and then obviously thought better of it and said, 'No, it's fine, have it on me. You're welcome to it; I've got lots of copies.'

'I bet you have, you scheming fecker,' Brendan hissed. And with that he was gone.

'Okay, lads, one last bit of business,' Mitchell began. 'I didn't particularly want Dixie hearing it. I'd like to suggest that you all stick together. I'd also like you to consider having Brendan as lead singer. Maybe you should also think about moving into the country music end of the market, that's definitely where the future lies in Ireland. You'd have to change your name and all, but I can tell you this, I've spoken to Thomas Boyle at City Records this morning, and he says he'd be happy to put out your records.'

Right there, in the time it took to snap your fingers, and with as much fuss, one band died and a new band was born. The dark clouds from the previous hour miraculously disappeared, and everyone reverted to their showband personalities. It was a thing to behold. Everyone became a head again, and Ben Lang crept back into the conversation.

'I think it's a great idea, sir,' Brendan announced, 'I'd like it to be a full co-op band with everyone on equal shares.'

'I agree with that,' Davy said, before the final word had left Brendan's lips.

'Listen, heads, no disrespect and all of that,' Barry announced hesitantly, 'but I've been thinking about this for a while, and what with me and Angela expecting a wain and all, well to be honest, I'd like to give up doing the ballrooms to be honest. I mean, I was planning to leave The Playboys when I could find a good time and now, well this just seems to be the perfect time.'

'We'll be sorry to lose you, Barry, we really will,' Brendan said, as all the others muttered agreement, 'but it's your call. Take some time to think it over first though, will you?'

'Thanks, Brendan, but I've been thinking about little else since Angela got pregnant. You know we kept meeting all these other showband heads who had families who would keep saying that their only regret was that they were missing out on their children growing up. I really don't want to be saying that in ten years.'

'What will you do?' Robin asked.

'I've made a few bob over the years…' Barry smiled as everyone laughed at his understatement, '…and I was thinking I might open up a wee electrical shop and sell records, record players, televisions, radios and maybe even some musical instruments.'

'Good on you, head, don't forget the discount for all your mates,' Brendan said, and then turned to face Mitchell. 'Will you be our manager, sir?'

Mitchell wasn't surprised that, although it was a co-operative band, Brendan seemed to be taking charge.

'Thanks, lads,' Mitchell replied, openly flattered, 'I'll certainly get you up and started on the circuit, make sure you've got a full diary, but these days that's all you really need. Treat the Dreamland with as much respect as The Playboys did and you can rehearse here all you want. My door will always be open to you, and if you still feel you need a manager beyond that I'll make sure you get the best.'

'You can't say fairer than that,' Brendan replied, going round to Jim Mitchell's side of the desk and shaking his hand firmly. They all did the same in turn. 'Right, lads,' Mitchell said in a very businesslike manner, 'if you're going to take The Playboys' residency, first Thursday of the month, you'd better get your skates on.'

As they left Mitchell's office, all were muttering about this musician and that. Brendan wanted a pedal steel player who doubled on piano and guitar. Just the one split for a band member who could play three instruments, Mitchell thought, that's not bad – he's learning. The hustle and bustle evaporated from his office. Just as the door was about to close, Brendan stuck his head back into

Mitchell's office and said: 'Oh yes, and the next time you see that Martin McClelland chap, can you tell him we're going to need a few of his tunes for our first recording session.'

When they were outside the Dreamland, and out of earshot of Gentleman Jim Mitchell, Smiley pulled Brendan to one side and said: 'That was nice of you to make that offer to Martin. But I can't understand why you made it to Jimitch. Sure he told us Martin's gone away for good. So why do you think that they'd ever be in contact again?'

'Oh,' Brendan said with a sly wink, 'something about blood being thicker than water.'

'What?! Mitchell and Kathleen McClelland?' Smiley said in disbelief, 'No never?'

Brendan nodded knowingly.

'Well, actually now you come to mention it, I suppose it makes sense,' Smiley said, though clearly flabbergasted, 'How did you know?'

'Me auld man used to fancy her,' Brendan admitted, 'he always talks about it when he's drunk and me ma's not around. He always claimed that Mitchell beat him to her bed.'

'Gosh,' Smiley said, 'now there's something Robin didn't know.'

'Nor ever will know, head,' Brendan said, winking again.

'Nor ever will know,' Smiley agreed.

CHAPTER FORTY

You really did have to be there

Selrahc Luap

From that day on, The Playboys Showband from Castlemartin started to slip into obscurity. In terms of their career, their timing was probably perfect. The days of the big crowds and big fees were numbered. In terms of securing their place in history, their timing was lousy. In truth, the showband and ballroom scene peaked in Ireland that year. The reality was that the movement was coming to an end, and The Playboys hadn't made a big enough impact on the scene to have permanently etched their name on the showbands' roll of honour. Even at their peak, they'd never been discussed in the same breath as The Royal, The Freshmen, The Dixies, The Capitol or The Drifters. Added to which, the circumstances of their demise gave the historians the perfect excuse to dismiss the band and all their work.

Brendan, Smiley, Robin, Mo and Davy recruited Vincent, a younger musician who was a bit of a boy genius and could near enough make music on any instrument. He was definitely on his way somewhere greater, but was happy to start his journey with Brendan & The Good Guys, and together they enjoyed another four years of good crowds and great money. Their biggest hit, which reached number four in the Irish charts, was a new recording of 'There's Always A Song At The End Of A Teardrop'. They had taken Mitchell's advice and managed themselves, which ensured that when the band ran its natural course, they all had enough money stuffed in their mattresses and in various plots of land and buildings around the county to be financially set up for life. Brendan then put together his own little four-piece, pure country outfit, to play the lounges. Smiley and Robin joined a popular, already-famous show-band, and Mo and Davy moved to London where they joined a progressive band.

And Dixie? Well, Dixie came out worst from The Playboys. Was it poetic justice or just bad luck? It's hard to say, but they do say that we make our own luck. Colette put up with him trying to get it together for a couple of years before she advised him, in no uncertain terms, that it was time to hang up his saxophone and get a proper job or she'd leave him, the most humiliating ultimatum you can give to a gigging musician. The Blairs weren't penniless, or anything near, but Dixie's wife knew her husband was too young not to have a focus to his day and to his life.

Together, they opened a small grocery shop, and within six years they had built it up to be the biggest grocery store in Mid-Ulster. Colette was packing their shop with new lines as quickly as Dixie could get the contractors to build the extension. Now and again, Colette would find herself having to politely interrupt Dixie with, 'Now, dearest, I'm sure Mrs Fleming is very interested in your gory, sorry did I say gory? Of course I mean *glory* days with The Playboys, but she does need to be home in time to get Trevor's dinner on the table.'

Ireland went to Eurovision in 1967 with Sean Dunphy (of The Hoedowners but not accompanied by them) and you'll never guess who won… no, sadly not Ireland and Sean, but England with Sandy Shaw and a song co-written by Bill Martin, a young lad from Scotland, and Derry-man Phil Coulter, who had just added another page to what was to become a fabulously successful songbook.

Over the counter in Dixie's grocery store and in the back of Brendan & The Good Guys' wagon, it was often discussed just how far Martin Dean and The Playboys would have gone in the contest if it hadn't been for what RTÉ had euphemistically referred to as 'Martin's irregularities'. The debates were often long and always passionate. And the conclusion to such discussions? Well, the consensus over the years seemed to favour the opinion that perhaps Martin McClelland's 'Did She Say Anything To You?' was just a wee bit too good for Eurovision.

And what became of Jim Mitchell? Well, he too saw the writing on the showband wall. He always considered the ballroom scene to be very similar to the gambling scene. The main attribute of a great gambler is that he knows when to keep the money in his pocket and walk away. By the end of the sixties, Jim had sold off his chain of ballrooms; all that is except the jewel in his crown, the Dreamland Ballroom by the shores of Lough Neagh near Castlemartin. Mitchell still went to his office in the Dreamland every day. The Castlemartin locals hadn't a clue what he was doing in there, because he'd stopped running dances in December 1972. People knew he was in his office because Scotty Connelly could be seen polishing his Vauxhall VX490 most days. When his beautiful car wasn't outside the Dreamland, he was off travelling around Ireland, just as he did in The Playboys' halcyon days, only now, instead of visiting ballrooms and ballroom owners, he was visiting racetracks and also, or so the rumour went, still doing a bit of business in Dublin.

The showband scene peaked around 1967. In its heyday, well over 10,000 people were employed directly and indirectly in the business. There are many reasons given for its demise: the showbands blamed the ballroom owners for not looking after the dancers properly; the ballroom owners blamed the showbands for being too greedy. The other main gripe the owners claimed was that by the showbands using relief groups and not taking to the stage until 11.30 p.m., the dancers found themselves going into the nearby bars to while away the time until that magic hour. Over the years, these bars grew more comfortable, and some of the more entrepreneurial bar and hotel owners turned them into comfortable lounges. Eventually, the owners started to put on entertainment in these lounges – more cabaret and folk shows than the ballrooms. The dancers took to them in a big way. You have to understand, by this point, the ballroom boom had enjoyed ten years, which is also a generation. If your older brother and sister went out to see showbands in ballrooms, then human nature dictated that you would seek out something different for yourself.

In the early days, booze hadn't been a major factor on the ballroom circuit, but as it became more popular with both musicians and dancers, it slowed down the musicians and made the dancers happier to be elsewhere, and the lounges provided the perfect venue.

Additionally, both showbands and the ballroom owners blamed the government for not giving grants to an industry that supported 10,000 people. But in the days of big money, you'd never have heard a musician or a manager utter the words 'tax incentive', 'grants' or 'tax breaks'. You have to remember that these people were wild, wild rich. And the other contributing factors to what many would call the crime of the decade? The taxman was growing cute to the money being generated in the ballrooms.

The growth of country music in Ireland was another major contributing factor. The Mighty Avons and The Mainliners were the back door through which country music entered Ireland. Country was a genre more suited to the lounges than the ballroom. Before them, country & western music would have constituted maybe 10 per cent of a band's repertoire.

The changing face of the English and American music scene wouldn't have helped the showband cause either. England, probably a generation ahead of Ireland in terms of developing its music scene, had now progressed from their own copyists and wannabe Yanks to a host of original and interesting artists. The music of these new bands didn't lend itself to being covered by the showbands.

The Royal Showband, for instance, was never going to sound or look comfortable trying to cover ELP, Pink Floyd, Jimi Hendrix or Cream for instance. The Freshmen could probably have made a brave attempt at it, but then again Billy Brown was often quoted as saying that he never considered The Freshmen to be a showband in the first place. To him they were always a *group*. In general, Ireland's home-grown original talent just wasn't quite ready to emerge and, sadly, hardly any of the showbands had concentrated on writing original material, and as a consequence few were actually building what today you could call a career.

When The Royal started out, it had all been tremendously exciting. They had obviously taken the showband format as developed by The Clipper Carlton and The Johnny Quigley Allstars. But the primary difference between The Royal and these bands was that the established bands were getting on a bit. Yes, they were the crème de la crème of musicians, but unlike The Royal they were hardly going to send the wee girls' hearts fluttering – and don't forget the golden rule: the bands brought the girls and the girls brought the boys, and that's how you filled the ballrooms. In the early days, The Royal were considered to be young, vital, exciting and sexy. Mind you, that's sexy in a repressed Irish kind of way. But as the sixties prepared to make way for the seventies, well, all the members of The Royal had also grown older. The showband format had grown tired and jaded because no one was pushing the boundaries; they had all been doing the same thing – night in, night out – as they had been doing for the previous ten years.

The border problems couldn't have helped either, and a lot of the southern showbands stopped travelling north. Also, there were now just too many bands on the road. In the early days, a bunch of mates got together because they enjoyed each other's company, they loved music and they wanted to have a bit of craic, so they formed a band. But the one thing that all the original showbands had was the fact that they were musicians, and were music-led bands. Then the businessmen started to become interested, due understandably to the vast amounts of money being turned over. These bread-heads started to put together *their* bands. They'd nick a popular singer from a big band, pay him an amazing salary to tempt him away from his mates, pay the rest of the band peanuts and keep all the folding money themselves. The majority of these bands were naff because essentially they were being told what to play by the businessmen. Gimmicky bands like The Indians and Light started to turn a part of the showband scene into a bit of a joke.

In truth, when Brendan Bowyer was nicked from The Royal Showband, not only was it the saddest day of the decade, but it marked – in extremely large pound signs – that the showbands' days were numbered. Following the English and American trends, the showbands became more liberal in their dress sense and presentation, losing a lot of their unique identity in the process. International travel became a lot easier, so it was not only easier for people to travel farther afield to concerts, it was also a lot easier for the original artists, who the showbands had been copying, to come to Ireland to play their own concerts. Singer-songwriters and 'progressive' bands became the preferred artists of the seventies. Irish traditional and Celtic music became the passion of the Irish youth. Even *New Spotlight* magazine started to favour pop artists over the showbands.

And then, of course, there were those new Irish artists of undeterminable talent who decided that badmouthing the showbands could act as a leg up for their own careers.

But all of this is probably *how* the showbands disappeared, not *why* they disappeared. Trying to figure out why the showband world slumped so drastically is like trying to explain why thoroughbred racing pigeons can find their way home from a strange drop-off point hundreds of miles away. They just can – in the case of the pigeons finding home – and they just did – in the case of the showbands disappearing.

If pushed for a quick answer on why the showbands fell out of favour, I'd have to say that all generations want and need their own music, their own fashions and their own heroes. Each generation *needs* to find its own way. What was good enough for the older brothers and sisters is never good enough for them. Years later, they'd probably happily go back and reassess what their older siblings or parents were listening to. The problem with the showbands, or with the vast majority of them, is that when you go back to re-examine what they left on vinyl, it doesn't hold up; as *copies* of the original music of other artists, it doesn't really stand the test of time. I suppose what I'm trying to say is: you *really* did have to be there.

And some of the fans who were there do still turn out to see Brendan Bowyer or Dickie Rock throwing whatever moves they can still throw. For the most part, though, the showbands faded into history.

This was a luxury not afforded to The Playboys Showband from Castlemartin. It's not even that they weren't forgiven for Martin's and Dixie's sins, it was more that they were simply forgotten.

CHAPTER FORTY-ONE

When you saw her
Up the street
Did she say anything
To you?

Martin McClelland

And that was that. It is not, however, the end of *our* story. When I was researching the disappearance of The Playboys Showband of Castlemartin, I obviously wanted to try and talk to Martin McClelland. He hadn't spoken to any member of the media since *before* the RTÉ Eurovision incident. But try though I did, I just couldn't trace him anywhere. The last known sighting of Martin McClelland was at his mother's funeral in Castlemartin in the autumn of 1987. Apparently hardly anyone recognised him. He'd grown his hair longer and had a beard and was quite slim. Certainly no one bothered him. After the funeral, he got straight in a car and drove away without saying a word to anyone.

The other person I was anxious to speak to was Sean MacGee. Again I searched in vain. However, when I had completed most of my work on this story, I received a telephone call from Smiley, The

Playboys' trumpet player. He told me that Sean had been in touch with him, and he'd heard I was writing this story and felt it was important that he and I talked. Smiley reckoned that Sean was the only person he knew who was still in touch with Martin and Hanna. Smiley also told me that Sean said something about it being time people knew what had really happened.

I suspected that he wanted to spin me a yarn just to earn himself a bit of cash for another boozing spree, but I agreed to his request for a meeting, mainly because I felt it was important to at least pick up parts of the story from his perspective. I felt it was my job to see through whatever tale Sean MacGee had, and hopefully glean some truths in the process.

We met in Bryson's pub in Magherafelt. I had a pint of Guinness, Sean had a pint of orange juice. He looked incredibly fit, if a little overweight and very sharp mentally. His pale skin, thinning hair and missing teeth testified to 'his drinking years'; his words, not mine. He claimed not to have had a drink since August 1966. He looked me straight in the eyes as he said this, and he defied me not to believe him. I believed him.

'I don't want to appear rude or anything, but I really don't want to answer any of your questions,' Sean MacGee said when we settled down to our drinks. He paused and took a large gulp of his orange juice, sighed loudly and continued. 'What I do want to do is give you a little bit of information, which I feel might help with the story you are writing. No, actually make that *vital* to the story you are writing.

'I don't want any money for this, but in order to convince you that what I'm about to tell you is the truth, I have no problem with your quoting me directly. If you can accept my conditions, I'm happy to continue.'

'That's perfectly fine with me,' I replied, 'can I record you?'

'I insist on it,' he said, searching into his windcheater and producing a Sony Professional Walkman. He declared, 'I'm going to record it too.'

'Okay,' I said.

'Okay,' Sean MacGee said, 'let's go. The first thing I have to tell you, and the single most important piece of information I am going to give you, is that Martin McClelland *never* tried to steal *any* of my material.'

'Wow,' was all I could say (I didn't even realise that I had said it, but it's there on the tape so I've included it).

'However, equally, Dixie was not lying when he said that he had discovered a sheet of paper with the lyrics to 'Did She Say Anything To You?' written in my handwriting.' I looked at him and he obviously picked up that I was thinking to myself that drink had obviously damaged part of his brain.

'Confused?' he asked.

'Yes.'

'And so you should be,' MacGee laughed. His laugh was halfway between a wheeze and a whistle. He laughed like someone who was short of breath and should not really be wasting their breath on laughing. 'Here, let me explain. As was often the case when Martin brought one of his songs to me, he had all the music and about 60 per cent of the lyrics completed. In those days, Martin always had trouble completing his lyrics, so he'd come around to my house or I to his and we'd work on them together. That's what happened with "Did She Say Anything To You?".

'So, I'd take his bit of paper and he'd have something like: "When you saw her / Up the street / Did she say anything / To you? / Blah, Blah, blah / Something, something, something / Something … love her still / etc. etc. / Did she say anything / To you? / Did she look at you? / Was there any clue? / Something etc." Do you get the picture?'

'Yeah,' I replied.

'So, I'd write all over his attempts and flesh it out a bit, and, line by line, we'd finish the lyrics. By the time we'd completed them, the page would be in such a mess with both our scribbles, so I would take a clean page of paper and write out the completed lyrics again, this time in my best handwriting. I always wrote the final version of the lyrics. Martin's handwriting was atrocious. If he wrote it, we'd both have a bit of a hoot trying to decipher his scribble two days later.

'Now, I don't know if you know this part yet, but Martin came round to see me – it would have been in August 1966, a big month in all our lives. He came to see me about entering what he considered to be *our* song as the Irish entry for the Eurovision Song Contest. In those days, any song we worked on together credit-wise we'd consider a song we'd both written. This was before all the crap about, "I wrote a verse and a chorus and the middle eight, so I own seven and a half sixteenths of the song". We were never into any of that. And you know why? Because I believe – and I think Martin does too – that the songs are already out there, and sometimes we are lucky enough to be the ones to 'catch' them and put them down on paper.

'Anyway, I can see that didn't fall on very receptive ears with yourself, so moving swiftly along, when Martin came around to see me to discuss this Eurovision contest... well... I was out of it, totally out of it. I think I even tried to pick a fight with him and take a pop at him and in the process I fell over in a complete and utter mess. There are no other words to describe it. I was a fecking disgrace. That's a great word, isn't it? *Disgrace*, the second part of that word is so elegant and beautiful, but by sticking those three letters in front of it, you make it into something ugly and repulsive, don't you? And... what's your name again?

'Paul Charles.'

'Yes, Paul, what I was going to say to you, Paul, was, that's exactly what I was, ugly and repulsive. So, what Martin did was he went home, got out his guitar, his pen and a bit of paper and what he did was he re-wrote my contribution to the lyrics of "Did She Say Anything to You?".'

'Shit, so that means the final version was a genuine Martin McClelland composition?' I heard myself asking.

'Natch,' MacGee agreed, 'all his own work from start to finish. I'd like to be able to say that he ruined the song by bastardising the lyrics, but, hand on heart, I'd have to say that he made it a much better song entirely, no doubt about it.

'And that superior version of 'Did She Say Anything To You?' was the song The Playboys had recorded for Eurovision. That was of course until Dixie Blair got the wrong end of the stick and dropped Martin in the smelly stuff you so eloquently referred to a few seconds ago.

'If he or the band or the manager had only bothered to check the lyrics on the page Dixie stole out of Martin's guitar case, they would have realised they were the original lyrics and *not* the lyrics on the version they'd submitted to the Eurovision Song Contest. My point would be that if anyone had bothered to look and figure out what had happened, they'd have discovered that the song was totally legit and well capable of winning Eurovision then or any year since.

'Now there's more, that's if you need more to show you exactly what kind of character we are dealing with here. Do you know where I was on that memorable day, not to mention half the night, in August 1966 when Jim Mitchell was desperately running around looking for me? Do you know where I was? Where the only person who could definitely have cleared all this up for Martin was? Where the only person who could have helped him come out of it whiter than white, and possibly even at that stage, as I say, go on to win the Eurovision Song Contest, was? Do you know where I was when I could have helped to clear my mate's name?'

'No,' I replied.

'I was in a very expensive clinic down in Carrickfergus. I was drying out and having my life saved,' MacGee said, and as all this was sinking in, he continued, 'Hi, guess what? There's even more. Guess who it was who came and kidnapped me and took me down and checked me in to that very expensive clinic in Carrickfergus in the first place?'

MacGee stared at me, his eyes moistening up a little, and said: 'Yes, you're right, sir; give a prize to the man with the moustache and glasses. It *was* the very same Martin McClelland, helped by none other than our other great schoolmate, Hanna Hutchinson. And no prizes this time, Paul, for guessing who paid my bills while I was in there for several months convalescing. Of course, I didn't know all this at the time, but Martin could have saved his own bacon by telling the world where I was, and I've often asked him why he didn't, but he'd never tell me. Hanna once told me that after what happened to Butch Moore – you know, when the press hounded him in the middle of his Eurovision glory, after they found out that he was married, although for some strange reason he wasn't meant to be – apparently Martin's fear was that the same press would show up at the clinic, and I'd take one look at them and go back on the drink again.

'Martin chose instead to go to ground. Everyone assumed he had gone to Scotland. I believe that's because someone spied him when he was flying up there to see his friend Anne in Glasgow when he was working out what to do. But Martin McClelland is a Lough Neagh man, and he never likes to be too far away from the Lough shore, so he bought a wee hideaway on the east shore of the Lough near Crumlin, and he and Hanna did it up. It wasn't too far from Queen's, where Hanna was studying. They came down to see me in Carrickfergus once a week, and he'd spend the rest of his time in his wee cottage on the Lough shore writing songs.

'He took on another pen name, and continued writing his songs, which have been covered not just in Ireland, but also in England and even America. After Hanna and Martin saw Dylan perform live, Martin knew for a fact that he didn't want to be, that he couldn't be, a showband singer any longer. Luckily enough he'd made enough from his song-writing royalties to get by on. In the early seventies, Hanna graduated. She won an English Literature post in Oxford, and so they moved over there and are, right now, literally living happily ever after. He continued writing songs. Some of them are very famous, and you know them I'm sure. It's just that you don't know that it was Martin who wrote them.

'His mother told Martin who his father was, and Kathleen and Jim Mitchell lived together for the last nine years of her life. Isn't it just amazing how people are prepared to wait all their lives for the ones they love? Mitchell took care of all of Martin's business interests until he retired, and now Martin's affairs are run by a wee girl in Dublin who's been Mitchell's business partner since the late sixties.

'Funnily enough, over the last eight years or so, Martin's taken to painting landscapes, usually when he's down at their cottage on the Lough shore. They still keep the cottage as a retreat. He uses a different name again for his paintings, and the last I heard he was picking up a good bit of change for them as well.'

'Did Martin and Hanna ever marry?' I asked.

'God, no,' MacGee replied automatically, and then pulled himself up. 'You've only gone and broken one of our conditions. You weren't to ask me any questions, remember? However, I started to answer you, so I'll finish, but I'm afraid that will have to be an end to our chat. No, they never married; they'd no need to. Hanna keeps claiming they'll get around to it one day, but they now know they are together for life. Sure I always knew that, even when we were hanging around as kids. It just took *them* quite some time to work it all out though. But, hi, I'll tell you this for nothing: there was *never* a couple I've met who were more meant for each other than those two.'

CHAPTER FORTY-TWO

And you said,
"He always takes the first dance."
But when there's no last dance
There's no commitment
So, here's to our
Last dance in Dreamland

Martin McClelland

Somewhere on the shores of Lough Neagh (we're not allowed to say exactly where) a dark blue Golf crunches its way up the gravel path through a well-attended garden to a small but perfectly built cottage. The list price for a brand new Golf is £15,850, but Hanna Hutchinson spent a considerable amount of time sourcing her pride and joy. She eventually located a pristine model of the cute and compact car, complete with heated leather seats, air-conditioning, hi-tech radio and CD player, 101,873 miles on the clock and with one previous owner for an absolute steal at £5,400.

The sky is blue, nearing the end of a glorious day with only 40 minutes to sundown, which is why Hanna is in a little bit of a rush. She exits the car, trying to carry two bags of shopping and get the keys to the house out of her Mulberry shoulder-bag at the same time. She struggles with her complicated balancing act until she eventually succeeds, and floats quietly through the lounge, tastefully peppered with antiques, and deposits her load onto the old oak table at the centre of the open-plan kitchen and dining area.

She smiles to herself because she can hear Martin (she no longer thinks of him as Martin Dean, or even Martin McClelland for that matter, just Martin) out on the decking, which they built together and which connects their cottage with the lapping water of the lough. She is smiling because she knows just how happy Martin is to be back by the lough shore again. Yeah, she accepts that he likes their place in Burford in the Cotswolds, and she does too, but for both of them this is home.

Martin is sitting in his favourite American Ginger Bread chair – favoured by Martin because there are no arms on the chair to knock his guitar against and because it's not comfortable enough to doze off in. He's leaning over his guitar gently swaying from side to side, quietly strumming, occasionally singing, occasionally scatting, sometimes humming, but all the time searching for words to fit his sweet yet relaxed melody.

He sings:

There's no last chance,
Only the last dance
In Dreamland.

He's still using the same Hofner guitar his mother bought him for £4-19-6 in Tone Sounds in Magherafelt. Yes, he's most certainly had more expensive guitars in his life, but none with as smooth or friendly a tone as the original. Martin feels, if anything, that the sound is bettering with age. He's happy sitting by the lough shore strumming away and singing. Age has not been as kind to his voice as it has to the guitar, and he looks positively in pain as he tries for some of the higher notes. Hanna is always telling him to leave those ones to the divas and to follow Leonard Cohen's low and whispery approach.

Hanna pauses for a time by the French door, she is keen not to disturb him and equally keen to drink in some of the pleasure he is clearly experiencing from his endeavours. But as ever with Hanna, Martin enjoys a sixth sense and he stops mid-chord, mid-lyric and turns to see her. He smiles, betraying immediately how happy he is to see her even if it's only been a little over an hour since she went off shopping. She still takes his breath away. He's long since stopped trying to figure how why; he is now just totally content that she does.

'You've been working on that song for as long as we've had the cottage.'

'I made a bit of progress on it today,' Martin claimed.

'Really?' She grins and starts to undress, revealing that she's already wearing his favourite two-piece white bathing suit under her stunning black-and-chalk cady dress.

'Well every time I start to make progress you start to do this,' he said, nodding at her discarded dress.

'If you think you're going to crease my new Stella McCartney dress you've got another think coming.'

'And what might the other think coming be?'

Martin is now on his feet, the Hofner secure on the lush cushion of the chair. He is standing still, just staring at her, drinking in this vision before him. She's never done anything like this before, and he's as shocked and as speechless as he was the first night she undressed for him in the half light up at old man Hutchinson's (no relation) hay shed.

'Perhaps, wee boy, when you manage to pick your jaw up from our expensive decking you'll join me for a wee swim in the lough and you'll find out?' she said as she walked over to the edge of their decking and dived in.

Twenty minutes later both are still in the water. Hanna, her head secure in the nook of his neck, is clinging on to Martin for dear life as they make love. Now, with the advantage of their years, they know exactly how to pleasure and be pleasured by each other. Yet for all their years their passion for each other has never dampened and maybe it's even more intense from the fear that it someday may wane.

But today is certainly not that day.

Still holding on, but now glowing in the golden sunset, she sings his melody back to him, adding a wee bit of her own to his work-in-progress lyrics:

> *By the lough shore*
> *You got me*
> *Just before the last dance*
> *In Dreamland*
> *Before the last dance*
> *In Dreamland.*

Acknowledgements

Oh my goodness, where to start with the list of people to thank?

I suppose it has to be with the (very sadly) departed Dixie Kerr, a dedicated musician, husband, family man and the man who got me started on the trail, way back when. And then Eamonn Regan: a man generous with his time, advice, humour, equipment, bookings, not to mention having the patience of a Saint with a 15-year-old manager. Dixie and Eamonn's band, The Breakaways, showed me from the inside how amazing it was to belong and be part of a showband.

Also thanks to Vince McCusker my sidekick at the beginning of my adventures in Wonderland. And then Paddy Shaw, RIP, a soulful singer, in my humble opinion up there with the best of them. Sammy Barr, may you also rest in peace, you'd certainly one of the best ballrooms on the circuit – the Flamingo in Ballymena – and positively the best hot dogs in Ireland! To *Cityweek*, *Thursday Mag* and *New Spotlight* and, in recent years, *Hot Press*, for being there when you were needed.

When I was working on the story, Jim Aiken and Brendan Bowyer were both very, very generous with their time, their stories and their excellent company. Jim sadly passed away a few years ago, and I still miss our chats and our endeavours to right the wrongs of the music business over numerous cups of tea.

To Edwin Higel for helping get the wheels on the wagon; to Eoin Purcell and the New Island gang for getting the show on the road.

To Chris Charlesworth for support and encouragement. To Justin Corfield and Lucy Beevor for the eagle eyes. To Edward and Zara for press cuttings. John McIvor for the cameo.

To Billy Brown for being the inspiration for not only this story, but also the majority of the musicians on the showband circuit. I count myself to have been extremely lucky to have seen and heard Billy on several occasions in ballrooms up and down the country; he was absolutely nothing short of brilliant on every single occasion.

Thanks are also due and offered to Catherine for the red-pen work and more, to Andy and Cora for turning on the bright light, the radio too and turning me on to Emile Ford and his hit record, "What Do You Want to Make Those Eyes At Me For?".

And finally, goodnight and God bless from The Playboys from Castlemartin: Martin, Brendan, Dixie, Robin, Barry, Davy, Smiley & Mo, or whoever they may have been.